Client Service

a novel by

Shelby Tucker

For Tommie Tucker, fellow
Mustang, with love

Memphis   13 Nov 2012

STACEY
INTERNATIONAL

STACEY INTERNATIONAL
128 Kensington Church Street
London W8 4BH
Tel: +44 (0)20 7221 7166; Fax: +44 (0)20 7792 9288
Email: info@stacey-international.co.uk
www.stacey-international.co.uk

ISBN: 978 1906768 92 8

CIP Data: A catalogue record for this book is available from the
British Library.

Printed in Great Britain by TJ International Ltd, Cornwall.

For

Thor Thorsson, Bill Bunting, Jim Barnes,
Larry Humphries, Anthony Brontë Blemings,
Ticia Bernuth, Francie Bullard, Allen Reed,
Fritz Schas, Geoff Wood and Brian Jones,
companions with briefcases
and our many aggrieved clients.

By the Same Author:

Among Insurgents: Walking Through Burma

Burma: The Curse of Independence

The Last Banana: Dancing with the Watu

'This is a world inhabited not by people who have to be persuaded to believe, but by people who want an excuse to believe.'

—John Kenneth Galbraith, *The Great Crash*

'The greatest of all gifts is the power to estimate things at their true worth.'

—Le Duc de la Rochefoucauld
Quoted in the Fund of Fund's prospectus

'If you want to make money, don't horse around with steel or light globes – work directly with money.'

—Bernie Cornfeld
Charles Raw *et al.*, *Do you sincerely want to be rich?*

CONTENTS

PART I Fall Contest

1 Financial Genius	2
2 Big Orange Country	21
3 Captive Audience	39
4 Sugar Bowl	70
5 Breaking the Ice	90

PART II Spring Training

6 Double Trouble	112
7 WoFing WoFers	145
8 Eastward Ho	166
9 Flotation	191

PART III Liquidation

10 Bad Karma	210
11 Sir Vyvyan to the Rescue	231
12 Apocalypse	249

Topical Postscript	279

Part I

Fall Contest

1

FINANCIAL GENIUS

'CALL FOR YOU from Ouagadougou, Mr Baroque.'

'Tell them to call back.'

If Baroque was sometimes blasé about his harried salesmen, scarcely a day passed without their thinking of him and World of Finance's Stock Option Plan. All that morning, Bob Bleitgeist had been musing on the value of his shares.

The Promise of the Public Offering endowed the moment with beauty and tranquillity. He floated in a rheumy euphoria, in trance-like opacity. The radio was on, but he wasn't listening. The gaping pits of Man's denudation of the hills about swept by unseen. Tennessee's Area Manager was bound for Big Orange Country in his Targa.

Two years before, at the time of Bumper's predecessor's arrest, Marty Rubin, the president of World of Finance Management Company, the sales subsidiary, had awarded him the Volunteer State. He had proved more than worthy of that exalted commission. The contrast between Tennessee *before* Bleitgeist and Tennessee *after* Bleitgeist, Bob knew, neatly expressed the returns on his discerning supervision. His huge hands, large mouth, thick neck, heavy eyebrows and slightly crinkly black hair were not disabilities. What was important was motivation and discernment, which, in common with his managerial colleagues, he had in abundance.

Before Tennessee, he had worked in Europe VIII. He could not pretend that he opened up Europe VIII. Handschuh had passed through Madrid on a rapine visit, picked up a few Plans and dispersed his calling-cards; and once, en route from Angola to

Paris, Tom Stamp had touched down at Lisbon and struck the Embassy Market there. But no one before Bleitgeist had thought about Europe VIII's Maritime Market.

In devising different ways of gaining entry to the docks without a permit, in boarding ships without the shipping agents' authorization, in defying captains' orders to disembark, Bleitgeist had shown, as was stated on his personnel record, 'more than average intrepidity in making and maintaining contact with prospects'. Seldom, and with tankers never, did turn-around permit a Call Back. Accordingly, he had tailored the Sign-or-Tear-Up Close for mariners who feared making snap decisions.

'Mr Worth, you've never had a financial plan designed for you like this before, have you?'

'No.'

'And you agree that it makes sense?'

'Yes.'

'Thank you. I have completed my part of the job [indicating all the Financial Work Sheets and clipping them together with the application form on top], but only you can make your Plan work. My experience is that things that don't get done at the right time never get done at all. You have two alternatives: to okay the Plan now or tear it up. [Place the papers and a pen in front of him to sign, then remain silent.]'

If his prospect hesitated, Bleitgeist struck him with the Parable of the Two Seamen, also of his own devising. One seaman went from port to port all his life frittering away his wages, never holding back a drachma, while the other prudently made regular monthly remittances into the Fenner Biddup Offshore Fund.

Bleitgeist had often felt incongruous and ill-at-ease in mariners' society. Tattoos repelled him. And certain dark memories would haunt him for the rest of his life. Such as that fruitless Group Presentation on the Japanese ship when he had to read aloud the whole Fenner Biddup Ofshore Fund prospectus and wait while each sentence was translated. Such as that painful incident with the stoker he had followed ashore and accompanied from bar to bar, chatting about financial planning. Only a Financial Counsellor with a strong sense of Goal could sustain such humiliation. There were occasions when, even the most critical supervisor would concede, he cut a fine figure of a man standing by the taffrail, briefcase in hand, expounding the advantages of Vertical Diversification and the Automatic Withdrawal Plan.

Opening up Nashville had absorbed the better part of a lonely six months during World of Finance's Year of Growth, 1966, when special *Growth Awareness Bulletins* featured stories with alliterative titles such as 'Sensational Sales in Seychelles' and 'Fabulous Funding in Formosa', and double bonus points were awarded during the *University of Modern Money Contest*. He established the nucleus of an organization in Nashville and moved on to Chattanooga.

In October, the company changed its policy on DGPINS. Previously, these Plans opened with the life cover feature subject to the underwriter's approval. 'Instant DGPINS' now provided the client with life cover from the moment he signed the statement of health. Bleitgeist explained this fine distinction to his men and trained them vigorously in the new selling techniques set forth in the Informogram. Tennessee in consequence made a respectable showing in the Professional in Action Contest when triple bonus points were awarded for DGPINS.

The Year of Professionalism, 1967, was 'the year that witnessed the greatest number of major accomplishments in WoF history'. It was also the year that Bleitgeist made Regional Manager and established his office in Memphis. Regional Manager was only two ranks below General Manager.

Still reflecting on the ceaselessly increasing value of his stock, he reviewed the past nine months of 1968, the Year of Total Planning.

January. WoF launched Fiduciary of Fiduciaries (FoF), a mutual fund investing in other mutual funds.

February. WoF launched Kapitalsfonds, 'an investment vehicle for German investors', and Commodities Fund, 'an investment vehicle for investors trading in commodities futures seeking to balance risks'.

March. WoF's banking subsidiary, Anonymous Depositors Bank, extended the range of its services to include nominee investment accounts.

April. WoF launched Orbis Fund, 'an investment vehicle tailored to the needs of Italian investors', and Stars and Stripes Fund, 'an investment for American investors'. WoF's investment bank subsidiary, Finance Bank, participated in its first underwriting.

May. WoF added three proprietary funds to FoF's portfolio: Natural Resources Fund, Venture Fund and Hedge Fund. (FoF could not be sold in the United States, but 'special buys' using overseas addresses were allowed clandestinely.)

June. Half-year results for WoF funds. Fenner Biddup Offshore Fund up six per cent. Fiduciary of Fiduciaries up eight per cent. Folkestone Plan up six per cent. Stars and Stripes Fund up an electrifying sixteen per cent. Orbis Fund up eight per cent. Kapitalsfonds up five per cent. Total assets under WoF management surpassed a billion dollars.

July. WoF's real estate subsidiary, Redevco, announced commencement of construction of Solymar II, a luxury apartment development on the Costa Brava. More than seven thousand Associates participated in the WoF Olympiad Contest, producing a spectacular increase in cash flow, contest winner Noam van Zilver writing nearly a million dollars in Contest Volume with thirty-seven Fully Paids and seventeen Anonymous Depositors Bank Securities Safekeeping Accounts.

August. WoF's investment bank subsidiary, Entrepreneurs Bank, participated in its first underwriting. Peter Gass, the noted American economist, and Sir Harvey Nobody, the company's top field echelon, gave Keynote Addresses at the General Managers Conference, 'advancing and evaluating scores of vital ideas to help guide and implement future WoF growth'.

September. Twenty per cent of WoF Management Company stock offered for sale to the public. Listings obtained on the Amsterdam, Luxembourg and Toronto Exchanges, and vigorous over-the-counter trading in London and Zurich indicated a market value for the parent company more than twice formula value as determined under the Stock Option Plan.

September was also the month in which Bleitgeist made Divisional Manager with Group Volume of $1.3 million, an amount exceeding the total production of all of WoF during the same month exactly a decade before. The *Bulletin* showed him in his new car. 'DM Bob Bleitgeist's new Bahama yellow Porsche "Targa" blisters the interstates at better than 130 mph. Deluxe equipment includes a license plate with the initials "BB".

According to Bob, in addition to its prowess on the parkways, it's an excellent way to meet new clients in sports car circles.'

Bleitgeist was still absorbed in his reverie – the Volunteer State was on the brink of becoming a Major Market Area, a mirror image of the company, offering the company's mutual funds, insurance, real estate and banking services – when he sighted, rising above the dogwoods in the distance, an enormous sign depicting a man with a pony tail clad in animal skins holding a breech-loading musket. As a trainee Financial Counsellor he had neglected his lunch quite often. Now never. He shifted his foot to the brake and the Targa began a gentle deceleration. It was time to eat.

*

Innocent of the need to plan for the future, the only hint of ambition in Belvedere Beauchamp was his resolve to publish a novel. He was in Barcelona boarding at the Pension Porsepina, teaching English at the Universal Languages School ('Uners') and writing an autobiographical hagiography entitled *Our Times*.

Writing novels had been all the rage at Eton. None of his contemporaries, however, could draw on his broad range of experience. There was that time his housemaster blamed him for inscribing obscene words on the lawn ('All right, Beauchamp, own up. Where did you get the weed-killer?'). That kind of adolescent prank wasn't his style, he protested. ('Come off it, Beauchamp! Why did you do it?') Not until he revisited the incident in *Our Times* did he admit his guilt. He and Ankers had done it. Poor Ankers, he was a barrister now.

He wondered if his life was not too rich and passionate to be compacted within a novel. Perhaps *Our Times* would be the first of a trilogy.

After Eton, there was Oxford. Oxford was all parties. Parties and parties, then more parties. Pre-disco, dark, riotous parties where everyone arrived with a bottle and left with a girl. A bottle for a bird, they said.

It was at one such party that he met Philippa. The in-word that year was *soignée*. Philippa was the quintessence of *soignée*. Undergraduates were not *soignée*, hanging about Blackwell's and crowding the bar at the King's Arms, always talking about their weekly essays. Philippa inhabited an urbane world of altogether grander scale beyond the porters' lodges, where really serious things were *done*, not just talked about.

They met during the last week of his last Michaelmas term. He failed his collections at the start of Hilary term and abandoned, finally, his idea of getting a First. None of his friends aspired to a First – except Alistair, who struck an orator's pose at the Union and cut a dashing figure in OUDS. Everyone thought Alistair romantic and idealistic. Not Philippa. For her, Alistair was simply 'heavy'.

They spent Easter in Rome. Fatuous conversations about art between mouthfuls of pasta and a too memorable hackney cab ride through the Borghese Gardens with the horse fouling the road behind them.

Then back to Oxford and the pageant of Trinity term, the parties now spilling over onto the Cherwell. Moored beneath the embowering willows, while the sun sank behind the golden spires, huddled wet but warm beneath blankets, Belvedere was more and more bestial, Philippa alternately affectionate and amused. 'Dear me! The *things* men *expect* women to do!'

In the course of writing up these adventures, Belvedere discovered: first, that fact was *not* more interesting than fiction; second, that, broad though his experience was, it resisted transformation into interesting fiction; third, that he lacked Evelyn Waugh's natural talent and the discipline and perseverance to write such a novel as *Put Out More Flags* in thirty days; finally, that he was a shirker, his guiding principle being, *Never do today what you can put off doing until tomorrow.* He was twenty-three and could defer *sine die* whatever demanded more than cursory concentration. Hence, *Our Times* proceeded slowly.

Much of it concerned Philippa. She understood him best. She gave him more rope and coped with neglect better than other women. Once past the preliminaries, other women lost heart and sank to petty recrimination, reproaching him with accusations of indifference or infidelity. Those ambitious creatures went their separate ways. Philippa stayed the course, and with her in London, as an earnest vow to return, were several boxes filled with his books, including many cherished Pelican Specials.

Even so, Philippa's understanding and patience were not absolute, as shown by the description of their last evening together in *Our Times*.

> Outside the weather was already inclement. The homogenous bricks and television aerials of White City took on the peculiar drabness of an English urban winter.
>
> I had known for some time that I could not endure another winter in White City. This room, the few books that I had read here, the bed on which I lay, the nameless and forgotten girls who had shared it, had brought me little, if any, joy.
>
> And it was even worse in summer when the hard, bleak scene beyond the rotted sash window served to remind me that elsewhere was all the beauty of sheep-cropped knolls, the elder blooming, fields deep in barley, poppies peeping above golden undulations, oaks spreading their long shadows in the late afternoon.
>
> I had never regarded this room as more than temporary, a place where I might sift through what survived of my classical education and resolve some New Plan. I recognized now that it was a mistake to have come here at all, to have cast myself in the role of the impoverished seer. There was no strength to be gained from self-imposed squalor. I waged here no heroic struggle. I needed the stimulus of beautiful surroundings in which to work, not the sound of Arthur's radio through the wall. We were both on the dole, but Arthur was an Irish labourer and I was an Old Etonian and Oxford graduate.
>
> Philippa beside me chilly despite the electric fire, her goose-pimpled nudity shadowed and neglected on this last evening together, was quite resolved on her own New Plan, which excluded me. She had tried to warn me, in vain. Nor did any of my many explanations make sense to her. If a change was needed to lift me out of my doldrums, and certainly a change was needed, then let me move to Chelsea or with her into the country, where a writer

belonged. Alas, none of her schemes for my rehabilitation held the least interest for me. She had not pressed the marriage issue. That was for me to decide, in the leisured way men decide this important question, but, in my ingratitude for this concession to the male's prerogative, I had ceased to speak of it altogether and now seemed solely intent on living apart from her. Beside me, staring up at the crumbling ceiling plaster, were the wide awake burning eyes of a girl deranged by thwarted hopes.

*

These sessions with his secretary were less impersonal than talking into a dictaphone. With Virginia, Nelson could always be confident of a sympathetic audience, the comfort of a hired hand. She did not mock his ambition to settle in France and write poetry after the Public Offering.

'Ready?'

'All set, Mr Rock.'

'The policy of the Fund is based on the belief that basic trends in increased taxation, as well as real economic growth which has prevailed in the United States since the close of World War II, are likely to continue unabated in the foreseeable future. It will be the policy of the Fund to seek situations that offer savings in the form of tax relief, tax rebates, write-offs, deductions and deferments and, in particular, situations which are tax exempt.

'How does that strike you?'

'Mr Rock, you always ask the most challenging questions. But, since you ask, why it's poetry! *Continue unabated in the foreseeable future* sounds exactly the right note of inevitable disaster. No one else could have written it.'

'Not even Baroque?'

'If you want my honest opinion, Mr Rock, not even Baroque.'

Nelson smirked. He had just received a rebuke from the Founder for sloppy drafting. She meant inevitable growth, of course, not disaster. He gratefully resumed fondling a gold ballpoint pen awarded to him for 'administrative excellence' by vote of the Board of Directors from which he had punctiliously abstained.

'Can you do me a rough?' he said. 'We'll see how it looks projected on paper.' Then, turning in his swivel chair, he gazed out the window at a Goodyear blimp and thought poetically of the *Tour Eiffel* and the *Arc de Triomphe*.

*

Down the corridor in the Leadership Room, Baroque was in conference with the rest of the Executive Committee. Others might rise late, but these important men had been consulting since dawn. The subject of their consultation was *New Products for 1970*. Baroque, Sleek McCool, WoF's legal counsel and its master of detail, and Fenner Biddup, the president and CEO of Bidwell and Biddup, which managed the Fenner Biddup Offshore Fund (FBOF), were pre-eminent at all meetings of the Executive Committee. Marty Rubin, Herb Beck, who managed the Deep South, Clovis Hoof, Pierre Sansjoy, Henri Sansloy, Hans Strumpf, Gerhard Handschuh, Michele Mafia and Vincenzo Vendetta were there, as was Wally Whitmore, who once induced WoF to reimburse a client robbed by a Regional Manager. Everyone present noticed Nelson's absence. Baroque refrained from explanation. He knew the value of keeping his men guessing and tasting the threat of exile.

*

Exile was Bumper Peabody's punishment for inadvertently leaking news of a FBOF reverse to a journalist in the hire of the Competition (the Quarterly Report had to be revised on the eve of dispatch), and he was tired, *very* tired of being pursued by SAVAK for currency infractions.

He drew back the curtains and peeped out apprehensively at the four police officers who shadowed him. They stood in the dim yellow light of the corner street lamp armed with pistols, rifles and moustaches. Why did *all* Iranian policemen have moustaches? He thought about his predecessor; how he had been placed on a rack and forced – Bumper shook his head sadly – *to disclose the names of his Clients!*

He closed the curtain, ascertained that no one was in the closet, went to the bathroom, bolted the door, removed a waterproof box from the cistern and re-counted the transmittal slips.

*

The most successful of Bumper's protégés and his self-appointed successor, Noam van Zilver, was on safari. He had travelled by boat to Alexandria, train to Aswan, steamer to Wadi Halfa, train to Khartoum and hitchhiked from there. Five months hence, he would enter Equatoria via Nimule on the Uganda border disguised as a lorry driver's assistant and tap yet another untapped market, the Shuka Dancer Warriors Market.

For the time being, though, he had eschewed the river to swing over to Ethiopia and tap the Falashas, an unassimilated pre-Talmudic people who claimed descent from Solomon and were suspicious of a deviant usurper regime with like pretensions in Addis Ababa. Vaunting his own Solomonic pedigree via the Dutch line, he appealed to the wider family loyalties of these praeternaturally covetous, credulous people and motivated them to buy Plan after Plan.

Not many Regional Managers travelled thus; van Zilver always. His rucksack contained a collapsible briefcase and a glossary of words in all the main Hamitic, Nilotic and Bantu languages for 'Swiss bank', 'high return on investment', 'liquid', 'with or without insurance', 'in your own name or jointly with your wife (tribe)', 'absolutely guaranteed' and 'yes'.

*

Another of Bumper's protégés, recently reassigned to London but over whom Bumper was still drawing a Continuing, was lecturing at an Advanced Training Seminar sponsored by the company's insurance subsidiary, WoF Insurance Holdings Limited.

'Winston Churchill once said, "to carry adequate life insurance is a moral obligation incumbent upon the great majority of citizens",' declared Ernest Gloom.

'Each of us here is keenly aware of the responsibility that we have to our clients in making certain that their families are adequately protected. Certain phrases can prove highly effective when you sit down with a prospect to help him provide for his family's future security.

'If he says that he doesn't believe in insurance, ask him if he believes in dying.

'If he says that he doesn't need more insurance, tell him that *he* never needed insurance. You are not talking about *him*. You are talking about his wife and children, because he is their provider.

'If he asks you to come back next month, tell him if he doesn't need insurance now, he won't need it next month.

'And then you can tell him about a letter you once saw which said, "Please don't think my husband didn't love his family. *It's just that he didn't plan to die at this time.*"

'In the great majority of cases,' continued Ernest, 'selling a DGPINS, a Dynamic Growth Plan *with Insurance*, requires no more than a couple of sentences at the end of a presentation. "We want to be certain, Mr Worth, that, if something unforeseen happens to you, your Plan will be completed. Does that make sense to you?"

'Sales of DGPINS increase the value of our Stock Options, of course, but just as important as the material benefits we award ourselves is the pride that we can take in knowing that we have provided a vital service for our client, the best protection that WoF has to offer. Who else guarantees as many widows a lifetime free of charity? Who else provides so many young men an education which permits them to follow rewarding careers? Who else is responsible for so many dignified retirements, for so much genuine peace of mind?'

*

While the Executive Committee was meeting in the Leadership Room, Jacques Sansfoy was lecturing in the Golden Opportunity Room to Pre-Icebreakers at a Financial Training Seminar.

WoF had brought Jacques to New York to serve as Director of Training owing to his renown at Situation Control, which he defined as the art of taking command of an alien domain and reordering it to suit your aims.

'Suppose that you arrive at a prospect's office for your appointment and he is on the telephone. Don't just stand there. Pretend that you are as busy as he is. Open your briefcase and start filling out transmittal slips. Continue until he is free of distractions and impatient for your appointment to begin. Then ask him for a glass of water *with two cubes of ice in it*. This is an example of Situation Control.'

Sansfoy was lecturing this morning on Closes.

'Some of you may be wondering what, exactly, is a Close. Signing a document is a difficult decision for most people, particularly if they don't know you or the Plan you are offering. A Close is a leveraging technique used to calm your prospect's fears and help him to make that decision.

'"Mr Worth, would you like to do this with or without insurance? . . .

'"I know it's a personal question, but – are you in good health? . . .

'"If you were given a medical examination, do you think you would pass it? I hate to push the point, Mr Worth, but are you *sure* that there's *nothing* wrong with you? Because if you elect to take the Plan with the insurance endorsement, the company may request a medical examination, and the insurance endorsement will depend entirely on your physical condition."

'This is an example of what is called the "Assumptive" Close. It *assumes* that the prospect has assented to buy a Plan when he has not assented to buy a Plan. You have him focused on his health, and he allows to go by default the question as to whether he *wants* a Plan. The Assumptive, you'll find, is especially useful with elderly prospects. You'll discover new phrases as you become more adept at helping people to plan their estates.'

*

Five storeys below the Golden Opportunity Room, Art Director Hef Hughes was admiring the cover of *The WoF Monthly Bulletin* – a bee at the centre of a flower. 'Baroque will like this,' he reflected. 'Everybody will like it, Sleek, Fenner, Nelson, Wally, Marty, Herb, Clovis, Pierre, Henri, Jacques, Hans, Gerhard, Michele, Vincenzo. We are a family, always busy, always extracting the nectar like this bee at the centre of the flower.' Hef was credited with having designed the company logo, a bull and a bear prancing around a globe.

*

'Call for you from Teheran, Mr Baroque,' issued a voice from a speaker on the conference table, interrupting an impromptu sermon the Founder was giving on the Australian interest rate.

It was Bumper again.

'Talk about paranoia! You'd think he was the only General Manager under police surveillance. Tell him to call back,' said Baroque.

*

The Founder's story can now be told. There are different versions, but no one had attempted to express it as a diagram. Herb Beck, who had majored in symbolic logic at Fordham, recklessly ventured this idea.

'I was thinking of a straight line pointing up,' he said. Although he was joking, no one laughed.

'Herb, my life is more complex than a diagram,' countered Baroque. 'It's more interesting than a straight line. There is no subtlety in a straight line. Besides, nobody believes in straight lines any more. My success rests on the proposition that men can use reason to improve the structure of their lives. That can't be represented by a diagram or by a line.'

The problem with the Founder was, you never knew when he was serious.

His earliest memories, of the slums of Gdynia and Amsterdam, before his family crossed the Atlantic and settled in Brooklyn, imparted to him an enduring understanding of the importance of money and stamped him with a social conscience. The social order was in ferment. The rich exploited the poor and mutual funds provided the panacea. Concern for the injustice of Capitalism and the victims of oppression, not avarice, was the reason the Founder started selling mutual funds.

The story, enhanced by the lush inventions of the popular press, was told repeatedly and effusively at Financial Training Seminars:

1. To strengthen the resolve of new recruits rebuffed at their first presentations;
2. To Reps daunted by shyness or cowardice;
3. To Managers apprehensive of other Managers pirating in their territories;
4. To anyone whose selling zeal was flagging.

General Managers and Divisional Managers used a modified version to solace Regional Managers and Branch Managers cheated of Overrides. Embellishments, modifications, fantastical episodes, optional versions were fashioned according to need.

The Founder's real story, though rarely heard, was more inspiring. He had never known poverty. Born Melvin Abrahamski in Gdingen (Gdynia) in 1930, his father, Abe Abrahamski, was a Polish impressario and film producer, a pioneer of the film industry in Central Europe, his mother, a Viennese actress. Following the fortunes of the film industry, the Abrahamskis moved to New York in 1933 and settled among other affluent immigrants. Had Abe, who was much older than Sarah, lived, New York would have been no more than a stopover en route to Hollywood. But Abe died suddenly when Melvin was eight years old, and responsibility devolved on Sarah for keeping the family intact.

Their modest house at the corner of East 189th Street and Avenue B had no back yard and tree where a lad might build a tree house. For Melvin, there were only brick walls and solitary handball. Saul Dressler, a counsellor at PS 112, the primary school he attended, remembers him: 'Team sports and all those group activities that interested the other boys never seemed to make much of an impression on the kid. He went through an electronics phase, a stamp collecting phase and a ham radio phase, and, at one time, I thought he was going to be a professional photographer. Kids grow out of these fads, of course. You can't be *too* dogmatic about a boy's future on the basis of his childhood enthusiasms. I'm told he's quite changed.'

Lou Doniach, who knew him through Boy Scout connections, recalls: 'One thing he *wasn't* was an athlete. I remember he had trouble getting his life-saving certificate. He wasn't studious, either. I'd say what he liked most was organizing people.' And the principal of PS 150, where Melvin completed junior high school, recalls: 'He was a little on the quiet side and kept to himself. Definitely *not* a mixer. Not so much trouble as some of the bigger boys. I think he had a problem with awkwardness, and he had a stammer. Of course, everyone at One Fifty is glad the little runt has done so well.' 'An average student', 'Satisfactory work' and 'Does not participate in sporting activities' were recurrent notations in his teachers' progress reports at Lincoln High School. There is a picture of him taken at commencement ceremonies in the basketball stadium there. It is the picture of an inconspicuous laureate among others in black robes and crowned with mortar boards.

We do not know when he developed the stammer to which the principal of PS 150 alludes. Dressler does not refer to it, but does mention Melvin's habit of pursing his lips. What is known is that his mother engaged a therapist who diagnosed the stammer as classical Adlerian 'organ inferiority compensation', a 'plea for mercy' and the lips pursing as an 'invitation to kiss his rosebud mouth' and 'signal to admire him'. 'Our goals determine our behaviour,' he told Melvin. 'We *become* our goals.' He also told Melvin about *Gemeinschaftsgefuhl*, or community spirit, 'without which we will never govern. When one baby in a crèche begins to cry, all the other babies begin to cry. When we walk into a room where people are laughing, we too begin to laugh.' Thereafter, instead of asking his teachers not to question him in class, Melvin encouraged them to question him. His stammer slowly disappeared, and he pursed his lips less and less.

At Atlantic City College, he joined the Socialist Youth League, which was a natural progression from his high school membership in the Yipsels (Young Peoples Socialist League). They met every day in the student cafeteria to share meals and invigilate the militants of the Peasants and Workers Soviet, the American Socialist Party, the Atlantic City College Soviet of the American Communist Party, the Youth Association of the

Leninist Fourth International and the Socialist Labour Party, who also met in the student cafeteria.

'The Republicans and the Democrats were not an option after the rise of anti-Semitism in Europe. There was only the Left. We wrote tracts, which we mimeographed and circulated. During my sophomore year, there was a national election. We all wanted Henry Wallace, who had been Roosevelt's and Truman's Secretary of Commerce, but the press reported that he wanted to share atomic energy information with Stalin and destroyed his candidacy. So we backed Norman Thomas, who had studied under Woodrow Wilson and was one of the founders of the American Civil Liberties Union.'

The stamp collecting ham radio enthusiast of PS 112, the humble loner of PS 150, the stammering cub photographer of Lincoln High School, now showed his mettle as a leader and conceptual thinker.

'Why should I be diffident about this? Dressler didn't know what he was talking about. After I joined the Yipsels, I became their leader. At college, I formed the Psychology Club and was its leader. I wasn't elected. It was spontaneous. The other guys interested in psychology just looked to me to take their decisions for them. In every group, there were some big guys and some little guys. Okay, I was short. So I was the big little guy.'

What happened to Melvin next? The years that witnessed the end of the Korean War and the CIA-supported overthrow of the Moussadeq Government in Iran and the Arbenz Government in Guatemala are a black hole in this story. We do not even know if he graduated from Atlantic City College. 'Look, let's just say that I disappeared.' When he emerges, he is in Paris leading an organization that will become World of Finance. Marty, Henri, Jacques and Herb are his lieutenants and will be known as Pioneers. They rendezvous at different sites by prior agreement. Melvin's 1949 Plymouth station-wagon serves as their headquarters.

Others who had been Melvin's acquaintances since his ham radio days join them, enticed by the prospect of living in France. They work pseudonymously and without permits. Henceforth, Melvin will be known as Baroque or, simply, the Founder. A police investigation shakes their confidence and it takes the full measure of his genius to restore harmony at their first Key Associates Conference. 'Sure, they don't trust us. They're scared we're going to come up with something they hadn't thought of. But we have to keep on expanding.' Denouncing authority as small-minded, Capitalist, recidivist and anti-Semitic will become the company's axiomatic defence to allegations of tax evasion and exchange control violations.

The installation of an office in a room overlooking Place Muette, the company's bronze nameplate beside a *sonnerie* at the front entrance and the purchase of a typewriter seemed to augur a new era. Advertisements were placed in the *Herald Tribune* for people with 'sales ability, a sense of humour and a willingness to work hard in a fast-growing industry'. Clovis joined the company. Michele and Vincenzo joined, but most new recruits were Americans who had come to Paris as students under the GI Bill of Rights and stayed on. To keep their resident permits alive, many of them had enrolled in *Civilisation Française*, a course at the Sorbonne without compulsory classes or lectures. All were aloof from practical affairs and had time on their hands. They breakfasted late on croissants and spent their afternoons and evenings playing pinball. Three decades earlier might have seen them at a Gertrude Stein *salon* debating Cubism with bullfight *aficionados*.

As new Reps came on board, Sansfoy began conducting Financial Training Seminars. Earnings were not high, but Potential was ubiquitous. Baroque partitioned the world. Clovis got Britain; Michele and Vincenzo Italy; Henri, Pierre and Jacques France. Then one of Herb's trainees attempted a presentation to a Rotarian ('I didn't know they had them in France'), and *les bulots* renewed their persecution, raiding the office, seizing files and arresting staff even as the second *Spring Contest Special Bulletin* went to press. Herb and Henri escaped by pretending that they had called to ask about the *Herald Trib* ad, but Marty was caught *in flagrante* reading a Volume Report and hence became the first of a long cortège of deportees.

Wally Whitmore, now a General Manager credited with fifty-six SSEs (Successful Supervisory Experiences) and three million dollars in Personal Volume, was one of those who rubbed shoulders with the toy vendors on the Boul' Miche, haggled with chestnut vendors for modest deals, tarried by the Quai Notre Dame peeping over the berets of derelict painters adding daubs of pink to compositions of the Pont Neuf. 'We'd hoof it over to American Express the first thing every morning to check our mail,' recalls Wally. 'Maybe there'd be a cheque. Then we'd celebrate. Or maybe there wasn't, but we'd celebrate anyway. Maybe we'd just mosey around. I remember that we used to argue a lot about Becket, Ionesco, Pirandello, Obey, Henry Miller, about all the really avant-garde writing. An opinion was the only thing we never shared. Everybody was writing novels.'

Tom Stamp was a playwright before the Founder shared with him his zeal for funds, gave him a pseudonym and sent him to work in Bolivia. Bumper Peabody was a teacher. All these men soon adapted to their changed roles. Pierre Cardin suits and Jacques Fath neckties replaced denims and tee-shirts, save for rare moments when there was no prospect of making a sale. They still patronized the commodious bathrooms at the Café de Flors and Les Deux Magots. Now, however, they also sat at tables and ordered drinks.

The first Reps were mostly transients. The second generation included men of a different social order. Before joining WoF, Sleek McCool was a corporate lawyer, Nelson Rock an advertising executive.

Strumpf and Handschuh worked for a manufacturer of shock absorbers. They opened up Germany and established the WoF Academy, which provided an 'intensive, graduate-level study programme in economics, business, banking, law, psychology, government and real estate' spanning four terms of four days each. Strumpf won that year's Big Game Contest and, repressing his excitement at receiving the parchment Citation for Entrepreneurial Excellence and the Silver Blazon awarded to Key Associates, demonstrated 'Contest-winning Situation Control' by closing the photographer sent to take his picture for the *Bulletin*. Germany, the beneficiary of two decades of *Wirtschaftswunder*, joyously embraced a concept that seemed to embody every post-war virtue and overtook Brazil as the world's top producing Territory.

Meanwhile, a letter from an *inspecteur d'impôts* addressed to Melvin Abrahamski decided the Founder return to the

United States. The Pseudonymous Reps Code was lost during the transition and pandemonium broke out among Reps. Some gained, some lost and some were so angry that they defected to Investors Overseas Services, a rival organization operating out of Geneva. Informograms were dispatched to the Reps, asserting that everything would be rectified and urging them to be patient. '. . . Just keep on selling, and the next formulation under the Stock Option Plan will reflect a very substantial increase in the value of your shares. . . .' Sleek was deployed to convince the Securities and Exchange Commission that WoF would not use its overseas affiliations to assist gangsters. WoF became a holding company owning all the shares of a holding company owning all the shares of companies registered in Canada, Panama, the Bahamas, Switzerland, Luxembourg and the Netherlands Antilles. Volume quadrupled.

Now ready to sponsor its own fund, it acquired the Fenner Biddup Offshore Fund as part of a package enticing Fenner to join WoF, decorated its literature with a new, bolder coat-of-arms and offered its shares to the public through an intermediary holding account called the WoF Investment Program. The offer was timed to coincide with a market phase of optimistic outlook and rising prices. The market rose as expected, but the price of FBOF shares remained stubbornly sluggish and, the following quarter, was bearish. A year later, they were still depressed. FBOF was 'reorganized' and an entirely new concept applied to the computation of its shares' net asset value. Henceforth, the price was marked up fractionally on days when purchases exceeded redemptions and discounted fractionally when redemptions exceeded purchases.

'Admirable,' said Sleek.

'Baroque's a genius,' concluded Herb, Marty, Clovis, Michele, Vincenzo, Henri, Pierre, Jacques, Strumpf and Handschuh.

World of Finance spread and vindicated its name.

2

BIG ORANGE COUNTRY

It was Saturday. All over America people rose late, lunched on hamburgers, then sank lugubriously into cushions to watch the game. In turquoise and rose-pink cars speeding along interstates, on Florida beaches, in the Ozarks, they turned on the radio. No one was more eager for the kick-off than Coach Moose Henning, head coach of the University of Tennessee Volunteers. In the past six games, the victory-loving Big Orange had suffered but a single reverse. They had been penalized ninety yards for unnecessary roughness, unfairly in Coach's opinion.

A bowl bid depended on the result of today's game, and every sports writer in the state had addressed himself cautiously to the issue. Vance Williams, a celebrated Knoxville columnist, predicted a Vol victory, but reported his interview with the Razorbacks' coach as a warning of what *could* happen.

'We've got a real fine bunch of kids,' the Arkansas mentor had claimed. 'They're fighters and winners at heart. They've done a fantastic job so far, but now we've got to fight harder than ever before. We thank we can, but this is a young team, and we'll have to experience it together.'

Vance Williams believed that such enthusiasm augured badly for Tennessee.

The Sports Editor for the *Commercial Appeal* allowed that the Razorbacks were 'real stout and real sound', while Charlie Rapp of the *Nashville Banner* seemed to rest hopes for an Orange victory on its linebacker.

Bone Saxon Upset, So Look Out Arkansas

'There's one thing about this football season that really irritates Tennessee Monster Man Bone Saxon. "I'm not getting as many tackles as I'm used to," used to complain the 6'1", 205-pounder from Humboldt' [wrote Rapp].

The reason is simple. The Opposition just isn't running Saxon's way as much. Over the past two years Tennessee opponents have gained a tremendous amount of respect for no. 71.

Coach Harold Voight of Auburn has said: 'He's the best at Monster we've run into. You don't want to try him too much.' It is significant that Voight has had some pretty outstanding teams during the time Saxon has been at Tennessee. Thus the Volunteer Monster Man has impressed Voight against people such as Sandy O'Connor, Jerry Butler, Bob Brown and Bob Burleigh.

Modest

When asked about teams running away from his side Saxon modestly passes the subject, saying: 'Well, I don't know about that, but I'd like to believe it's so.'

Coach Jerry Hamilton, who handles the defensive backs, has special words for Saxon because of his ability. Then, too, Hamilton recruited Saxon.

'He's the kind of player who makes a coach look good,' says Hamilton. 'He's a leader and has the respect of his fellow players, and the opposing players too. He lines up the other team's strength every time, and much of the time, especially this year, they run away from him.'

The Credit

Bone credits Hamilton and Coach Moose Henning with a great deal of his success. 'They've put up with a lot from me,' Saxon explains. 'If it wasn't for Coach Henning, I'd probably be just going to school and goofing around. Coach Henning is the kind of coach you like to play for.

He'll go a long way for you. All the guys who play think a lot of the coach. Of course, if you don't put out, he's on you, and he should be. You've got to work for him, and, if you do, he's going to be in your corner all the time.'

*

Bleitgeist arranged his napkin about his neck and tucked into a plate of meatloaf; then, amiably, invited the proprietor of the Davy Crockett Drive-In to join him in an order of pecan pie. 'Nice restaurant you've got here,' he observed.

'We try,' said the restaurateur, little accustomed to praise from his customers.

Bleitgeist solicited his name and continued, 'It must pose pretty much of a challenge, Mr Hill?'

'What kinda challenge?' asked the restaurateur.

'To know where to invest the profits.'

Mr Hill stared at his customer. Was he dissatisfied with the food and trying to humiliate him? The drive-in was losing money. The restaurateur removed his cigar from his mouth, tapped it softly into an ashtray, let it linger there, put it back in his mouth and, being a decent type, loath to condemn his fellow man out of hand, looked hard at his customer again. His customer was looking at him.

'Well?' asked Bleitgeist.

'What mightn't you be driving at?'

'Would you be interested in hearing about an exciting new idea?'

'I guess I'm always interested in hearin' new ideas,' replied the restaurateur rashly.

Bleitgeist calmly finished his pie and cleared the table; then, extracting from a briefcase at his feet a tablet of white paper headed 'Financial Worksheet', said: 'Before I get started, Mr Hill, I wonder if you could ask the waitress to bring me a glass of water with *two* cubes of ice in it?' He waited in silence until the waitress had fetched the water, then asked the restaurateur: 'Maybe you've sometimes wondered how banks make money?'

Simultaneously, a voice familiar to all Big Orange fans, familiar to Mr Hill, came on the radio. '*Tennessee's great All-American, Bo Pearson, member of the 1940 Rose Bowl team, talked with*

Bone just before we came on the air. We'll bring you that interview on tape. . . .'

'Have you any idea how *much* they make?'

'*. . . Bone, I understand that Arkansas is out to really upset the Vols' chances for the choice of number one team in the nation. Of course, they are out of it, but they're determined to play the role of spoiler. . . .'*

'Would it surprise you to learn that they make more than six per cent on your money? I have to tell you that some banks make as much as *fifteen* per cent on your money.'

Hill was longing to hear the pre-game discussion between Bo Pearson and Bone Saxon, but he thought he had better listen to this Yankee fellow's opinions about how much banks earned.

'*. . . Wail, that's right, Mr Pearson. Arkansas's got a rail fine bawl club, but we thank we're ready. . . .'*

'Do you think that, as an individual choosing your own investments, you could make as much money as a bank?'

'*. . . Bone, I understand that Arkansas's got a big right guard over there named Ricky Dickson, who everybody says is the most underrated player in the Southwestern Confrunce, and if he had been on a winning team would probably have been an All-American. . . .'*

'I don't guess I could.'

'Certainly not! A man of your general business experience recognizes at once that a bank has certain advantages that you lack. What are those advantages, Mr Hill?'

'*. . . Wail, he's a real fine bawl-player,'* said Bone. '*As a matter of fact, we played against each other in high school, and he's the kind of guy that really gives it that extra effort. . . .'*

'That's right, Mr Hill. A bank knows what it's doing. Let's write that down on our Financial Worksheet. A bank has Professional Management.'

'*. . . Wail that's right, Bone. Word is that if yawl win today's bawl game, you just about got a Sugar Bowl bid sewn up. And your likely opponent in the Sugar Bowl will be Texas A & M. Now my question is this, Bone. Can the Volunteers handle that great team of Coach Jimmy Rice?. . .'*

'That's right, Mr Hill. A bank can invest in many different things. Speaking technically, it has diversification. Let's write that on our Financial Worksheet, Diversification.'

'. . . *Wail, I understand that they've got a real fine team over there, but we played Tampa and beat them by seventeen points. But when Texas A & M played them, they only beat them by three, and Tampa has a fine bawl club. . . .*'

'And thinking about these advantages, to what would you ascribe them, Mr Hill? . . . Exactly! A bank can afford to engage experts and a diversified portfolio of investments, whereas, acting alone, you are limited to one or two investments and can't afford experts. However successful you are, and,' looking brightly around the empty dining room of the Davy Crockett Inn, 'it appears that you have been *very* successful, you cannot hope to match the kind of resources as an individual which a bank brings to the business of money management. Is that not correct, Mr Hill?'

'That's true,' conceded the restaurateur.

'Now, Mr Hill, let me ask you this. If you had millions, instead of only thousands of dollars to invest, you could expect to earn the same rate of return on your investments as a bank. Isn't that true . . . *Exactly!* So the problem essentially boils down to assembling a large capital sum under one management. Right?'

Bleitgeist had completed Phase I of his presentation. He now tore off the page of Financial Worksheet on which he had been writing and proffered it for his prospect's inspection. It was a diagram of Phase I.

Professional Management

Capital =

Diversification

'. . . *Wail, I'm sure we're goin' to see some fine bawl playing from Bone Saxon and the whole University of Tennessee defensive team this afternoon,*' said Scroggs Kelson, radio announcer for WVOL.

'*That's right, Scroggs. I think they're going to do everything in their power to win this one and that they will go on to win on New Year's Day, when their likely opponent will be Coach Jimmy Rice's Texas A & M's Aggies. . . .*'

Bleitgeist now designed a pictograph and showed it to his prospect, to whom it resembled a rather clumsy drawing of a snowman.

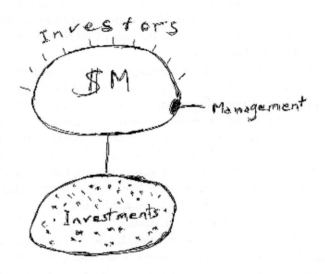

'This is precisely what a mutual fund is, a union of small investors,' he explained. 'By pooling their resources, they can have the advantages that financial institutions like banks have, experts to invest in a portfolio of securities ranging over the entire economy at a fractional cost to each investor. Instead of paying you, say, four per cent for your money and keeping whatever your money earns in excess of four per cent, a mutual fund returns all its profits to its members. Does that make sense to you, Mr Hill?'

Bleitgeist sipped from his glass of ice water, gave pause for the great themes of his dialectic to take hold of his prospect's imagination, then resumed.

'Another way of looking at this, Mr Hill, is, mutual fund shareholders *are* bankers, only they run their banks as a cooperative, instead of a business earning big money for its shareholders. Mutual fund shareholders number in the tens of millions. Twenty-six per cent of all Americans' – a number drawn out of the air – 'now enjoy participation in professionally managed mutual funds. Note the concentric circles by which I have indicated the future growth of that fund's portfolio.'

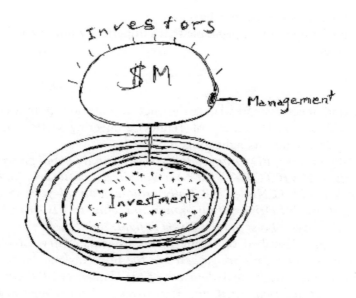

'Do you think the fund's portfolio will grow, Mr Hill?'

'I don't railly know.'

'Do you think that the American economy will grow?'

'Yes sir, I thank that the American economy will grow.'

'Has there ever been a time in the past when it has failed to grow?'

Thoughtfully: 'Not over the long haul.'

'"Not over the long haul." Exactly! Aren't we continuing to make new technological discoveries? Isn't the population steadily increasing? Isn't it true that people today, just as in our grandfathers' day, want to improve their standard of living? . . . Exactly! Then I think we may accept that the American economy is growing and that money invested in an expertly managed portfolio diversified over the whole American economy will grow, too. Don't you agree, Mr Hill?'

'Sounds awl right to me,' said Mr Hill.

'Have you invested a substantial part of your savings in the share market?'

'Not a lot.'

'Has anyone ever acquainted you with the principle of Vertical Diversification?'

'I don't reckon as they have.'

'It's an investment principle that's imperfectly understood and appreciated.'

*

A kind of ecstasy spread over the huge, orange pom-pom waving crowd, as the University of Tennessee cheering section broke rapturously into its fight song.

'*Big Orange, Big Orange, don't be shy, stand up and give your battle cry! VICTORY! That's our Volunteers' battle cry. All hail to dear old TENN-es-see! Rally around with all your might! might! might! Drive on! oh orange and white to VIC-to-ry! We are the boys who show the FIGHT! fight! fight! . . .*'

Scroggs described the scene to his listeners. '*Fifty thousand cheering sports fans are gathered in the Bob Neyland Memorial Stadium to watch the Volunteers of the University of Tennessee meet a traditional rival, the Razorbacks of the University of Arkansas,*' he shouted over the tumult. Then he began a recitation of the starting line-ups. '*. . . At left defensive tackle, sometimes linebacker, six foot one inch, two hundred and five pounds, a senior from Humboldt, Tennessee, Lawrence Saxon . . . .*'

The Big Orange cheering section saluted its favourite linebacker.

'*Give me a B!*'

'*B!*'

'*Give me an O!*'

'*O!*'

'*Give me an N!*'

'*N!*'

'*Give me an E!*'

'*E!*'

'*What does it spell?*'

'*Bone!*'

'*Bone WHO?*'

'*BONE SAXON!*'

Below ground in the locker room, meanwhile, Coach Moose Henning was concluding his pre-game address.

*

Mr Hill studied a table that the Tennessee Area Manager had crafted.

FINANCIAL WORKSHEET

Monthly Investment	Share Price	Shares Purchased
$ 200	$20	10
200	10	20
200	5	40
200	2	100
200	5	40
$1,000		210

'In five months you have invested a thousand dollars, right? You started buying at twenty dollars a share, and the price is now five dollars a share. You have lost money, right?'

Mr Hill said, 'I spoze so.'

'*Wrong!*' exclaimed Bleitgeist. 'You have bought 210 shares that are now selling at five dollars each and are worth $1,050. You have made $50, even though the shares have fallen to a quarter of the price you started buying them at.'

'How's that?'

'Every month you invest a fixed cash amount. When the price of the shares rises, the fixed amount buys fewer shares. When the price falls, the fixed amount buys more shares. So you buy shares at an average price which is lower than the average price over the period of purchase. See?'

Mr Hill studied the table, pronouncing each figure aloud as he carefully checked and rechecked the calculations.

*

The crowds roared and their feet pounded the grandstand, as the University of Tennessee team emerged from the locker room. Bone and Mule Henderson, the fullback, were jogging together, both silent, both aroused. Out of the corners of their eyes they detected the cheerleaders, but, unlike Lot's wife, did not turn to look at their legs. They had a job to do.

All stood and faced the Flag for the playing of the *Star Spangled Banner*, the Big Orange and Razorback teams with their helmets in their hands, the flag fluttering in a strong wind. Bone was not thinking of the *Star Spangled Banner*. He was thinking of Coach's instructions to elect the south end if they won the toss.

Another mighty roar arose from the stands and Bone thought of Coach's game plan: 'Keep to the ground until you feel you can confidently take to the air.' And his advice to the defence: 'We've got wet weather. The ground's damp, and the bawl's hard to handle. Hit hard and aim for the bawl.'

*

'In other words, whether the price goes up or down, you still make money. Whatever happens, you achieve the long-term goals of your estate planning. Now let me ask you, Mr Hill, how many children have you?'

'Two.'

'Are they boys or girls or one of each?'

'Both of 'em's girls.'

'And how old are they?'

'One's thirteen and the other's eleven. The littlest one's birthday's next month.'

'And do you want your children to go to college, Mr Hill?'

'Wail, that depends on ifn they're smart enough.'

'But you would't want to deny them the advantages of a college education?'

'Nor ifn they're smart enough.'

'Have you any idea how much a college education costs, Mr Hill?'

'I know it's expensive.'

'Am I also right in thinking that one day you and your wife would like to retire? Or maybe you intend to work for the rest of your life?'

'Not if I can help it! I reckon on retiring sometime, once the girls're gone and the home's paid for. The way inflation's goin', though, you gotta give it a purty hard lick to retire decently. We got us a little vegetable patch and my wife bakes her own bread.'

'How old are you, Mr Hill?'

'Thirty-eight.'

Bleitgeist wrote '38' on his Financial Worksheet.

'And at what age would you like to retire? Sixty? Sixty-five? . . . Fine! To send each of your children to three years of college will cost you about $12,000, and a four-year course still more. Just to give us an idea of how much money might be involved here, let's budget for two children, each receiving three years of college. Will that be all right? . . . What are your children's names, Mr Hill?'

'The oldest one's cawled Mary Lou, and the littlest is Barbara, but we cawl her Babs.'

Bleitgeist wrote on the Financial Worksheet: 'Mary Lou's + Babs's Col Ed = $24,000'.

'And what are your living expenses?'

'At the moment, I'm payin' off the notes on the house. They come to three hundred a month.'

'Let's assume that you've finished paying off your house and your children are grown. Would $10,000 a year be a reasonable estimate of what it costs to support yourself and your wife?'

'Somethin' around that figure, I guess.'

'You would expect to receive about $3,000 from Social Security, which leaves about $7,000 a year towards retirement to provide from your own savings. Mr Hill, for that kind of return on capital we are talking about an estate in the region of $70,000 in today's money, or $140,000 in tomorrow's money.'

'That's a lot of money.'

'That's right, Mr Hill. It's a *lot* of money. And that's what we at World of Finance are here for, to help you analyse your financial goals realistically.'

Bleitgeist had now completed Phase II of his presentation.

'We offer two types of Plan,' he continued. 'Our Fully Paid Plan is for investing a lump sum of a thousand dollars or more – money that you have in a bank account or in certificates of deposit earning an inadequate return. For investing regular monthly amounts, money that you are able to save from current income, we offer a Dynamic Growth Plan. How much money do you happen to have in the bank?'

''Bout eleven thousand.'

Bleitgeist wrote '$11,000' on the Financial Worksheet.

'And how much are you able to save every month?'

'It depends on how wail we're doin'. Just at the moment, we ain't doin' too wail.'

'Let's assume that you leave $1,000 in the bank for immediate contingencies and invest $10,000 in a Stars and Stripes Fund Fully Paid Plan. For that amount, you receive the benefit of a twelve per cent discount off the usual acquisition charge. As the Fund's sponsor, World of Finance deducts only seven and a half per cent to defray the cost of selling and buying back the shares, which is to say that, when you decide to withdraw your money, it costs you nothing. Let's assume also that you set aside $150 every month and invest that money in a Stars and Stripes Fund Dynamic Growth Plan. Is $150 enough? Or would you prefer to aim for $200?'

'Keep to $150.'

'Based on past performance' – Bleitgeist exhibited a report of a rival mutual fund showing its past performance – 'you could reasonably expect $10,000 to be worth $20,000 in four years, when you start paying for your daughters' college educations, while $150 a month ought to be worth $30,000 to $35,000 in ten years, when you would stop payments. Allowing the money to continue growing, it ought to be worth $100,000 to $150,000 by the time you are ready to retire. Can you see how this is a practical way towards achieving your investment goals?'

'Looks purty good,' admitted Mr Hill.

'Do you carry life insurance, Mr Hill?'

''Bout $30,000.'

'So, were you to die tomorrow, your wife would *not* have an income of five thousand a year? . . . Our Dynamic Growth Plan comes in two forms, with or without insurance. Suppose you take the insured Plan. Should you happen to die before completing it, World of Finance will complete it for you in one lump payment. Wouldn't you like to challenge yourself to save more than $150 a month?'

'A hundred and fifty's enough.'

'Would you like the Plan with or without the insurance endorsement?'

'I'd right like the extra life cover. Whut do you thank?'

'I think you need it, in which case let me ask you this. I know it's a personal question, Mr Hill, but are you in good health?'

After the salesman's departure ('Hurry back to see us'), Mr Hill sat for a while behind his cash register meditating a liquidity problem of which, until half an hour previously, he had been ignorant. Behind him was an aluminium facsimile of the drive-in's namesake: a lean, heroic pioneer dressed in animal skins. Mr Hill was chewing pensively at the stump of a dead King Edward cigar when he heard Scroggs announce: '*With forty-eight seconds remaining to play in the first quarter, the score is the University of Tennessee nothing, the University of Arkansas nothing. We pause now for station identification.*'

*

Detectives broke into Bumper's apartment while he was in the shower and arrested him. Others belonging to his organization were already at the police station, all handcuffed and dressed in pyjamas. As soon as they saw their General Manager, they lifted their manacled hands and began denouncing him, engraving the moment on Bumper's mind.

*

The Vols scored on a brilliant end run by Buddy Askew. However, a spectacular line buck by Bronco Jackson diving into the end zone over the centre's head was nullified by a penalty. When yet another scoring sprint by Mule Henderson on a delayed handoff was called back for a penalty, Coach Moose Henning protested.

There the first quarter ended. Early in the second quarter, a sustained drive carried the Volunteers in twelve plays from their own fourteen yard line to the Razorbacks' one inch line, but they failed to score.

Up to this point, the Big Orange limited its attack to a ground game. Now it took to the air. Bronco, who had taken a lateral from Buddy, passed to Buck. The Razorbacks, observed Scroggs, were ineffective against such razzle-dazzle, but they were helped by penalties. A long pass to John Murray might have been ruled complete due to defensive interference. Instead, it was ruled intercepted for interference with the pass defender. There followed another incident involving Coach Henning.

*

During halftime Scroggs summarized the game for his listeners and discussed it with Bo Pearson.

'We have been seeing some fine footbawl this afternoon, Bo,' said Scroggs.

'We sure have. Have you noticed how every time Tennessee gets possession of the bawl, they just have to score?'

'That's right, Bo, and in spite of some fine defensive play by Arkansas. They're a really scrappy bunch, and there's no faulting them on tactics. Did you notice how they automatically pulled the extra linebacker when they expected the screen pass to Murray?'

'Yes I did. Tommy Tackett, the defensive captain for Arkansas, has called the right patterns all the way. And their passin' game is just as strong as their runnin' game. Coach Henning's decision to keep them to the air during the second quarter proves that. Perhaps we'll see a return to the ground durin' the second half.'

'I think we can expect to see more running plays during the second half and that we can look forward to more fine defensive play from Tennessee.'

'It's the defensive team, of course, that comes in for most of the criticism and little of the glory.'

'That's right. But I suspect that today's statistics are going to show a diffrunt story. I don't think Tennessee has yielded more than thirty yards all afternoon. They've rushed hard and tackled hard the whole way.'

'They've been helped, of course, by the loss of Pete Calhoun. That must have been a heartbreaking setback to Coach Charlie Boone. But what a tremendous tackle that was by Bone Saxon.'

'He's been in on almost every play.'

'Yes he has. He's really earned the title to his position as Monster Man.'

'*That's right. And UT has certainly had the backing of their supporters. Just listen to their cheering.*'

'*. . . Strawberry shortcake, gooseberry pie, V-I-C-T-O-R-Y! That's the way you spell it. Here's the way you yell it, VICtory! VICtory! . . .*'

*

The oncoming traffic prevented Bleitgeist from turning left. He revved the motor impatiently, waiting for the light to change. A block further on, he had to wait for another light, then found himself behind a tractor. 'That's the trouble with these Southern states,' he thought irritably. 'Too many tractors on the road.'

*

Bone resumed his position on the field for the second half, his teammates ranged alongside toeing a stripe of powdered chalk. He stood in a tense, crouched posture, left shoulder-pad aimed downfield, tense padded rear aimed at Lester Blount, the right guard, and the buckle of his hip pads overlooking the tense padded rear of Blaize Bullings, the right tackle. Downfield, the Razorbacks defiantly clawed the earth with their cleats. Then Steve Talbertson broke the tense silence with his honking challenge: '*Lez gitum, Arr-ange!*'

The whistle blew simultaneously and the pigskin spiralled end over end into Razorback territory. Bubba Marples, Arkansas's All-Southwestern Conference back, returned it to his fifteen before the first Volunteers reached him. Marples neatly sidestepped, and Blaize and Lester collided. Steve got a shoulder in his thigh, but Bubba swivelled and survived him and looked as though he might break clear. Then Bone caught him with a shuddering shoulder-in-the-stomach lunge.

Exhilarated by the tackle, Bone sprang to his feet, and the Razorbacks went into the first huddle of the second half.

'*Pork chop, pork chop, greasy, greasy, we'll beat your team easy, easy. Gotta go, go! Gotta go! Gotta fight, fight! Gotta fight! Gotta win, win! Gotta win! Gotta, gotta, gotta, gotta, gotta go! Fight! Win!*' roared the Razorback fans.

The Razorbacks came out of the huddle. '*The centre over the ball. The quarterback calling signals. The Big Orange in a six-two-two-one defence. Man in motion to the left. Quarterback back to pass. A late handoff to Marples up the middle to the twenty, a gain of one yard on the play.*'

'How'd they feel?' Coach Jerry asked Bone when the Vols resumed possession. He wanted to get the feel of the other team after its halftime conference with Coach Charlie Boone.

'I didn't notice all that much diffrunce,' replied Bone.

Coach Jerry looked thoughtful.

'I thank they mean to give us a mean time,' said Bone.

Coach Jerry looked troubled.

Matters now improved for the Volunteers. They enjoyed a period of play immune from penalties. Mule took a handoff, broke into the secondary, found a convoy of blockers, gained another twenty yards and was only driven out of bounds at the Razorbacks' thirty. Tennessee scored six plays later on a pass from Askew to Murray, and Maurice Chron converted for the extra point.

The Big Orange defence then forced the Hogs to punt, and Bronco returned the ball to the Arkansas twenty-five. '*Go B O! Go B O! Go B O! Go BIG ORANGE!*' screamed the Volunteer fans. Arkansas called a time-out.

*

'*Suddenly it's a diffrunt bawl game,*' said Scroggs.

'*It sure is,*' said Bo. 'If the Vols score a third time, it's hard to see how Arkansas can overcome a margin of three touchdowns and come from behind to win the game.'

'*Although against Texas Tech in 1967, Coach Charlie Boone's offensive eleven did exactly that. The score was 21 to 0 at the half, and Arkansas came from behind to win an upset victory 22 to 21 over the Red Raiders.*'

'*That's right. Few college teams in the country have Arkansas's capability for pulling the game out of the hat at the last minute. They know how to play sixty minutes of footbawl.*'

*

Noam van Zilver inspected various hotels. None was satisfactory. Those fronting the market square crawled with informers. His accommodation needs were more furtive than commodious. Some students from Gojam directed him to the YMCA.

'We're not getting any reply from Teheran, Mr Rubin.'

'Please try again in an hour.'

*

'*Get fired up! Get fired up!*' screamed the Razorback fans.

Arkansas was at the Vols' forty-five stripe and its cheerleaders were going ape. A pass complete to Haynes took the ball past the thirty. The clangour of cowbells had not died before the Hogs came out of the huddle again. A line buck by Burleigh produced another five yards and a deafening roar from the Hogs' supporters. '*Pow Woodridge, number seventy-three, a junior from Greenville, South Carolina, made the stop.*'

Arkansas called another time-out to interrupt the running of the clock.

'*And the question on everybody's mind here in Bob Neyland Memorial Stadium with less than ten minutes remaining in the game is whether the revitalized Razorbacks of the University of Arkansas will sustain this drive for a touchdown and keep up their enthusiasm to come back and win this game with two more touchdowns and a two-point conversion,*' said Scroggs.

Now everyone on the Arkansas team was in the grip of this new spirit. The same thought was on every linesman's mind as he dug his knuckles and cleats into the dirt; on the quarterback's mind as he called out the signals and waited for the snap.

'*What's deceptive about Bone is, he's a good accelerator.*'

'*That's right, Bo. And he's a very durable player. He hasn't missed a game in two years.*'

'*A battering ram! Last year, I'm told, he suffered from severe headaches. They had to devise a special helmet for him.*'

'*This football game is brought to you by Sears, home of the Diehard battery, and Gillette. Ejector shaving is just ahead of you, the best shave of your life.*'

The snap.

'*Morse back to pass. He moves. He takes his time. He can't find daylight. Looking downfield for a receiver – the blitz is on! Morse elects to run. Mercury Morse, there's nothing he can't do!*'

Mercury negotiated the Orange rush, reached the line of scrimmage, and it looked as though he might go the distance. The Arkansas fans were on their feet. Then Bone shot out of the secondary. There was a pile-up. Bone felt a sharp pain in his leg. Everyone seemed to be taking his time getting up.

'*It looks like there's been an injury on the play. The referee's called an official time-out.*'

Bone could hear the eerie silence in the stadium as they carried him to the locker room.

At the hospital, the doctor informed him that the tibia and the fibula were broken, that the tendons around the knee were torn, that the leg would have to be set. Bone was conscious the whole time, staring morosely at the swelling and the blue muscle. But all he thought about was whether Mercury Morse had made the first down.

3

CAPTIVE AUDIENCE

Finding accommodation in Big Orange Country on weekends when the Vols were home was difficult. Bleitgeist, practical in all things, stopped outside Knoxville, short of the heaviest congestion. The Great Smokies Appalachian Inn stood in the bed of an abandoned quarry surrounded on three sides by mounds of rubble, but inside were pile carpets, thick upholstery and soundproofing. Like most motels, it bore the reassuring badge of affiliation with a national chain. Bleitgeist attempted a presentation to the desk clerk and was rebuffed, and to the bellhop and was rebuffed. He did not solicit the bellhop's help with his bag. He believed that tips degraded both parties to the transaction.

He found his room, confirmed that the towels were clean, that soap was provided and that the lock on the door worked, then posted the PLEASE DO NOT DISTURB sign. He wanted to finish reading an article in *Business Week* advocating the abolition of the front load.

The article vexed him. Its whole attitude and tone were offensive. 'What does this schmuck know about funds? Always criticizing the load. So, if no load, how do they pay the Override?'

The telephone rang. It was the desk clerk responding to his query about a room for conducting interviews.

'I can give you the Green Room,' the clerk said. 'We normally charge twenty dollars an hour if you intend to use it for business purposes.'

'What other kind of purposes are there?' asked Bleitgeist.

'Meetings with guests connected with sporting or athletic activities entitle our guests to use the Green Room compliments of the house.'

'This kind of facility ought to be free to *all* your guests,' replied Bleitgeist indignantly. 'The price of a room includes use of the swimming pool and sauna, right? So, why not the Green Room? So, why don't you charge for the lounge?'

'I'm sorry, sir. If you'd like to speak with the manager.'

Bleitgeist spoke with the manager, told him that he was in Knoxville to open up the Big Orange Market and obtained a discount.

Hardly had he resumed reading before the telephone rang again. It was his New Man, Levy Levin. 'How'd you know where I was staying?' he asked.

'Whaddaya mean, how'd I know where you're staying? I figured it out, that's how. You couldn't get a room in town, so the Great Smokies Appalachian is the most likely place, right? Like the company's paying your expenses.'

'You should've been a detective. So, what do you want? I'm in conference.'

'Come off it.'

'Well anyway, I'm busy.'

'Betcha you're reading a magazine. What I want to know is, maybe it's okay if I bring a friend and meet you at twelve instead of ten?'

'I have an appointment at twelve,' said Bleitgeist. He did not want to pay for Levy and the friend's lunch. 'What's your friend's name and what's he do?' he inquired politely.

'Whaddaya mean, what's his name? Fitz. And whaddaya mean, what's he do? Nothing. He's a student. What I want to know is, who gets the New Man Bonus?'

'No problem. You recruit him. He reaches $50,000 in Personal Volume. You get the New Man Bonus. Now if that's all that's bothering you, I'll hang up.'

'Okay. See you at ten tomorrow,' said Levy.

As long as Bleitgeist was hunting for prospects, making presentations, recruiting and supervising or contemplating his stock options he was content, and when he received his monthly commission statement, he was ecstatic. Then he went to bed boasting to his wife and fell asleep, happily planning the allocation of his winnings between different WoF-sponsored funds.

It was not so most nights, though, and tonight was particularly troubled. He tossed and turned, wrestled with the pillows, rearranged the pillows, was almost asleep, then was wide awake again. Sounds of the Johnny Carson Show from a neighbouring room prompted a quest for earplugs. *He had forgotten to pack them*! He turned on the radio. It was all advertising jingles. He took a hypnotic. He had little faith in the drug, but, mercifully, it had the desired effect and he slipped into unconsciousness, only to awake soon afterwards from a nightmare. Joe Stamp, who managed Atlantic II (Pennsylvania, Delaware, Maryland and Virginia), was poaching his prospects and Overrides. Turning on the light, he attempted to read an article about the outlook for tobacco futures. The outlook was bleak, said the article. Consumers were wary of cancer. Balkan imports were a worry to growers in Virginia and the Carolinas. He should have been a professional instead of a salesman, he reflected: an architect, like his brother; or a lawyer, like his cousin; or a doctor, like his other brother. Yes, he should have been a doctor. But doctors had not cured his insomnia. They always advised him not to worry, especially at night. Night was intended for repose, not for worrying about WoFers poaching his prospects and Overrides. The advice was sound, but it had not conquered his insomnia. Clearly, Stamp was scheming with Levin to cheat him of his Override. Why else was Levy so anxious about the New Man Bonus on Fitz?

*

While Bleitgeist fretted, John Fitz studied. He was in his room at the Francis Ellsworth Haynes Memorial Graduate Students Dormitory studying the charge structure of the Dynamic Growth Plan with Insurance. He had devoted the evening to the DGPINS.

'The DGPINS', he read, 'is offered in varying monthly investment units, ranging from $25 a month for ten years (the $3,000 Plan) to investment units of $500 a month for fifteen years (the $90,000 Plan).'

Fitz underlined 'DGPINS' and 'investment units'.

'Ten-year Plans with a face amount in excess of $60,000', he read, 'may be insured up to and including $60,000. Fifteen-year Plans with a face amount in excess of $90,000 may be insured up to and including $90,000.'

He underlined 'face amount'.

He was preparing for an important interview with Mr Levin's associate and wanted to understand the Plans' charge structures in case this man with the peculiar name should ask him about it.

*

The Founder worked late, too. The hours between midnight and four were often devoted to managers on Regional Schedule or above who brought their problems to the Top of the Spirals. Joe Stamp was with him tonight. Joe wanted to annex East Tennessee to Atlantic II.

'Please understand, I have nothing against Bob personally,' said Stamp. 'It's just that I think he's neglecting the Territory. How much Volume are we getting out of there?'

'A system is needed whereby everyone participates in the fruits of production without feeling constrained by the means of production,' the Founder replied.

'I have ten men I could send into East Tennessee tomorrow,' said Stamp.

*

Bleitgeist awoke, sat up and, as he had seen Goofy do, pinched himself. He examined his watch, saw that it was past one, got up and opened the window onto a damp, still evening suffused with metallurgical effluents. Exhausted, fearful of renewed attempts at sleep, unable to read *Business Week*, he dressed and went down to the bar. It was softly lit and empty, save for the barman, a humble employee plainly needing financial advice. Speakers buried in its spongy walls dispersed soft music.

'Not a very busy evening,' observed Bleitgeist without conscious irony.

'Quiet as a crematorium,' replied the bartender. 'It's always like this. Beats me why they keep the joint open. We lock up at two unless a customer shows up. You just made it.'

'You've not had a customer all evening? Not one?'

'Not here, mister. It's like a morgue. And it's Saturday night at that.'

'You must get lonely,' offered Bleitgeist.

'Loneliest job I ever had. Good thing I'm not scared of ghosts! Did you ever read that book *Blind in Dusty Wraps*, about the mummified pharaoh who came back to life four thousand years after he died? They made a movie out of it. This pharaoh woke up, all wrapped up in dusty bandages, like they use on mummies, but in the meantime they had already sealed up the pyramid and made another guy pharaoh. I can't remember what happened, or how he finally escaped, or if he got his throne back. I just remember him feeling around in the dark of that tomb and his old grey bandages. Talk about scary movies! That was the scariest movie I near ever seen. Anyway, this place kinda reminds me of *Blind in Dusty Wraps*.'

Although he had not read *Blind in Dusty Wraps* nor seen the film, the Manager for Tennessee empathized. 'I know how you feel,' he said and, after a couple of companionable Budweisers, added, 'Ernie, has it ever occurred to you how banks make money?'

*

Elsewhere, the company prospered. Weekends were a banner time for Volume. Clients put down pick and shovel and, in *Gasthaus* and *Weinstube*, Strumpf's and Handschuh's trainees were signing them up between drinking songs. The Folkestone Plan was 'selling like hot cakes', in Clovis's happy phrase, while General Managers, Divisional Managers, Regional Managers and Branch Managers all over the Orient expounded inspirational advice, lending credence to Baroque's celebrated maxim that the sun never set on Training.

Thus a GM in Tokyo, advising trainees to make a service call on Client within three months of a sale and use it to sell him another Plan: 'Client's financial position may have changed in the meantime. There may be new WoF products tailored to his needs. The follow-up is not a luxury. It is a necessity.'

In Manila: 'Only when you convince a man that he *needs* what you are offering can a presentation be successful. And that means a careful, systematic analysis of his Total Financial Goals.'

In Bangkok: 'Your target should be a minimum of a dozen Client Calls a day, including Cold Calls, Call Backs and Service Calls. It all boils down to the question that every Associate has to ask himself: "Am I really serious about wanting to sell more than a million dollars a year?"'

In Hong Kong: 'Closing the credibility gap is often the first step in a presentation, especially with people accustomed to low, fixed-interest returns on capital. I show annual reports, newspaper clippings and our advertisements to prove that we are an established, highly reputable firm.'

In Taipei: 'I don't just sell investment plans. I sell professional management. We have the world's best. So regardless of what happens in the stock market on any day, our clients can be confident that their money is in good hands.'

*

Bone was wheeled from the operating room on a trolley, his leg in a cast. It was covered by a plain white sheet, illuminated by the blue night lights in the hospital's corridors. The nurses were circumspect. Blaize Bullings, Buddy Askew, Mule Henderson, Lester Blount, Bill Yancey, Chubby Gross, John Murray, Steve Talbertson, Bronco Jackson and Coaches Henning and Hamilton quietly awaited news in the waiting room.

*

The presentation to Ernie, although wasted on an insolvent, calmed Bleitgeist's nerves. He arranged the covers snugly around him and fell asleep, his dreams relaying music, his cheeks and lips pink and puffy, delivered at last from both fear and insolence, the clouded brain behind the lidded eyes now cherubically innocent of the vexations of recruitment, supervising, mediating his salesmen's quarrels and keeping his standard paramount in his Territory. Who, seeing him thus, would have thought that his repose was to be disturbed again?

The Razorback fans had travelled far for their team's reputation to be tarnished so badly. About the time of Bone's injury, the rain which had been falling in a fine drizzle all afternoon bucketed down and the Hogs had been dragged through the mud. Their fans, huddling close under drenched newspapers and plastic bags, had the gruesome experience of watching the Four Moosemen romp over All-Southwestern Conference defensive guard Roy Wethersby and around Associated Press Second Team All-American defensive end Jimmy Hasselle. The ordeal had proved too much for them. Something was needed to exorcize the ghost of their shame, something by way of atonement.

Their first plan, extreme even by their standards of vandalism, was to set alight the UT Administration Building. It took the full force of Coach Charlie Boone's position and influence to dissuade them from that rash enterprise. He warned them bluntly that they were in the heart of Big Orange Country.

'Some of yawl are *drunk!*' said Coach Boone. 'Wail, I guess we're awl purty disappointed. Wail, I'm just as disappointed as yawl are, but is that any reason to *break the law*? I'm sure none of yawl realize whut yawl're doin' or I wouldn't have to come out heah at this hour and remind yawl that yawl are about to commit *arson*! Yawl *heah*?' And even as he spoke, some Orangemen passing in a car threw a bottle at them and yelled, '*Go B O!*'

'*Woo pig SOOie!*' the Hogs' fans retaliated and leapt into their cars to give chase.

The provocateurs eluded them, but round the sleepless city they drove, until they reached the Great Smokies Appalachian Inn. From the window of his room, Bleitgeist saw them in the parking lot erecting a straw effigy of Coach Moose Henning, saw them set the effigy alight, saw it engulfed in flames. What was going on out there? Was this a meeting of the Klan? Was he about to witness a lynching? Were those fools going to *set fire to his Targa*? He heard a gun explode, followed immediately by another pig summons. *What was that?*

He rang the desk clerk. 'What's going on out there?'

'Nothing to worry about, suh,' replied the desk clerk reassuringly. 'They're just boys.'

*

Bumper knew by the behaviour of the prisoners sharing his cell that dawn was approaching. They washed their arms and feet in a slop bucket and prostrated themselves on the stone floor. Had Sher Mirza betrayed him? *He* was not in custody. Bumper knew that Sher Mirza chafed under grievances against him. He had deprived Sher Mirza of the right to manage his own Territory. He had showed partiality in handing out Referrals.

'Call for Baroque from Johannesburg. Think we should wake him up?'

'Tell them to call back in maybe a couple of hours.'

*

Daylight in Knoxville. Potted imitation judas trees with bright green plastic leaves. A nylon carpet resembling a golfing green. An imitation walnut table beneath a photograph of an Old Master framed in moulded gilt stucco. Bleitgeist selected flapjacks and decaffeinated coffee from a morocco-bound menu, then turned, groggy but awake, to the local newspaper. '*VOLS BEAT HOGS 21–0 BONE SAXON INJURED*'.

Standing by the lift after he finished breakfast was a short, sharp-featured man of ashen complexion. Bleitgeist evinced no surprise. Only in mock amazement at a prospect's imprudent estate planning did he evince surprise. He gave his trainee a quick glance and decided that he was dressed adequately. Levy studied his Area Manager and made the same observation. Both men were wearing identical suits.

'*Ten o'clock*, I said.'

'So, what's it matter if I turn up early?'

'You are *two hours* early.'

'So, just be glad I'm not late.'

They entered the lift and waited in silence until the doors shut. Then Levy announced, 'I got a *prospect*.'

'Fine,' said Bleitgeist, feigning equanimity.

'So, maybe you'd like to supervise the presentation?'

Bleitgeist accepted opportunity as and when it arose. He inquired little into causes. He was a pragmatist.

'I'd hate to lose this one on account of lack of experience. Why don't you make the presentation and give me the credit?' said Levy.

'First, you ask me to supervise the presentation. Now, you want me to make the presentation. What's the percentage?'

'There's not going to be a percentage.'

'So, I take my time, my professional knowledge, skill and experience and make the sale for you, and you wanna keep all the commission?'

'That's what I want.'

They got in the Targa and drove to meet Levy's prospect. Pursuant to Levy's directions, Bleitgeist parked the Targa at the rear of the building, near the ambulances. A rush of cold wind struck them as their feet touched the asphalt. The Area Manager shrank inside his overcoat. Had a detective been following them, he might have reported of their progress at this stage: 'Two short white men with sallow complexions, one middle-aged, one in his twenties, were seen leaving the car together, each carrying a briefcase.'

Leading Bleitgeist exultantly up a ramp and onto a landing supporting half a dozen bins filled with soiled bandages and other refuse, Levy pushed on through twin swinging doors into a glossy corridor. Beyond a bend in the corridor was another pair of swinging doors; beyond that, an open area buzzing with activity. Were they in a kitchen?

'You know the way?' asked Bleitgeist.

A sombre circle of prospects in wheelchairs detained them. They wore Government-issue pyjamas and dressing gowns and were parked in front of a television. The television was on, but no one was watching. Conversation absorbed them. They spoke in flat, accentless voices which the Area Manager associated with the Military and Public Employee Markets. He assessed them as being war veterans and whispered to his trainee, 'Wonder what sort of benefits they're getting?'

Levy, who was thinking the same, said, 'We'll get them on the way back.'

The two Estate Planners explored another corridor crowded with nurses carrying trays of instruments and dressings and porters pushing trolleys laden with bodies under sheets, and came to a door posted Operating Room. Here they doubled back.

'This has gotta be it,' pronounced Levy before another door in another corridor.

'Are you sure?'

'Man, it's gotta be.'

'Maybe we, like, oughta knock?'

Levy pushed open the door and peered inside.

'Wrong room,' he said.

'Don't you think we oughta go back to the veterans?'

*

Bone was dreaming about the Sugar Bowl. The sky was brilliant, the air warm and balmy, Tennessee was ahead 28 to 0, and he had led two goal-line stands, recovered four fumbles, blocked two punts. He was leading interference for Blaize, who had picked up a fumble and was romping downfield towards another touchdown, when these two weirdos entered the room. Bone's first impulse was to cover himself. On further consideration, though, he thought that they might be pro scouts.

One of them asked him, 'What if I was to present you with a cheque for fifty thousand dollars, Bone? Would you be happy?' Only pro scouts would start talking about big money straight off the bat like that, Bone reflected.

What gave selling its zest, what made it so exciting, Bleitgeist so often told his trainees, was its unpredictability. Rarely were two presentations the same. Every new door opened onto a new world. Here was his first prospect with a leg in a gesso cast.

'I sure do appreciate yawl coming to talk with me,' said Bone. 'I railly do. But the doctor says I'll never play again. But don't thank I don't railly appreciate yawl coming to see me. I jus' wish yawl hadn't had to come all this way for nothin'.'

'We're sorry about your injury,' said Levy.

'It's very sad,' added Bleitgeist. 'Sad, but not tragic. What's needed is to convert defeat into victory.'

Both men advanced to the bed, their right hands extended to shake Bone's, on their faces an expression of consternation and compassion.

'Mr Bleitgeist's going to offer you something that will convert defeat into victory,' said Levy.

'That's right, Bone. You must be pretty downcast. Yesterday, you were the star of the team. The world was at your feet. Today, your leg's broken, and your career is in ruins. I can imagine how you must feel. In your position, I'd feel terrible.'

'Mr Bleitgeist's going to show you how you can make a lot of money,' said Levy.

'No doubt you've been wondering exactly what you're going to do once you get out of the hospital. So much has changed. First the injury. Then the cast. Then discovering that you will never be able to play football again.'

'All that's very sad,' added Levy.

'That's why we have called on you, Bone. To help you meet your changed circumstances in a positive spirit.'

'So that you don't let your crushed leg get you down.'

'I'll bet that one of your worries, Bone, is how you're going to make a living now that you are no longer able to play football. Have you been worrying about that?'

'Mr Bleitgeist wants to tell you about mutual funds,' said Levy.

'What is it you've always wanted – wanted more than anything, Bone?'

'You mean for rail? Or jus' supposin'?'

'For real.'

'To be an Awl-American.'

'Is that what you want more than anything?' In the Area Manager's experience of Goals, his prospect's ambition was unique.

'What Mr Bleitgeist is trying to say,' prompted Levy, 'is there anything that you've always wanted to *own*. Something that you can buy for *money*? See what I mean?'

'Can't thank of anythang,' said Bone.

Bleitgeist had an impressive battery of weapons to strike down opposition, and his trainee was looking on. Yet his guns were silent. Suddenly, he had an inspiration. 'Bone, how'd you like to own *your own pro team*?'

'Mr Bleitgeist's going to show you how you can own your own pro team,' chorused Levy.

'Would you like that, Bone?'

'Sure,' said Bone.

'That would be just wonderful, wouldn't it? Perhaps almost as wonderful as being an All-American. Bone, what do you think stands between Bone Saxon, the injured athlete we know today, and the Bone Saxon of tomorrow, whose own pro team has just won the Super Bowl?'

'Money, I guess.'

'Owning your own pro team would be simple if you had fifty million dollars to invest; right, Bone? The problem is getting together fifty million dollars,'

'I guess so.'

'Bone, do banks make money? . . .'

*

The silence from Teheran began to trouble even the Founder.

Marty: 'We've been trying to contact Teheran for twelve hours. It looks like Bumper has, maybe, taken a powder.'

Baroque: 'Keep trying.'

*

Having perceived that Bone was not a prospect, Bleitgeist began a presentation to recruit him as a New Man.

'Can you see how you would be performing a real service to your friends and former teammates by pointing out to them the many advantages of investing in mutual funds?'

Levy: 'Now that you know that you can never play football again, Bone, doesn't it make sense to use your intelligence and influence to help others who are too busy playing football to manage their estates properly?'

Bleitgeist extracted a New Man application form from his briefcase and completed it on Bone's behalf. 'Who would you like to give as a reference?' he asked.

'Mr Moose Henning.'

'How do you spell Moose?'

'M-O-O-S-E.'
'Is that a real name or a nickname?'
'A nickname, I suppose.'
'Address and occupation?'
'UT Athletics Department, head coach,' said Bone.
'And for a second reference?'
'Mr Jerry Hamilton . . . .'

*

'Gee, that was *beauti*ful!' said Levy, returning to the motel in the Targa for their appointment with Fitz. '*Really* beautiful. You really closed him.'

'Successful presentations, successful New Man recruitment, success at every level depends on your ability to assess your prospect's needs correctly, which, in turn,' said Bleitgeist, 'implies a systematic analysis of his Total Financial Goals. Most people, you will find, harbour a secret dream that can be so important to them that they are afraid to talk about it. Our job is to assemble the facts in such a way as to translate that dream into reality, and the best way of accomplishing this is by interrogation. How much do you earn? How much are you paying on your house? How would you like to own your own pro team? How much are you willing to sacrifice to own your own pro team? Prospects are often unaware of their deeper needs or incapable of acting on a proper understanding of their deeper needs. Our job is, first, to help them understand their deeper needs, then to define the practical steps for accomplishing their goals, and finally, to help them overcome the difficulty of making a decision.'

'He probably won't get his leg out of a cast until February.'

'No problem. Call on him again before he leaves the hospital and give him more brochures to read. Explain to him the principle of Vertical Diversification and ask him if he understands how the withdrawal privileges work. Give him a Wiesenberger to study.'

'What's a Wiesenberger?'

'You've been selling funds a month already, and you don't know what a Wiesenberger is? Whatsa matter with you?

A Wiesenberger is a study by a highly reputable firm of stock analysts of all the mutual funds in the country. It tells how all the different mutual funds perform so you can make comparisons.'

'So how does that help me sell the Stars and Stripes Fund?'

'It doesn't, but it can help you introduce a New Man to a new hobby which, like any other hobby, can become an obsession. The more he knows about funds, the more obsessed he gets, the more he will want to try to sell them. See?

'Okay, so who gets the credit for the New Man Bonus?'

'No problem. You found the guy, you get the bonus.'

'Okay, who gets the credit for the Successful Supervisory Experience?'

'I do.' Accumulating SSEs, awarded after a trainee's Volume reached $150,000, was the easiest way to rise in schedule. 'But the good news is that you get the Override. Because when you reach Senior Schedule, you get Senior over anyone working in the Knoxville area.'

'Okay, so when do I reach Senior Schedule?'

'When you reach $300,000 in opened Volume. You sell a $1,000 Fully Paid, and you get credit for $1,000 in Volume. You sell a ten-year $100-a-month Dynamic Growth Plan, and you get credit for $12,000 in Volume. When your Volume totals $300,000, you reach Senior Schedule. The Schedule Tables is something you ought to know about.'

'So what happens to the Override?'

'What happens to the Override? Once you've reached Senior, your commission on Fully Paids rises to 4½ per cent. A New Man just starting out makes 3½ per cent. You get the difference between his commission and yours. If he sells a $5,000 Fully Paid, he makes $175, and you make $50. That's how the Override works.'

'What happens if he catches up with me?'

'Then for that trainee you automatically get the next schedule up. Only if he passes you in schedule do you stop drawing an Override on his sales. The quickest way to get rich is to think territorially and build your own organization. That's how the system works. And by the way, did you notice how I kept nodding? It helps to generate an atmosphere of agreement. Mr Worth, can you see how a comfortable retirement tomorrow demands prudent and systematic investment today? Nod your head. Mr Worth, doesn't it make more sense to gamble on the future of the entire American economy than to risk all your eggs in one basket? Nod your head. It helps to put him in a Yes-Frame-of-Mind. See?'

*

Van Zilver presented his passport, one of several issued to various pseudonyms, and received from the clerk at the Poste Restante *guichet* of the General Post Office at Addis Ababa three large parcels stamped 'Printed Matter'. He took them to his room. They contained prospectuses and annual reports for the Fenner Biddup Offshore Fund, Fiduciary of Fiduciaries, Orbis Fund, Kapitalsfonds, Stars and Stripes Fund and Commodities Fund in four of the languages in which van Zilver was fluent; Folkestone Plan Questions and Answers brochures, WoF Investment Program and Redevco applications, specimen signature cards for opening current accounts, deposit accounts and securities safekeeping accounts at Anonymous Depositors Bank, Financial Worksheets, Designation of Beneficiary forms, Letters of Intention, reprints of articles written by journalists in WoF's pay praising WoF products and, for freebies to prospects, Coinage of the World calendars and ballpoint pens inscribed with the company's name and logo. Van Zilver consulted the gold watch awarded to him when he reached Branch Schedule. He just had time to make his appointment at the British Embassy.

*

'Still no reply from Teheran.'
Baroque: 'That's funny.'
'You mean strange, or funny?'
'Both.'

*

Irregular even during peak hours, Knoxville City Transport on Sundays was entirely capricious. Fitz rose at first daylight to be certain of reaching the Great Smokies Appalachian Inn in time for his interview. It was a serious deviation from his regime and, when the two Financial Counsellors found him waiting for them in the motel's lounge under a rubber palm tree, he was looking a little haggard, an impression fortified by his uncombed hair.

'Who's this schmuck?' thought Bleitgeist with disgust, immediately sizing up Levy's trainee as a Time-Waster.

After a preliminary exchange of questions, answers and compliments, Fitz revealed his major.

Bleitgeist: 'English majors have a notable record of success in our business. The ability to articulate that comes from the formal study of the English language and English literature is a great advantage in financial counselling.'

Fitz nodded his head sagely. 'I'm about to finish my doctoral dissertation,' he said.

What a dummo! thought Bleitgeist. Who does he think will read it? Four, five years gone, and nothing in the bank to show for it. 'What's the topic?' he asked.

'The Problem of the "ure" rhymes in Hoccleve.'

'Now isn't that interesting! How far have you got?'

'Nearly finished.'

'That's *amazing!* And now, I suppose, you are looking for a way to earn a little money on the side, while continuing your research? A way to supplement your father's allowance, perhaps?'

Levy nodded appreciatively. To supplement his father's allowance so he could complete his study of the 'ure' rhymes in Hoccleve: that was a good one.

'Why do you believe you would like to work for World of Finance?' asked Bleitgeist.

Fitz: 'I can't give you anything like a complete answer to that question without digressing somewhat into some of the background and personal aspects of my situation.'

'Okay, go ahead. Shoot.'

'For a long time now', said Fitz, 'I've been thinking of changing to another discipline. English literature is a meaningful investigation, sure, but I seriously wonder if it isn't the kind of discipline which exacerbates the problem of relating to your fellow human being. By fellow human being, I mean ordinary people, people without the advantage of a college degree. I had a discussion about this with my supervisor, and he didn't have anything meaningful to offer. I discussed it with Blonstein – he's the president of OCAAD, On-Campus Association Against Discrimination – and he had nothing to offer. Then I met Levy, and we discovered that we were both depressed over the same problems, what to do about prejudice against the poor, and so on. Levy said that the only way to combat the situation was to take a more positive, active role. I could see the meaning and asked him if he had any concrete suggestions. He said he would have to come back to me on that one. He thought it over, then he said mutual funds. He mentioned this mutual fund thing.'

Bleitgeist: 'You could see the relevance?'

'Not at first. But, gradually, it began to impinge, began to come clear. As soon as Levy mentioned the possibility, it started me focusing in a different direction. I think I can see it now.'

Bleitgeist extracted a New Man application form from his jacket pocket.

'When would you like to start?'

'Everything's a question of getting your priorities right. My dissertation's due in December. I have been wondering if I shouldn't postpone submitting it and go straight into this mutual fund thing, or whether the degree would enable me to make a more significant contribution later. That's what I have to decide.'

'I would be inclined to act now,' advised Bleitgeist.

'You don't think I should aim first at getting my doctorate and defer the concrete manifestations of loving my neighbour until later?'

'The degree as such is not the important thing,' said Bleitgeist. 'We have successful Financial Counsellors who already have their doctorates and we have successful Financial Counsellors without even a Bachelor of Arts degree. It's how much you really *care* that counts. Can we discern a truth here?'

'I think I'm reading you!' Fitz signed the New Man application.

'That's the principle of the thing.'

*

Bumper was indignant. Not only was his arrest irregular and uncouth, but they had required him also to wear pyjamas. A warder escorted him to a bleakly furnished room where a dim light burned. Behind a desk sat three policemen with truncheons masquerading in the plain clothes of civilians. They wore black gloves and those abominable moustaches. They looked at him with unsympathetic eyes. On the desk was a whip.

'I demand an explanation! I insist on an apology!' said Bumper.

'Please sit down, Mr Bartridge,' said the one with the black patch over his eye. Jeremy Partridge was Bumper's pseudonym.

'Obviously, their leader,' thought Bumper.

The warder left. The man with the patch extended the stump of his right hand, a thumb and a finger, for Bumper to shake. 'Perhaps you think we are angry with you, Mr Bartridge?' he said.

'You arrested me without a warrant, you know? You handcuffed me in the privacy of my own bathroom.'

'That was unfortunate, Mr Bartridge. Allow me to explain. It is the work of the Minister of External Accounts. He has the ear of the Shah. The Minister is a powerful man, a cousin of His Imperial Highness. His Highness has placed him in charge of all external bank accounts which many of our citizens use to conceal their money from our tax collectors. I believe you have information that can lead to their arrest. No?'

'No,' replied Bumper defiantly. The principle of Client confidentiality was inviolable. Moreover, he had decided to deny everything.

'It will be easier for you if you cooperate, Mr Bartridge. Perhaps you recognize my colleagues' faces and mine? Have you not seen us looking at your window? We know that you are associated with the man Sher Mirza and that you are frequently in the company of the money changers in the bazaar. We have the tiny, water-tight box which you tried to conceal from us. You hid it in the water closet cistern.'

Bumper was silent. He was thinking: 'So Sher Mirza is not in on the game.'

*

'Any news of Peabody?'
'Not yet, I'm afraid.'
'Are you getting through to the local operator?'
'No problem.'
'And still no answer?'
'I can't figure it out, unless . . .'
'Why would he want to take a powder? . . .'
'Still no reply from Teheran, Mr Baroque.'
'Keep trying.'

*

'Whaddaya mean, bringing me this dumbo?' said Bleitgeist, rounding on Levy after interviewing Fitz. 'So he wants me to worship him for being a concerned human being. So let him join the Department of Welfare and Human Resources. Sanctimonious do-gooders, we already got too many of.'

*

It was business as usual with Noam van Zilver.

'Your papers appear to be in order,' said the colonel commanding the palace guards, 'and I accept that the subject that you wish to discuss with His Imperial Highness is of a confidential nature. But you must understand, the Emperor will not see you unless you first make an appointment.'

'Hang it, man! Here's my card. Tell His Imperial Highness I'll call on him at ten sharp tomorrow morning. If he can't see me then, that's his pigeon. Who else is around the palace?'

*

While Bumper chaffed in captivity and van Zilver was opening up the Lion of Judah Market, WoF en France was giving a romp. The festive Sansjoy was in charge of preparations. Buses provided for the clerical staff departed hourly from the Area Office at the Place Vendôme, and, for the guidance of guests who chanced the journey on their own, patrolmen dressed in bright blue and gold livery for easy identification were stationed at all important junctions en route.

These were joyous occasions for the waiters, who vaunted their silk perukes and sang ye-ye tunes. They were so keen to supplement their modest wages with the surplus bottles of champagne and the ermine stoles and the diamond brooches that might be left behind, so candid in their reminiscences of past acquisitions, that the *maitre d'hôtel* was obliged to remind them of their duties to the name of the house whose trays they bore. Sleek was in Vancouver setting up a deal and would not be present. Nor would Marty Rubin. After last week's celebration in Miami, he and Wally had flown home with hangovers. Clovis and Ernest were sure to be there. Their lust for parties almost equalled Sanloy's. Fenner was coming as part of the Founder's entourage and bringing with him an important person with whom he shared finder's fees for procuring unregistered stock for FoF's portfolio. Strumpf and Handschuh were coming, too. More than a hundred Override disputes between them had stirred up so much mutual distrust that neither risked allowing the other unguarded access to the Founder.

Nelson was not coming. Having boarded Baroque's aeroplane and ordered the mini-skirted stewardess to bring him a Bucks fizz, the Founder decided that he needed to keep his roving eye on the job and peremptorily ordered him back to the Top of the Spirals. Obedient as a dog to his master's whims, the Executive Second Vice-President treated himself to an apple fritter at Horn and Hardart's and was soon busy composing Model Telephone Techniques. Baroque, thought Nelson later, was right to proceed to the party without him. *Someone* had to stay behind and compose Model Telephone Techniques. He accomplished his best work on Sunday afternoons.

*

'What's the difference between a mutual fund and a unit trust?' asked Her Britannic Majesty's Ambassador to the Court of the Lion of Judah.

Van Zilver: 'There's no difference, Your Excellency.'

'What's the difference between a programme and a plan?'

'One example of a plan, Your Excellency, is the Folkestone Plan, a unit trust investing in equities. Owing to its life cover, UK law treats it as an insurance policy. Hence, it is not offered for sale under the WoF Investment Program.'

'You should tell the emperor this, Mr van Zilver. His Imperial Highness is a great admirer of the UK. . . .'

*

It is midnight in France, and Baroque is thronged by sycophants. His ears are buzzing with their adulation, ambition and intrigue. Sansjoy imparts to him a sad *nouvelle* and tarries, studying the Founder for a hint of alarm. He detects a barely discernible crinkling of the skin round the eyes. A portent of imminent sorrow? The issue hangs in the balance! Sansjoy's eyes dart back and forth like searchlights probing inimical skies. The All Clear sounds. The Founder has a genius for concealing his fear. Accountants can wait. The party must go on.

*

'. . . The WoF Investment Program serves as a curtain between the investor and various nationally registered unit trusts,' continued van Zilver. 'Suppose, for example, that an investor wants to hide his ownership of shares in Fenner Biddup Offshore Fund for income tax, estate duty or other reasons. The WoF Investment Program acts as custodian of shares purchased under his Dynamic Growth Plan. It applies each monthly remittance received from him to the purchase of Fenner Biddup Offshore Fund shares and retains the shares on his behalf. His name does *not* appear on the Fund's register of shareholders. In that sense, Your Excellency, a programme *is* a Plan. . . .'

*

The party goes on. Clovis pauses in discourse, smoothes his sparse grey hair and continues the story of his WoF career.

'Deals were everywhere. We lived, breathed and fed on them. Like a few months before we had lived on ham sandwiches and *croute*. We picked up whoever we happened to meet and closed her. My clients that year included no fewer than sixteen schoolteachers, all of 'em craving both funds – and fun! It was a happy, exciting time to be alive.'

In big groups, in little groups, everyone was talking and laughing, laughing and talking. Only Strumpf and Handschuh remained aloof from the general confabulation.

'. . . If you'da told me ten years ago that today I'd be a millionaire with a town house in London, I'da said you was nuts.'

'You got a town house in London? I got a friend who's got a town house in London. Nice set-up my friend's got.'

'Who's your friend? . . .'

And so on into the night.

*

They were still talking and laughing in the early hours of the morning, while Baroque slept, folded into a tiny ball like a koala bear. On a tray beside him was a clutter of miniature cognac bottles, a *berlingot* of white wine, a cup of tepid coffee and assorted snacks. Blue lights implanted in the bulkhead and the orange glow of a stewardess's cigarette aft.

The aeroplane struck an air pocket and jolted sharply. Baroque awoke, looked out the window into obscurity, turned over and went back to sleep.

*

'. . . And the difference between the Fenner Biddup Offshore Fund and Fiduciary of Fiduciaries?'

'The Fenner Biddup Offshore Fund, like most unit trusts, invests directly in the shares of public companies, whereas the Fiduciary of Fiduciaries invests in the shares of other unit trusts.'

'Wouldn't an investment in Fiduciary of Fiduciaries be a safer way of investing?'

'Safer, but perhaps not as dynamic. I recommend a first investment in the Fiduciary of Fiduciaries for security, and a second in the Fenner Biddup Offshore Fund for growth.'

*

Daylight was breaking in a diffuse glow through the metropolitan fog at Kennedy International Airport, grey, colourless cloud spray and drizzle. The Customs and Immigration officials were disrespectful. No one was on hand to meet him. Baroque impatient and in bad temper and complaining of obstructiveness. No limo. Taxis too much hassle. Morosely alone and conspicuous in his gold-brocaded cape in a Corey Transport bus, watching the cloud spray trickling down the window.

At the Top of the Spirals, the Latvian cleaners were busy vacuuming the shampooed carpets.

'Good morning, Mr Baroque,' they sang in unison.

Whereas other executives were supercilious in such encounters, owing, perhaps, to his Gdynian origins, Baroque always found time to chat with the Latvians. 'Hi, fellows,' he said. 'They keeping you busy and out of trouble?'

'You bet we're busy,' they replied above the roar of their machines.

'They giving you plenty of coffee and doughnuts? You getting enough recreation?'

'No sir,' they shouted. 'We don't have too much time for breaks. We're too busy vacuuming.'

'That's the spirit, fellows.'

It was marvellous how these simple workmen went tirelessly about their simple chores, thought Baroque. He decided to send them some of the prizes left over from the University of Modern Money Contest. If only his WoFers were so dutiful!

A valet had laid out a change of silk shirts. A barber stood waiting to shave him. Candy Matthews, the weekend secretary, sat on his desk beside the outgoing tray, awaiting dictation. Baroque tossed her his cape and sank wearily into his chair. He was in no mood for dictating. The bleak agonies of the bus ride from the airport were fresh in his mind. The barber tied a bib about his neck and lathered him in peppermint foam. Baroque stared into the mirror and reflected on the benefits that might accrue to society, given a wider attachment to Latvian cleaners' values. Corruption, excess and foam stared back at him.

'No one except immigrants is willing to work anymore, and even they are quickly demoralized,' he declared.

Candy's pencil was poised above her notebook. Was he dictating? Or was this another outburst?

'Where's decency? Where's integrity? Look at the Arts. Nothing is so sad as the general decline in artistic standards. You tell me the name of one contemporary composer of the stature of Salamone Rossi. Look at politics. Where are the Disraelis and the Madame Lupescus?'

It was another outburst. The barber held his blade.

*

'I still say we ought to give him one more chance.'

'Why should we? As far as I'm concerned, he's terminated.'

'Why are you terminating Bumper?' asked Baroque.

'He's stopped sending us Activity Reports. He's neglecting his trainees. He doesn't answer his correspondence.'

'What are you doing about his commissions?'

'The usual thing.'

'Garnishment?'

'I don't see why not.'

'We can always settle out of court if his widow decides to bring suit.'

*

About nine o'clock, Nelson's secretary came to him with the proofs of the new Model Telephone Techniques.

'Aw Mr Rock, they're *beautiful*' she exclaimed.

'You really think so, Virginia?'

'Oh *yes*, Mr Rock! I especially liked *Approach to Orphan Clients*.'

'Read it to me, willya?'

'Mr Worth, this is Joe Counsellor of World of Finance. How are you? My records indicate that it has been some time since you have had an opportunity to check your WoF Program account with us. Since I now have the pleasure of looking after your account, I am just calling to find out when you will have a few minutes so that we can get acquainted and I can bring you completely up-to-date on your Fund. Would Tuesday at seven or Wednesday at eight-thirty be better for you?'

'I like that one too, Virginia. Listen, would you mind reading out the others? It helps me evaluate their effectiveness.'

'Sure, Mr Rock. I don't mind. It is always a pleasure to read what you have dictated. You missed your calling. You should've been a poet.

'"If the prospect says, 'Where did you get my name?' you reply, 'That's a good question, Mr Worth, and I am glad that you asked it. Your area was selected, and you were one of those in your area chosen. Would Tuesday at seven be better, or Wednesday at eight-thirty?'" . . .'

*

The clank and rattle of steel as the warder opened and closed the cells. Rice and lentils for breakfast. Rice and lentils for lunch. 'Hey, don't you fellows know how to cook anything but *poloadas*?'

After lunch, the officers resumed their interrogation. They wanted to know where Noam van Zilver was.

'How'm *I* supposed to know?' replied Bumper. 'I'm not my brother's keeper. Somewhere south of Cairo and north of Cape Town. . . . No! Please! *Don't* hit me! *Please* don't hit me! I didn't mean to be sarcastic. Hold it! I think I'm going to vomit!'

*

Bumper's travails were a symptom of wider distress. Ostensibly, the company was enjoying the zenith of its prosperity. The sales subsidiary anticipated Volume in excess of $4 billion. Germany alone was producing $130 million a month. Fifteen thousand Associates were commencing three new presentations a minute in more than a hundred countries. However, the message that Sansjoy whispered in Baroque's ear, which brought the Founder scuttling back to the Top of the Spirals, presented a different picture. Gargantuan Volume notwithstanding, WoF had lost control of its spending, precipitating a cash crisis. Where were they to find the money to pay the staff?

Baroque received the proofs of the Model Telephone Techniques clipped to Nelson's Inter-Office Memorandum and read them approvingly between conferences with his interior decorator and his biographer. Then he dictated a memo referring the proofs to Marty for a second opinion. Then he summoned Angus Anstruther, the Comptroller.

'Angus, I understand that the sales company's profits for last quarter aren't going to match up to expectations?'

'That's about it, Mr Baroque. We're up to making a bluidy great loss.'

'Do you realize what you're saying, Angus?'

'Aah do.'

'The men would never tolerate a reduction in the value of the shares they've bought under the Stock Option Plan. They have foregone commissions to pay for them. They will feel cheated,' said Baroque.

'Aye,' replied the dour Anstruther. 'We'll nae blather oor way ou' o' this one.'

'It will show up in our annual report. It could cause a stir. Our Clients might start withdrawing from our mutual funds.'

'Aye, right enough.'

'We have been fortunate so far in enjoying a favourable press. All the leading financial editors are our buddies. A loss would embarrass them. They might turn on us.'

'That's right.'

'D'you hear, Angus? A loss is completely out of the question.'

'Weel now, had you not best tell that to the braw column of figgers over there? I'm just the wee man who tots them up.'

The portion of WoF's revenues from the 'front load' and other charges deducted from clients' investments diminished as its Managers rose in schedule, but, Baroque knew, they would not condone a reduction in their commissions and overrides. Unless this cash drain was reversed, there would be no Public Offering. No underwriter would underwrite the shares, fearing that the capital raised by the Public Offering would be used to subsidize the company's sales operation. They would want a full investigation before committing themselves.

Baroque discussed the matter with Fenner and Sleek.

*

During the first week in December, Hoof, Mafia, Sansfoy, Gloom, Strumpf, Handschuh, Sansjoy, Vendetta and Sansloy arrived at the Top of the Spirals for a Key Associates Conference.

The last time that they had gathered for a Key Associates Conference, Baroque referred to the company's 'unprecedented success in bringing professionalism to little people the world over' and imputed the credit to 'those hard-working Key Associates who, by their sacrifice, have risen to high positions in our company. And', he had added, 'who can begrudge them their larger share of the rewards?' The applause was thunderous. Every Key Associate felt that Baroque was directing the tribute to himself. None omitted to congratulate him on his speech. Vick Johnson, who managed Argentina, called it a 'fine example of human oratory'.

Now those same Key Associates heard from the Founder an address very unlike that which had raised them to their feet clapping and cheering the previous year. It began gloomily – 'A man in my position has many responsibilities, some not so pleasant' – and continued in that unsunny mode about outlays, rather than New Products. The speech was replete with numbers that none of the Key Associates understood or cared to understand. '. . . Estimated expenses on telephone calls alone will exceed . . .' Worst of all, the speech lacked flattery. It lasted for almost half an hour, and there was not a word of praise in it. This was *not* what they came to hear. No one minded, at first. It did no harm to stress the importance of frugality. Only a Key Associates Conference seemed an odd occasion to bring up such a dull topic. Baroque seemed to have lost his flair for inspiring Leadership.

Slowly, as they realized that the value of shares acquired under the Stock Option Plan was threatened, boredom gave way to alarm. Perhaps they *had* been a bit extravagant.

The really overwhelming revelation, however, was still to come. After concluding the grim preliminaries, Baroque tabled a motion to cut Overrides. The silence that settled over The Bull and The Bear Conference Room was so profound that one might have heard a Key Associate's Gold Pen drop.

It was Ernest who broke the silence.

'*Aw, boss!*'

Increased stringency over expenditures, certainly. Firing some of the staff, why not? But a *cut in Overrides*! It was too much to ask. Even Strumpf and Handschuh stood shoulder to shoulder on this one. 'It kinda makes ya wanna cry,' said Vincenzo.

More silence, disbelief, more hostility.

Baroque: 'If there are no further objections, will someone second the motion? Then we can vote it as proposed.'

But there *were* further objections. 'It looks to me like there's lotza alternatives,' said Michele. The Key Associates prided themselves on their candour.

The conference fell to discussing alternatives.

Sansfoy thought that they were spending too much on scholarships to send undeserving young Associates to the WoF Academy. 'Also, we pay for too many Board meetings. There are now more than eighty separate companies in the WoF Family. Do we need such a large family? Must all the family members have Board meetings?'

Sleek lowered his meerschaum long enough to advise the Conference on a company's legal obligations with respect to Board meetings.

'Nevertheless,' insisted Sansloy, 'there's got to be some scope for reducing expenses there.'

Beck wondered about the value of 'all these seminars and conferences. Back in the old days we got along perfectly well without them. Now we have Supervisor Seminars, Advanced Training Seminars, Professional Sales Seminars, Managers Conferences, Millionaires Conferences, Divisional Managers Conferences, General Managers Conferences and Key Associates Conferences. I figure we could do without some of these seminars and conferences.'

There was general consensus that one or more of the seminars and conferences could go.

'Another way to economize would be on Contests.'

'I emphatically disagree!' trumpeted Herb. 'Here is *one* area where we *shouldn't* stint.'

'Stink?' asked Strumpf.

'No, Ludwig. Stint. Save on outlays.'

'But can we be sure that these figures are accurate? Has anyone checked them, apart from the accountants?'

'I table a motion that an independent check be made forthwith.'

'I second that.'

'I move that we fire Angus.'

The discussions were protracted and fierce, with many proposals and counterproposals, none derogating from the Override, however, and ended without any award of a Founder's Medal for Quality Business or a Citation for Entrepreneurial Excellence.

*

That same evening was Bone's first out of the hospital, and he and Blaize were at the SAE house. The fraternity houses ranged along College Street, where the action was. The Big Orange had just trounced Vanderbilt in the final game of the season, and the icy streets around Volunteer Hill resounded with the enthusiasm of Vol supporters. Although the co-eds just held hands and behaved sedately, the males more or less ran amuck, shouting, '*Go B O!*'

'Got any idea whut you're goin' to be doin' next year?' asked Blaize.

A fan: 'We won't forget whut you done for us in the Arkansas game, Bone.'

'Jus' did mah best,' replied Bone. Then to Blaize, 'Goin' into bankin' and finance.'

'That was a great game you played against Arkansas, Bone. Bone, you're *great*!'

'Jus' did mah best,' replied Bone. Then to Blaize, 'It's an opportunity to do some rail good.'

'Hope your laig gets wail soon, Bone.'

'Thanks. . . And the pay is rail good.'

Blaize wanted to know what the pay was.

'Dunno,' said Bone. 'This fellow said that one of his men made forty thousand dollars his first year at it, but it all depends on the person.'

'We'll never forget whut you did for us, Bone.'

'Did whut I could.'

'Sounds like a rail good deal.'

'Sorry about your laig, Bone.'

'It's healin' up rail good.'

'That was a railly great game, Bone.'

'Sure 'preciate your sayin' so.'

'You railly thank you might go into this?' asked Blaize.

Bone described his meeting with Bleitgeist and Levy. He went into all the pros and cons.

'It's not like ordinary bankin'. Instead of stayin' indoors sittin' at a desk, you're out workin' among people, helpin' them to save in a way that benefits them more than the bank. Did you know that only one American in ten is able to retire on his own savin's? The fellow who manages Knoxville has only been at it a year and says if he was to cash out now he'd be a millionaire. But you railly got to hustle.'

'How's it feel to be back on your feet, Bone?'

'It feels rail good.'

'Can I get in on this, too?'

'I dunno, Blaize. You'd have to talk to Mr Levin. He's the fellow who manages Knoxville.'

Next day, Lester and Mule also expressed interest in a career in banking and finance. They were on the way to Portuguese class, a yard of shoulder span on each narrowing to a foot at the waist, the shoulder supporting a small nodule bristling with fine flaxen hairs and two large ears, Bone between them on crutches.

'And you know whut you stand to make in your first year?'

'Whut?'

'Forty thousand, and that's only the *first* year, Mule. If you're good at it, in your second year your earnin's should *double*.'

'No *shee*-ut!'

'That's whut he says. And all the time you're helpin' people retire.'

'Who else's in on this?'

'The only one I've met is this postgraduate creep.'

'They also pay your expenses?'

'Naw, you gotta pay your own expenses, Lester. But that's *good!* That way you're your own boss. You earn whut you earn.'

The conversation resumed after Portuguese class.

'Whut's the work like?'

'I understand that all you do is go around callin' on diffrunt people and talk to them 'bout this Stars and Stripes investment.'

'And they pay you forty thousand a year just for doin' *that*?'

'After the first year, it goes up.'

'That sounds like a purty good deal to me,' said Mule. 'Who runs this thang?'

'Some fellow up in New York. They say he's a *financial jaine*ous.'

'No *shee*-ut!'

4

SUGAR BOWL

A hundred miles or so north of the Top of the Spirals, massive, bulky and dominating a bend in the Hudson, lies Mountain Close. It belongs to Baroque, who bought it after launching the Stars and Stripes Fund.

He has little opportunity to enjoy its granite and oak amenities. Key Executives and Key Associates, though, are frequent visitors, flying up in the company's Cessna or speed-boating up in the company's launch, and the weekend before Christmas found Nelson, Marty and Wally sitting before the inglenook fireplace under a stuffed elk's head in the larger 'drawing room' discussing the chief hazard in selling WoF funds internationally, incarceration.

There were two schools of opinion in the company. Marty, Nelson, Michele, Henri, Vick, Ernest, Jacques, Pierre, Herb, Clovis, Strumpf and Handschuh believed that the fault always lay with the Rep for getting caught. Wally, who was regarded as the company's conscience, was in the camp that imputed the blame to society.

'It seems to me that it takes minimum common sense to stay out of the jug,' said Marty.

'Absolutely!' concurred Nelson.

They were discussing Bumper.

'Noam was in Teheran, and *he* wasn't nabbed. I say don't blame the *system*; blame the *man*.'

'Absolutely!' concurred Michele.

'That's all very good, but look at Johan,' countered Wally. 'He was forever shifting apartments and changing aliases. He screened all his men before allowing them to work the Territory. All mail went to him by special courier. All transactions were in code. No follow-ups were ever made on unverified Easy Money Referrals. But these precautions did not prevent him from getting nabbed. All I'm saying is, if the company had a policy, these things would *tend* to happen *less*. That's *all* I'm saying.'

'What do you suggest?'

'For a start, there ought to be a limit on what you can take out of a Territory. Most Managers become blinded by greed and can't resist making that one presentation too many. When you can't say no to more, that's when you oughta be *made* to quit.'

'Whaddaya wanna do, limit incentive?'

'Anyway, Bumper is in a bad way and we're doing nothing to help him.'

*

Bumper *was* in a bad way. The prisoners in neighbouring cells, broken men under sentence of death, were terribly inconsiderate. Some prayed aloud, although it was difficult to know whether they were praying or just lamenting. Out of the general devotions and wailing, he detected the voice of the previous Manager. Distant, but not faint, it came to him through the troubled acoustics as desperate pleas for help from someone who was suffocating.

'George, is that you?' cried Bumper.

He thought that he heard a gurgle. Then, abruptly, the gurgle ceased.

Bumper tried again. 'It's Bumper Peabody, George. The new Area Manager! Remember?'

Could George hear him? Was George deaf? From some macabre punishment administered to his ears? Had he died, perhaps in the very instant that Bumper had called out to him? Had they choked him to death? Was the gurgle he heard the rattle?

*

'Of course, we can't be *sure* he's in the clink. Officially speaking, he's just disappeared.'

'He's in the clink, all right. No one takes a powder if he's drawing thirty thousand a month in Overrides.'

'I still say the prisoner's to blame.'

'We're supposed to be a family, Marty.'

*

Detention had forced Bumper to reassess his position fundamentally. His tormented imagination toiled with vexing, fundamental propositions about the fundamental purpose of existence. Why go on? Was this all that life was about? He had spent many anxious hours wondering if he would be tortured, if he would be beheaded.

*

After Wally went to bed in disgust, Nelson and Marty talked freely. Each knew the other's mind.

'It's getting harder and harder to relocate General Managers. Most of them want to come back to the States.'

'Bumper won't like having to accept a drop in schedule. Whadda we charge him, forty thousand?'

'At least. Don't forget, they're *torturing* him. That's the SAVAK, man.'

'Well I guess we can decide on the exact amount once we find out just how desperate he is. We might have to cut Herb in on the deal. Who's next in line in Iran?'

'Noam van Zilver.'

'Wow! They won't catch *him*. Where's van Zilver?'

*

Noam had spent the preceding night at a guest house in Moyale, exchanged his Ethiopian dollars for Kenya shillings at a good rate and caught a lift with a Somali trader driving a Peugeot, driver and passenger beguiling the journey's tedium by deploring the condition of the road – reduced to sand as fine as silt in places. It was even more deplorable during the rainy season, the Somali said.

At Marsabit, Noam put up with the Italian fathers, who delighted in entertaining a stranger who discoursed so freely and suavely in their language. He now sat surrounded by goats in a box-shaped wooden armchair of local make on the grass in front of the mission's refectory.

'It's hard to dispute the basic tenets of your religion, father,' conceded Noam, resuming at lunch a conversation that had started at breakfast.

'Are you a Catholic, Mr van Zilver?'

Noam smiled. He had bathed and shaved and put on a clean shirt. A difficult road was behind him, another Close in front of him. He felt relaxed. He smoked a cigar provided from the mission's endowment.

'A lapsed one, father.'

'I will say a rosary for you, my son.'

Noam drew contentedly on the cigar and contemplated his many evident blessings. If only everyone were so fortunate. His contentment expanded and embraced his companion.

'What happens when you retire, father? Will you be able to depend on your superiors to look after you? Or does prudence dictate that you lay aside a little something now and invest it in a good mutual fund?'

*

'Whadda you think's the percentage there?' Marty asked Nelson. A change of management always offered an opportunity.

'Not a hope in heaven,' replied Nelson. '*Not* with van Zilver.'

*

Van Zilver reached Nairobi and walked out Uhuru Avenue to the roundabout joining the Mombasa Road. An Indian gave him a lift as far as the Athi River turn-off. From there, traffic was sparse. Noam sat on his rucksack and studied a Folkestone Plan *Questions and Answers.*

At sundown, a Kikuyu lorry driver bound for Namanga stopped and gave him a lift. Giraffes crossed the road in long, loping strides. Gazelles pricked up their noses. The driver turned

73

on the headlights. Van Zilver learned that he had served in the East African Rifles. They discussed the transport business, ivory poaching and the price of flour in the *dukas*.

'These *wahindi* charge too much for everything, *bwana*. The old man ought to expel them.'

They discussed motors, how to cure mange with a shrivelled monkey's foot, tribal overlappings and animosities, and the nocturnal perils of giraffe, zebra and bucks crossing the road.

*

Came the day when Bone learned that he had passed Portuguese 1510. He was majoring in Supply Chain Management, with a minor in Advertising, and had signed up for Portuguese 1510 at the suggestion of the Department of Phys Ed's Academic Supervisor to meet his foreign language requirement. It had caused him no end of grief. His heart was in Marketing 4510 and Phys Ed, not in Portuguese 1510. Model sentences, such as 'I am a man' and 'She is a woman', humiliated him. Whenever he pronounced '*Eu sou uma mulher*', everyone in the class except Mule and Lester giggled. The instructor exacerbated his humiliation by greeting him at the beginning of each class, '*Bom dia, senhor Saxon*', instead of just plain 'Good morning, Bone'. Nor did he share that little egghead's enthusiasm for the Golden Age of Portugal. Exactly similar difficulties had beset Mule and Lester. It was therefore something of a triumph when all three teammates got Cs in their final examinations.

This wonderful result, posted on the bulletin board in the Department of Modern Languages building just as Bone was leaving Big Orange Country for the Christmas break, gave him something to talk about other than football when he arrived home. It elicited his father's congratulations. His mother, though, was more reticent – that Christmas might be Bone's last Christmas at home for many years. After graduating, he would be eligible for the draft and might have to participate in that awful war overseas. Bone hobbled about the house, trying to ease his mother's anxieties. With his new disability, he said, cheerfully exhibiting his cast, they might reclassify him. The military didn't want cripples.

*

Christmas Eve in the Saxons' living room. Bone's mother is reading selections from her favourite authors to Bone and his father.

'Twas the night before Christmas, and all through the house
Not a creature was stirring, not even a mouse. . . .'

*

Marty: 'You don't think Noam's put the screws on Bumper?'
Nelson: 'I wouldn't like to say. I've only met the guy once.'
Wally: 'He's a dark horse. Likes to do things his own way.'
Marty: 'Yeah, difficult to fathom.'

*

'. . . *The children were nestled all snug in their beds*
While visions of sugar plums danced in their heads,
And Mama in her kerchief and I in my cap
Had just settled down for a long winter's nap. . . .'

*

'. . . We've just made two hundred thousand on Comsat.'
'We'd better tell Fenner. . . .'
'Mr Biddup, we've just made two hundred thousand on Comsat.'
'Sell.'

*

On Christmas morning, Mrs Saxon drew back the curtains and made the men get out of bed to see what Santa Klaus had brought. They trooped down to the living room still in their pyjamas. Three large red felt stockings bulging with walnuts and tangerines hung from the mantel over the gas heater, a bowl of red and silver glass balls was on top of the piano, a Santa in a sleigh and a set of plastic reindeer on top of the television. Streamers of tinsel, coloured lights and angel's hair adorned the tree. A pile of gaily wrapped presents lay beneath it.

Everyone emptied his stocking and opened his presents.

Bone received from his mother a leather briefcase with matching writing folder and a cable-stitched pullover. His father gave him aftershave lotion. From Bone, Mrs Saxon received a box of Whitman's Sampler chocolates. Her husband gave her a Kelvinator bathroom fan heater. She gave him a pair of fur-lined slippers, a fashionable wide-girthed tie and two boxes of Remington twelve-gauge shotgun shells. Bone gave his father aftershave lotion.

After everyone had opened his presents, the men went upstairs to dress, while Mrs Saxon picked up the wrapping paper and put aside the ribbon she wanted to save. Mr Saxon dutifully put on his new tie and Mrs Saxon brushed her hair, put on lipstick and, checking that the turkey was roasting nicely, turned down the oven. The whole family then got into the Chevrolet pick-up and went to the Methodist church.

It was the first service that Bone had attended since Easter and the first time he heard the controversial new preacher. Bright sunshine streamed in through the stained-glass windows, spraying the congregation with a rainbow of colours, and the choir sang robustly *Hark! the herald angels sing, Glory to the new born King!* Richard Dixon, who owned Dixon's Dry Goods Store, read the Scriptures. Then the preacher mounted the pulpit and, under the ferocious head of a brass eagle, denounced the congregation for its headstrong resistance to racial integration. After the service, everyone stood outside the west door and chatted affably, ignoring the preacher. Bone and his father then hurried home to shoot the shotgun, a rite commemorating the shotgun Bone received as a Christmas present from his father when he was twelve. Dinner was served: turkey and dressing, cranberry sauce, sweet potatoes mixed with raisins and topped with marshmallows, peas in a cream of mushroom sauce, followed by ambrosia and fruit cake. Then the two men sat in the den and watched the North-South game.

They were still watching the game when the McCallums arrived. Everyone said, 'Merry Christmas!' then the McCallums inquired about Bone's leg. Sarah McCallum was going to UT next fall, and she and Bone had a serious conversation. What was it like at UT? she asked. It was important to get in with a good group of girls, he advised, and he mentioned the names of several good sororities. Another good thing, he said, was to be an ROTC sponsor. Sarah listened attentively to all his brotherly advice. Bone said that if she could come up sometime in the spring, after his leg had healed, he would show her around.

That evening, after the McCallums left, the Saxons played Bing Crosby singing *Silent Night* and *White Christmas* on the record player and watched *A Christmas Carol* on television. They cracked walnuts and ate them and Mrs Saxon passed around her Whitman's Sampler. She baked Sally Lunn, and they ate that and her fruitcake. Then Mrs Saxon made everyone a cup of hot chocolate and sat down to sew Bone's name into the collar of his new pullover.

'Sarah Jo's nice,' said Bone.

'I thank so, too,' replied Mrs Saxon. 'Cute as a bug! And she sure thanks the world of you, son.'

It had long been her hope that Sarah Jo would turn out to be the Right Girl for Bone.

*

Knowing that most people are at home, Christmas Day found Levy in Knoxville making presentations. He crossed briskly to his prospect and, like a mechanical toy, raised his hand to shake hands, while his lips began to move in tandem with his wrist. 'Nice to meet you, Mr Adams.' He had chosen the prospect at random from the telephone directory.

'I don't believe I've had the pleasure,' said Mr Adams, rising from the chair where he was watching the North-South game.

Levy came straight to the point. 'Mr Adams, I'm here to talk to you about money.'

*

Noam was spending Christmas in Chaggaland with his friend, Fritz. Annihilating time and distance, the two friends had renewed their bonds, Fritz out of nostalgia and affection, Noam from cupidity. They met as undergraduates at Leiden University.

Fritz's family, reputedly, owned so much land that, when Fritz went for a walk in his front garden, he went on safari, but their estates were about to be confiscated. A guillotine hung over the white farmers in Chaggaland.

*

'Wail, I suspect that the average person is a lot more interested in money than he likes to admit. Won't you sit down, Mr . . . ?'

'Levin.'

'I was jus' watching the game.' Mr Adams turned off the television as a courtesy to his uninvited guest and said, 'Care for a cup of coffee?'

Levy fetched a straight-back chair from a set surrounding the dining room table, placed it in front of the easy chair where his prospect was sitting – the Model Technique for Bridging Distances – and requested a Situation Control glass of water.

'Sure,' said Mr Adams, and calling to his wife, who had returned to the kitchen after admitting Levy to the house, said, 'Peg, would you please bring our guest a glass of water with *two* cubes of ice in it.'

'Aw, never mind,' said Levy, embarrassed almost for the first time in his life.

'Sure you wouldn't like some water?'

'Thanks just the same.'

'How about a Coke?

'No thanks, I'll do without a beverage.'

'Seven Up?'

'Thanks anyway,' said Levy. 'Mr Adams, do banks make money?'

*

Bleitgeist was in Memphis composing Inter-Office Memoranda to Commissions about unpaid Continuings over Reps he had trained in Barcelona, and to Herb and Marty about an SSE dispute involving a Rep who reached Advanced Schedule after he relocated to Tennessee. '. . . It was strictly defined and agreed between us before I ever left Spain . . .'

*

Herb was addressing an Advanced Training Seminar in Dallas. Christmas afternoon was the only opportunity for an ATS that his busy agenda allowed.

'People and their interrelationships are the focus of our business and the basis of our success. A Manager is only as effective as the people he's responsible for. That's why recruitment, training and more training are such an important part of our job. A man becomes a Manager in the true sense of the word only when he demonstrates his ability to lead others – which means setting an example, delegating authority and transmitting ideas.'

*

Ernest was supervising a New Man.

'You have only two financial problems, Mr Worth. One is life is too short – too short to earn all the money you need. The other is life is too long – you may live too long for the money you can earn.

'If Mr Worth says he has no money, tell him, "I didn't realize, but, if it's *that* bad, I could lend you a few pounds to tide you over."

'If he says that he doesn't need insurance, prompt him to think realistically: "Let's lean over your executor's shoulder for a moment, Mr Worth. How long is it before your widow is working?" Or tell him about the letter you once saw which said, "Please don't think my husband didn't love his family. It's just that he didn't plan to die at this time." . . .

'. . . Don't say "Good morning" meekly, like you were afraid of your prospect. Let your confidence ring out loud and clear, "GOOD MORNING!" Let your greeting boom like a cannon. "GOOD MORNING!" . . .

'. . . *Never* sit where you have to look *up* at your prospect. Your head relative to his is *critically* important. Your head should be even with his or higher.

'Now what was his Objection?'

'He asked me to leave the literature with him and promised to contact me after studying it.'

'That's what we call the "I'd Like to Think about it Objection". So how did you handle it?'

'I gave him a Questions and Answers and said that I looked forward to hearing from him.'

*

Bone told his father about Bleitgeist.

'The thang that railly impressed me, Dad, was the way he laid his cards on the table. He didn't try to fool me at all. If I don't work, I don't earn. It's as simple as that. After a year or so I can be earning four thousand a month, if I hustle.'

'That's purty good pay, son.'

'He says that I'm just the type of person who'll do wail at it, if I work hard. My low grades actually *impressed* him. Mr Bleitgeist says that he has grateful clients all over the world, who even write to him.'

'And you pay all your own expenses? You're on commission only?'

Father and son went by Central Drugstore to visit Bone's uncle. He had the habit, odd in a pharmacist, of dressing in overalls. It was the town joke that the last time Ned Saxon mixed an honest potion was during President Hoover's Administration, when tight money policy had an adverse effect on distribution of cherry cokes. All post-Hooverian drugs were 'new-fangled' to Uncle Ned, and when, as rarely happened, someone consulted him about one, he would shake his head and advise gloomily, 'That whole side of the business has jest about *pla-y-*yed out on me.' His speech, like his overalls, was much influenced by the cinema. He was an ardent fan of Gabby Hayes.

'Merry Christmas, Uncle Naid!' said Bone. 'How's life treating *you* these days?'

'Life has its ups and life has its downs, Bone. I heah you bust your laig. Now how come you want to do a thang like that?'

'Jus' one of those thangs,' Bone replied.

'Good lands, Bone! You weren't trying to get in front of a *train*?'

'Shoot!' said Bone, modestly.

'I heah you stopped a whole pack o' them boys from over thair in Arkansas. Were you trying to show 'em who's the toughest?'

'Wail, they were a pretty tough bunch of fellows, Uncle Naid.'

'But you showed 'em anyway?'

'Wail, I don't know 'bout that,' replied Bone, modestly.

'You don't, eh?' Uncle Ned firmed his false teeth and fixed his lame nephew with an expression of mock ferocity that had been one of the recurrently fearful experiences of the first six years of Bone's life. 'You mean you jest gone and bust your laig for *nothin*'?'

'Wail, we won the game, Uncle Naid, and that's whut counts.'

'Looks to me lak you don't know your Scripture, son. It says thair, "an eye for an eye, and a tooth for a tooth".'

'I know that,' said Bone.

'That means a laig for a laig. I'll bet some ole boy over thair in Blytheville's jus' struttin' around laughin' his doggone haid off about bustin' your laig.'

'Why's that, Uncle Naid?'

''Cause he's cruppled you and you ain't cruppled him, that's why.'

'How's Aunt Mag, Uncle Naid?'

'She's on one of her durn diets. Them Weight-Watchers been naggin' her to death 'bout how fat she is. She'll be wantin' to see you. Why don't you come over and share a bowl of prunes with us?'

'Uncle Naid, it railly doesn't look like I'm goin' to have the chance.'

'He's leaving tomorrow for the Sugar Bowl,' Bone's father explained.

'Yawl thank yawl can whup them Aggies?' asked Uncle Ned.

'I thank we can,' said Bone. 'They're big and they're hustlers. They've got a rail fine bawl club, and they're going to put up a rail good fight. But I thank we're ready. Our defence is looking rail good, and so is our offence. We'll have to watch our muhstakes and stay on the bawl. With a team like Texas A & M, you can't afford to give away too much. But I thank we'll win.'

'Wail, I sure hope so,' said Uncle Ned. 'Not too many of us ole folks'll be going down to the game. But we'll be pullin' for you all the same. We'll be drinkin' thet prune juice and settin' at thet TV shoutin', "Go *B O*! Go *B O*! Go for a *techdown*!"'

*

'When we leased this land from the Canadian Government,' said Henry Yates to the other directors of the Henry Yates Corporation, 'many of you were sceptical. What good, you asked, was a treeless plain of sedge, moss, lichen and shrubs frozen solid for most of the year and becoming a bog during the short summer thaw, what the Russians call tundra and the Algonquian call muskeg? Who, you wanted to know, was going to finance such a venture? If hydrocarbons were present in any significant quantity, they lay at depths beyond the economic feasibility of existing extraction technology. You said that we lacked the resources needed for it.

'Since our last meeting, I have been involved in negotiations with WoF and, I am pleased to tell you, we have concluded an agreement. You all know that WoF sponsors the Fiduciary of Fiduciaries. What you may not know is that one of the funds in FoF's portfolio, the Natural Resources Fund, invests in property instead of shares. Gentlemen, we have sold half of our leased Arctic acreage to the Natural Resources Fund for a dollar an acre, reserving to ourselves an Override of twelve per cent on our partner's share of the profits from any production. In other words, before committing a single dime to the venture, we have recouped all our expenses to date and all the expenses that we are likely to incur, while retaining what amounts to a sixty-two per cent interest in the acreage.'

Sleek had conducted the negotiations for World of Finance. He explained the deal to Fenner.

'We don't intend to extract minerals from this land. Our aim is to revalue our investment and pay ourselves a Performance Fee. Everybody is excited about the fact that oil has been found at Prudhoe Bay, and one thing is absolutely certain: *nobody* is going to go up and investigate what we have there.'

Fenner explained it to Marty.

'Explain it to me again,' said Marty. 'The land is worthless, right?'

'Right.'

'Why buy land that's worthless?'

'Because no one will find out that it's worthless. The Natural Resources Fund buys the acreage from the Henry Yates Corporation, sells a tenth of it to CGR at an average price per acre that is twenty times the average price we paid for it, then *conservatively* revalues the nine-tenths it retains at ten times the average price paid for it. We then take a Performance Fee for the increased value. See?'

'Who are CGR?'

'Capital Growth Resources. It's a company beneficially owned by Yates, a Yates-associated company, Baroque and Sleek.'

'GCR is putting up the money?'

'Anonymous Depositors Bank puts up the money. We are just borrowers.'

'Why "beneficially owned"?'

'Ostensible title vests in a nominee.'

'How come?'

'To conceal the identity of the buyers.'

'So no one will realize that the party buying the acreage is linked to the party marking up the value of the rest of the property?'

'Exactly.'

*

Financial Counsellors all over Tennessee who had taken a Christmas break resumed prospecting. 'Mr Johnson, I will be more than happy to send you something in the mail, but can I make a suggestion? I'm going to be in your neighbourhood on Thursday evening anyway. I'll drop in and leave some material. You can then go over it at your convenience. It might be of some value to you in the future. Would Thursday at seven or eight-thirty suit you? Or, if I can manage it, would you prefer Friday morning?'

*

Levy, who had taken no break and who could be extremely adept at Telephone Technique – 'Hello Mr Golden, this is Levy Levin with World of Finance. . . . That's right, you guessed it, mutual funds. Whadda *you* do for a living? . . . Ah, you in the rag trade? I used to sell threads myself. You make a lotta money in the trade. You must be cleaning up. Listen, whaddaya doing with your money? . . . You need a good mutual fund. . . . Too expensive? Whaddaya mean, *too expensive*? . . . Sure, I'll give you a discount. I'll come over and kiss you, too!' – was in the middle of a presentation.

'So, whad about taxes? Well, the thing about taxes . . .'

Levy broke off in mid-sentence. They were at it again, talking behind his back. It was a tribute to the Spartan manner of his upbringing that he was able to abide such rudeness. He sat stoically staring at the coat rack and the mouldy wallpaper, waiting for them to finish. 'So now you understand about taxes?'

'Vy I understand about taxes? That's vat I ask you, Mr Levin; vat about taxes?'

'And, if you'd been paying attention, instead of flapping your lips like a trained gibbon, you'd understand about taxes.'

Golden, his son and Levy were in a room crowded with changing mirrors and haberdashery. All three men sat together on a threadbare sofa, Levy in the middle radiating authority.

'So what's your full name?' he asked. . . . 'Whaddaya mean, you're not sure? I said what's your name. So you don't know your own name?' It wasn't that he minded Group Presentations, but leaning and talking over his back interrupted flow. . . . 'Individual or joint? . . . *Vat I mean*? I just explained.'

'You come back in maybe a veek, Mr Levin, and maybe ve do business. Ve like first to think about it. Ve got doubts.'

'Doubts we all got. *Sign*!' ordered Levy.

Mr Golden was not intimidated by the salesman's imperious style. He was an old man, thoughtful and cautious. Only after studying the prospectus and talking over the matter again with his son did he consent to sign the forms. He liked investing in a mutual fund with such a patriotic name as the Stars and Stripes Fund.

'Now you are a shareholder,' said Levy radiantly. 'I promise to come back in a month, Mr Golden, and explain everything you don't understand. A promise is a promise.'

But Levy was not the type of estate planner to relax and savour a Close. 'Gee, you sure got some beautiful heaters there,' he said, indicating a row of synthetic wool jackets. 'Who's your supplier?'

The haberdasher stared at the salesman with big, round, paternal eyes. He was thinking, 'Vy not? This is a fine Jewish boy, and smart this Mr Levin who vants so much that I give him the names of my suppliers. So vy not?'

Levy thus obtained a Referral and proceeded to his next telephone call.

'Hello Mr Levinson, this is Levy Levin with World of Finance. . . . Ah, you've heard of us. That's wonderful! I've just been talking to your customer, Mr Golden. You sure have stocked him up with some fine-looking garments. I got to compliment your good taste. In my conversation with Mr Golden, your name was mentioned. I'm just across the street and felt I oughta continue the conversation with you. I've only got a few minutes, so would it be convenient to see you in, like, five minutes? . . . That's wonderful. Also, Mr Levinson, could you tell your partner, Mr Benjamin, that I will be wanting to see him too? . . . He's out of the office? Then can you telephone him and tell him I want to speak to him? In, like, about an hour? . . . Gee, that's wonderful. I'll see you in about five minutes, Mr Levinson.'

*

Upon learning that Sleek had closed the Arctic deal, the Founder called Henry.

'Henry, Sleek's just told me the good news. I hope that you will be able to address our top salesmen on the theme of natural resources and the role they have to play in promoting world peace. . . .'

'I welcome the opportunity,' replied Henry. 'It's a very great honour to be asked to speak at a Millionaires Conference.

Over the next twelve years, economists foresee a forty-three billion dollar gap between the total amount invested by existing natural resources companies and the amount needed to meet the demands of an expanding world population. This is nearly equal to the total assets of the entire US mutual fund industry at present. Through its Natural Resources Fund, WoF will be in a prime position to fill a major part of this forty-three billion dollar vacuum.'

Baroque: 'This promises to be perhaps the most exciting investment ever made under WoF management.'

'The location of the property has been noted by people around the world because of the geological similarity of the area to the Alaskan North Slope, where discoveries within the past two years project vast quantities of oil. Preliminary drilling by major hydrocarbon companies indicates the presence of huge reserves.'

Baroque: 'We are living through very exciting times, times of challenge, times of opportunity, times in which we can demonstrate to each other, to ourselves and to the world what the creative process can yield.'

'We are betting on the growth of the free nations and want to be a part of this growth. The old exploitation approach in the development of natural resources in the developing nations is clearly not appropriate to either the needs or tempo of today's world.'

Baroque: 'To be merely an international business entity is not enough. The corporate entity must be willing to share its growth with the countries in which it seeks natural resources.'

*

At Folkestone Plan Towers, Sir Harvey Nobody, Ernest and Clovis were among those who watched the video of the Founder's pre-recorded New Year's Day speech. It was always a treat to see the Founder's face, even if only on video. He wished them happiness and prosperity for 1969 – the Year of Total Financial Service – and coyly advised them to look out for a hike in the price of shares of Fiduciary of Fiduciaries.

Bleitgeist had made a renewed, but in the event unsuccessful, effort at getting on better with his wife. He was alone with her on New Year's Eve, but, despite his good intentions, he found that he was incapable of exhibiting even a courteous interest in her. He understood why she hated him. She had too little to do. Like all wives, she imputed to him responsibility for her happiness and blamed him for ruining her life. She had countless small ways of vexing him, such as never turning off a light. He even suspected her of deliberately annoying him to gain his attention.

*

John Fitz was not among the revellers ubiquitously celebrating the advent of a New Year. He remained in the dorm studying Wiesenberger.

*

'Man, it's *cold!*' said Bone.

The Texas A & M band was endeavouring to keep warm by playing *The Eyes of Texas Are upon You*. It stopped playing, and the Texas A & M fans carried on cheering, '*Give 'em a lick! Give 'em a lick! Harder! Harder!*' Their team was leading; still, there was little enthusiasm. Everyone was feeling the cold.

Two minutes remained to play in the third quarter. Coach Moose Henning and all his assistant coaches looked glum, but most glum of all was Coach Jerry Hamilton. It wasn't as bad as against Auburn in 1961, when Coach Henning had benched the entire first and second teams for eating candy, but it was bad. Lester Blount and two others had broken curfew. They were caught returning to their rooms after midnight and, unrepentantly, despite Coach Henning's severe reprimands, broke curfew again.

'I guess I jus' sort of gave in to my desires, Coach,' Lester had pleaded in vain. 'We'd been having a rail good time in the French

Quarter, when we had to leave to go to the rally. I won't do it again. I promise. This is the last time. I'm railly sorry, Coach. I railly am.'

'You know the rules, Lester. I've already let you off once. You're benched.'

'Aw, Coach!'

'We sure could use you at a time like this,' Coach Jerry confided to Bone.

The Aggies had crossed the midfield stripe again and were threatening the UT thirty-five yard line.

'How's it feel not to be out there with your buddies?'

'I'm getting my unemployment compensation right now,' said Bone wryly. 'Coach, don't think I'm gittin' nosey, but I wonder if you've ever thought about how you're goin' to provide for your family when you retire?'

A television reporter intruded. *'How about a few words for our viewers? . . . 'I know what a big disappointment it must be for you, Bone. This was the game you had all looked forward to.'*

'Sure was,' said Bone.

'And, of course, this would have been the last game of your college career. Well, Bone, I know your teammates miss not having you out there with them, especially in a moment like this. And your defensive backs must also be moaning the loss of Lester Blount, Bill Yancey and Chubby Gross. Coach Hamilton doesn't seem too happy. I understand that Coach Henning has kept them out of the game for violating curfew.'

'That's right. You gotta do whut Coach says. Otherwise, there wouldn't be any dissuplin'.'

'Still, that's a big disadvantage for your team. And the Aggies are really fired up tonight and playing to win. Do you think the Volunteers can stave off this strong Texas A & M team and go on to win?'

'I thank so. I don't feel too nervous. Out thair is one of the finest defensive teams in the country. But you're right, Texas A & M's got a rail strong team, and they're showin' that tonight.'

'We all know how much you'd like to be out there with your teammates, although Jack Boyden has done a wonderful job

at monster. In the last two games of the season Tennessee actually reduced their averages allowed to one hundred and fifty-two yards and three point seven five points a game.'

'That says a lot for Boyden and our team.'

'One more question, Bone. How's the leg?'

'Doin' fine.'

This interview cheered Bone up for a while. It was as though his leg were not in a cast and he were out there in his pads and cleats with the others. When the third quarter ended, though, the Aggies were on the Vols' twenty-yard line, and, on the first play of the fourth quarter, they drove to the UT nine-yard line. Coach Hamilton looked glumly at defensive line coach Bobby Voss, who looked glumly at Coach Henning, whose attention remained riveted on the field. Would Coach Henning finally relent and let Lester, Bill and Chubby into the ball game? All was silence and anxiety on the Big Orange bench.

Big Orange supporters had swarmed to New Orleans, the women in orange dresses, orange tweed trouser suits, leather coats and fur collars dyed orange, waving orange pompoms, the men in orange cowboy hats, cotton shirts printed with UT, orange socks and white shoes with UT cut into the toes. A dark cloud hung over all this loyal enthusiasm. Would Coach Henning relent and let Blount, Yancey and Gross into the game?

5

BREAKING THE ICE

The loss to Texas A & M caused Coach Moose Henning no serious annoyance. It was an acceptable price to pay for team discipline and he was now free of responsibilities until the team reassembled in April for spring training. Recruitment had ended with the acceptance of the last of the scholarships offered under UT's Athletic Program, and he was not coaching in the Hula Bowl. It was off to Key Vaca for the winter: three months of beaches, palms, sunshine and deep-sea fishing. Being a strict disciplinarian, he indulged himself only an occasional can of beer, and even during this idle interlude would swim half a mile every day.

*

Noam was still at Fritz's coffee estate on the slopes of Mount Kilimanjaro, for they had many subjects of mutual fascination to discuss, including the Tanganyika African National Union, Julius Nyerere, *Uhuru*, the Arusha Declaration and the Fenner Biddup Offshore Fund.

'How imminent do you think confiscation is?' asked Noam.

'It's a job to say. They nationalized the banks and import-export firms in 1967. They nationalized the sisal plantations in 1968 and commercial buildings and large hotels in 1970. The coffee estates will be next. In the past decade, the Chagga population has nearly doubled. Everyone wants them to remain on the land, but they drift to the towns and become criminals, and Nyerere is coming under pressure to provide them with *shambas*. This is why your proposition interests me, Noam. But how would you get the money out of the country?'

'How much were you and the other settlers around here thinking of investing?'

Fritz posited a figure.

'For that amount, interesting procedures go into operation. Perhaps you are already familiar with our scheme for shipping water to East Africa?'

'Explain to me how that works.'

'We will arrange for you a shipment from Rotterdam.'

'Of water?'

'Doctored to look and smell like pesticide. The Central Bank of Tanzania will approve a remittance of foreign exchange to pay the invoiced amount. Pesticides and other agricultural chemicals are on their approved list. You are then credited with the amount of the remittance, less the cost of shipment and a handling charge of one per cent. The customs officers at the port of discharge – Tanga presumably – will examine the bill of lading and sniff the concoction to confirm that it's pesticide. You spray your crops with it after taking delivery, just as you would pesticide. It's smelly, but quite harmless. The remittance and the costs of off-loading and forwarding are all tax-deductable expenses. Your saving in taxes will more than offset the cost of the shipment and our handling charge.'

'Very clever. You chaps aren't connected with the Folkestone Plan, by any chance?'

'We are, but you can't invest Tanzi *shillingi* in the Folkestone Plan. It would be different if you had Kenya currency. Folkestone Plan policyholders are credited with sterling equivalents for premiums paid in Kenya *shillingi*. The *shillingi* are used to purchase Kenyan real estate for the Plan's portfolio, its "Equity Unit Account".'

'Doesn't that rather work to the disadvantage of the UK participants?'

'That rather depends on how you value the future of Kenyan real estate. Have you Kenyan money to invest as well? . . .'

*

Baroque in conference with Sleek and Fenner: 'Now that the Arctic deal is in the bag, we'd better see about going public. Let's get out a *Bulletin* to say that the decision was taken on the same day that we landed on the moon.'

*

Bumper was doing yoga contortions to steady his nerves. Execution was at dawn. A *mullah* assigned to console him during these final hours asked him if he wished to shave under his arms before his beheading. Perhaps, being so recent a convert, he was ignorant that such was the custom of the Faithful? No, said Bumper, if it was just a custom, and not the law of the Faith, he would forgo that additional purification.

'Shaving is better, *huzoor*.'

'I suspect it is,' Bumper conceded. 'But it can't matter too much now. Only a few hours to go.'

'It is when you give of yourself that you truly give,' said the *mullah* above his beard.

'Shall we get the prayers over with?'

Ever since his conversion, Bumper was resigned. Without any show of resistance, he had assented to the Precept that Allah was One and Muhammad was His Prophet and renounced the contaminations of alcohol, pork, fowl with webbed feet, scaled creatures that crawled on their bellies and various patterns of behaviour repugnant to the prejudice of the Faith. The *mullah* now guided him through a complicated prayer ritual which recalled the daily exercise regime he had experienced while serving as an airman in the Pennsylvania Air National Guard; then read to him in Arabic long passages from the Qur'an, while he lay with his nose to the floor; then recited from a stock of homilies. '. . . *What shall tomorrow bring to the over-prudent dog burying bones in the trackless sand, as he follows the pilgrims to the Holy City? In their fear, our forefathers have bunched us too near together. That fear shall last only a little while longer. A little longer will our city walls separate our fires from our fields. . . .*'

Bumper fell asleep. . . .

A fly buzzed in his ear. He opened his eyes and saw light through the window's iron bars. Dawn! His last. Outside, the city he had exploited for Contest-Winning Volume and grown to loathe, its ugly streets soon to be congested with traffic, every car blowing its horn and belching exhaust. At least there wouldn't be traffic jams where he was bound. Or maybe it would be like Teheran there? The *mullah* was still at his side. 'I suppose he thinks it's considerate staying with me until the last moment,' thought Bumper.

'. . . *The wind and the sun will trouble you no more. You will have thirst never again. All your hours will be wings beating in the space from self to self. . . .*'

'I know,' agreed Bumper.

'How much longer must my trials endure?' he wondered. 'What more can they want from me? Nothing remains to confess. My bones are beginning to ache from lying on the floor so long.'

'. . . *Your friends and loved ones will be forever linked to you with shackles of purest silver and gold that can never break. Only when you cease to think of freedom as a goal and a fulfilment will you become truly free – free of the harness of seeking freedom: when such thoughts as "I am hungry" or "I am cold" girdle your life, and yet you rise above them naked and unbound. And how shall you rise beyond your days and nights, unless you break the chains which you at the dawn of your understanding have fastened around your noon hour?*'

'Yes,' allowed Bumper. 'I am ready to break the chains.'

*

There was little consternation at the Top of the Spirals concerning Bumper. Assuming a worst-case scenario, he was dead, another manager gone to the firing squad or the gallows.

'Shouldn't we, like, mention it to Baroque?'

'We've just received a cable from Teheran, Mr Baroque. There's speculation that our GM there has been beheaded.'

'Remind me, who's in Teheran these days?' inquired Baroque.

'You might recall the conversation we had on this subject in November. It's Bumper Peabody – or *was* Bumper Peabody.'

'Ah yes, Bumper. Of course. Don't worry about Bumper. They'll never behead Bumper. He's sly as a fox.'

Marty and Nelson discussed the implications.

'You think we should drop the plan?'

'Why?'

'If they haven't beheaded Bumper, Bleitgeist won't want Asia II.'

'We can always sell the Territory to somebody else.'

*

Financial Counsellors all over Tennessee were busy that morning. Some were prospecting for prospects and some were making presentations to prospects. Levy had proved so effective as a trainee Financial Counsellor-cum-Manager that he had already reached Senior Schedule and was rising rapidly towards Branch.

And his was not the only star in local ascent. Adjusting slowly to the rigid limitations of his gesso cast, proudly marking the days that he was able to stand, to take three consecutive steps without crutches and to run on his steel heel, it was by a similar hobbling growth in confidence that Bone, too, was becoming an effective WoFer.

The results of his first month of activity were not impressive – without a sale, in fact – but Bleitgeist had forewarned him; 'The first month is the period when Counsellors lacking will-power fall by the wayside.' Bone, therefore, did not lapse into despondency. Instead, he plugged on. He used the telephone to arrange appointments. He spoke to ten people for everyone who granted him an appointment. Most of the others hung up on him.

Bleitgeist prepared him for this also.

'This is the period when Counsellors who are excessively sensitive to rudeness fall by the wayside. . . . A wrong concept of dignity is the greatest single failure factor in the industry. . . . All rudeness has its source in ignorance. . . . Exposure to rudeness is the hazard of any forward marketing position.'

Bone's efforts that morning were yet to yield an appointment. He had reached the Greggs in the telephone directory. He dialled the next Gregg number and pondered which valediction to use while waiting for his prospective prospect to answer. The Informogram on Model Telephone Technique provided a variety of choices. Bleitgeist had advised him to commit them all to memory, and, in more than four hundred calls so far, only four prospective prospects had asked questions for which there was no Model Reply.

'Mr Gregg, this is Lawrence Saxon. I'm in Knoxville this week, and I'm callin' to arrange a suitable time for an appointment. Would Thursday morning at elevun, or Friday afternoon at foar suit you?' It was one of his best deliveries, but the words were spoken to the prospect's secretary. This happened sometimes.

'Would you spell your name, please.'

'S-A-X-O-N, as in Anglo-Saxon.'

'Just one moment, please.'

The call was switched to another, less agreeable voice: 'Does this concern insurance?'

'It concerns money,' replied Bone firmly.

'You want to lend *me* money? Or you want me to lend *you* money?'

'I want to show you how to make moar money, Mr Gregg.'

'In that case, I'd have to pay more taxes.'

'Savin' taxes is partly whut I'd like to talk to you about, Mr Gregg. My clients generully find that the money they save in taxes is one of our investments' neatest features.'

'What are you selling? Municipals? Municipals are the only investment that's tax-free.' Bone had learned all about municipals in Finance 1001, but the Informogram on Model Telephone Technique had forewarned him against drifting into debate. 'Can you show me a way of getting out of Social Security?' Gregg continued.

'Social Security is partly whut I'd like to talk to you about, Mr Gregg. At our confrunce, I'll be able to iron out any special difficulties you have. Would Thursday morning at elevun, or Friday afternoon at foar suit you? Or would you prefer Thursday afternoon at three?'

Although Bone was still young in his new career, the tirade issuing from his prospective prospect was already familiar to him.

'We pay thirteen direct taxes and forty-three hidden taxes. We pay taxes on everything we buy, sell or earn. Then we pay taxes on what we give away and what we leave to our children. The company is taxed, and so is the shareholder. Whatever companies earn, the Government reduces by half and takes a further cut on dividends distributed to shareholders. Now the President says we *need* this new excess profits tax to keep down inflation. If the money were spent on retiring the national debt, even if it were spent on national improvements, like more dams, it might work. But do *you* think the Government's going to retire the national debt? *Ha*! It's going to hire more experts to hire more experts to hire more experts to find more ways of giving away our money. As soon as the Government gets its hands on our tax dollar, back it goes into circulation. The only way to beat inflation is to leave the wealth in the hands of the producers of wealth and let competition take care of prices.'

Bone waited patiently for Gregg to finish then said, 'Inflation is partly whut I'd like to talk to you about, Mr Gregg.'

'And who does inflation hurt the most Mr . . . Who did you say you are?'

'Saxon. Lawrence Saxon.'

'The *poor*! That's who!' resumed Gregg. 'The very people the Government *claims* it's trying to help. People who work all their lives and save so they can provide for their *own* welfare without looking to the Government for a handout when they retire.'

'That's another thang I'd like to talk to you about, Mr Gregg. Retirement.'

'Sir, I don't know who gave you my name, but I've been been retired for the past six years. Now I have to go back to work, because inflation's so high I can't live on what I've saved. The Federal Government depreciates the purchasing power of the currency by giving away what I pay to it in taxes, and it is still figuring out new ways of taxing me.'

Bone put down the receiver.

Later, he consulted Bleitgeist about this exchange. 'The fellow had a thang about taxes.'

Bleitgeist: 'Even with cranks you learn the importance of zeroing in. Let's run through it again, Bone.'

'Again?'

'It's the only way.'

They ran through it again.

'Now let's see how you get on with the next Gregg.'

The telephone directory described the next Gregg as 'Atty'. Again, the Informogram on Model Telephone Technique provided guidance. 'Mr Gregg, this is Lawrence Saxon. I'm in Knoxville this week contacting architects, doctors, attorneys and other professional people. . . . Since you ask, Mr Gregg, it concerns you, and it will take about twelve minutes to cover the essentials. . . . I understand, but let me ask you this. If I could show you how to get as much life cover and more return on investment *for the same money*, don't you think, *as an intelligent professional man*, this would be somethang you should look into?'

After working on Bone's Telephone Technique, Bleitgeist worked on his Close. '"However polished your Telephone Technique, however thoroughly you have researched Prospect's Background Data, however professional your presentation, it all counts for nothing without an effective Close",' he said, reciting from the Informogram on Model Closes. 'There is no problem with what you are selling. The problem is getting your prospect to make a decision. He understands rationally what in his heart he cannot bring himself to do. Your job is to *help* him. Make him feel your enthusiasm. Put him in a Yes-Frame-of-Mind. "Does this investment make sense to you? – Yes." "Can you see how your savings would have multiplied had you known of this opportunity before? – Yes." "Can you see the advantage of the inheritance feature? – Yes." "Do you see the purpose of the insurance feature? – Yes." "Can you see how such an investment can protect your savings against inflation? – Yes." "Can you see the advantages of Diversification? – Yes." "Of Vertical Diversification? – Yes." Don't ask him *if* he would like to buy a Plan. Confront him with a Positive Alternative, whether he prefers the investment with or without insurance; in his own name or jointly with his wife; in units of $300 a month, "Or is that overly optimistic?" So Bone worked on putting prospects in a Yes-Frame-of-Mind.

He soon found that he was able to fill his spare time with appointments. However, he was yet to make a sale.

'I want you to tell me exactly what happened at your last presentation,' said Bleitgeist.

Bone described his last presentation.

'Did you smile when you entered his office?'

'I thank so.'

'Don't smile. Too hearty an approach can make a Rep look silly. Affability has to be tempered by solemnity.'

Bone began to premeditate his smiles.

'Never sit where your head is below the level of your prospect's head. Avoid sofas.'

Bone began to premeditate his choice of seating.

'Never start a presentation while a third party is present. Wait quietly until the prospect has finished his other business, prompting him only if it goes on too long. "I'm sure you'll appreciate that this is a matter to be discussed in the strictest confidence, Mr Worth." Demand his *full* attention. Your presentation is not effective unless he hears it. If his mind wanders, stop talking. He will notice the silence. Convict him with his own rudeness.

'Never accept an expensive drink. People offer hospitality to strangers because they think it's the correct thing to do, but they will resent you accepting it. Don't forfeit a thousand-dollars commission for a bourbon and water costing two dollars.'

Finally, on St Valentine's Day, ten weeks after his first presentation, Bone electrified his Manager with the announcement that he had made a sale. They met at the Thelma Houk McGrory Student Center. Bleitgeist was checking the *Knoxville Sentinel's* divorce columns for leads when Levy's trainee hobbled in and gave him the precious completed forms. Bleitgeist held them reverently in his hands. He had fondled more than four million dollars of sales during his WoF career, but a soon-to-be-processed new Plan never failed to excite him. It was the sensation he craved. He examined the forms as an exhausted but elated mother first looks on her new born baby. His professional eye alighted first on the client's cheque and Bank Instruction Letter. Next, it scrutinized the Application. Finally, it turned to the Designation of Beneficiary. He gave no hint of his discovery, saying only, 'Bone, that's wonderful! How does it feel to be an Icebreaker?'

'It's a funny thang, Mr Bleitgeist, but I thank he felt sorry for me.'

Bone spoke sincerely and with modest intention, but, disappointingly, his words diminished the magnitude of his achievement. 'A Close is a Close,' said Bleitgeist.

'The Stars and Stripes Fund is a rail fine investment,' persisted Bone.

'Yes, it is. But however fine the investment, the final credit belongs to the Rep who makes the Close. I always knew you were going to become one of our leading Financial Counsellors.'

'Gosh, Mr Bleitgeist, it's only my first sale.'

'But that's the Big One, Bone. It's only your first, but it won't be your last.'

'Gosh, Mr Bleitgeist, it was just like you said, like a fish on a hook.'

The Area Manager succeeded in projecting a look at once beatific and wise, the look that he had tried in vain to project for the photographer sent to take his picture for the article about him in the *Bulletin's* Meet Your Fellow Counsellor column. He kept the forms and, when Bone was gone, forged the client's omitted signature on the Designation of Beneficiary, and prepared a transmittal slip for sending to Processing and an index card for his Override records.

*

Twilight over Serengeti. Mingled herds of zebra and wildebeest. Jackals emerge from their holes. A dik-dik sniffs the air. A lion moves. Hyenas scatter.

'Call for you from Bujumbura, Mr Baroque.'

Van Zilver was spending that evening at the *manyatta*. No cool veranda for him. No fireside chats under trophies of kudu and eland hunts. No convivial evening squandered in cigarette haze before the dart-board at Fritz's club. He was busy. None before him had attempted the Maasai Market. Ferociously xenophobic and contemptuous of all forms of wealth that did not walk on cloven feet or jangle as ornaments, the tribe had foregathered on sacred grazing grounds within menacing distance of a sacred hill adversely occupied by the Government for an Ujaama village. *Bwana* van Zilver was seated on a three-legged wooden stool outside the chief's hut, where the *moran* were paying homage to the chief's new investment, a novel investment celebrated by traditional means. They slaughtered a cow and drank its blood. They shaved a virgin's head and all her other parts, performed on her the beneficent rite of clitoridectomy, clapped hands and presented her to *Bwana* in holy matrimony. Then they slaughtered another cow and drank its blood. *Bwana* drank *naishi* and received gifts of plates of fried flying ants, strips of raw beef and a wife. All round the brushwood fence of the *manyatta*, the *moran* beat drums and shuffled. They clapped and chanted in low moans hymns of ancestral praise. They broke into frenzies as though possessed by spirits, thrashed themselves with thongs of buffalo hide and cursed the immigrant races, the Wakikuyu, Wameru, Wakamba and Wachagga. The ground throbbed with the pounding of feet, and the sky was orange with the glow of their fires. It was, to date, van Zilver's most successful Group Presentation.

*

'Inter-Office memo to Herb. Subject: Bumper Peabody, 6114.' Nelson was dictating. 'It has been confirmed that the subject Area Manager of Asia II is alive. You will recall, he's in difficulty with the Iranian police for currency violations, working without a permit and tax evasion. Therefore, we are withholding all commissions and New Man Bonuses owing to him pending further developments. *Vide* my memo to Commissions dated Jan. blank, copy of which was sent to you with my memo of Jan. blank. I have advised him that the company, in principle, is sympathetic to his request for another Territory.

'New paragraph.

'According to more precise information received today from Teheran, Area office remains closed and all WoFers working the Territory on Branch or above, except Noam van Zilver, 7111, whereabouts unknown, remain in detention.

'New paragraph.

'Company policy calls for rendering assistance to Area Manager, quote, whenever consistent with company's interests and the interests of its clients, unquote. *Vide* Adminogram dated October or November 1967. Get the exact date from Phyllis. Clients' interests and our own are best promoted in this instance by reaching an accord with the Iranian Government which might include, colon offset, clarification from the Iranian Government of the exact legal status of our operation in that country; semi-colon offset, if appropriate, mutually agreed parameters within which we can operate in future; semi-colon offset, formalization of existing or alternative channels of remittance; semi-colon offset, negotiations, if appropriate, for the establishment of a national fund under joint Iranian Government-WoF sponsorship and linked on the investment side to the exploitation of that country's natural resources.

'New paragraph.

'Any agreement along the proposed lines would necessarily involve immediate release of all WoF personnel detained on charges arising out of WoF activities. Company money should not be sent for local attorneys' fees, posting bond or any extraordinary prerequisites necessary to that end, except in the last resort and only after determination that such expenditure is in the best interests of the company and its clients. End of memo. Copy to Sleek.

'Second memo.'

Virginia changed pencils.

'To: Jim Chumney. Subject: Asia II. Dear Jimmy, I would appreciate it if, as a matter of utmost urgency, you could ask someone in your department to assemble the Activity Reports on all Associates who have worked in the above Territory during the last twelve months, as well as copies of the print-outs of all investments by clients of Iranian nationality, whether currently residing in Iran or not. End of Memo.

'Third memo. Leave date blank. To Sleek. Subject: Bumper Peabody, 6114. I enclose copies of relevant Activity Reports and clients' investments and my Memo of today's or yesterday's date, as the case may be, to Marty, setting forth my general ideas re the above subject. Our violations are obvious, and I understand that all detainees have been subjected to prolonged and intensive interrogation. It may be assumed, therefore, that the Iranian police will have compiled a fairly complete and accurate dossier on our activities. Immediate action should be taken to resolve the present difficulties. End of memo.

'Fourth Memo. To Marty. Subject: Bob Bleitgeist, 5242, and Tom Stamp, 5186, semi-colon, East Tennessee. You will be aware that this Territory remains the subject of contention between the above Reps. As East Tennessee is to me a *terra incognita* – T-E-R-R-A I-N-C-O-G-N-I-T-A – I am unable to judge the merits of their respective claims. The easiest way round the problem might be to reassign one of the Reps to another Territory. Any such move, of course, would need your authorization. Perhaps you will want to suggest a different solution. End of memo. Copy to Herb.

'Next memo. . . .'

*

While Nelson dictated, the wires between Bujumbura and the Top of the Spirals were busy with the mundane affairs of tardy processing.

Jean-Baptiste Mwambutsa, Area Manager for Burundi: '*Nous n'avons pas reçus les cartons suisses*' – meaning that he had received no confirmation of a Fully Paid negotiated through local agents of the bank handling Special Collections for Anonymous Depositors Bank.

Baroque: 'What was the date of the order?' – meaning, 'When did you send the papers to Processing? . . .'

The extreme delicacy of the situation required Baroque's special touch.

Baroque: 'What kind of response are you getting on the other cartons?' – meaning how much Volume was the Territory producing. The Founder's interest was always aroused when Volume was in jeopardy.

Mwambutsa: '*Il-y-a beaucoup d'interêt mais très peu de réponse*' – meaning Volume remained strong, but Admin was weak.

Three men in Baroque's office, who had waited twelve days to see him and felt uneasy in his presence, were appalled to see him quake violently and to hear him bellow into the telephone. They feared the onset of one of his rages. Baroque's rages were like typhoons. They blew out of nowhere, scattering innocent and dishonest alike.

The storm passed.

It transpired that the premier of Burundi had imposed a curfew and troops were combing the streets looking for Hutus, rounding them up and shooting them. 'It sounds like another case of genocide,' said Baroque. 'The newspapers tell us nothing. South Africa is a story. Burundi is not. We are keeping our fingers crossed that none of our Reps will be shot.'

Minutes later, the scandal broke. The Top of the Spirals throbbed with the news. Mwambutsa had not received a Confirm on a Special Collection.

Baroque: 'Martha, who's looking after Special Collections these days?'

. . . 'Martha, Irving says you want me to check out Mwambutsa's Special Collections. . . .'

'Okay, on first September . . .'

'Are we talking about Mwambutsa's Special Collections?'

'His Special Collections gotta show up on his Activity reports, right?'

'Not necessarily. Not if he gets the Confirms direct from ADB. Find out, willya, and call me back.'

And thus it emerged that Noam van Zilver was pirating in Africa IV.

'Inter-Office memo to Marty Rubin. Subject: Noam van Zilver, 7111. I stated in an earlier memo of today's date that this Rep's whereabouts were unknown. Information just received suggests that he may be in Africa IV working the Territory without Mwambutsa's knowledge or permission. Mwambutsa has received no Confirms on Plans sold via locally approved procedures for Special Collections. Steps already taken have not resolved the present dispute, and, to avoid further difficulties, perhaps you will want to cable 7111 and advise him where and under what circumstances he may work pending re-integration into a reconstituted Asia II. . . .'

*

Bone had a light load that quarter. He was taking only two courses, Transportation 3110 and Finance 4520, and his growing Client List included his parents, the McCallums and Uncle Ned. Steve Talbertson had opened a now delinquent Plan with a minimal down-payment, while two of the other linesmen had taken out Pendings. Altogether, it was an impressive performance for a part-timer on Trainee Schedule.

Noam was contemptuous of Marty's cable. WoFers no longer able to recruit, train and supervise New Men or make presentations either quarrelled with Baroque, cashed in their stock at extortionate prices and left the company or retired to the Top of the Spirals and wrote bumf. Mwambutsa was just one more jealous, avaricious Area Manager. 'The fellow doesn't even speak Swahili!'

Noam had been a week at the *manyata* drinking milk and *damu joto* from calabashes and enjoying other honorary tribal elder privileges, while the *moran* herded. He retired at dusk to a fumigated earthen hut with his giggling bride, who cauterized her tick sores, greased her taut skin with cow lard, wore coils of nickel wire round her neck and ankles and spat on him to thank him at each ejaculation.

Now bidding his adoptive brothers and sisters and his wife of a week farewell, and having explained the Fenner Biddup Offshore Fund once more to the chief's satisfaction, he departed for the tribal lands of the Wairaqw, Wambulu, Wasandawe, Wahehe, Wangoni, Wanyamwezi, Waweno, Wakahe, Washambaa, Wayao, Wasukuma and Wagogo.

He did not delude himself. His work had no moral or aesthetic purpose. He was Top of the Bonus List and a Contest Winner because he liked imparting his enthusiasm for WoF products, especially the Fenner Biddup Offshore Fund.

*

At Levy's urging and owing to Bone's impact on the Athletes Market, Bleitgeist decided to hold a Financial Training Seminar at Knoxville. So the third week in February, after mid-term exams were over, found Bone, Blaize, Lester, Mule, Fitz, Levy and Bleitgeist round a table in the Green Room of the Great Smokies Appalachian Inn. The table was set with bowls of peanuts and crisps. Financial Worksheets and balsawood blocks engraved with the trainees' names contributed an element of professionalism. A blackboard bore the words 'ALWAYS BE POSITIVE'.

Bleitgeist explained DGPINS, Vertical Diversification and Dollar Cost Averaging. He reviewed the Application, Automatic Withdrawal Plan and Designation of Beneficiary forms. Then he read aloud the portfolio of the Stars and Stripes Fund. The diversity of companies in this portfolio, he said, exemplified the nation's economy; they accounted for its miracle drugs, packaged foods, new houses and office buildings. 'You make a profit for yourself every time you go to the dime store. Is it possible that *all* these companies will lose money?'

'In the short run,' answered Bone. As senior Financial Counsellor under Bleitgeist and Levy, he felt relaxed and confident. His leg was free of its gesso encumbrance now, and success at his chosen career seemed assured. It was a novel experience seeing Mule smoke in class. 'Whut I was aimin' to say was that, in the short run, you can't always bank on thangs turning out like you want them to.'

'The Mutual Fund isn't the proper vehicle *for a quick return*?' hinted Bleitgeist coyly.

'That's whut I meant to say,' replied Bone.

Bone made a note on his Financial Worksheet, 'Don't depend too much on Diversification in the short run'. He passed his Financial Worksheet to Blaize to copy the notation. Blaize passed it to Lester and Lester passed it to Mule. Blaize, Lester and Mule had also decided to make banking and finance their careers.

'That's right, Bone. Am I not right in thinking that you are really saying that we needn't be concerned with next month or next year, because we have an investment vehicle that contemplates the *whole* future? We don't have to pick and choose between different securities. To pore over stock market reports. To consult Standard and Poor's ratings. To make comparisons of dividends and earnings ratios. To evaluate past management. To judge when to take and when to get out of a position. That we may confidently leave such worries to experts and, even if they fail us, we are still protected. That all we need ask ourselves is, "Will the economy grow over the next ten or twenty years?"'

'The economy's growing now. I apprehend that it will continue to grow,' declared Fitz.

'I figure it'll keep on growin',' said Bone.

Blaize, Lester and Mule concurred. 'The economy's goin' to go on growin'.'

Bone wrote on his Financial Worksheet: 'Diversification safer over the long haul.'

'I've lectured at plenty of seminars, but this bunch of dildos absolutely takes the cake,' Bleitgeist confided to Levy, while the 'dildos' refreshed themselves with free coffee, peanuts and crisps and discussed sports during the mid-session break.

'Why not talk about how much money they can make?' said Levy. 'Nobody wants to hear about Diversification.'

So after the break, Bleitgeist spoke on Career Prospects. He furnished examples from his own experience.

'Not only was my Supervisor great at his job. He also believed in *enjoying* his work, and that was something that I had never thought about. Hardly a day went by that we didn't take time out for a swim and a little nap on the beach. At night, we went mambo dancing at the *Dos Pájaros*. Or maybe we would just walk up the hill to the *Paragueña* to hear the *mariachis*. Even lying on the beach or sitting at the bar, we often met someone who needed a mutual fund. Acapulco is where I made Branch Schedule.'

'Show them your gold watch,' prompted Levy. 'A gold watch is what WoF gives you when your Volume reaches a million dollars.'

Bleitgeist cheerfully retracted his jacket sleeve and revealed the glittering prize. He loosened the band, took off the watch and passed it round. Everyone admired it in turn, Blaize, Lester and Mule tapping it with a fingernail, estimating its purity in carats.

'They engrave your name on the back' said Bleitgeist. 'And, after you've done two million in Volume, they give you a silver blazon.'

Later, when Manager and Supervisor were alone again, Levy said, 'That time I think you impressed them. Was it true what you said about the average earnings of Key Associates exceeding the combined earnings of the Packers' first string line?'

'I don't have the actual figures at my fingertips, but it wouldn't be far off the mark.'

'It sure was a neat way to bring the point home to them.'

'I thought so, too.'

'Was it Mexico or Spain where you made Branch?'

'Spain, but I figured it was too far away for them to conceptualize. So I substituted Mexico.'

*

The Second Session of the Financial Training Seminar was devoted to the *World of Finance Financial Counsellors Production Analysis* booklet. On the blackboard were the words:

Calls + Knowledge + Ability = Success

and

Structure to Work With – The Five Steps to a Sale:
Attention
Interest
Desire
Proving the Case (Find and Fulfil the Prospect's Needs)
Action (Write up the Sale Immediately)

*

Fitz in his room at the Francis Ellsworth Haynes Memorial Graduate Students Dormitory preparing for the Final Session of the Financial Training Seminar.

The Ten Golden Rules For Successful Salesmanship:

1. Act Enthusiastic.
2. Organize Your Work: Plan Carefully.
3. Watch Personal Habits and Appearance.
4. Improve Your Speech Habits.
5. Create Confidence: Deserve Confidence.
6. Attitude: Expect Business.
7. Concentrate Your Effort: On the Key Issue.
8. Ask Questions: Instead of Making Positive Statements.
9. Silence: Listen to What Prospect is Saying.
10. Improvement: Spend Time Regularly for Improvement.

*

The Final Session of the Financial Training Seminar opened with brief rehearsals of Sincere Smiles and Firm Handshakes.

Next came a review of the Mutual Fund as an Investment Concept, Investment Feature Analysis Techniques, the Difference between Closed-End and Open-End Investment Companies, Net Asset Value, Tombstone Advertisement, Partial Liquidation, Diminishing Term Insurance and Volume Bonuses.

Attention was then paid to the Importance of Correct Choice of Terms: 'Direct Call', instead of 'Cold Call'; 'Client', instead of 'Customer'; 'Help', instead of 'Sell'; 'Dynamic Growth Plan', instead of 'Contractual'; 'When Something Happens to You', instead of 'Dying'; 'Imaginary 'Fears', instead of 'Objections'.

Next discussed was Tactical Positioning. 'Sit next to your prospect, where it is easier to win his confidence.'

Bleitgeist then turned to the Three Types of Imaginary Fears and How to Deal with Them.

'The best way I have found for overcoming *I don't believe you* is to show the prospect old newspapers and clippings from magazines showing past results.

'*I can't afford it.* Mr Worth, do I understand correctly that you cannot save even twenty-five dollars a month to protect your wife and family's living standards?

'*I can do better.* In our business, Mr Worth, we often hear success stories. Unfortunately, we also hear a lot of stories that end in tragedy.'

The Area Manager concluded with a review of Graduating Commissions According to Schedule, Entitlement to Stock Options, the Record of Growth in the Formula Value of Stock acquired under the Stock Option Plan and the World-wide Compass of World of Finance Products and Services.

'But just because the company gives you a piece of calfskin with a red seal on it certifying . . .'

'And a briefcase,' intruded Levy.

'. . . and a briefcase, it doesn't mean that you will become a successful Financial Counsellor. The emblems of official status in themselves can never guarantee success. Something *else* is needed. Who can tell me what that something else is?'

Bone supposed that it was influence in one's own community; Fitz, a pleasant personality. 'Always be positive,' offered Mule.

'True, all these things matter. But what is the really *vital* ingredient, the cornerstone and mainstay of steady achievement, the bedrock of successful financial counselling? Would anyone else like to take a guess?'

Silence in the Green Room.

'Hard work,' announced Bleitgeist, 'and . . .?'

'Mr Bleitgeist doesn't mean you got to work hard *all* the time. He means if you work harder, you get to be a millionaire quicker. That's all he means.'

'Well, up to a point, Levy. You can make a presentation and think you've closed. Your prospect has revealed his Need, and you've matched it to a Plan. The forms are completed and ready for signing. Then, for no obvious reason, he changes his mind. Gentlemen, at such times you may be assailed by doubts as to whether Stock Options are really worth it. My advice to you is . . .'

Bone wrote in his notes, 'Expect disappointments and push on.'

Part II

Spring Training

6

DOUBLE TROUBLE

Belvedere came out of the woods, his body in a tuck, head forward and craning a little. He straightened, skated flat over ice, took the moghuls in three quick jumps and was in the woods again, travelling at speed. His manner, a spirited nonchalance, proclaimed that mountains and a soft purr from crunched snow edging his skis was all that were needed to perfect him in contentment and self-esteem. Far below, the lights of the village came into view. He stopped to clean his goggles and wait for Hugh.

Presently, Hugh caught up with him and said: 'Christ, that's tremendous!'

'Fantastic!'

'Fantastic snow!'

'Stop at the Brosser for a *Glüwein*?'

'Race you down!'

Belvedere soon regained the lead, looked back over his shoulder and shouted, 'Don't get lost in a cloud!' then saw Hugh, taking a bend, crash into a tree.

'Bit tricky that,' Hugh explained later at the Brosser. 'Must have lost control.'

'About that money I owe you,' said Belvedere happily.

'Yes, thanks for reminding me. I've been meaning to ask you about it.'

'You might have to wait.'

'Fine! Send it to me.'

'Sure you don't mind?'

'Send it to the Alpenhof. I always seem to end up there sooner or later. I don't expect you'll be much in funds before next year.'

Four months had passed in this pleasant way. In December, Belvedere had left his job teaching English at the Universal Languages School in Barcelona for a fortnight's holiday from 'the grindstone' and, when the Christmas break seemed to be drawing to an end too soon, decided to extend his holiday in order to perfect his stem Christy. New Year's Day had seen him composing a letter to the Principal (*'Muy amable señor'*) pledging to return to work quite soon. But January had passed and he had been unable to leave the mountains. His funds depleted, he had begun borrowing: first Neville, then Christopher. An amiable Swiss girl named Karin had supported him for a month to work on his jump turn. Hugh – Hugh was a brick – had made it possible to perfect his slalom. Now the snows were melting and, in less than a week, all but the top runs would close. He had no morbid desire to stay to the end.

It was dark when they finished 'the parting *Glüwein*'. Hugh paid and they bade Frau Brosser goodbye (*'Bis nächstes Dezember'* . . . *'Bis Morgen'*). Then they stepped outside and into their bindings and, for the first time since the first run of the day, zipped up their anoraks. An unseasonable snowfall had begun, reminding Belvedere how this now gloomy wooded trail had looked on mornings in February. He remembered the Himmelspitz gleaming and covered in fresh powder, the run markers desolate as high Himalayan prayer flags. He skied the slush at the end of the trail in silence as befitted his melancholy. He thought sadly of the lifts functioning for Hugh's sole benefit.

'Lucky bastard!'

'What d'you say?'

'I said you are a *lucky bastard*!' he shouted.

'That's what I thought you said.'

Hugh accompanied him to the station that evening.

Later, in a first-class carriage on the *Flèche d'Or,* while passengers in the corridor remonstrated about his usurping their reserved compartment, Belvedere lay awake reminiscing.

At Lyons, he changed trains and went to sleep. Some hours later he awoke, looked out the window upon an insipid landscape and thought, 'This time yesterday, I was racing Hugh down the M1.' The M1 was what they called the run from the top of the Blauhorn.

He changed trains again at Perpignan, the sun a ball of fire above the Pyrenees. Moustaches, hairwash and shaving soap at the border.

His circumstances, thought Belvedere, were satisfactory. His task was merely to perpetuate and even improve them. He didn't relish returning to Uners, but accounted it the price he must pay for literary ambition, for he was not merely an athlete; he was also the author of the mostly unfinished *Our Times*. Both his ambition and his predicament were the same as that of many young men. What he *really* wanted, beneath all the cant that he proclaimed about the freedom to develop his own ideas, was the freedom to pursue the whims of each passing moment – and that required money. He wanted to be rich, and neither pedagogy, fiction nor inheritance would ever make him rich. None of his numerous girlfriends, except Philippa, was rich. Philippa was very rich.

Dazzling light alternating with pitch black as the train waddled in and out of tunnels. Windows jammed shut and prised open. Black clouds in the carriage, everyone coughing and spitting; later, sharing tangerines; Belvedere sullen and unfriendly.

Although he had considered various jobs appropriate to his training and abilities – modelling, translation, broadcasting – none had interested him greatly. Soldiering in one of the newly independent African countries held a certain romance, but the remuneration offered was manifestly incommensurate with the risk. Further dependence on his father could lead only to further acrimony. His father was an aristocrat of the old school who believed atavistically that privileges deriving from birth entailed obligations in the public good.

There was a stampede of animated Latins at Barcelona station. *Christ*, it was awful to be back! Paunches, raven hair neatly trimmed and combed, gold teeth, wild embraces, shoving and pinching, oratory and olive oil. Belvedere sat tight.

The crowd dispersed. He hoisted his rucksack and skis onto his shoulders and alighted onto the platform. It was a warm evening, full of secret fragrances, a mild breeze blowing from the sea rustling palm leaves and flowering oleanders, but Belvedere was indifferent to the beauty around him. Tonight he might have been rampaging and stomping in the cellar of the Alpenhof.

Widows in black on benches of wrought iron fell silent and stared at him as he passed. Children playing football beneath arc lamps rushed about his feet. Hawkers touted lottery tickets. There was something like calm in the parks and clamour and the vapours of copious frying in the streets. He made tedious progress.

He stopped at the *bodega*, the scene of his skirmish with the longshoreman, Enrique – obscured now by a haze of alpinism; a tiny commotion because of a little spilt brandy eventually requiring Don Vyvyan's intercession with the Guardia Civil to spring him from prison, all but obliterated by snow. Affectionate recollection of the affray led him to peep through the door and hail the *padron* with his free hand, but the vile Catalan of the one dangling tooth only scowled and drew back against his hogsheads.

'My felicitations to The Drunk,' said Belvedere observing that his erstwhile antagonist was nowhere present.

More vapours and congestion, more henna-tinted curly hair and gold teeth, and no snow. Don Vyvyan's green Porsche was parked outside the Florida. Deciding that he would unload his gear and return, Belvedere continued nonchalantly up the Ramblas through a tremendous roar of traffic and turned into Calle Union. At the Porsepina's massive doors he paused before mounting its familiar steps. As usual, there were no lights on the landings. They have the Spanish disease, he thought: *no funciona*. He pressed the buzzer. Doña Teresa answered. She was a handsome woman with an open face, now worn and disillusioned by the hobos who lodged at her pension. The heavily encumbered, unshaven man who stood before her seeking re-admission was one of her disappointments. He had deserted her, as other without-shames, without settling his bill, leaving his possessions behind for her to look after.

'He has returned,' she reported to her daughter, Almira.

'The Englishman?'

'The without-shame.'

*

About the time Belvedere was changing trains at Perpignan, three Managers were standing at the window of Clovis's office surveying a drenched Market.

All that day it had rained. Crowds took refuge in tube station entrances or stood trembling in bus queues with newspapers folded over their heads. In squares and crescents and along the Embankment, trees dripped and everything smelled mouldy. It was not like the Spring Contest of the previous year, when the sun had shone brightly on their enterprise. Then there had been no holding the men back, and Call Back had followed presentation and Close with unremitting cupidity. Now only the few who could not afford not to ventured out. It was a grey day for insurance salesmen.

'All me men 'av lumbago,' complained Ernest, imitating the local dialect.

'All mine are 'oarse,' jested the Manager for Wales.

'That 'ud be bronchitis,' advised Clovis. 'It's Volume 'ut suffers most,' and all three Managers sighed deeply. Garrulous by profession, they now stood as silent as coffins in a Magritte painting.

They had a lot to be grateful for. When Clovis opened up Britain, he had found the situation as bad as in most places: ignorance of the company's name, exchange control laws, patriotic sentiments about the plight of the local currency impeding the natural flow of money. Worst of all, door-to-door selling of all forms of securities, including unit trusts, was prohibited. Then the Founder proposed selling the investment as a with-profits insurance policy.

'So, we can't sell DGPINSes door-to-door. Okay, we'll stand the thing on its head and sell INSDGPs.'

The lawyers implemented his idea, and the salesmen adapted to a new vocabulary. Thenceforth, remittances were called premiums and Plans were called policies. These changes wrought no significant difference in the investment. Great Britain being a net exporter of actuarial services, the Bank of England even gave its permission to invest the equity pool outside the country. The Crown rejected WoF's application for Special Appointment to Her Majesty to purvey insurance. Nevertheless in Britain, as elsewhere, the company expanded by leaps and bounds.

*

Belvedere dined at his favourite tavern and, ordering *mariscos* and a jug of *sangria* to chase them down, chatted affably with all the waitresses.

'He is *not* a without-shame, Mama. Why else would he come back to the Porsepina?'

'To reclaim his possessions, that box of papers and other junk.'

'If he were a without-shame, Mama, why would he want to reimburse you?'

'Your father was like him, my daughter. Always talking good intentions and always deferring his obligations. Spending the money needed for his family's food on other women. Gambling on bulls. Drunk at his daughter's first communion. Always showing off.'

'Belvedere is not like that, Mama.'

Having eaten to repletion, Belvedere decided to give Don Vyvyan a miss. He stumbled back to the Porsepina and went to sleep.

Sometime after midnight, Almira opened the door to her room and peered cautiously out onto a ghostly scene. A solitary, ten-watt bulb burned in the corridor. Under her pink and black lace *peignoir* was a starched petticoat. Her hair was shampooed and swept into a *chignon* and tied with a bright nylon bow. In one hand were her slippers, in the other, two soft-centered, chocolate bonbons. Reassuring noises of slumber came from her mother's room. She slipped noiselessly across the linoleum floor and into Belvedere's room.

It smelled wonderfully like the lion's cage at the zoological garden. A dismal glow from the street defined a heap of canvas bags in the middle of the floor and a litter of discarded clothes, like washing blown from the line. Belvedere was snoring heavily. Almira nestled into bed beside him.

'Calm thyself,' she whispered.

Belvedere making pelvic thrusts while asleep. Almira testing to see if she still loved him.

Presently, satisfied that she was still in love, she wriggled out of bed and dressed. She had trouble finding her nylon bow. Then, leaving the two bonbons on the bedside table, she crept back to her room to dream about Belvedere.

*

Barcelona, early morning. A tolling in the cathedral belfry. The *basureros* in blue overalls sweeping the Ramblas. Bales of newspapers outside tobacconist stalls. Steel grilles over shop windows.

Buttoning on a black cotton dress, Doña Teresa rose and lit the paraffin heater, inspected the corridor, kitchen and bathroom to ensure that no one had left a light burning overnight, listened outside the doors of some of the rooms to confirm that the occupants hadn't bolted, then offered five Hail Marys and an Act of Contrition to the image of the Sacred Heart of the Holy Mother and went to early Mass.

At eight o'clock, some time after the Señora returned from receiving the Holy Sacrament, the first of Belvedere's alarm clocks went off. He groped for it in vain, turned over and went back to sleep. Half an hour later, the second alarm went off. He lay comatose, as the various disorders of the previous night gradually took shape in his mind. Rising onto his elbows and detecting the two bonbons, he ate them, incuriously. By nine o'clock, he was more or less dressed. It was a big day for him, yet what did it matter if this morning, of all mornings, he arrived at work a little later than usual? If the job was still his, it could wait another half hour or so for him to take coffee at the Florida and read the morning paper.

After breakfast, he engaged a boy to polish his shoes. They haggled about the price, Belvedere deprecating the quality of the work. They were standing beside the monument of the Generalissimo in the Plaza Cataluña. This plaza, where the pigeons feed on grime, reflected Belvedere, must be a kind of haven for this shoeshine boy, who walked off muttering, 'It is not even enough for *un espreso.*'

Onward. The Avenida José Antonio, the ugliest street in Barcelona with its bullring at one end and its bullring at the other and, between them, only banks and office buildings. The flagstone steps of Uners. Belvedere contemplated the dreary prospect before him and was struck anew that anyone of his experience and ability should be employed at such menial tasks as imparting moronic English idiom to foreigners.

Later, between model sentences, he thought, 'It makes one despair of the future of Literature.' He remembered Klaus saying, *'Eine Stunde auf den Pisten wert sechs Monaten in den Klasse.'* Klaus was an Austrian ski instructor he had met at the Alpenhof.

'I put the pencil on the table.'

'I poot thee peenzil on thee *tay*bool.'

'The pencil and the pen are on the table.'

'Thee peenzil and thee peen arr-r on thee *tay*bool.'

'Not peen. Pen. Now repeat after me. The pencil and the pen are on the table.'

'Thee penzil and thee peen arr-r on thee *tay*bool.'

The Principal's decision to reinstate him confirmed his opinion that Uners did not remunerate him adequately. Still, the work had its compensations. It demanded no preparation and he was free during the middle of the day. One of his students usually paid for his lunch, and after lunch he returned to the Porsepina for a nap. That was the Spanish way. Evenings were his own. Then he sometimes worked on *Our Times*. More often he pursued what Don Vyvyan called *Nachtkultur* among the dark alleys of the city, or just strolled and looked at the luminous fountains.

*

In London it stopped raining.

'Cor, stone me! 'Ere we go again,' Charley said to Flo.

'Bleedin' thoughtless is whut I call it. Wouldn't 'urt 'er to turn it down a bit. Give 'er a piece of my mind one 'o these days.'

'Good 'iding's wot she needs.'

'Never did us no 'arm.'

Philippa Young was at home. She had returned from her art class laden with lavender- and magenta-striped tote bags containing the purchases of an impulsive shopping expedition that had lasted most of the day. Swinging from her little finger on a blue ribbon was a box of Razinsky's *petits fours*, under one arm a brace of pink suède Elliott boots and, precariously wedged under the other arm, an LP.

No one had seen her arrive, but everyone felt the impact when the throbbing sounds of Big Beat burst upon the calm of Belgravia. Hardly had she put disc to turntable before she was at the telephone telling her friends all about her new suède boots and the trouser suit of *corde d' éléphant* that she had found at Biba's. The music stopped, and while Philippa turned over the record, Lady Tessa Lonsdale had to wait breathlessly for the rest of the details of the darling *crêpe de Chine* Gina Fratini frou-frou.

At half past seven, people began to arrive at Philippa's house, other young things in E-type Jaguars and Lotuses. Philippa had just finished speaking with some of them over the telephone. As soon as they saw her, they began screaming. Philippa went to her room to change. It was already occupied and bolted against her. 'Oh damn!' she said, and hurried back downstairs. All the girls who in the first excitement of reunion had somehow missed noticing her boots screamed again, and Philippa proudly agreed. 'Yes, *rather super*, aren't they?'

Tessa's fellow that evening was Clovis – twenty years older than Tessa but so jaunty and right-dressed that no one really minded. He seemed obsolete only when he spoke. However, he said very little, his jauntiness deriving from a manner of gesticulating while silent. In any case, Philippa and Tessa were always reciprocally tolerant of the other's fellow. They had known each other all their lives and been best friends for a year now, ever since that miraculous afternoon of rediscovery in the Health Juice Bar at Harrods. They both loved and despised the same people and were wild about the same albums. Philippa knew all about Clovis, and Tessa had heard, more than once, the deeply alarming truths about Belvedere. Both girls were positively brimming with new revelations – for, apart from the too, *too* brief conversation on the telephone, they had *absolutely* not spoken for ten hours. And crowning all their rapture this evening was the happy expectation of meeting Ernest.

Clovis was emboldened to predict that his dashing colleague might arrive at any moment. On the other hand, being a Manager and shouldering the heavy responsibilities of a Manager, Clovis cautioned, Ernest might arrive late.

'Oh bother!' said Philippa.

The hubbub of shrieks and stereophonic sounds grew louder. Mabel, who pulled pints at the Manley Arms in the mews, was inspired. The racket recalled the daft escapades of her own raucous youth. 'Wha' a lark it was, too,' she said mistily. But across the street, in a drawing room bedizened with kukris and group photographs, Colonel Fitzjames, frail and maimed veteran of many bombardments and distracted from his reading of *Railway Magazine*, suffered his wife to soothe his nerves with a cup of Horlicks, while down in the basement, Charley and Flo turned up the telly.

'Bleedin' stick round 'er backside's wot that young lady wants.'

Ernest finally arrived a little before midnight. Of all amusing get-ups, he was wearing a suit, starched shirt and tie. He was everything that Philippa had been led to expect, and more. He sought to make himself popular with a repertory of lewd stories. '. . . Have you heard the one about the Irishman who couldn't get it up? . . .'

'Oh what goodies!' shrieked Philippa.

'*Aren't* they!' cried Tessa.

Then somebody said, 'Nosh!' and somebody else, 'Scoff!' So off they went to a *trattoria* in Jermyn Street known to Clovis and ate lasagne, and Ernest ordered a bottle of Chianti and discoursed Italian to the waiter, who kept nodding his head and raising an eyebrow. When they returned to Philippa's house, it was full of strangers. Philippa wondered if she ought to expel them, but Clovis and Ernest pleaded with her to let them stay. Then Ernest began a Folkestone Plan presentation to a couple who were pretending to be asleep behind the Buhl sofa.

'Now just pay attention, willya? This will only take about twelve minutes without obligation to either party. I'd like to talk to you about money.'

'Let's get the fuck out of here,' they said and left in disgust. Some of the others went with them. After that, there was more room for Philippa and her friends. 'Isn't this a gas!' said Tessa.

'*Isn't* it!' agreed Philippa.

*

Philippa awoke next morning about the time that Belvedere began his Model Pronunciations and thought: 'How too, *too* shaming.' It was still too early to telephone Tessa and tell her what really *terrible* news Ernest was. Well, she thought, she had experimented, and it would *not* happen again.

Tessa was at her dressing table re-ordering a face swollen from an exactly similar misadventure when the telephone finally rang.

She freed one hand from a bottle of Monsieur Charles's Touch 'n Glow and picked up the receiver.

'Guess what?'

'You *didn't*!'

'Guess what else. Got a letter from Belvedere!'

'You *didn't*!'

Here Philippa paused to allow Tessa opportunity to digest fully the implications of this important intelligence. Then she read the letter.

After many shrieks and squeals, Tessa said: 'My *dear*, isn't it all a hoot!'

'Too too! Plus plus!'

But Philippa was not really amused, and in the course of another busy day shopping at Harrods and seeing the printer about invitations for a little party that Mummy had persuaded Daddy on and placating her bank manager and having lunch with Patrick at Bishop's and hunting all over Chelsea for the right pink suède fringed waistcoat to go with her new boots and a visit to the hairdresser's, she suffered all the passion to which a girl of her pampered and fashionable position was prone. In truth, the letter which had reached her in the morning's post and which was all about skiing had disconcerted her. More, it demanded something in the way of punishment. She rang Tessa again just to hear her *real* opinion. Then, under the hairdryer at Vidal Sassoon, she decided not to send Belvedere another penny.

There would come a time when Belvedere was really *old. Then he would inhabit a room even smaller and less central and even darker than that student's lodging near White Stadium.* Philippa was particularly susceptible to bouts of cynicism under the hairdryer. *A few dozen paperbacks between the bricks on a shelf would represent all that remained of the many girls to whom he had once given devoted, if ephemeral, service, and who, in turn, had tried to contribute to his moral growth. Marking the passage of years: a pile of yellowing papers stored in a cardboard box. And the skis, once defiant decoration of the wardrobe top, long since exchanged for necessities – including soap for his sponge-down bath at the wash basin, pencils for calculating each day's expenditures and postage stamps for keeping in touch with those who no longer cared to keep in touch. No suspicious landlady would lurk in the gaining shadows to spy on the diminished train of women who sought his murky abode for evenings of elderly, fatherly advice,* thought Philippa with particular relish. *In this environment and with feelings pardonable at his time of life, he would cast his mind back to that sultry afternoon when Philippa, her circumstances also impoverished, withdrew to her bedsitter, took three bottles of gin and put out the light once and for all. These phantoms would comprise his choicest recollections,* thought Philippa with tears in her eyes. *Throughout the years, they would remain his loyal, involuntary friends. The sky would glower, dusty, midsummer leaves toss restlessly and the heavens weep a few unrepentant tears as Belvedere, now long in the tooth, veins standing out on his forehead and unable to bear his solitude, would stumble down the successive flights of stairs and out into the street. Where now that famous delight in eclecticism? Contracted to the narrow span of an old man's pleasures. And the Hamlet who had struggled in vain for life and its elusive meaning? Forever mute. Though a dull pain of remorse would press against his old heart, his failing eyes, exhausted by misuse, would dimly register the passing girls, his racked and wrecked brain that they had passed (for he would not lightly surrender his image of himself as the village bull). Lovers brought out by the warm weather would stream past, elbow him aside, push him into the gutter. Scraps of newspaper would drift across the street and cling to his patched jeans, as though intent on impeding his progress. Cats and dogs on furtive evening sorties would avoid him. Even other old vagrants, bored with hearing about all the places he had been and all the girls he had known, would repudiate his tiresome company, while the lustrous stars looked down on this alien not with disdain but with brutal indifference. As bodies human, animal and celestial fled from him, the very stones would be repelled; vegetable matter would snap at his heels, then wilt. . . .*

These reflections brought Philippa a measure of relief, and the tears stopped. Perhaps she would not commit suicide after all. She appeared suddenly to herself in a new, more positive light. Her hair, now worn up, retained its golden glow.

A ragged tramp passed her on the street. It was, of course, Belvedere. Recollection spurred him to action. His mouth was always dry now. Nevertheless, he attempted his friendly dog's greeting, but Philippa passed by on the other side in myopic safety. So long the Mover of the Spheres, once the fixed point of a world that was everywhere shifty, he was no more to her now than an unpleasant memory, a white dwarf consumed by his own fires, his face as pitted and inhospitable as the moon's, alone and eminently resistible.

*

Philippa's apocalyptic vision bore little resemblance to her entrepreneurial man, who was busily experimenting with new ways of supplementing his wages. He raffled pieces of chewing gum to his students. He conducted a lottery and a pari-mutuel over the results of football matches. He imposed fines for omitted or sloppy homework.

'Young Jorge has accused you of charging him in excess of the tuition advertised,' said the Principal. 'Is he speaking the truth? Or is this accusation malicious?'

'It's an incentive scheme, sir, to encourage the boys to work harder.'

'No doubt this method is used elsewhere – in England perhaps, but not here. In Spain, it is not customary to charge differentials according to academic performance. Our fees are fixed.'

'Sir.'

'I also understand that you have introduced gambling in class. Would you like to explain?'

'As a means of alleviating classroom boredom, sir.'

'I see. Well, I am sure that you will be able to devise other means of alleviating boredom. By paying more meticulous attention to the syllabus, perhaps? Universal Languages School is not a bookmaker.'

'Sir.'

Belvedere at the Porsepina writing up his diary, his first serious authorship in almost four months. The pen moved awkwardly in his hand. 'Waterloo at Uners. Scenes with the Head,' he wrote, mindful of the implications for posterity.

*

Some territorial definitions survived the company's pioneering phase. Because very little business was done there, for example, Asia II, in addition to Iran, comprised Afghanistan, Pakistan and India. Reps en route to other destinations occasionally stopped there to tap the Expatriate Markets. Owing to exchange controls and the poverty and paucity of the middle class, the Local Markets were not interesting, comprising almost entirely Referrals from Asians living in Kenya or Fiji who had bought Plans and written to WoF asking it to contact their relations in the motherland. A part-timer, Hunter Sacks, represented WoF in Afghanistan, and a part-timer, Lucivius Williams, represented it in Pakistan. Bumper wanted to retain the Continuings over them and to claim them as SSEs if their Volumes reached $150,000.

He imputed the commutation of his sentence and release from prison to the Founder's intervention, not to Islam, which he had now renounced.

'Time brings changes,' he told Hunter. 'It's a pity, because I was the one who recruited and trained you, Hunter.' He had taught Hunter how to fill out an application form. Hunter worked for the Food and Agriculture Organization but sold mutual funds in his ample spare time. 'Do you remember the first time we had dinner here?'

They were dining at the Otel de Nuristan, a *chaikhanna* with a reputation for local colour. When in Kabul to buy bullets in the weapons bazaar, Afridi tribesmen were drawn irresistibly to the smells of mutton grease there. They would not return from trans-Khyber until the peach trees blossomed, and now the hotel was nearly empty.

'I remember well,' said Hunter. 'I was putting all my money in certificates of deposit.'

'I like to think that our friendship transcends business,' said Bumper. 'I like to think that my men trust me. I've always believed that *you* trust me, Hunter.'

'Trust is not the cornerstone of our relationship,' corrected Hunter.

'Okay, maybe you don't trust me. Have you considered how much less trustworthy your *new* Area Manager might be? At least with me you know where you stand. You send me your

Plans and, if necessary, I go to a money changer and see that the money gets transferred. If you send me a Plan for processing, and the cheque is drawn on a convertible currency account, I send it direct, along with the application, and a couple of weeks later you *always* get your Confirms. If there's a delay in processing, the problem gets dealt with quickly and efficiently through the Area Desk. Don't underestimate the human element, Hunter. It could be different with my successor. You won't know *where* your Plans might wind up.'

Hunter acknowledged that Bumper was efficient and was grateful that he (Hunter) was not financially dependent on World of Finance.

'You know, I have that feeling that I used to get watching those ambush scenes in those old cowboy flicks,' continued Bumper. 'Two guys are riding on top of the stagecoach, and the one with the rifle says, "I don't like it, Joe. It's too quiet." Then, *zoom*, he gets an arrow in his back. That's how I feel, Hunter. I'm Joe and you're the guard who gets the arrow in his back. It's too quiet.'

'Eat your shishkebab, and maybe you'll feel better.'

Presently Bumper asked: 'What's your Volume now?'

'A hundred and thirty-five thousand.'

'Opened?'

'Twelve thousand's pending. I sent in a DGP yesterday. The guy's arranging his own remittance.'

'Never count your Plans before they hatch. Wait a few days and make a Call Back. He'll appreciate your professional seriousness.'

The two men ate for a while in silence under the baleful scrutiny of the whiskered, turbaned man behind the abacus, indifferent to the fact that he was not a client. Then Bumper said, 'The new Manager might want to terminate you.'

'What for?'

'Some Managers have the idea that part-timers are a drag, that the Overrides they produce are not worth the time spent on training them, that they discourage more productive Reps from working the Territory, that they spoil the Market.

'Frankly, I don't foresee a problem there. The Market here wouldn't support a full-timer. Anyone who thinks otherwise is welcome to try.'

'Yeah, but he might want your clients.'

Very occasionally, and at their own initiative, Hunter's clients paid more money into their existing Fully Paids or purchased new Plans. Then, as a kind of bonus, he got the credit. Moreover, he got the Referrals when clients wrote to the company requesting free calendars for their friends.

'Listen, Hunter, tell you what I'll do,' said Bumper, who was well-versed in the arcana of World of Finance Admin procedures. 'You are twenty-five thousand short of reaching Advance Schedule, including your pending DGP. Your reaching Advance Schedule before I leave the Territory is in our mutual interest. Technically, you pass out of my supervision as soon as I leave. So I'll buy a $12,000 DGIP and a $15,000 DGP from you to make up the needed Volume.' As Bumper intended to pay only the initial payments, and as he drew GM Overrides on the sale, the Plans would cost him very little – less than dinner at any restaurant except the Nuristan; less than the sheepskin coat he had purchased in the leather bazaar that afternoon.

Hunter signed the letter requesting transfer to Tennessee.

'It's up to me who I want to take with me.'

'They're bound to find out I'm still in Kabul.'

'Not soon, they won't. And when they do, it won't matter any longer.'

His business in Kabul satisfactorily concluded, Bumper left early the next morning for Lahore to negotiate a mutually advantageous arrangement with Lucivius Williams.

*

Meanwhile, back at the Top of the Spirals, Nelson and Marty struck a deal with Herb.

'Herb, we just thought you would like to know that Bob Bleitgeist is about to make GM.'

A GM in Tennessee meant a reduction in Herb's Override.

'I have nothing against the guy personally,' said Herb. 'He's a good man at opening up a Territory. But he's an inefficient administrator. He's no longer making a contribution.'

'We have an opening for Bleitgeist elsewhere if you can afford to lose him, Herb.'

'I can afford to lose him.'

'We can suggest somebody to replace him.'

'I don't need anybody to replace him,' said Herb.

'We'll have to do a deal, Herb.'

'What's the deal?'

Marty explained about Bumper.

What's his schedule?'

'General Manager.'

'Don't need him, Marty.'

'The deal is he takes GM only on his own sales. He gets the next Schedule up over the guys he inherits from Bleitgeist – BM over Senior, RM over BM, DM over RM. He's a good man, Herb. He's willing to pay ten grand.'

'I can use him.'

*

'Write a personal cheque drawn on your bank here in Lahore, Mustafa, and don't tell Mr Williams. As you know, he's the US Consul General here.'

Mustafa's hand sprang to his heart. 'It is my duty!'

'Use your own chequebook. Make the cheque out to a fictitious payee. Any ordinary sounding Pakistani name will do. And, of course, make it out in rupees, not dollars. ADB will negotiate the cheque through a correspondent in Pakistan, who will present it to your bank guaranteeing endorsement. A Swiss franc amount for the free market value of the rupees, less a small commission, will be credited to an ADB account opened in your name.'

'Please explain, Mr Beabody, what is ADB? I am not knowing it.'

'Anonymous Depositors Bank. It's a Geneva bank we use to conceal depositors' identities. It sells the rupees to someone needing Pakistani currency – say, an international contractor who has won a bid in Pakistan and, naturally, prefers buying at the free market rate instead of the official rate. The rupees never leave Pakistan. And be sure that you give no hint of this to Mr Williams. I'm doing this for you as a personal favour, Mustafa. Don't let me down. If Mr Williams finds out, both of us are in trouble.'

'It is my duty!'

*

'No luck, eh?'

'I'm sorry, Lucivius. I tried every trick in the book, but he wouldn't budge. I did my level best.'

'Gee, and just yesterday he seemed all set to buy. I guess telling him that I couldn't use the diplomatic pouch to smuggle money out of the country put him off. If you couldn't close him, I guess nobody could.' The loss of the sale to Mustafa Khan was a *huge* disappointment. He had gone to very considerable trouble, and even some expense, cultivating the friendship of the cotton exporter, fertilizer manufacturer, camel trader, planter and judge of the Punjab Supreme Court; had entertained him at diplomatic fêtes, at his youngest daughter's birthday party and twice at family picnics. Mustafa Khan was reputed to be the richest man in Punjab and one of the most influential in all Pakistan. For Lucivius to have caught him as a client would have meant getting his leg into the door of the Millionaires' Market.

Supervisor and trainee walked side by side, Lucivius with his hands in his pockets, kicking a stone as he ambled along. They were dressed so dissimilarly that not even the shrewdest observer would have guessed that both were WoFers. Only Bumper carried the usual badge of belonging, a briefcase.

'Just goes to show, the best laid plans can go astray.'

'Cheer up,' counselled Bumper.

'I was counting on the commission to buy a sailboat for the kids.'

'Buy 'em a sailboat next month.'

They worked on Lucivius's Close during lunch. Bumper enlarged on some arrestingly interesting ideas he had heard expounded at the General Managers Conference. ('If you should die in an automobile accident, Mr Worth, how long could your wife afford to stay home with the children?') They discussed WoF's latest product, Taxpayers Fund ('targeting clients aggrieved by oppressive rates of taxation'), the performances of Fiduciary of Fiduciaries and Fenner Biddup Offshore Fund relative to world stock market indices, the higher commissions earned at Advance Schedule, the hazards attendant upon a change of Manager ('Some of these fellows just steal your sales'), and the scheme whereby Lucivius could continue working under Bumper. Then Bumper insisted on paying for his trainee's lunch.

'Put your money in your pocket,' he ordered. 'This is on me.'

'How about each paying his share?' proposed Lucivius.

'I wouldn't consider it.'

'Why should *you* pay?'

'Because I *want* to buy your lunch, Lucivius, that's why. I know that the Consulate gives you vouchers. Never mind. Don't let it be said that Bumper Peabody supervised you without ever once standing you a meal.'

'I don't deserve it. Certainly not after sending you off on that wild goose chase this morning. Listen, I'm really very sorry about that.'

'Forget it. Rules of the game. Only wish I could've closed him for you.'

'Look, it's decent of you, but I insist on paying for my lunch.'

'Have it your way, then.'

'In fact, since I wasted your time, I'd like to pay for your lunch as well. If you don't mind.'

'Are you sure?'

'I won't have it any other way, Bumper.'

Lucivius paid for the meal.

'Why don't you call me LW?' he said. 'All my friends call me LW.'

'All right, then. From now on, it's LW.'

Lucivius looked at his watch, a simple Rolex Oyster Perpetual without the date feature. Time was getting on and he was due back at the Consulate to resume his responsibilities.

'You can't imagine what it's like, reviewing applications for visas, renewing passports, writing reports on reports in the local press day in and day out. I never get to do anything or go anywhere. That's why I was sort of banking on something working out with WoF. But I guess I'm not very good at selling mutual funds. All I'm good for, it seems, is diplomacy.'

'Goodbye, Lucivius.'

'LW, remember? . . . Goodbye, Bumper. It's been a genuine pleasure working with you. I sincerely hope we'll meet again. And don't you be upset about Mustafa Khan. You did your best. I'll send you my Plans.'

'Goodbye, LW. And good luck.'

'All the best.'

Supervisor and trainee walked a short way together towards the Consul General's office before Lucivius said finally, 'Well, goodbye.'

Bumper returned to the restaurant and obtained a receipt to support a claim for reimbursement from the company. Continuings secured over two part-timers, another Successful Supervisory Experience and General Manager schedule commission on a $155,000 Fully Paid, plus the Personal Volume, together with his claim for reimbursement of expenses: not a bad tally for his last week in Asia II. He looked at his watch – the Million Dollar Gold Watch. His flight was that evening. He took a taxi to the Moghul sites at the western edge of the city.

The glare reflecting from the floor of the Badshahi Mosque's great courtyard was blinding. Bumper removed his shoes and explored within with the experienced, contemptuous eyes and ears of an ex-Muslim. He observed the *mu'minin* prostrating themselves and heard the reverberations in the hollows of the *mihrab*. Beating off a mob of beggars at the gate, he then proceeded to the fort and mounted its steps with the same determination that had taken him to the pinnacle of financial counselling. Pausing at the elephants' stables to catch his breath, he wondered how the new Manager would get on with Noam van Zilver. He (Bumper) was not bad to work under. He believed in encouraging his men to take initiatives and allowing them maximum clearance, only intervening to compose their quarrels. But van Zilver defied all laws of discipline. Or rather, he cast himself as Lord of Laws. The least serious thing that could be said about him was that he lacked *esprit de corps*. Who else would give the opening address at a Financial Training Seminar dressed in a loin cloth as a disciple of the Hari Krishna movement? Nothing about that brilliant, but afflated and stubborn man was commonplace, ordinary or predictable.

Passing the derelict cannons, Bumper wondered how many steps remained before the summit.

On reaching the summit, he gazed about him. Pink sandstone, relieved here and there by outcrops of white marble, walls rising sheer on three sides. The *Diwan-e-Aam* was empty, the grounds deserted. He placed his ear against the barrel of a cannon and listened for the echo, inspected the flower-beds, walked to the machiolated rampart and, peering over, stared blankly at the city, as all Iranian, Afghan, Pakistani and Indian cities, covered in a patina of dust. He took a snapshot, then decided that he'd better move on to Jahangir's Tomb.

The taxi was waiting for him outside the Alamgiri Gate in the shade of a tree next to a confectioner's stand, the driver squatting beside it chewing betel. Beggars thronged him, and again at the gate of the mausoleum, one wretched woman pinching her baby to make it cry. More perforated screens. More tiles. More calligraphy. He had now seen all he wanted to see and was free to concentrate his thoughts on fetching his suitcase from the hotel and catching his flight to New York. He wouldn't be coming back.

*

Saturday on the Nile. Crocs sunning on the banks, hippos poking their pig eyes and nostrils above the water. The Juba Market lacked lustre. Van Zilver replenished his supplies and moved on.

The ensuing journey on a flotilla of barges lashed to a paddle-wheeler was very dull, his fellow passengers unlettered to a man. They passed the time at simple card games, chewing sugarcane, spitting and fighting. They pressed him for *dawa* and were curious to inspect his teeth – coal black savages who scarified their skin, dyed their hair orange and wore saw-tooth ivory necklaces. Everything seemed hilarious to them. Once, sighting a tribal kinsman on the bank – a naked giant covered in ashes to repel mosquitoes and brandishing a spear – they hurled their half-masticated sticks of sugarcane at him and laughed. The privies were ineffably awful iron closets with a hole in the floor, the ordure clogging the hole and overflowing onto the women and babies' deck. The flotilla rebounded clumsily from bank to bank, pushing day by day through drifting islands of water hyacinths. The sky pink at dawn and silver during the day; long files of egrets at sundown and rain on the roof at night. Between Jonglei and Shambe one of the rudder cables broke.

At Malakal, van Zilver found a marooned Greek storekeeper acutely in need of financial counselling. His qualms were for the fate of his money once it left his bank. Such childish posers were nugatory before the thrust of the WoF *Olympiad Contest* winner, a pile of sand to a bulldozer.

*

Saturday in Knoxville. Blaize and Mule had cut their Handball Lab, as Bleitgeist was taking them on a Cold Call. Fitz did not come along. He stayed in his room at the Francis Elsworth Haynes Memorial Graduate Students Dormitory studying *A Union of Small Investors*.

'Be sure to fix the prospect's name firmly in your mind,' advised Bleitgeist from the front seat of Levy's Chevrolet. 'Don't call him Mr Worth, like one Rep I heard about. Everybody likes to be called by his right name.'

Levy parked the Chevrolet in a bay reserved 'For Clergy Only'.

'You'd better button up your shirt, Mule. Watch your personal habits and appearance. If you look sharp, you feel sharp. Okay! Everybody ready?'

'*Lez gitum!*' said Blaize.

They all got out of the car.

Mule was nervous. 'Mr Bleitgeist, are you sure, no matter whut happens you don't want me to say anythang?'

'That's right, Mule. It could divert the prospect from the presentation. Just watch and pay attention.'

'Whut do I do if he asks me a question?'

'In that case, Mule, your reply should be as brief as possible. Now,' continued Bleitgeist, 'we have chosen this neighbourhood at random. First, we look around us.' Bone, Mule and Blaize looked around. Around them was urban squalor. 'Next, we choose a house.' They chose. In its front yard stood a plastic shield with green neon tubing over white painted letters.

THE REVEREND WILLARD DONLEAVY
WEDDINGS FUNERALS
BAPTISMS CHRISTENINGS
DIVINE HEALINGS CONFESSIONS
ALL RELIGIONS WELCOME

Bleitgeist advanced to the front door, pressed the buzzer, then turned to his trainees and said: 'Your attitude is important. Expect business.'

A child opened the door an inch and immediately shut it again.

'Is your daddy at home?' shouted Levy. 'We want to talk to him about your education.'

After a while a woman appeared and asked, 'Is you the gentlemens whut wants to see the preacher 'bout divine healin?'

'We would like the opportunity of a conference with the Reverend Donleavy as soon as he is released from his pastoral and other commitments,' replied Bleitgeist.

'Say *whut*?'

'We'd like to speak with your husband.'

'He ain't heah. He gone.'

'We have not come about the car payments or the rent or anything like that,' said Levy, reassuringly.

'Saturdays he be out ridin' the bus.'

'Riding the bus?'

'Look like hit.'

'That's most unfortunate, Mrs Donleavy. When will he be back?'

''Fo long. Is you fom the insurance company?"

'No!' replied Bleitgeist firmly. 'Although your child's welfare may eventually depend on us. We represent World of Finance. Haven't you heard of us, Mrs Donleavy? Our services are especially designed to protect a man's dependants in the event of his untimely death. You and your child's safety and comfort are what we want to see the Reverend about.'

'Thas right. Wall, he ain't heah. He gone.'

*

Homeward bound, Bumper's first destination was Majorca. Some years before, after a selling Safari in West Africa, he had met and spent a long, physically demanding week with a magnificent leggy blonde named Ulla there. She returned to Scandanavia and the husband to whom she claimed to be happily married, and the affair ended. He had gone on to another successful but lonelier safari in South America. However, he had not forgotten Ulla, and it was with the stimulating recollection of her that he revisited Majorca. Sadly, it had changed beyond recognition. It was now Promoter's Modern, instead of Spanish Insular. No one was even faintly interested in loving him, for, unawares, he too had changed, Jaded Impressario instead of Plain Man.

*

The Porsepina's guests lingered late in their rooms on Sunday mornings, listening to the radio. Belvedere rose on the stroke of ten and distressed the Señora by singing in the shower, unsparing use of the hot water and strutting in the corridor wrapped in a towel.

'The English heretics are without-shames,' she complained bitterly to her son Julio, an ordinans.

'It is what they say.'

'The women are even worse than the men. They do not cover their heads during the Mass. Even their arms are bare.'

'It is an aspect of the general lack of piety which disgraces the age, my mother.'

'Although a professor, he conducts himself like a mendicant.'

'Even mendicants clad themselves in more than towels while going to and from the shower, mother.'

They were in the kitchen. Julio, seated on a high stool chatting, as was his custom, while his mother and sister chopped carrots. His cassock and wholesome conversation were a balm to Doña Teresa, but could not altogether divert her thoughts from the transient who had haunted her life for six years, six years of legally contracted marriage to an alcoholic, a philanderer and a deserter from her and the municipal fire department, Julio's father.

Belvedere emerged from the shower and strode to his room, slamming shut its door. He never did anything quietly. Another burst of song. After dressing, he summoned the Señora and informed her: 'I will be lunching with Sir Vyvyan. I do not know at what hour I shall return.'

'Good,' she replied, as though registering a fact of historical significance.

Once Doña Teresa had consulted a wise old woman with a wart on her nose, who had told her that she was fated to suffer domestic calamities until a tall, swish, rugged, handsome professor of musical disposition from another land made his abode in the Porsepina and put an end to her troubles. She had paid that ugly woman fifty pesetas for her advice, and, according it a place alongside the hopes she cherished for Julio and Almira, had nourished it over the long years of privation, loneliness, anxiety, futility and disillusionment. There it still lay, an ember smouldering in a dungeon, a candle in a grotto, a prophecy unfulfilled.

The handsome professor of musical disposition left his room shortly before noon with his skis on his shoulders.

'He is a without-shame,' declared the Señora.

'Calm thyself, mother.'

Belvedere was in a light-hearted mood this morning, the mood of the young unemployed. He strode down the Ramblas, where, even at this late hour, a few obstinate mariners were stumbling from the doors of the *cantinas* and squinting painfully in the natural light, exhaustion writ horribly in their sunken and unshaven cheeks. He shuffled through the swarms of pigeons emitting crapulous moans and was soon crossing the little square at the bottom of the avenue beneath the statue of Columbus. He rarely entertained speculations of an historical bent. When he did, as now, they always concerned major personalities, such as Columbus – like himself, a man dependent on a female's munificence for the means of sustaining his grand designs, another visionary, a navigator in unchartered waters, a foreigner on his own ship.

One of the vagrants occupying a public bench accosted him and was rebuffed. '*Poderoso caballero es Don Dinero,*' grumbled the tramp, shuffling resentfully back to the bench.

Belvedere walked on. A light breeze stirred the oleanders. Past the Customs House, a place of fractious disputes and prodigious corruption. Past the rusting destroyers. Past the crates and bales and stacks of timber. A blast from the funnel of the Baleares passenger liner all gleaming white and hung with bunting from stem to stern. Another blast. The gulls swooping low. It was just such a day.

*

Sir Vyvyan was relaxing on a deck chair on what he liked to call the poop dressed, as always, in the uniform of an officer of the Senior Service, gold braid on his jacket sleeves, on his head a brimmed cap, around his neck a pair of binoculars. Very little happened in the harbour of which he was ignorant. His circumjacent inspection now caught sight of his compatriot entering the sunny space between the near side of the Customs House and the first stack of timber. 'I wonder what that young scamp's been up to?' he asked himself, elatedly. 'Raul, you had better stand by with rations for three,' he instructed his deckhand. 'I have an idea that Señor Belvedere may be joining us in the mess.'

Vyvyan Drake-Chichester once seemed destined for high adventure. He had put out fires while preparing for his eleven-plus and soldiered in the Cadet Training Corps at Rugby. No one was surprised, therefore, when he joined the Royal Rhodesian Constabulary straight out of Rugby. Better that than the French Foreign Legion, everyone said. He soon discovered, however, that policing the African bush would not requite his longings. The long nights spent under mosquito nets were more solitary than adventurous, the 'sort of lark that [was] all right for Boers,' he said, drifting errantly into the calm waters of academia, where family connections would sustain him like a log.

Parents, great-uncles, great-aunts, their ancestors and cousins once and twice removed on both sides were Vice-Chancellors, Regius professors, men and women of learning. A place was found for Vyvyan in the benevolent charge of his paternal Great-Uncle Roderick, who was Master of Balliol. Three idle years later, Vyvyan sat for his final examinations in the Honours School of English Literature. At his Viva Voce, another Drake-Chichester commended him for a shining faculty of memory. On the recommendation of the Warden of All Souls, his father, he was appointed to a lectureship at an Australian university where the family reputation for sound scholarship could suffer no lasting harm, for by now the lad's opacities were a topic of general concern. Came the war. Vyvyan felt again the old stirrings for adventure and thought about joining one of the Forces, but didn't, and about becoming an air raid warden, but didn't. He thought about applying for a job at another university, but didn't, and the product of the years when Malaya, Burma, Guam, the Philippines and Borneo were overrun and New Guinea, the Marshalls, the other Mariannas, Iwo Jima and Okinawa were fiercely contested, was a cook book integrating the principles of Near Eastern, Middle Eastern and Far Eastern cuisine.

Other men might have stopped there and rested on their laurels. Not Vyvyan. He was already busy with another *oeuvre*. It was long delayed in coming, did not appear, in fact, until the year of his retirement, after three more sabbaticals had passed unobtrusively. It was Uncle Frederick's turn now to rally to the family flag by interfering in the affairs of the periodical, of which he was the editor. The *Critic's Quarterly* was supported by public funds. No idea need suffer for lack of an advocate; it demanded little from its contributors except blandness, and Vyvyan's articles, with some help from Uncle Frederick, met its minimal requirements. A mythical battle was fought with an illusory enemy; no sacred reputations were destroyed, and no immutable dogmas affronted. No Dr Leavis rose to challenge the few incontrovertible conclusions, and Uncle Frederick's audacious nepotism had a success that exceeded even his own sanguine expectations. In due course, thanks to a cousin on whom the Prime Minister relied for advice in such esoteric matters, the author of *The Imagery of the Sea in Conrad* was awarded a KCG and the Prix Babylon for services to Literature. As a result of the publicity generated by the knighthood, the cookery book received a second printing, and *The Best Jokes of 1950* by the same hand was accepted for publication by one of the many publishers who had rejected it.

Vyvyan was now willing to rest on his laurels and, to the astonishment of everyone who had ever known him, declined the post of bursar offered to him by his old college. A cousin twice removed, the Dean of Christ Church, exercised his influence with the Bishop of Chichester, and he was offered the post of Principal Librarian of Pusey House. It was the first time in the brief history of that dynamic institution that the post was offered to a layman. Nevertheless, Vyvyan, now Sir Vyvyan, declined it. The onerous duties of the office, he protested, demanded the zeal and stamina of a younger man.

Throughout his years of exile, unwelcome letters from his twin sister kept him abreast of the distinguished careers of his cousins.

Belvedere had heard all about this sister, in childhood inseparable as a Siamese twin and so similar to Vyvyan in manner and appearance that a myopic aunt once asked him if classes in needlework were still offered at Roedean. In the nursery, they played together more like cherubs in a Rubens painting than ordinary toddlers. Celeste, being the pushier, prescribed the rules for the games they played, a behavioural defect that morphed into offering him unsolicited advice. On returning from Australia, he learned from her the outrage caused by the rebuff to his alma mater ('They offered you the post out of courtesy to the memory of Uncle Rod, you know') and by the rejection of the sinecure arranged by the Dean of Christ Church for his retirement.

Never mind. Sir Vyvyan had another idea, born triumphantly, like the Hippocrene, from impulse. He bought six Land Rovers fitted with extra petrol tanks, extra tyres, five-gallon jerry cans with lock taps riveted to the chassis and heavy duty shock absorbers; two tons of tools and spare parts that slowed the caravan to first gear on bitumen, attracted duty at borders, were rendered useless by the desertion of the mechanic at Palmyra and were too heavy for lugging over the desert; sand panels, cross-cut saws, shovels, axes, a bundle of barbed wire, primuses, pressure cookers, camp tables, aluminium flasks, a samovar, salt tablets, water purification tablets, anti-venom serums, dehydrated food rations, tents, a compass, sextant and sandproof chronometer, inflatable air-bags for fording rivers, a wireless apparatus, transmitter and receiver, crampons, three miles of nylon parachute cord, a Sten gun and 400 rounds of ammunition confiscated at the Syrian border, a camera with twelve different lenses, light meter and tripod and a movie camera with 300,000 feet of film confiscated, along with his Land Rovers, at the Iraq border. On the premature termination of *Overland to Ur*, he returned to Europe.

'Squandered half his inheritance on that idiotic expedition,' chorused the family.

Sir Vyvyan was not discouraged. 'You can take the girl out of Chinatown, but you can't take Chinatown out of the girl,' he was fond of saying, and thus it was with his spirit of adventure. He bought *Luna* at a price that made yacht club news from Børnholm to Positano. The round-bilged, gaff-rigged, double-ended craft had been damaged in a collision with a destroyer while doing service as a seaplane tender in Scapa Flow. The hull latitudinals were split and warped, rabbets of both stem and sternpost had separated, and she was spewing her deck caulking, corroding about the gudgeons and pintles and accumulating barnacles and sea lettuce. With emotions in part antiquarian, he determined to make her seaworthy. The shipwright advised laying a new keel. 'Best not to skimp now and be sorry later, sir,' he said, painting a grim picture of the implications of false economy. The cost of the repairs greatly exceeded the shipwright's estimate. Even so, the old whaler sprang leak after leak on her 'maiden' voyage. Bilge stringers, futtocks, decks, wiring, plumbing, joinery, ballast, fittings, rigging and sails were overhauled or replaced at various ports, as the extent of the shipwright's duplicity slowly impinged on Sir Vyvyan's naivety.

At Barcelona, where he was fortunate in obtaining a mooring next to the hot water shower at the Club Maritimo, he decided to call a halt. All went well for a time. He became the doyen of the little band of yachtsmen berthed there and came to enjoy a popularity that was new to him, deferred to for his advice about chandlers, eating places and such things, and it was always Sir Vyvyan who composed the quarrel when trouble arose between one of them and the port's authorities. Three or four evenings a week he made excursions into the town, where he was always popularly greeted. It was on one of these outings that Sir Vyvyan met Belvedere. The two men recognized instantly that they shared common values. Both were incontinent in their enthusiasms. Both had a talent for evading or deferring almost indefinitely all those responsibilities that tamed and ultimately defeated others. And now, for the first time in months, they were together again on *Luna*'s poop.

'Enjoy yourself in the Alps? . . . Well, I daresay it must feel wonderful to be back on the Med. Reason why I decided to retire. So I could live as and where I choose. And people say there's no happiness in retirement. Absolute poppycock! However, I must tell you we have had a very tiresome winter. Raul is of the opinion that I need a change. Seven years at the same mooring, he says, is quite long enough. I rather think he misses his family.'

'What news?' asked Belvedere.

'Nothing is ever news when you've knocked about as much as I have, but, since you ask, a chap by the name of Grigio has interested me in making an investment in some mineral properties in the Canadian Arctic. All very hush-hush, you understand. Can't see any harm in telling you, though. They've started drilling for oil. He showed me some photographs.'

Raul came on deck looking swarthier and older than Belvedere remembered him. They exchanged tidings.

'I think our friend here would like a little lubrication. . . ' Eh? Same as always?'

'*Semper fidelis*,' said Belvedere.

'Raul, bring Señor Belvedere *un volcano*. I was afraid you'd ask for kümmel or some such nonsense.'

The deckhand slunk away and returned with a bubbly concoction. Belvedere sank it in one swallow. 'Just hit the spot,' he said gratefully.

'I *thought* you might do with a little lubrication. Raul, bring Señor Belvedere *un otro volcano*.'

'You can leave off the cherry,' said Belvedere. 'That sort of embellishment is wasted on me. Augment the gin! More champagne!'

'Get much reading done while you were away?' asked Sir Vyvyan.

'Hardly time for it,' replied Belvedere. 'Once, during a blizzard, I had a crack at a book called *Herzog* this American chap recommended. He said it was the greatest book he'd ever read.'

'Did he, by Jove?'

'I can't say that I agree with him, but I only managed about twenty pages. They were all about some intellectual Yank who suffered from *Angst*. This fizzy stuff is more expendable than kümmel. How's Bantam Rooster treating you these days?'

Bantam Rooster was a girl who worked the *cantinas*.

'Badly, old man. Badly.'

'Still on at you about buying her a leopard coat?'

'Worse. Her ambitions have turned matrimonial.'

'That *is* bad.'

'I've had to return her picture.'

He was referring to a snapshot Bantam Rooster had given him, taken in a kiosk when they were on holiday in Madrid.

The two men sat for a moment in silence while Belvedere wondered how he could decently bring up the subject. He decided to rush in. 'I don't suppose you know anyone who would be willing to relieve me of a pair of skis for a couple of months?' He explained about his rupture with his employer. 'It has placed me in a rather awkward position.'

'Quite.'

For nearly a quarter of an hour they discussed what Belvedere might do with his skis. Then Sir Vyvyan said, 'Tell you what. I'll ask the Commodore of the Club to keep them. He's a jolly sort of chap and won't mind a bit, and they have masses of room. In fact,' added Sir Vyvyan, 'it could be described as a warehouse with shower and bar attached.' This mild jest sent him into transports of mirth.

'Well, that's settled.'

At the sound of a gong, they went below. Raul, who had laid a new tablecloth, appeared in a Cunard liner's steward's livery bearing a silver tureen on a tray.

'*Gazpacho*!' cried Sir Vyvyan, as though the tureen contained diamonds. 'I leave the catering entirely in Raul's capable hands, and he always surprises me.'

'Raul's a brick,' acknowledged Belvedere.

'Don't know what I'd do without him.'

'Competent, loyal help is hard to come by these days.'

'Good servants are a dying breed. Everyone's so keen on getting an education. But what good will an education be to them? Can you see Raul as an art critic? Or a historian?'

'Maybe a novelist.'

'Like the author of *Herzog*.'

'Exactly.'

'Have some more of this very excellent Blanc de Blanc.'

'Don't mind if I do.'

Sir Vyvyan poured. They touched glasses and drank. It was not without emotion that they drank. They discussed the implications of the Butler Education Act over the main course, *filet de carrelet Louis XIII*, Raul shuffling between table and galley, then resumed the discussion of Literature and came round to topics dear to Sir Vyvyan's heart, which had earned him his knighthood, the gist of lectures expounded to two generations of undergraduates in the antipodes.

'*The Secret Agent* looks inward, deep into plastic emptiness.'

'Yet one is glad for a change from impenetrable forest and vanishing horizons.'

'Just so.'

'*Jim* needs a clear focus.'

'The ear is strained almost to deafness by the dirge of jungle sibilants.'

'It stops listening for the unspeakable. I think I'll just help myself to more flounder, if you don't mind.'

'My dear boy, go right ahead.'

'I'm very fond of Jim. . . .'

'Only you think that he goes on with his woes rather?'

'Exactly.'

A thump on *Luna*'s deck.

'Raul,' said Sir Vyvyan, 'see who it is. . . . And when Axel Heyst commits suicide grieving over that tiresome woman's death, you'd sooner he'd done it before? You feel that too much martyrdom to gallantry is up for display? Couldn't agree more. That sort of thing is all right for wartime stories of commando attacks, but Literature demands more.'

'In your opinion it demands a Comrade Verloc?' said Belvedere, producing another name recalled from past conversations with Sir Vyvyan.

'My dear boy, you are mistaken. That is *not* my opinion, and, if it were, I would have a great deal to retract. Comrade Verloc is drawn far too crudely to deserve a place beside *Emma*, *Tess*, *The Mayor of Casterbridge* and *Nostromo*. He is too Slavic!'

Raul returned and identified the visitor as *Consejo Financiario Grigio*.

'What on earth can the fellow want at this hour? Fancy barging in on a man's lunch like that!'

'It could signal the start of another depression,' said Belvedere, helping himself to more wine.

'Raul, tell *Señor* Grigio that I shall be very glad of his report, whatever it may be, but just at the moment I am at lunch.'

Raul trotted off to evict Financial Counsellor Grigio.

Later, sitting out on deck, Belvedere lying back in his chair, his eyes closed under sunglasses, one arm lying langourously across a side-table, while Sir Vyvyan read aloud to him.

'. . . *Emaciated greybeards rode by the side of lean dark youths, marked by all the hardships of campaigning, with strips of raw beef twined round the crowns of their hats, and huge iron spurs fastened to their naked heels. They were a good sample of the cavalry of the plains with which Pedro Montero had helped so much the victorious career of his brother the general. . . .*'

The wasps hovered close, the ice melted in the glass, the bubbly concoctions stirred memories of other yachts at Juan-les-Pins, Cannes, Santa Margherita Ligure, Ischia; of ochre-plastered stone villages surrounded by vineyards; of the tinkle of water at night before he fell asleep and the rattle of the anchor chain in the morning. A woman sunbathing recalled a girl of forgotten name and the taste of suntan cream. Soft music came from beneath the awnings of the Club Maritimo.

'. . . *His opinion was that war should be declared at once against France, England, Germany and the United States, who, by introducing railways, mining enterprises, colonization, and under such other shallow pretences, aimed at robbing poor people of the lands, and with the help of these Goths and paralytics, the aristocrats would convert them into toiling and miserable slaves, and the leperos, flinging about the corners of their dirty white mantas, yelled their approbation. General Montero was the only man equal to the patriotic task. . . .*'

Belvedere sipped wine and ate from a bowl of salted peanuts. The gulls flew over. The sea sparkled.

7

WOFING WOFERS

Mutual cupidity united World of Finance and the financial press. When WoF wished to announce a quarterly report, the launch of a new fund or the appointment of a film celebrity, former astronaut or former ambassador as a non-executive director, Marty Rubin rang two or three of half a dozen financial editors whom the company entertained liberally and often and said, 'I got a story for you.' The story broke that afternoon or in the morning editions. Marty relished the power he thus commanded. He even boasted about it to his wife.

'So what if it's not exactly proper. So who's complaining, Hadassah?'

'I'm just telling you, Marty, you got *noive*.'

The news of FoF's Arctic transaction was released in this way. Managers were provided with stocks of brochures depicting drilling activities in the Yukon in advance of the jump in FoF's share price, and the salesmen were soon closing Plan after Plan on the strength of this exciting news. Existing clients took advantage of the Family Conversion Feature to switch their investments from other funds in the WoF stable to FoF. It was the topic of conversation wherever staid men discussed financial matters. Even bankers seemed affected by the general enthusiasm. Noam van Zilver saw a reference to it on the bulletin board of the USIS office in Khartoum and divined the implications from the *Sudan Vision*.

'Baroque's a genius,' they said in London, where Now Generation insurance executives stuffed themselves with caviare and toasted him with the pink champagne flowing from a fountain in the ballroom of Folkestone Plan Towers. Everyone was attending the gala in honour of the Genius, and the arrangements were as tasteless as money could buy.

It was the Founder's first visit to Europe I since the August 1966 Bank Holiday, when, stepping down from his aeroplane, he predicted that Volume for 1966 would double Volume for 1965. 'Boy, that was *some* stopover,' Clovis and Ernest reminisced happily. Alone of the current Board, these two had been present in the visitors lounge at Heathrow. 'That was *some* flying visit,' they said in unison.

Then they had celebrated, now they were celebrating, for, wherever the Founder happened to be, there were celebrations. He was looking his dapper, chipper, stylish self in a beige-pink Pierre Cardin safari suit, accompanied, as always, by his Great Dames. That afternoon he had taken them on a little tour.

'We really did see some fine sights,' he was saying to Ernest. 'I had seen them before, of course.'

'Did you see the Tower of London, Mr Baroque?'

'Yes, we did.'

'What did you think of that tower? Isn't it something?"

'It's a great tower, a fine historical splendour.'

'Did you see Westminster Abbey?"

'We sure did, after the Tower. We lost our way but hadn't gone too far before a cab-driver pointed out the right direction. The London cabbies are something else. We ought to tailor a Plan for their special needs.'

'What did you think of that Abbey?'

'A fine historical splendour. Perhaps you could tell me, how much does it take to get buried there?'

'Clovis, a burial plot in Westminster Abbey, you got any idea how much they charge?'

'I don't know. Let's ask Tessa. Hey Tessa, what's it cost to be buried in Westminster Abbey?'

'Oh tons!'

'It's expensive, Mr Baroque.'

'Find out for me, will you? JoAnn and Pam jumped up and down and trembled all over when they saw the memorial to Abraham Lincoln.'

'They went ape, huh Mr Baroque?'

'They sure did. JoAnn and Pam are very patriotic.'

Philippa asked in a loud whisper: 'Who is Mr Baroque?'

'He's a genius,' replied Tessa.

'A genius at what?'

'Haven't the faintest. Ask Clovis. He's always going on about him.'

'Clovis, why exactly is Mr Baroque thought to be a genius?'

'Haven't you chicks heard about the Arctic deal?'

Clovis had not made a presentation all day and was eager to counsel somebody, so he told them what he had read in the Informogram.

Many other guests at the gala were also keen to hear about Operation Thaw, but only Baroque knew the inside story, and he kept his own counsel.

*

They were also discussing it in Japan, where Yukihisa Fujita, the leading Volume producer of Asia III was meeting stiff I Don't Believe You resistance from an old Client.

'Mr Yukihisa, please, kindly explain. How is possible with existing heavy-mud technology to counter deep subterranean Arctic pressure? Water solvent not like other solvents. Expand when freeze and break pipe.'

*

It was discussed in Italy, where Michele felt obliged to lay a proper foundation in his address to the Milano Womens Gymnastic Team.

'We have now seen how the performances of different mutual funds vary according to the skill of their portfolio managers and the compatibility of current market conditions with their respective investment objectives. But outstanding past performance is no guarantee of future performance, so, naturally, you are wondering *which fund to choose*. Ladies, World of Finance has solved this problem for you by creating a super fund *that invests in other mutual funds*.' He drew a diagram on a blackboard and explained: 'Circles one to five of the middle tier are independent mutual funds. Their managers are paid a percentage of assets under

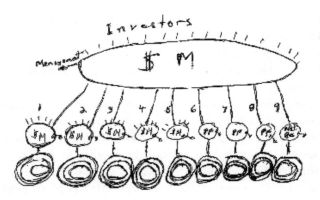

management. Six to eight are World of Finance proprietary funds. WoF is paid a percentage of the income and gains generated by its management decisions. The circle at the right end of the middle tier is a proprietary fund investing in natural resources, and one of its first investments was in mineral prospecting permits. A recent sale of some of these permits has shown that Management acquired them at a fraction of their real value. The unsold portion has since been revalued, increasing the value of shareholders' equity in FoF by more than $100 million.'

*

They were discussing it at the SAE house in Knoxville.

'It's called Operation Thaw, and it's a hoss of a different colour.'

At the reference to horse, Mule Henderson perked up his ears. In recent weeks his interest in WoF had abated, but, as one of five officially appointed on-campus Financial Counsellors, he felt an obligation to attend Bone's Panhellenic Market Group Presentations. On these occasions, there was always lots of work handing out prospectuses, obtaining particulars of brothers interested in hearing more about the investments and being friendly.

'You mean to say that awl we gotta do to git in on this thang is jus' put up the money?' Mule asked impetuously.

Bone knew from previous Panhellenic presentations that success depended on stimulating a dialogue with the audience. 'That's right, Mule, jus' put up the money.'

'And I don't have to watch it?'

A light joke to ease tension: 'Shoot, Mule, there's nothing to watch. It's awl buried under the ice!'

'And they do all the paperwork?'

'That's right.'

'And you say this thang's tax-free?'

'That's whut's called a feature of the Plan.'

'Whut happens when you want to git rid of it?'

'How to withdraw your money?' Bone read aloud from the prospectus. '"An investor may terminate his Plan at any time by instructin' WoF to liquidate the Fund shares held for safekeepin'." In other words, Mule, awl you gotta do is write to WoF tellin' them you want to git rid of your shares, and they send you a cheque for whutever the shares happen to be worth.'

'I still don't see how they can pay out whut's invested in rail estate. Looks to me lak that Arctic stuff's illiquid,' observed Lester, who was majoring in Business Administration.

Bone saw the dilemma and dismissed it with more light humour. 'I guess they jus' melt you down a piece.'

*

At Folkestone Plan Towers, the celebrations attending the Founder's presence continued through the night. Baroque interrupted his conversation with Pam to look about him and exult in the sight of so many Managers and Counsellors – *his* Managers, *his* Reps. Some were sitting, some were standing, some whispering to one another in what they took to be professional restraint, while others were their natural brash selves. Most drank prodigiously of the free champagne, but, noted the Founder with approval, not Clovis and Ernest. They kept themselves busy developing leads and making presentations to new trainees, to other Financial Counsellors, to their girlfriends, spreading the exciting news of Operation Thaw hither and yonder, and, when they chanced to encounter scepticism, they became especially sober.

'What is it, exactly, that you don't understand about the Plan?'

'I understand the Plan perfectly. It's your colleague who puts me off.'

'Mr Gloom? How much were you thinking of investing?'

'About fifty thousand pounds.'

'Is it that you don't *trust* Mr Gloom?'

'That's one way of putting it.'

A sigh. 'Do I understand correctly that you want the transaction to be handled without his knowledge and involvement?'

'I haven't said that I have agreed to invest yet.'

'But, assuming a decision in principle, you would not want Mr Gloom to be a party to the transaction?'

'That's putting it mildly.'

'That can be arranged.'

Ernest was preoccupied with Philippa. Their relationship was still young, and certain ambivalences needed clarifying.

'Of course, I understand,' she said. 'Bankers must be *mad* about "maximizing returns on investments". But it's no use to me. Daddy takes care of all that.'

'What does Daddy do, baby?'

'He owns breweries and department stores. That sort of thing.'

'Do you think he's given sufficient thought to the problem of inflation?'

'Oh Daddykins is *always* harping on about inflation. Is Clovis a kind of manager?'

'I should say he is, baby. He's almost the biggest Manager we have. He was almost one of our Pioneers.'

*

It was company policy that what was decided at the Top of the Spirals was always in the salesmen's best interest. Reassignment of humble Counsellors required no special conciliation and was left to the adroitness of the Area Managers concerned. Reassignment of Branch Managers and Regional Managers, though, was referred to Marty or Nelson. Above RM, the Founder's personal touch was indispensable.

Thus it happened that Bleitgeist waited anxiously at the Top of the Spirals, while Baroque amused himself with the Great Dames. He had been there before on similar negotiations; indeed, was a familiar, if slightly comic figure to the permanent staff, whose friendly attitude was useful in that important arena where the recurrent battle for unpaid commissions and overrides was fought. These visits were not as fun as Advanced Training Seminars, Supervisors Conferences and Managers Conferences, and entertaining all the Key Clerks, even at Horn and Hardarts, was quite expensive. Accounts were churlish about reimbursing such disbursements.

The Founder usually received visiting Managers between ten in the evening and midnight, but his routine was subject to many imponderables. Waiting in Money Makers Lounge and smiling whenever he happened to pass improved Bleitgeist's chances of an early audience. To be noticed was not to be forgotten. Amenability, moreover, could prove advantageous should Baroque have one of his freakish bouts of bonhomie. It had sometimes happened that a Manager waiting thus had been spirited to the Founder's office, or his car, or his aeroplane and awarded a new Territory, new Supervisees and new Stock Options, just because he was sitting nearby when Baroque was in a good mood. WoF was nothing if not adventurous, reflected Bleitgeist.

The days passed, while Bleitgeist patiently awaited an interview. The trick was to out-wait the others waiting for interviews. At first, he kept himself alert, watchful for the opportunity to remind the Founder of their appointment. Later, he beguiled the hours reading magazines. Baroque emerged from time to time but always accompanied by body guards or JoAnn and Pam. Then Bleitgeist would bolt upright, affect a pose that best projected the image of a Manager competent to handle major responsibilities, and smile. Very late one night, Baroque came over and shook his hand. Bleitgeist worried afterwards about how responsible he had appeared, and his fears were not allayed until a week later, when the Founder looked in his direction and, quite unmistakably, nodded. The Manager for Tennessee rejoiced in this fleeting recognition. He did not reproach Baroque for detaining him so long. He was not resentful that others arriving after him were interviewed before him. He accepted that his appointment to see Baroque was an obligation unilaterally binding on him. Nor was there an order of precedence. Even portfolio managers and bankers had to wait. It was enough to sit in the proximity of these waiting grandees and study the uniform expressions on their faces signifying calm under pressure, clarity of purpose and discretion.

Old-timers passing to and from Administration sometimes cast nods of recognition in his direction. Marty approached once with a friendly smile and warmly shook his hand. Nelson inquired after the health of his wife.

Every morning, and again in the afternoon, a woman with purple-varnished nails recomposed a bulletin board disclosing the sponsored funds' latest share prices and assets under WoF management. Bleitgeist had the satisfaction of knowing that he was privy to these computations before the general public read them in the newspapers. The woman's name was Gladis. Bleitgeist imputed to her a more glamorous role than her humble duties suggested. Another exquisite creature with shrimp-pink hair who was taller than Gladis routinely sprayed the flowers, and another pushed a trolley bearing manila envelopes, bouquets of clipped papers and wire baskets of Inter-Office Memoranda. One of the receptionists told him that the Founder himself chose the music dispersed through speakers camouflaged as part of the soundproofing. 'Last month it was all Stephen Forster, and, gee, did I get tired of *Ole Black Joe*!' she said. JoAnn, Pam, Gladis, the flower-sprayer, the trolley pusher and this jaunty receptionist, all the girls at the Top of the Spirals, were among the most statuesque women Bleitgeist had ever beheld, but in such a place one could not be too careful.

Baroque went to Stockholm, and when he returned, the mood in Money Makers Lounge brightened, as again the candidates for favours went forward to their interviews. It would not be long now, thought Bleitgeist. Then one night, as he was about to leave Money Makers Lounge to return to his hotel room, the night receptionist told him to prepare to meet the Founder. A long-distance telephone call frustrated that meeting, but the incident lifted his hopes, and a few evenings later he was granted an audience.

*

On the aeroplane returning to Tennessee, Bleitgeist reviewed every detail of his wonderful interview.

'. . . I was once a trainee mutual fund salesman, Bob. There's no better way to learn the business. . . . Go out and meet the ordinary little guy who buys our Plans, insures his life with us, banks with us. Dig him out, get into his problems, agonize with him about the interest his savings account pays him and the distributions he receives from his with-profits policy with Mutual of Idaho. Point out to him the hundred different ways he's been insulted, humiliated and swindled. Then create for him the life he might have lived had he met you instead of that other guy. He *needs* you. That's our policy, and it works. We are an army led by natural leaders who have come up from the ranks. We even dress alike. . . . You'll do well in India, Bob.'

'*India?*'

Had he projected the image of someone competent to assume major responsibility? Had he projected a personality that was forceful, persuasive and amusing? Had he shown sufficient gratitude for his new assignment? He had found opportunity for none of the witticisms rehearsed so often during his long anticipation and he had forgotten to raise certain questions. Presumably, he would receive Continuings over his Tennessee trainees. For how long? Presumably, the company would pay his relocation expenses, but up to what amount? Presumably, it would underwrite the expense of setting up a new office. He should have asked for additional Stock Options, but his confidence deserted him at the critical moment. He had committed the uninitiated's error of failing to ask for the second Close.

He would want Bumper's Activity Reports and a list of WoF clients currently residing in Afghanistan, Pakistan, India, Ceylon and Nepal. Did they speak English in those countries? He would want prospectuses printed in Afghanistanian, Pakistanian, Indian, Ceylonese and Nepali just in case. He would have to see which of his men were willing to re-locate. He was sceptical of success there. Afghanistan, Pakistan, India, Ceylon and Nepal were too large a concept for them. He would have to decide where to set up. He would need a map.

*

'Double trouble!' exclaimed Philippa, when she found in her letterbox among the bills, invitations and police notices a letter from Belvedere. She opened it cautiously and read it thrice over. A quick perusal first to see if it contained a proposal. Then, more philosophically, to decide about its little wounding hints of indifference (the letter was mostly about 'Uners'). Finally, for its few austere expressions of sentiment. 'It's too ridiculous,' thought Philippa. 'I've somehow got myself tangled up with Ernest, and now Belvedere's coming back.'

Lady Tessa Lonsdale was in her bath when the news broke. 'Well, he'll just have to accept it,' she counselled. 'Ernest just *isn't* the kind of chap you can hide under the carpet. It's either tell Belvedere, and keepers weepers – or give up Ernest. You can't have your cake and eat it too.'

That evening Philippa talked it over with Ernest.

'Listen, baby, I didn't realize there was another guy. Who is this jerk? What's his worth?'

Philippa explained.

'Drop him, kid. He's going *nowhere*. These guys are a dime a dozen.'

Ernest's 'technique' was part-impresario, part-mortician. Even at the best of times it was never more than interesting. This evening it left her feeling numb.

'What's the matter, kid? You not in the mood or something? You want another highball? Or maybe you're still thinking about that other guy?'

'Do you mind if we don't?' said Philippa. 'I'm bored.'

They were in his apartment with the wall-to-wall, white shag carpet, long black leather Habitat couch, gold end-tables, bar in the corner and lights always on dimmer; Philippa in her Janet Reger peach satin panties and bra eating yoghurt.

'I'm not exactly the type who has to beg for it,' said Ernest huffily.

'You're a *darling* boy. Can't think why I don't like you,' said Philippa. 'Maybe if I have some more gin I'll feel more "in the mood".'

*

'Call for you from Honolulu, Mr Baroque.'

'Why aren't you in Tokyo, Fenner? I've been trying to get you all evening. We closed the deal tonight. Five per cent cash, the balance in two-year warrants with an option for earlier redemption. Yeah, the entire Board is resigning. No, there won't be any golden handshakes.'

To Sleek: 'That was Fenner. Now all that remains to be settled is the price of the shares.'

The company's two most Key Associates were discussing the long-awaited Public Offering. The conversation with Fenner referred to an agreement to buy a rival mutual fund group with the proceeds.

'If eight fifty a share, why not nine and a quarter? Why not ten? Which one of the underwriters is the problem?'

'Calhoun, Faloon and Balloon.'

'Who's the head guy at Calhoun, Faloon and Balloon?'

'Abe Balloon.'

'What's his problem?'

'He says that our past profits, our profits outlook and the book value of our tangible assets do not justify a price exceeding eight dollars a share. And that's on the high side, he says.'

'Total sales have more than doubled every year, and Marty tells me they are up a hundred per cent again this year.'

'Yeah, but the sales operation doesn't cover its expenses. Where would we be without the performance fee from Operation Thaw?'

'There's magic in ten dollars. Think how inspired the men will be when they compare the formula value with their shares' offering price. Sales will rocket. It will more than make up the difference. I'd better have a word with the schmuck. Jack me up some figures, willya?'

'No problem.'

While Baroque and Sleek laboured late into the night on the Public Offering, WoFers were reading the advance publicity in the *Bulletin*. As Public Offering Decision Date reputedly coincided with the moon landing, Wally had used a blurred picture of the helmeted astronauts superimposed over the backs of General Managers listening enraptured to a speech by a Key Associate on the cover. 'On July 21, 1969, the date of Man's triumphant first step on the moon, the 25 Directors of World of

Finance met at the Top of the Spirals to prepare one giant leap for our company,' proclaimed the Bulletin. 'Their mission – to shape plans and major projects for the rest of 1969, to evaluate results of the most successful six months in company history and complete final details of the widely awaited Public Offering of WoF stock.'

'The very sweep and panorama of history is expressed in this layout,' said Nelson. 'Gee, isn't that wonderful,' thought Levy. Yukihisa liked it, as did Bumper Peabody, holidaying at a Redevco apartment in Torremolinos and van Zilver in Cairo. Michele announced to a Financial Training Seminar in Bologna that the Public Offering would be 'the most important single event in the history of capitalism'. Sansloy told an audience in Monte Carlo that it 'marked the beginning of a New Era'. Handschuh said that it would 'make the successes of the past seem very small compared to the potential and challenge of the future'.

Clovis explained how the Public Offering would affect the Stock Option Plan. 'It will continue as before with WoF formula shares being offered and repurchased on the same terms on the basis of formula value. But it will make recruiting New Men much easier as they will be able to compare and see that the market assigns a value to the stock that exceeds by several times its price to WoF Associates under the Stock Option Plan.'

*

The forthcoming New Era also excited Bleitgeist. For the moment, though, he thought mainly of his change of Territory. The Founder's words haunted him.

'*How much do you know about Asia II, Bob? Our Iranian operation has been shut down. All our men there are in jail. We've procured the Area Manager's release, but only at some considerable expense. He's been deported.*'

Baroque had a wonderfully easy manner of sharing confidences, thought Bleitgeist.

'*It's created a vacuum in this Major Market Area. Before the crackdown, we were doing around five million a month there, half of it in cash. The Area also comprises Pakistan, Afghanistan,*

India, Nepal and Ceylon, but these second-tier countries have been neglected. The number of inquiries our Client Service Department receives from them suggests that they could make an extremely significant addition to our profits. Their combined population is nearly ten times that of Brazil – our next largest Major Market Area. It wouldn't surprise me to see you doing two million a month from India alone in the first year of setting up there.'

Two million a month!

'Building a new organization in Iran when it reopens will be the other part of your assignment. You will collaborate with Sleek, Fenner and the Shah in establishing an Iranian fund. How much do you know about our National Funds Program, Bob? Broadly, the aim is to create an Iranian fund investing partly in stocks traded on Western exchanges and partly in Iranian natural resources and natural resources futures. The fund's shares will be sold all over the world through the WoF Investment Program. Iranian nationals will be free to invest in it and any of our other funds. Inflow of capital into Iran through this medium is expected to balance outflow. It's a revolutionary concept and damned exciting, an extension of concepts that have already proved their value in other areas, a concept tailored to the needs of the international community of small investors. It will protect the savings of our clients by insulating them from the chronic inflation that has accompanied rising prosperity throughout the world and afford Iranians the opportunity of participating in the growth and prosperity of Iran's economy.'

*

Once the Founder decided about a concept, it was left to other Key Associates to implement it. Bleitgeist was now in almost daily communication with Nelson and Marty.

'He wants a list of all clients in Pakistan, Afghanistan, India, Nepal and Ceylon. Can he have it?'

'He can. Ginny, Inter-Office Memorandum to Client Service. Subject, Bob Bleitgeist, 5242. . . .'

'He wants to know what special literature is produced for the markets in Pakistan, Afghanistan, India, Nepal and Ceylon. Is there any special literature?'

'Beats me!'

'Find out from the boys over in Supplies.'

'Ginny, Inter-Office Memorandum to Supplies. Subject, Pakistan, Afghanistan, India, Nepal and Ceylon. . . .'

'Mr Rock, on your inquiry about relocation expenses for Bob Bleitgeist, 5242. I've been onto Accounts and they say they need a voucher from you or Mr Rubin.'

'Ginny, Inter-Office Memorandum to Bleitgeist, 5242. Subject, Relocation Expenses. In principle, personal expenses incurred by a Manager in relocating to another Territory are not reimbursed except in very special circumstances and never in advance. This will have to be sorted out between you and Accounts once you have settled in the Territory and are able to substantiate your claims with stamped invoices and receipts in the usual way.'

*

Bleitgeist was en route to Knoxville to see what could be salvaged from the operation there. Nelson's memorandum had not gone down well with him. It was what he had become accustomed to from Key Associates: always so friendly to your face, always so obstructive in correspondence.

His thoughts drifted to his wife. Ingrid had threatened to leave him and he had caused outrage by grinning. Her desertion was his best hope of escape, but he was not optimistic. She would stick to him like putty, accusing him all the while of failing to live up to her expectations. Exactly what was expected of him he had never been able to determine. He knew only that her anger was unappeasable. For him, the marriage bond was fear of forfeiting his property in a divorce settlement. She was the bride-price paid for retaining his Stock, while, for his wrinkle-lipped, blame-men-for-your-troubles, chain-smoking, useless wife, the bond was want of a better alternative. After leaving high school and before her first marriage, she had worked as a hairdresser. Nine to five every day but Sunday with a measly hour's break for lunch between rinses and facials for a measly seventy-five bucks a week: she did not recall that brief interlude of independence as other women remembered their young ladyhoods. She knew that she was onto a soft touch compared to hairdressing. Besides, by filching from her housekeeping allowance, she was accumulating a nest egg against the day when he transferred his support to another woman. This phantom Other Woman loomed in her fetid imagination not as a threat to affection, of which there was none, but as a risk to her status: there lay the dark route back to the salon. Yet maybe, just *maybe*, she wouldn't come to India with him. *Maybe* she would stay in Memphis.

He shared his woes with Ernie that evening at the Great Smokies Appalachian Inn.

'I had a friend who went to the Orient,' said Ernie. 'All that stuff about eating all the food on your plate is a load of baloney, he said. They weren't starving at all. They ate all the time, rice and stuff like that. . . . Aren't they Communists over there?'

'I don't think so.'

'I always wanted to go to the Orient,' the barman continued. 'I always had a hankering to see the Great Wall of China. Do you know it took them over five hundred years to build that wall?'

'I knew that it took them a long time. I hadn't realized it was five hundred years.'

'That's what it says in a book I read, five hundred years.'

'What's preventing you?'

'Money, for one thing.'

Bleitgeist looked round the room as a vacuum cleaner salesman might inspect beneath a carpet. 'Have you ever considered changing employment?' he asked.

'Whad you have in mind, mister?'

'Have you ever considered financial counselling? It's just an idea. Perhaps it wouldn't suit you.'

'If you mean selling mutual funds, thanks just the same, but I think I'll stick to what I know. My old man tended bar in Boston and Pittsburgh before we moved down here, and he kinda raised me to the job.'

Bleitgeist had trained more than thirty successful Financial Counsellors and tried without success to train many others. The experience had taught him that not everyone was suited to financial counselling.

'Look Ernie,' he said, sharply changing the subject, 'you've given me excellent advice and it's kinda cheered me up. No one can know what it's like living with old Wrinkle-Lips. Tell you what, I'll roll you for a drink.'

Such mateyness was exactly to the barman's taste. 'Sure,' he said, 'go ahead and shoot. I can always see when a guy's in the dumps, no matter how hard they try to hide it. They can come in here bouncy as a tennis ball, and, if something's eatin' 'em, it always comes out. Nobody can hide his troubles.'

*

Bone demonstrated that the Stars and Stripes Fund applied banking principles in its investments but passed on the profits to its shareholders instead of keeping them, and asked for the sale. He was elated by the result and told Mr Bleitgeist about it.

'Bone, nothing has pleased me more than watching you develop from a raw Icebreaker into a productive professional about to reach Advanced Schedule,' said Bleitgeist.

Bone was never obliged, as Levy was often, to insert his leg when doors opened, so to speak, and his song-like Good Morning was worthy of a Contest winner. Even his unsuccessful presentations often yielded Referrals.

'And that's only working part-time,' said Bleitgeist, 'and in spite of your leg being in a cast, too. Not many trainees do as much business working full-time. Bone, do you know why I'm in Knoxville?'

'To make us hustle moar, I guess,' said Bone.

'That's right, Bone. But I have a still more important reason. What I'm about to tell you is confidential.'

'Sure, Mr Bleitgeist. I can keep a secret.'

Bleitgeist told Bone about his new assignment and offered him the opportunity of accompanying him.

'Mr Bleitgeist, I railly do appreciate awl you've done for me, and I feel specially honoured by whut you jus' offered, but I don't thank I could sell to Afghanistanians, Pakistanians and Indians.'

'Selling to them is like selling to anyone else, Bone. They are no different from Tennesseeans. They want to make more than bank interest on their money. All you have to do is zero in.'

'I wouldn't know whare to begin, and besides, whare would I get the money for the trip?'

Bleitgeist smiled and said teasingly, 'Oh, I think we could arrange it.'

'How much would it cost?'

'About a thousand dollars.'

'*A thousand dollars!*'

'We'd be stopping over in London, Paris, Rome and Athens.'

Bone had never been overseas. 'It's kinda sudden,' he said. 'When would you want me to go?'

'As soon as you can tie up your business here. When do you think you will be ready to leave?'

'Not befoar June.'

'Why hang about until June?'

'Hang about! Mr Bleitgeist, I *graduate* in June.'

'Let's discuss it over lunch.'

They drove to a drive-in renowned for its barbecue. A sign in front said: 'Three great things – God, the Family, the Big Orange'.

Bone had a chocolate milkshake with his barbecue.

'I'll bet you weren't allowed frappes when you were training?' said Bleitgeist.

'You sure weren't! Awl they let you have was steak and butterbeans. They were so strict they even made you put Sweet 'n Low in your coffee.'

'I'll *bet* they were hard on you.'

'The University of Tennessee Athletic Program is one of the best in the country. You sure feel good after you've been on Coach Moose's steak and butterbeans for a while.'

'To get back to what we were discussing,' said Bleitgeist, 'you won't be selling only to locals. There are a lot of Americans in Afghanistan, Pakistan, India, Ceylon and Nepal, irrigation experts and people like that. But instead of earning the kind of salaries paid here in Tennessee, do you know what these fellows make?'

'Whut?'

'Fifty, sixty thousand a year.'

'*No foolin'!*'

'At *least!* And tax-free, too. And what's more, Bone, there is absolutely no problem about finding prospects. Here's a guy who spends his day training Ole Black Joe how to drive forklifts and bulldozers, and there's not even a television to watch when he gets off work. Even the refrigerator runs on kerosene. His wife nags him about all the horrors she puts up with. They have run out of Bisquick at the commissary. He's bored, she's bored, then you pitch up in a starched shirt. "Sit down, Mr Saxon. Take a load off your feet. Where you from? *Wall Street!* Off she rushes to put on lipstick, while he offers you a Budweiser. Soon they're telling you why they are in Afghanistan, Pakistan, India, Ceylon or Nepal and their big plans for all the money they're saving. You listen sympathetically and counsel them how best to realize their ambitions. You're somebody *new*. You are like an apparition to them. You're a dude.'

'Whut's an apparition?' Mr Bleitgeist.

'Someone who shows up out of the blue to relieve suffering.'

'I still don't thank I could leave befoar graduating,' said Bone.

'Think about it.'

Later, as they were driving back to the campus, 'It's kind've a shame, 'cause I only need three credits to graduate.'

'Don't worry, Bone. They'll let you do it by correspondence.'

'I don't thank they will. Not Transportation 3110.'

'You could always fly back for a quarter, say in a year from now, after your organization is ticking over smoothly under your subordinate supervisors. The important thing is to hurry out there before anyone else beats you to it. Before the news leaks out to Levy and people like that. I leave next Wednesday, TWA from New York. You can come with me.'

'I'd better start packin'.'

'And I'll take care of the Advance.'

*

Overton Park Gothic, West Tennessee French Provincial and Junior League Georgian are the three classical architectural norms in east Memphis. Bleitgeist's house was, emphatically, Eisenhower Ranch, a modest bungalow among the columned, multi-storey mansions of Walnut Grove Road. He parked the

Targa in its circular drive. A half-moon shed a warm glow over immense trees. The air was heavy with the fragrance of honeysuckle – springtime in Tennessee. Bleitgeist sang aloud while looking for his house keys. He found them in the wrong pocket. His presence triggered an intruder light, eclipsing the moon, as he walked round to the back and entered via the double-locked door to the kitchen. He poured himself a glass of milk, found some iced doughnuts and went into the den.

He hoped that Ingrid was asleep. Nothing he said interested her, and what she said was intended to wound and demean him. It did not wound him, but he did not want to quarrel. He wanted to sleep. Mercifully, she was not awake.

He took the tablets prescribed for his rheumatism and thought of all that had happened in the past month. *'How are things down there in Tennessee, Bob? . . . An explosive situation is opening up in the East and we need a man to take command. Call my secretary collect, and she'll set up the appointment to suit your convenience. Sleek will help you with your visa.'*

The great Sleek McCool!

'Your responsibility will be . . .'

His responsibility! This confirmed what he had always known, that he was destined for special responsibility. What about his Nashville and Chattanooga trainees? What about Mule and Blaize? How would they take the change of Area Manager? Would they miss him?

He fell asleep.

*

Baroque spoke to Abe Balloon and the other underwriters. It was a long and difficult meeting exercising all of the Founder's tact and persuasive powers. He did not cajole, threaten or reason. He complimented. He exuded. The health of the world's economy depended on the health of the US securities industry and that in turn now depended on the health of WoF, he said. . . . Conventional measurements did not apply to WoF. WoF was a Revolution, not a business, a Revolution whose hour had come, a floodtide in the fortunes of mankind, a golden chain linking rich and poor of all colours and creeds, all nations and professions. 'The job that we are accomplishing reflects a spirit that exists in no other company in the world,' he said. 'Each of us' – including the underwriters, by implication – 'bears a part of the responsibility for ensuring that the world's savings are channelled into the hands of those few people who can and will manage them productively. . . . Our activity and growth over the next five, ten, twenty-five years will provide convincing proof that the free enterprise system can and does work. . . . In a real sense, the service that we perform contributes to the stability of the democratic process.'

*

While the Founder was closing the underwriters for ten dollars a share as the price of the public's participation in WoF's ownership, van Zilver worked the Cairene Conference Market.

His prospect had delivered an animated speech the previous evening denouncing Britain, France, the United States and Armenian, Greek and Asian businessmen as wolves in white sheep's clothing, Western decadence and Dr Banda's part in the cultural and economic subversion of Africa. He had called for the abolition of tariffs on primary products, more agreements for technical cooperation between member countries, more technical cooperation agreements between member countries, a sports embargo against Rhodesia participating in the Commonwealth Games and solidarity with liberation movements everywhere. He had branded criticism of Uganda's expulsion of Asians as yet another instance of neocolonial racism. The speech echoed every other delegate at the conference except the Malawi delegate, and everyone except the Malawi delegate had praised its courage and integrity. Even so, he was finding it difficult to follow *Mzungu*, whose vocabulary was notably deficient in ideological jargon.

'What you mean is, I make my cheque payable to a nobody?'

'Not a nobody. Just someone who doesn't exist.' Van Zilver explained the procedure of a Special Collection and concluded, 'A *shillingi* amount is sold for hard currency to someone requiring Ugandan currency. You are credited in Switzerland, exactly as though you had stuffed *shillingi* into a suitcase and exchanged it for dollars in Zurich.'

'Then the money is paid to somebody?'

'It's really quite simple, Your Excellency.'

Van Zilver shut his briefcase and returned to his hotel to fetch his rucksack. His bill showed an error of a few piastres. He protested to the manager, and the error was rectified. On the aeroplane to Damascus, he considered making a presentation to the diabetic Circassian lady occupying the seat beside him but turned instead to his paperwork. His Plans seldom failed to open and, unlike most Reps, who waited until they received the Confirms, he made up index cards with full particulars of his new Clients before sending the applications to Processing. He prepared transmittal slips and put them with the Plans in sealed envelopes ready for posting in Damascus. Then, reclining his seat and closing his eyes, he contemplated the strategy needed to take over Asia II. He had no intention of permitting the installation of a new Manager. He had not encompassed Bumper's expulsion to work under a successor.

8

EASTWARD HO

'**O**h *April showers* that bring *the flowers* that bloom *in May* . . .'

Not even the smoke-filled waiting-room of the Gare du Nord had chilled Belvedere's exultation. He had been in high good humour since leaving Barcelona. Players and the *Daily Express* on sale at Dunkirk, the clanking sounds of activity on the night ferry, two queues at the passports barrier, one chaotic, the other – for British subjects – orderly, restrained and dignified. Beyond the barrier, porters in dirty overalls were hauling linked barrows of baggage and a woman was handing out tracts. The ferry's passengers swarmed about her, some dressed in elegant tailored suits, others in *Lederhosen*. 'Home from abroad?' she said, presenting him with one of her tracts.

Never one to decline free reading matter, he took her hand-out and already she was eagerly telling him something scarcely audible – '. . . ten years ago . . . invested ten thousand pounds . . .' – that seemed to concern some kind of insurance. '. . . What do you think it would be worth today?'

He stared at her, blankly but benevolently.

'What?'

'Would you be pleased if it were worth twenty thousand pounds?'

'Ecstatic. But you see I haven't even ten pounds to invest. In fact, I'm rather in debt. One of the reasons I've come home is to see my bank manager about a loan.'

She immediately lost all interest in him.

'Sorry I couldn't be more help,' said Belvedere cheerfully.

Later, he heard her engaged with another traveller. '. . . Now that you and your wife have returned from holiday, I expect you will want to consider how you will plan for these holidays in the future?'

He saw her again on the Underground. 'You don't seem to be having much success,' he remarked.

'No one has any money.'

'Yes, I know. It's grim. The Welfare State has sapped the spunk from the British. People aren't interested in making a pile any more. That's why I'm poor. Do you suppose I'd be mucking around abroad if England could offer me a decent future? *No fear!* I'd be stashing it away, but what for? Public health? Mass education? Doctors and academics are the ones who end up with it, you know? My great-great-grandfather worked very hard for the money that sent me to Eton and Oxford, and I don't see why I should bestow the fruits of his labours on someone who's no relation to me, and who, no doubt, is a Socialist into the bargain. You ought to be flogging that thing in the Dorchester instead of the Tube, you know.'

'I have too little experience. I might spoil the Market.'

'What are you selling?'

'The Folkestone Plan. Ever heard of it?'

'I'm afraid not. To be fair, though, I've been rather out of touch lately.' It did not occur to Belvedere that this woman and Financial Counsellor Grigio might work for the same company.

She began a spirited version of Only Two Things Can Happen to You: You Can Live, or You Can Die, then thought better of it and said, 'It's so depressing to be in a profession in which nearly all conversation is shop.'

He was thinking of asking for her card, when they reached her station. Should he let her go or follow her out? Well, just this once. He watched her disappear, her sailor's collar and bobbing white beret conspicuous among the other costumed wreckage flowing through the circular exits. 'I could be happy with you, if you could be happy with me. . . .' he crooned on reaching his destination. '. . . I'd give anything and live anywhere, if only you'd be there.' The 'you', of course, referred to the girl in the white beret so bright and fresh in his mind, so soon to be forgotten. It was a flabbiness of mind that had shielded him from unforeseen perils all his life; that was to protect him now.

*

Philippa and Ernest were asleep when Belvedere rang. When she put down the receiver, Ernest was already dressed, briefcase in hand, ready to march, the picture of a man gallantly determined not to complain.

'Come here,' she commanded and, planting a kiss on his ashen forehead, said, 'You silly old thing! Now run along and sell another Plan. And ring me in a fortnight.' By remaining silent and tamely surrendering his forehead, he had won the right to a Call Back.

Philippa bathed, daubed her face with satin flow cleansing lotion to remove last night's make-up, daubed her battered cheeks with a velvet moisture film that softened, smoothed and protected the skin and applied an ultra-sheer foundation of exquisite lightness that blended with her natural complexion for a naturally radiant glow. From bottles of Dior, Lancôme, Balmain and Le Galion she chose a perfume that diffused an evanescent mist of subtle magic. She shadowed her eyes, brushed an offending particle from an overburdened eyelash, repaired her swollen lips and approved the result. Then the doorbell rang and, after a final approving sigh at the mirror, she descended guiltily to the door to greet her fellow. He was thin and suntanned, *very* unlike Ernest and the broken old tramp, imagined under the hair dryer.

'Parents not home?' he asked, striding in and depositing his backpack on a marble table in the vestibule. 'I expect you got my letter? I took the night ferry from Dunkirk. How about some breakfast?'

They went into the kitchen and, while Philippa prepared Lyons tea, toast, Wall's sausages and a fried egg, Belvedere expounded his plans. He hadn't quite decided what his next move would be, he said, but he had thought about it a lot. One possibility was that he would work as a ski instructor or alpine tour guide or even lift attendant and write *Our Times* on days when the weather was bad. There was room in that scheme for Philippa, he conceded. She could work as a cleaner for the guests at one of the luxury chalets, or, if she preferred, take a course at Cordon Bleu – it wasn't expensive – and cook for them. Once she was gainfully employed, the income from her uncle's trust could accumulate while they lived on her earnings. She might even save enough by cleaning or cooking to enable him to spend *all* his time writing. Or they could go to India and learn Sanskrit together. He had always fancied learning an ancient language like Sanskrit, Akkadian, Ge'ez or Nubian. She served him tea in a mug, butter and marmalade to put on his toast and gentlemen's relish to eat with his egg. It was just like when they lived in his flat at Lurline Gardens, before a sudden and very short-lived scrupulousness about their accounts compelled him to take that dingy room at White City.

After breakfast, he said that he wanted a bath. When he emerged from it wet and naked, Philippa giggled and said that he reminded her of the bowsprit of a Viking ship. She decided that, after all, she liked him very much. He, for his part, examined her anew.

Later, on her mother's four-poster: 'Isn't slalom where they zig-zag in and out between little poles?'

'It's a lot more difficult than it looks. The slightest bump can cause you to lose your balance and miss the gate.'

'It sounds fearfully difficult and clever to me.'

'The trick, of course, is knowing just how wide to gauge the angle of turn. I don't suppose you'd have a cigar knocking about the place?'

'What beastly, revolting habits you've picked up!' Philippa went in search and found that someone had depleted her father's stocks.

'Never mind,' said Belvedere. 'You can buy a box later."

They spoke about *Our Times*.

'It's a comprehensive examination of the contemporary world and all its woes,' said Belvedere. 'My protagonist has fallen into the hands of bandits in Mexico. He embraces their profession and finds the outlaw's life congenial. The question is, will he go back to university and pursue the curriculum of a solid, respectable student or remain a bandit?'

'*Rotter!*'

The subject of Ernest did not arise until that afternoon. Belvedere noticed a toothbrush with *World of Finance* inscribed on it in gold letters, then found a black silk dressing gown embroidered with the insignia of the *Fenner Biddup Offshore Fund*, prizes awarded to Ernest during the Year of Growth.

'That's a nice way to greet your fellow,' he said.

'Don't be daft. You can hardly expect me to sit at home darning while you're out playing musical beds. A girl has her own life to think about.'

'If you ask me, it's pretty thick in here.'

They went for a walk. However, the air outside did nothing to dispel his disappointment.

'You might at least have shown a bit of taste.'

They bickered back and forth with Philippa easily winning and retaining the edge. Since when, she inquired, had he begun worrying about taste? It was taste, she supposed, that had led him into the grasping arms of that doctor's assistant?

'Nurse,' he corrected.

'And the ballroom dancing instructress? And while we're still on taste, surely you can't have forgotten Polly, that floozy you made off with the night you made me go with you to the Hammersmith Palais, the night you absolutely swore to me that you had stopped seeing Helen? And when I *think* of how you had me ask Mummy to invite that tart, Harriet Whatshername, the one with the white rabbit coat, for a weekend at Cowes and then thoroughly humiliated me in front of Kit and Becky.'

'Those girls meant *absolutely* nothing to me,' said Belvedere, adding that monogamy was as alien to him as bee-keeping. 'Anyway, that's all past history. I've turned over a new leaf.'

'*Belvedere!*'

'Really, Pippa, I feel like vomiting.'

'Go right ahead. No one around here will care.' They were passing Whitehall. 'But if you can wait until you get to the bridge, you can lean over a railing and imagine you're at sea.'

'*Very* amusing. I *knew* that coming back was a mistake. I had a really great scene going in Barcelona, really great. Next time, I'll stay put.'

Later, in front of the Victoria and Albert, Philippa said: 'Haven't you ever been keen on two women at once?'

'No.'

'Big liar.'

'Interested, not keen.'

'Shall I chuck him?'

'It's as simple as that. . . . Well, have you decided?'

'Darling Belvedere, you are ever your most adorable self when you are being your most severe. Ernest wouldn't know how to be severe. He's too busy scheming how to sell you one of his Plans. Can't you see how for years and years the one and only man I really wanted was you? It had nothing to do with respecting you. It was craving, pure and simple, as in that ridiculous song, a *yearning, burning, churning inside of me*. It didn't matter what you were going to be, which in any case changed from week to week, or where we were going to live, just that you took me with you. I wouldn't have minded about your going off to Spain to learn the guitar if you had asked me to go with you. But when you said that you wanted to live on your own just to see what it was like and went bounding off, knowing perfectly well that a queue of other women was standing by to home in on what was mine, then I got very cross with you. You needn't look so gloomy.'

'There was no queue of other women, as you put it. I was far too busy working for that sort of thing.'

'*Belvedere!*'

'Anyway, there weren't as many as I'm used to.'

'That's better.'

'There weren't half a dozen different nationalities.'

'Enough boasting. If I hear of another bitch with ambitions of ironing your curtains, I think I'll scream.'

'Well? Are you going to chuck him or aren't you? I would have thought that's the least I'm entitled to expect.'

'You're not *entitled* to anything.'

He was still grumbling when they returned to the house. Renewed lovemaking restored his confidence. He was majestic, like a great ram, with lots of soft fur and green eyes. 'Top marks,' said Philippa.

'Better than Corpulent Finance?'

'Yum! Yum!'

'All forgiven?'

'Plus! Plus!'

That evening Philippa cooked dinner, a humbled and penitent Delilah refurbishing her shorn champion's strength, lit candles, turned off the lights and brought out a choice bottle from her father's cellar. She made sugared pancakes, which she called crêpe suzies, and brought out a *ballon* of brandy. They went into the living room and, although it was quite warm, Belvedere made a fire from kindlings and paper and lumps of coal left over from winter. He lay on the rug in an old khaki shirt with missing buttons, his arms back, his hands folded beneath his head, the dominant, happy male, just as Philippa wanted him to be.

*

For a time all went well. It was as though Belvedere had never been away. The days were overcast, damp and misty, but London was in flower, mayflower and cherry blossom, and the horse chestnut and laburnum were just coming into bloom. The days lengthened and passed slowly, ending reluctantly each evening in a riot of colour. Philippa put her active life in abeyance and they lived myopically, solely for their immediate happiness. Belvedere bought a velvet suit at a very contemporary boutique in Carnaby Street that smelled of incense and throbbed with Led Zeppelin, and they dined at the Ritz, pretending to the waiters that he was a pop star. They went to the Horse Guards Parade and stood among the crowds of mothers holding up their babies and inspected all the new amusements in the toy department at Harrods. Belvedere imposed on Philippa hamburgers, several tedious hours examining rucksacks and sleeping bags at army surplus stores and several listless afternoons at cinemas watching westerns, Belvedere as rapt as a schoolboy and discoursing afterwards on the battles between sheriffs and cattle rustlers as avidly as students of Langland debated the bitterness of invective in *Piers Plowman*. They became so preoccupied with themselves that even Tessa stopped ringing.

Once, when Philippa suggested, as an 'amusing idea', that they invite somebody over, Belvedere replied, 'There's nobody I want to see.'

'Toad in the hole! What about Richard and Sally?'

'Crumbs! The last time we saw them we ended up playing Scrabble.'

'Mickey and Anne, then?'

'Newly weds are grotesque.'

'You used to like them.'

'That was before they married.'

'Peter and Lyndy perhaps?'

'No,' said Belvedere, 'too rustic. We could try and find Hugh.'

'Who's Hugh?'

'Chap I met at the Alpenhof, a distinguished *alpiniste*.'

'No,' said Philippa flatly.

'You never seem to like any of *my* friends.'

'*Amazing*, isn't it?'

Ernest did not re-emerge from the shadows of equity-linked insurance plans and was soon forgotten.

*

In the Founder's office opinion was conflicting. The Market was down. It might rise, yet, equally, it might drop further. The performance of most mutual funds reflected its bearishness and, with dismal results to show, the opposition's salesmen were idle. Not so, WoF's Financial Counsellors. FoF defied the norm, its share price boosted by Operation Thaw and mark-ups of the proprietary funds' unlisted securities.

'These moves won't stand up to inspection,' declared Baroque. 'The Market better recover, or something's gonna give. If another rock goes, there'll be an avalanche!' WoF was out of cash. 'We better keep *all* our options open.'

They were discussing how much restricted and new stock to offer to the public. There was general agreement about the need to involve as many Counsellors as possible. 'Otherwise, it might look like we engineered the Public Offering just to unload *our* shares.'

'We can't afford to horse around too much,' advised Sleek. 'Selling too many shares entails the risk of deluging the Market. We need a formula.'

'Exactly. What will it be?'

'I thought we'd already decided on ten per cent,' said Baroque, whose shares were unrestricted.

'I want to be in a position to dump more, depending on how things go,' said Fenner.

'Me too,' said Sleek.

'We can't make a special exception for you guys.'

'No problem. As we'll be the first to know, we'll be able to unload before the others. We'll have to amend the Rules of Vesting.'

'Okay. Then how do we word it?'

'Any Member whose stock has vested under any of the foregoing rules must offer to the company for redemption not less than ten per cent of his stock and may offer for such redemption not more than fifty per cent in accordance with the same terms and conditions as are agreed between the company and its underwriters for the sale of stock to the public.'

'Sounds all right to me.'

'This'll need the approval of the full Board.'

'No problem.'

*

In an extremity of shyness at finding himself suddenly in his son's company, Belvedere's father resorted to reading aloud from the manuscript on which he had been working since his demobilization. '. . . *The news of Klugel's success against the exemplary resistance thrown up by Four Battalion was received with dismay in the War Office. As soon as the news was received, the decision was taken, and everyone for once was agreed, to send Sunderland immediate reinforcements. This entailed the drastic revision of our plans for Crossbow. . . .'*

He put down the tome, peered over his bifocals and asked diffidently after Belvedere's activities. 'All your plans working out as you had hoped? Finished that book yet?'

'Not yet. I've attempted a rather large canvas, perhaps *too* large.'

'Well don't give up, son. Never say die. Persevere until you are satisfied that you have done your very best. Perseverance is the soul of success.'

Belvedere told his father about his winter holiday.

'I did a bit of alpining in my youth. Spud Leaning's parents had a chalet at Grindelwald. Of course, there weren't any cable cars in those days. We walked up, and jolly hard work it was too!'

'Did you carry a packed lunch with you, father?'

'*And* a first aid kit. Not so much for ourselves, of course, as for some wretched unfortunate we might meet on the trail.'

The conversation lapsed. Belvedere did not seek to revive it. He traced the estrangement between them to his father's remarriage. It always depressed him to come here now.

'Good to find you looking so fit, father,' he said eventually. He thought the old boy looked like a fossil. He retrieved some possessions from a store in the loft and returned to Philippa.

'I really must buckle down to something,' he decided.

Lord Hurlby heard his son leave the house and looked up from his work. 'What did that boy really want?' he wondered.

*

'When is a harbour a haven, and when is it just another harbour?' Sir Vyvyan asked himself. Belvedere's departure, Bantam Rooster's ever-increasing importunities, an awkward suspicion that the mariner's role was best performed on the high seas and not among the creosoted slips of the Club Maritima, had filled him of late with misgivings about staying on.

'A harbour is a haven,' he decided. 'It is a place of refuge and repose. It is a shelter from wind and sea if a mariner is temporarily exhausted by seafaring, disabled by scurvy or must effect repairs that cannot be carried out under canvas. Otherwise, it is an abode for transients on a footing with,' he grimaced, 'a caravan site.'

He was sitting on the poop, hands folded over his bare paunch, pondering his sedentary circumstances, when Raul brought him the post. He put to one side the letters from his sister and his bank to read another letter addressed to him in an unfamiliar hand. Occasionally, and somewhat to his annoyance, former students wrote to him from Australia asking for a testimonial. More rarely, candidates for doctoral degrees wrote to him *à propos The Imagery of the Sea in Conrad*, but those letters always came from the United States in oversized white envelopes embossed with the name of a university in Gothic script and a stamp portraying the head of a dead president. The letter that he received that morning had the markings of a more intimate correspondence.

'The cheek!' he exclaimed. 'The *bloody* cheek!'

Hitherto, communications between his niece and himself had been confined to mandatory gifts and acknowledgements at Christmas and a note to congratulate the girl on attaining her twenty-first anniversary. Was this letter a joke?

It was not a joke, he decided.

Was it meant as a gesture of family solidarity? During a sabbatical year, after the war and before the publication of *An Academic Gentleman's Oriental Recipes*, he had wasted part of a month visiting relations. Had he perhaps been over-friendly towards the child? He had not a sufficiently clear recollection to know whether she was his eldest brother's second or his second brother's youngest daughter. By renewing the lapsed connection, did she perhaps hope to receive a legacy from him? Had his brother's wife put her up to it? Or, as seemed most likely, and as his niece had hinted in the postscript, did she really expect to sell him a Folkestone Plan? A shadowy pandemonium took wing in the knight's tortured mind. He looked at the date on his watch. He looked at the date the child proposed to visit him. He knew what to do.

Some hours later, after a fiery and costly farewell to Bantam Rooster, Sir Vyvyan stood behind the wheel, while Raul trotted about barefoot executing his commands muttering petulantly, 'One pubic hair!'

'Let go the fore and aft springs!'

'*En seguida, Señor!*'

'Let go bow warps! . . . 'Let go stern warps!'

The noise alarmed the Finns on the neighbouring yacht. They drew back curtains and peered out of portholes to see what all the fuss was about.

'Full astern!'

Luna was under weigh.

*

Ever doted upon, ever basking in sunlight, a stag that has wandered into a trap and forfeited a majesty ever taken for granted, Belvedere was also pondering his circumstances. Settled life was alien to him. A month with Philippa was a lifetime.

Each morning, he despatched her to play house with a vacuum cleaner and dusters or sent her shopping, while he retired to the great drawing room to prop his feet up on the fender, read the newspaper and *think*. She tried discussing Test matches and such subjects which she thought might interest him, in vain. She exercised on him her most amusing stories, only to see him grimace, turn away and yawn. Those famed green eyes evinced a melancholy so profound that she suggested he see a doctor. In the evenings he fell asleep early in front of the television with his mouth open.

Her dreams of their shared future, of a house on Cheyne Walk where they would live, of a house in 'Glocks' for weekends, of *his* and *her* children, no longer worked their magic. The *mesalliance* with Ernest had been a diversion from a love that led nowhere.

So many questions. so few answers: reviewing the long list of shattered hopes, it seemed at times almost as if she were addicted to suffering, the heroine of an endlessly protracted radio drama with a hopeless end. Dying of some awful cancer, with the housekeeper, instead of Belvedere, holding her hand, bravely cheering him to further accomplishment when he appeared briefly at the sickroom door between directors' meetings.

The *mesalliance* with Ernest was not her first; nor would it be her last.

*

'The tax's going to be *moiderus* if we have to sell ten per cent of our shares,' said Marty. 'I hope you've got something for us?'

Although most Key Associates professed Socialism, they were loath to pay the Government its tithe. Baroque was the Founder, but, in this instance, Sleek was the Provider.

'No problem,' he said.

The lawyers to whom he delegated the non-problem knew about irrevocable trusts, discretionary trusts, foreign trusts, Clifford trusts, investment credits, interest deductability, depreciation, used aircraft, oil-well drilling equipment, drilling syndicates, dry holes and depletion allowances. The documents that they prepared were long and complex, even by their own prolix standards.

An interesting question arose. A bill was pending before the Congress to eliminate some of these shelters. What if it became law *before* the Public Offering? How could the Key Associates qualify for participation in these schemes *now*?

'No problem,' counselled Sleek. 'Anonymous Depositors Bank will lend you the money. Just put up your shares as collateral.'

'I can't. I've just assigned them to a Bahamian trust.'

'No problem.'

*

It was the eve of Bone's departure. He had taken leave of his parents, Coach Henning and Coach Hamilton, had packed his clothes and sold his books and was making his last presentation in Big Orange Country. His prospect was a sergeant associated with the UT ROTC Program.

'Government bonds only protect you against investment losses. They don't protect you against inflation. If there's a depression, how do you thank the Government's goin' to meet its pay packets?'

'You tell me.'

'By issuin' new money, that's how. Like in Monopoly.'

'What happens if there's a war?'

'Only two thangs can happen, Sergeant. We can win, or we can lose. My own opinion is we will win. Has the United States ever lost a war?'

'Naw.'

*

'It's no good, is it, darling?' said Philippa, cradling Belvedere in her arms and regarding him with wide, moist eyes. 'Poor, poor Belvedere.'

But Belvedere was as mute as a coffin.

*

All of Bone's close friends, the glory of the Big Orange team, were at McGhee Tyson Airport to see him off. Blaize carried his suitcase, Mule, his briefcase. They were in festive mood, singing, *'Ninety-eight bottles of beer on the wall, ninety-eight bottles of beer. If one of those bottles should happen to fall, ninety-seven bottles of beer on the wall . . .'* They observed silence during the announcements, then resumed singing. *'Ninety-seven bottles of beer on the wall . . .'*

Lester bought Bone an Almond Joy and a Heath bar to eat on the aeroplane. Blaize issued an admonition: 'Don't go divin' under any of them saris. We don't wanna have to come over thair and pull you out by the nails.' Mule said, 'I hear that sari stuff's better'n snuff.'

They were all of an age when all adventures were good adventures and were glad to be in on Bone's.

*

Bleitgeist was raging against the incompetence of a woman named Trudy ('All I want is to see Peabody's Activity Reports. So why shouldn't she show me those Activity Reports?'), when Bone found him at the TWA pavilion at Kennedy.

'Say, whut's goin' on around heah?' thundered Bone.

Bleitgeist's spirits rallied. He always felt better in company.

'Okay, let's do a check. Got your passport?'

'Sure have.'

'Vaccination certificate?

'That's with my passport.'

'Ticket.'

'That's in my pocket.' Bone reached in his pocket and produced his ticket.

'Okay, everything seems to be in order. Where's your bag?'

'I checked that thang right on through to Bombay. Was that all right?'

Bone was excited by the prospect of flying over the Atlantic. He had never flown over water before.

He saw Indians for the first time in the boarding bay. The men wore normal clothes, but the women's shiny satin sparkling costumes reminded him of circus performers. One had a brass ring in her nose and her palms were tattooed. Why did she do that? They were all chattering, some in English, some in Indian. His intense scrutiny of a black-bearded, beak-nosed man wearing a stiff round homburg and black suit prompted Bleitgeist to ask, 'Haven't you ever seen a rabbi before?'

It was almost nine o'clock before they took off. After listening to various announcements about cruising speed and flight time and ordering earphones for the picture show, Bone turned his attention to the menu. He normally ate at six. 'Wherever we fly, we have the enviable opportunity to discover cuisines from around the world, and you are invited to share some of our all-time favorites on tonight's flight . . . Boeuf Stroganoff . . . A delicious dish of international fame . . . almond pineapple chicken . . . chunks of chicken in a Polynesian style sauce with pineapple, Oriental vegetables and toasted almonds . . . grilled ham steak Cumberland.' He asked Bleitgeist what he was having.

'I never eat while flying,' replied Bleitgeist.

'Don't you feel too good?'

'I feel fine. I just never eat on aeroplanes.'

'Wail, I'm having the ham steak. It looks purdy good.'

After watching the film and telling Bleitgeist to wake him if they flew over anything interesting, Bone went to sleep.

Dawn came quickly. Bleitgeist, who had the aisle seat, looked out over his trainee's massive slumped shoulder, the first glimpse through the window that he allowed himself. Down there was *nothing* but *water*.

He relaxed somewhat when they touched down at Rome. The worst part was over.

The crew changed and the new stewardesses introduced themselves. 'My name's Judy.'

They took off again. When it was safe to unfasten his seat belt, Bone went to the back of the aeroplane to talk to Judy,

'What d'you major in?'

'Supply Chain Management.'

'What will you be doing in India?'

Bone swelled with pride. 'Financial counselling.'

They landed again at Teheran. The new passengers were mostly Indians.

'Do you always fly this itin?' Bone asked Judy.

'Pretty much.'

'I guess you prefer some itins over others? Which itin do you like most? . . .'

There was another meal. Bone felt quite experienced at air travel now and requested an extra dessert.

Then came the final Fasten Seat Belts and No Smoking announcements. Judy was like a flame in the aisles, urging passengers to their seats and passing around gumdrops. Children were crying. Bone was looking out of the window straining to see India. Bleitgeist was thinking, 'Only ten minutes to go and it'll all be over.'

'*Christ Almighty, I wish they'd get this over with!*'

'Huh?'

'I said I wish they'd get this over with.' Were there lights down there on the runway? They seemed to be landing in total darkness.

'If we come in too low we might hit an elephant,' said Bone, but Bleitgeist was not amused. His ears seemed to be exploding. This was no moment for wisecracks.

A bump! Remembering the cabin steward's announcement ('Our touchdown speed will be approximately one hundred and fifty miles an hour'), Bleitgeist gripped the arm rests.

Another bump, the revving of the engines and rubber braking on cement.

Despite the captain's instruction – 'Ladies and gentlemen, Captain McPherson has asked that you please remain in your seats with your seat belts fastened until he has turned off the engines' – a rabble formed in the aisles. They ought to know better, thought Bone. 'D'you see how they *completely ignore* the captain's wishes?' he said. Through the window, he saw two men in boiler suits walking backwards, beckoning to them with flags, and pointed them out to Bleitgeist. One was wearing a turban. The land of palaces and maharajas, elephants, tigers and turbans – they had arrived!

'Ladies and gentlemen, on behalf of Captain McPherson and the entire crew, we would like to thank you for flying TWA and we hope that you have a pleasant stay in Bombay.'

'Goodbye, and good luck with your mutual funds,' said Judy as they left the plane.

'I sure enjoyed our conversation,' said Bone.

'Be good!' she replied, then turned and bestowed her personality on the next passenger.

'You sure you got everything?' asked Bleitgeist.

They walked down the gangway and across the runway into a crowded omnibus. Bone felt frizzled about the tips of his crew cut. 'Man, *it's hot!*' he said.

There was a delay while the baggage was transferred to the omnibus. There was another, longer delay, due to a flat tire.

'It must've melted,' said Bone.

*

Belvedere, also bound for India, removed his groundsheet from his rucksack and spread it on the forest floor. His new sleeping bag was a present from Philippa. His pillow was his new pullover, another present, wrapped in a shirt. Philippa had given him some money as well – not enough, she reproached herself later, imagining him begging at a crossroads.

On the Ramsgate-Ostend ferry, a German had offered him a lift to Munich and he had carried on hitchhiking – Salzburg, Graz, Zagreb, Belgrade, Sophia, Edirne, Istanbul. His rucksack and its contents were his only encumbrance, and they were less burdensome the further he travelled.

Philippa wanted to write to him, but inspiration failed her. Eventually, she gave up and her loneliness atrophied into indifference. Finding nothing at his forwarding address, Clients Mail, Wagons-Lits Cook, Istanbul, he checked out the Blue Mosque and the Santa Sophia and carried on travelling.

Anatolia was bare, windswept and bitterly cold, and progress was mostly in lorries, which stopped every few miles to load or discharge cargo. The other passengers were hearty creatures with sour breath who gave him cold, soggy discs of bread stuffed with onions and moist goat's cheese. Avenues of willows swayed in the wind, and the sky was always blue now. Wild camels looked up from their grazing and trotted away from the road, their snouts in the air. Erzinjan, Erzurum and a long, winding ascent of Mount Ararat, where baggy-trousered fellows on horses galloped across glistening wet meadows between snowdrifts.

The weather softened after Maku. Dogs behind high earthen walls barked at him in unlit villages. A man brought him a glass of hot tea and a saucer full of sugar lumps. He wore a sheepskin coat and thick wool stockings and carried a lantern.

In a dry place symbolic of his own abstinence, without silhouette or shadow, Belvedere lay cocooned in his sleeping bag with only his closed eyes exposed to the wind. There was a rustle of dry leaves and a smell of jasmine.

*

Van Zilver paid Oghab Yarhater the second instalment of the agreed fee. Oghab was the man with the black patch over his eye who had interrogated Bumper during the last week of the Fall Contest.

'Where have you detained Sher Mirza?' van Zilver asked him. 'Is he giving you much static?'

'We had to shoot him. He was a vulgar fellow, but he seemed to know a lot of big people.'

'Of course. They were his clients. Now they're orphan clients. I'll sort them out as soon as the heat's off.'

'I suggest you lie low for the moment. I'll tip you the wink as soon as the coast is clear.'

'Right. I'll sort out the rest of the Territory.'

*

Bleitgeist *knew* that every Territory presented a unique challenge. None, however, was more challenging than *this* Territory. He reflected on what had induced him to accept it. '*Bob, the number of inquiries received by our Client Service Department suggests that these countries could make an extremely significant contribution to our profits. India, for example, has a population exceeding . . .*'

'I'll say it does,' he thought resentfully, 'and most of them sleep in the streets. What do you motivate them to buy? A bigger mat?'

'I know what you're thanking,' said Bone. 'It don't look too good,'

They had been for a tour of inspection and seen slums more depressing than either of them had ever imagined possible, a vast spread of shacks, lean-tos, huts and shanties interspersed between refuse dumps, people defecating on footpaths, rats foraging for food beneath vendors' stalls, women laundering in a sewer outlet to the sea, scrubbing clothes in the sewer and beating them on rocks, eight- and nine-year-old prostitutes exhibited by their mothers as dolls in cages to lure customers. Bone missed his friends and the fraternity house. Having promised his parents to return to finish Transportation 3110 as soon as he reached Branch Schedule, he was wondering how much it would cost to fly back sooner.

'Let's face it,' acknowledged Bleitgeist, 'this has come as a shock to both of us. Nothing, *nothing* in our experience' – Bone shook his head in sorrow – 'prepared us for *this*! Those people we saw bedded down on the sidewalks! . . .'

'They didn't have beds,' corrected Bone.

'Those people camping four, five and six to a mat . . .'

'Camping right there on the sidewalks!'

'Those little girls in cages. Those temple fellows with shaved heads and nothing better to do than beat drums. All those people condemned to spend the rest of their days like rodents.'

'Rodents are better off than they are, Mr Bleitgeist.'

'Well, what are we going to do about them, Bone?'

'I dunno. Whut do you thank we oughta do about them?'

'Have we the right to live like kings, while they fight for survival washing our underwear in sewers?'

'I guess not,' conceded Bone.

'That's right, Bone. It would be callous of us just to ignore them. We *could* ignore them, of course. We could just go back to the States.'

'That's whut I was thankin' of doin',' Bone confessed.

Bleitgeist knew what he was thinking.

'But how would we feel about it afterwards? That's what you have to ask yourself. How would you feel, knowing, as you would, that you had left the whole responsibility for these people to' – Bleitgeist groped for the word – '*missionaries?*'

'Not too good, I guess.'

'You'd feel bad, wouldn't you, that you had done something wrong? Right Bone? Can you see what I'm driving at?'

'I thank so,' said Bone.

'Before I saw what we saw today, I guess that I kinda assumed that everyone enjoyed the comforts that we Americans take more or less for granted. Buying a hamburger, for example. I want a hamburger. I buy a hamburger and don't think twice about it. But now I *will* think twice about it. Now I know what people mean by *Third World*. This experience has shaken me out of my complacency. We really ought to count ourselves lucky.'

'I guess so,' said Bone.

'When you think about it, it almost seems like we were chosen. I mean, who else would face up to such a responsibility? Would Blaize or Lester or Mule? Would Mule have been willing to devote his life to helping Indians? *Think* about it, Bone. It is the wheel of our individual fortunes eternally revolving and demanding from us only humble acceptance. Each man is assigned a place in this great rotation. Some will step forward at the appointed hour, and others will step back. We should look upon this as our *opportunity*, our *privilege*!' But his words were otiose. Bone was already convinced, now that he understood the purpose behind it all. *He* wasn't going to let a little thing like lepers lick *him*.

*

Operation Thaw begat Operation Outback. The Natural Resources Fund bought a vast parcel of land in the Nullabor Plain of Western Australia, a wilderness 'rich in potential for mineral extraction', and sold a small portion of this wilderness to an insider masquerading as an outsider at a price fifteen times that of the purchase price per acre. FoF then revalued the portion of the acreage retained 'conservatively' at a price eight times the purchase price and paid WoF a Performance Fee of ten per cent of the profit accruing to the Natural Resources Fund.

Addressing the Millionaires Conference that spring, Baroque hinted that anyone seeking a fast profit should invest in FoF. How did he know that? 'A little bird told me.' The applause was thunderous, and the Sales Force, who were exempt from charges on purchases of the company's sponsored funds, bought FoF in such quantities that Processing was obliged to suspend other purchases so their applications could be handled in time for the expected announcement. Sixty per cent of FoF's portfolio was now invested in proprietary funds. 'Outback,' proclaimed Baroque, 'proves the soundness of this type of real estate investment and management operation.'

Anstruther objected. 'Now what's this Performance Fee you're all wittering on aboot? I canna warrant this tae be a braw sale at arm's langth. Man I wouldna' touch it with a barge pole.'

Strong language was used of Anstruther. The Founder told him that he was a frustrated, old fuddly-dudley with the atavistic mentality of a bookkeeper, incapable of grasping the larger concepts. 'If the world depended on schmucks like you, Angus, we would never have invented the wheel,' he said.

Anstruther resigned.

The underwriters were alarmed. Was this the sort of transaction by which WoF hoped to achieve its profits forecast?

'No problem,' said Sleek.

*

Belvedere awoke and lay for a while snug in his cocoon. As the sun peeped over the horizon, he unzipped his sleeping bag, sat up and surveyed a vast encompassing emptiness of land and sky. A chill wind blew. His hair was stiff with dust. The driver had stayed the night in the village and other lorries might have stopped overnight there.

He rose, danced around his little bivouac collecting his bits and pieces, and dressed. He confirmed that his money was intact at the bottom of his sleeping bag, rolled up his sleeping bag, wrapped some sweating cheese, a half empty jar of peanut butter and the hard remains of yesterday's ash-encrusted bread in a cellophane bag and repacked his rucksack. Then he hoisted the rucksack onto his back. Its familiar weight tugged at muscles stiff from his night on the ground. A quarter of an hour later, he sat on the rucksack by the road waiting for a lift. There was no sign of traffic yet. The drivers would be drinking tea now, dipping sugar lumps in it and nibbling them, while their assistants hammer-tested their lorries' tyres. Soon he would hear the lorries' motors starting.

*

Baroque met the underwriters' doubts majestically. 'Socialism has taken such a hold on our imaginations that suddenly the best brains in the country are the bad guys,' he declared. 'Our greatness as a nation ultimately depends on the freedom of a relatively small number of individuals to make the choices necessary to harness its reserves of wealth for the public benefit. If we place too many restraints on their judgement, we will soon find ourselves living in an economy where everybody grows what little he needs for survival and raids his neighbour's corn in times of scarcity.'

*

A solitary star in the west survived dawn's first light. This was a place for lizards, beetles and astrologer nomads: pebbles and sand, thorn bush and wisps of withered grass, rivers of dry rocks and salt pans. It seemed to him scarcely credible that sixty years ago, within his father's lifetime, almost all travel over these magnificent wastes was on foot.

Thesiger had claimed that it was the hardness of life in the desert which drew him there, but that was tosh, wasn't it? He immortalized his guide, who 'held out his hands and with uplifted palms' recited from the Qur'an. That was tosh, too, wasn't it? Describing a visit to the ruins of a Syrian palace, Lawrence wrote that his guides led him 'from crumbling room to room, sniffing the air like dogs', saying, '"This is jasmine, this violet, this rose"', but that 'the sweetest scent of all' was that of the 'effortless, empty, eddyless wind of the desert throbbing past' because 'it has no taste'. That was tosh, too, wasn't it? Pure *tosh*!

The sky was now robin's egg blue turning to silver. An hour from now it would be dazzling. An hour after that, if he was still under open sky, he would long for shade.

There were few, if any, nomads now. Thesiger perceived that they were already obsolescent in his time, their mode of life as expendable as the detritus of tin cans, bottles and the skeletons of wrecked cars littering the desert. Lawrence, Thomas, Philby, Thesiger – and Abraham and the Magi overlanding from Babylon – were all obsolete. The unblinking spirit of this place now, thought Belvedere, was a hitchhiker on an empty road.

He waited there all morning, then caught a lift and sat perched on the motor casing between the driver and his assistant. They endeavoured to be as pleasant as possible, offering him sticky gumdrops with stale centres, addressing him with soft words in Farsi. He reciprocated with grins and gestures signifying incomprehension.

The road bifurcated at Karaj, followed a river upstream, crossed the Elburz and descended by stages to the Caspian Sea.

Salt water, sand shores and seagulls. He camped outside Babol
Sar and reached Meshed two nights later. He would remember
all his life a mosque he saw there. It was turquoise-domed and
faced with glazed tiles depicting arabesques of vines and flowers.
He learned later that it was built during the Timurid Dynasty and
renovated during the Safavid dynasty, when Persian architecture
attained the pinnacle of its elegance.

He sustained a long wait outside Torbat-e-Jam, using his
handkerchief to shelter from the sun and entertaining himself
by throwing pebbles at a stone. There was another long wait
at the border, where he filled out yellow forms in triplicate for
Immigration Officers. He eschewed advice at Herat to take a
bus from the square near the fullers' market, trekked out to the
road and caught a lift with a Canadian bound for Kabul, who
was travelling fast. They sped through vast solitudes of rocky
outcrops and dust, overtaking the few east-bound vehicles
sharing the road.

'How long do you think it'll take us to get to Kabul?' asked
Belvedere.

'If you don't mind my saying so, the locals pronounce it *Ka*bul,
accenting the first syllable.'

Belvedere thought of the peacock-blue mihrab of the Masjid
Shohada at Tabriz, the ribbed and glittering minarets of Meshed,
the pendant lanterns and scalloped niches where the pigeons
roosted, the blind man sitting in the shadows chanting, the
Masjid al-Jum'a and tomb of Abdullah Ansari in Herat and all
the other sweet sensations of the past fortnight.

*

Bleitgeist made his maiden presentations in India, adapting
versions of If I had Met You Ten Years Ago (known as Baroque's
Own) and Do Banks Make Money? to local conditions.

'You must ask yourself: In another five, perhaps ten, perhaps
fifteen years, will I have to clean my own latrine? You don't
want to clean your own latrine, do you, Mr Sharma? What can
be more degrading than physical labour? But, if you don't act
now, you'll be *forced* to clean your own latrine. . . .'

'How many daughters do you have, Mr Gupta? . . . Six! That's
a lot of daughters. You will want them to marry. Your wife will

insist on it. . . . That's right, Mr Gupta, daughters have to marry. How will you pay for these marriages? Marriages are expensive. How will you provide for your daughters' dowries? You are not a wealthy man. Do you want everyone to say that you had to choose husbands for your daughters who are common clerks, maybe belonging to a lower caste, who maybe are even Jains, Parsees or Muslims, just because you weren't able to provide them with proper dowries? . . .'

'A Vaisya's *karma* is to make money, Mr Reddy. . . . You don't believe in caste? . . . Caste is old-fashioned? I see. Then maybe you don't believe in making money, Mr Reddy?'

*

Oblivious of Financial Counsellors and financial manoeuvres alike, master and crew of *Luna* rode the waves. They passed the point, a clump of coral, and hove in sight of another. All day, all week, all these past three months, coral and sand, sand and coral, water and blue sky, blue sky and water.

They had first put in at the little-frequented port of San Carlos de la Rapita, a village of whitewashed plaster beyond the treacherous Cabo de Tortosa. Sir Vyvyan had received intelligence, which proved fallacious, that certain brands of radios were obtainable from duty-free shops there.

The second rosy dawn out of Barcelona found them riding at anchor in the little harbour of Isla Cabreara. Brobdingnag-like, it was inhabited by monumental Swedes in abbreviated bathing costumes. Raul parading about in his striped boxer shorts, doing handstands and cartwheels and other ostentatious feats of skill, ogling, leering, returning late to his duties in the galley, and sluggish and aphasic while serving breakfast.

Setting a course for Ceuta, Europe was soon astern, the old whaler pitching ever onwards under canvas in the gentler trades, trailing a stern anchor at night, the gentle shores of Morocco merging by degrees of desolation into a procession of bleached sand dunes advancing to water's edge. Then the headlands of virgin forest out of which crawled huge turtles and flew iridescent birds with long, wispy tails. Seagulls crying in the wind, porpoises slithering in and out of the waves and melancholy fogs reminiscent of *The Rime of the Ancient Mariner.* They floated 'in a world shut off from the universe' and took soundings with a lead.

Here in the solitudes of the African littoral, the taciturn Raul was even more uncommunicative. '. . . Haul in on the lug! . . . Brace the yards! . . .' Sir Vyvyan gave the orders, and Raul executed them, obediently, promptly, but listlessly. Sir Vyvyan annotated the log. '22° N. Proceeding SSW at 5–6 knts. Crew showing signs of boredom.'

Each dawn they assembled on deck for devotions. Sir Vyvyan was conscious of imitating a tradition of the Senior Service and proudly aware that his illustrious namesake would have approved. He was even a little superstitious that *Luna*'s well-being and the success of their voyage in some way depended on the daily performance of this rite, for early in life he had formed the habit of attributing the gift of each new day to a protective power superior to his own resourcefulness. Each morning, he read aloud the same words from the Prayer Book.

O Eternal Lord God, who alone spreadest out the heavens, and rulest the raging of the sea; who has compassed the waters with bounds until day and night come to an end; Be pleased to receive into thy Almighty and most gracious protection the persons of us thy servants, and the Fleet in which we serve. Preserve us from the dangers of the sea, and the violence of the enemy; that we may be a safeguard unto our most gracious Sovereign Lady, Queen Elizabeth, and her Dominions, and a security for such as pass on the seas upon their lawful occasions.

Sir Vyvyan happily ate and looked at the sea, as *Luna*'s bow snatched sapphire necklaces from the indigo waves. He wrote happily in *Luna*'s log, happily revised what he had written, ate and looked at the sea. Water and blue sky. Coral and sand.

9

FLOTATION

Ever since his conversation with Bumper at the Otel de Nuristan, Hunter had been wondering how to increase his Volume without making more presentations – to increase it, moreover, commensurately with the new Asia II Manager's expectations. For he had reneged on his agreement with Bumper. A notional transfer to Bumper's new Territory invited the risk that the new Manager would discover his continued presence in the old Territory. It would be better to play straight and hope for decency. No, decency wasn't the ticket. Volume was the ticket. Nothing else could save him from Termination. But new Volume presupposed more presentations, and he just could *not* bring himself to make more presentations.

The problem was on his mind that morning as he left his desk at the Food and Agriculture Organization to call on Dr Karim Ghulam Reza Abbas at the Ministry of Agriculture. An auxiliary, not a trainee WoFer, he decided, was what he needed. An adjutant, an *aide commercial*, someone willing to work under his direction and *in suo nomine* for part of the commission. Someone young, energetic, unemployed and ambitious to improve his position. Someone intelligent, who would be a credit to WoF and not spoil the Market. Who was eager for the drab self-sacrifice of making presentations. Someone with a talent for projecting himself sympathetically, yet who happened to be in Kabul and was willing to remain in Kabul. Such were Hunter's thoughts when he spotted Belvedere.

Hippies were not rare in Kabul. They were altogether too common. But this one didn't have the lazy, bent, defeated and exhausted shuffle that distinguished the type. He walked upright, more like a trooper in the Brigade of Guards than a hippy, and, from afar, looked as though he didn't stink.

Hunter studied him again. Granted, he did not altogether fit the conventional picture seen month after month in the *Bulletin*'s *Meet your Fellow Associate* column, but he would do. Hunter crossed the road and doubled back. He could have coffee with Dr Karim Ghulam Reza Abbas tomorrow.

Later, at Hunter's house, a concrete block surrounded by high walls (an innovative architectural style in Afghanistan), Hunter concluded his presentation. 'Can you see how a unit trust investing in other unit trusts offers better value than one with a portfolio of ordinary equities? The expatriate community here *needs* professional estate planning guidance. You could make a mint.'

Belvedere topped up his glass with another frothy Tuborg from Hunter's refrigerator, leaned back on the sponge cushions of Hunter's sofa and said: 'Isn't it all rather hypothetical, Mr Sacks?'

'Not to me, it isn't. It just seems obvious. Why not delay your travels for a month or so and give it a try? If it doesn't work out, what have you lost?'

'How much do you think I could earn?' asked Belvedere.

'Three hundred a week, at least.'

'Dollars?'

'*Pounds!*'

'Just for flogging doobreyferkins?'

'Fiduciary of Fiduciaries,' corrected Hunter. 'Our *really* successful trainee Financial Counsellors actually earn two and three times that.'

'Nine hundred pounds a week?'

'I've seen it happen,' affirmed Hunter. 'Of course, they are more permanently career-oriented than you. Don't forget, FoF is not WoF's *only* product. We offer our Clients a full range of products, from Swiss bank accounts to Spanish apartments. But why get in a ferment at this stage of the game? Start with the basics. The questions you must ask yourself now are, *Do I need the money?* and *Do I need the money enough to work for it?*'

'And, presto, I'm a Financial Counsellor?'

'Not quite,' admitted Hunter, sensing that he may have overreached himself. 'But in principle, yes. A few hours' intensive training, and a chap like you, an Oxford graduate, ought to be raking it in. Well, what do you say?'

A surfeit of startling new possibilities opened before Belvedere. Poor one moment, rich the next. Why not? He disliked dismissing ideas peremptorily. What finally determined his decision were nomads. They were more exotic than flogging mutual funds. Dark, lean, hard men wearing robes and sandals . . . armed with knives and rifles, web belts studded with cartridges criss-crossing their chests and leading strings of camels tied tail to nose . . . switching the backs of their legs to couch them, the beasts roaring their displeasure as they dropped to the ground . . . bangled, bonded, barefoot women staring fixedly at the ground, as though habituated to seclusion, their plaited black hair greased with butter and their hands and faces stained with henna – out there with the nomads, and not flogging mutual funds, was where he belonged, decided Belvedere.

'Oddly enough, had you approached me a fortnight ago, I might have accepted your offer,' he said. 'Not now, though. I'm not in the mood for Fid Fids just now, Mr Sacks.'

And he remembered the *aivan* and *mu'rraq* tiles of the Goharshad Mosque, the ribbed minarets and scalloped niches. He remembered the blind man sitting in the shadows chanting.

*

No one in WoF was more debonair than Sleek McCool. Operations Thaw and Outback were two of his debonair creations. Another was WoF's investment banking arm: Finance Bank and Entrepreneurs Bank, incorporated in the Bahamas and the Netherlands Antilles in 1967, the Year of Professionalism.

The challenge of combining investment banking and fund sponsorship under the same roof daunted other lawyers, but not Sleek. 'No problem,' he said when Fenner raised the illegality issue. 'The beauty of operating offshore is you are not subject to such restrictions. Unlike onshore operations, our sponsored funds can pick up what our investment banks fail to sell to the public.'

It was another New Concept.

The financial press remained ominously silent, however. It just did not seem right to dump unsold stock on publicly-owned portfolios. By the end of the Year of Total Financial Service, it was clear that these ordinarily supportive commentators were right to withhold praise for the New Concept. The sponsored funds were larded with what Fenner called 'an unparalleled set of dogs'.

'If this gets out, we are dead in the water,' observed Baroque.

*

The Founder avoided the topic in his speech to those attending the Key Associates Conference on the eve of the Public Offering. His speech was a ringing testimonial of his belief in *them*. 'Soon you will all be millionaires several times over,' he said. 'But none of you is interested in becoming a millionaire for its own sake. What you are primarily concerned with is doing an important job well.'

He stopped and breasted the applause, noting with approval that all present were clapping at this tribute to their altruism. It was a speech that they would all remember, he thought, one of his best, a speech that would survive his time on earth. It was a speech that Mayer Amschel Rothschild might have made. It was a synthesis of all the other speeches that he had made over the past fifteen years. The noise subsided, and he continued. 'I maintain that our activity and growth over the next five, ten or twenty-five years will provide convincing proof that the freedom that we enjoy to invest our private wealth can and does work. Through our efforts, more and more of the world's savings will flow into the international capital market and contribute to the growth of the world economy. We are helping an ever-increasing number of people enjoy the fruits of this freedom. For this is the Promise, that everyone who is willing to work and to save can participate in economic development. That the dream of a more equitable distribution of wealth can be realized within the structures of the free enterprise system. That the dynamism of our economy will result in the knitting together of the shattered bits and pieces of our society.'

No one before had extolled the Key Associates' deep moral societal concern and breadth of wisdom so eloquently. We *are* contributing to the growth of the economy, they were thinking. We are a *unique* company, because *we* are unique people.

However, on the eve of the Public Offering, the long and eagerly anticipated 'cashing-in', this is how matters stood with WoF. The Sales Force had been expelled from most of South America, Mexico, Iraq, Iran, Spain, Portugal, Greece and the Philippines, and the company had been indicted or was under investigation in twelve other countries. It was depleted of cash, having wasted its last reserves supporting the convertible paper of a company purchased for a proprietary fund's portfolio to prevent that company from going into liquidation as WoF was about to go public. The proprietary funds' portfolios were full of properties marked up for Performance Fees. The sponsored funds' portfolios were laden with worthless stock underwritten by WoF's investment banks. And the Fenner Biddup Offshore Fund was about to reach its tenth anniversary, a prospect deeply disturbing to WoFers who had done their calculations. Clients redeeming their Plans were about to discover the exact weight of the 'front load' and other charges borne by their investments and wake up to the real truth about 'Baroque's Own'.

*

June 30th. Trading in the rights 'when issued' is in full vigour in over-the-counter bourses in Amsterdam, Zurich, London, Toronto, Johannesburg and Sydney. Anonymous Depositors Bank is acting for undisclosed principals. The big buyers are the big Managers, Sansjoy, Sansloy, Sansfoy, Strumpf, Handschuh, Hoof, Gloom, Mafia, Vendetta, and the big sellers, who know that the shares will not rise much above the offering price, not soon, anyway, are Baroque, Sleek and Fenner.

'30 June,' wrote Sir Vyvyan in *Luna*'s log.

A light breeze NW 3 pts. abaft stb. beam. . . . About noon a rusting freighter laden with extra cargo secured under tarpaulins and nets on all six hatch coamings hove in sight. She was steering southwest and making bad weather of it. I signalled her by running a flag up the main mast but received not the courtesy of a reply. She was plunging into the head sea and rolling like a barrel. From the way she yawed, one might have said that a wild steer was in charge. . . . The wind, NE as our little cargo floated past the island, was more than a little insolent, and, had we been flying more canvas, I would have reefed her sails snug and steered broad away from the atoll.

June 30th. Bleitgeist awards Bone a certificate signed by the Chairman of the WoF Foundation.

This is to certify that
LAWRENCE SAXON
has been named to the Honour Roll
of The WoF Foundation in
recognition of outstanding contributions
made to community services
and for active participation and
investment in humanity.

The certificate is embossed with a golden globe held aloft by two petitioning, slender hands, and encircling the globe is the motto, MORE THAN MONEY TO GIVE.

'June 30th, Bombay, India

'Dear Mom and Dad, The WoF Foundation has awarded me a certificate for "outstanding contributions made to community services and for active participation and investment in humanity. . . ."'

*

Belvedere took leave of Hunter. So generous and welcoming at first; so surly and inhospitable after his guest proposed 'another Tuborg to toast the ever-widening dissemination of Fid Fids'. They rode in silence to the junction of the road to Jalalabad in the FAO Landrover.

Other hitchhikers were soliciting rides, some awake, some comatose, some dozing peacefully on blankets. Those who were awake nodded to acknowledge Belvedere's silent greeting as he passed.

*

Although incorporated in Canada, FoF did no business there. A Lichtenstein company owned by a Luxembourg company owned by WoF managed its portfolio. Its 'Depository of Cash' was a Swiss bank, its 'Depository of Securities' a British bank. Baroque owned its voting shares, but title to its non-voting shares, as evidenced by the handsome 'counter-signed and registered' certificates that Clients received, vested in the WoF Investment Program, a WoF house account.

Bleitgeist explained the structural benefits to Bone. 'That's just in case of a disputed succession or double taxation. Since the shares are owned by The WoF Investment Program, nobody knows who really owns them.'

Sansloy explained them to Sansjoy: 'Where we see a situation developing which offers the attraction of a higher than average return on investment, we are free to act without fear of involving ourselves in complicated and costly legal disputes with regulatory agencies, such as the Securities and Exchange Commission.'

Baroque explained them to Vendetta: 'We don't anticipate differences between Management and our clients, but should such differences arise, we are free to act according to what is in their best interests.'

Sleek explained them to Abe Balloon: 'Ordinary investment companies can't borrow money, buy on margin, sell short, lend out fund assets, participate in underwritings and trade in unregistered issues, commodities, real estate and the securities of companies in which the fund's officers, directors, sponsor or management company have a financial interest. But we would be doing our clients a disservice to ignore opportunities of this kind simply because such transactions are prohibited onshore.'

*

Levy was still disputing Bumper's authority two months after he was installed as Tennessee's Area Manager, nor was he Bumper's only problem. Another was a trespasser that Stamp had established in Oak Ridge during the interregnum. Appeals to Herb, Marty and Nelson failed to dislodge him.

Nelson's response was unworthy, a flagrant violation of both the letter and the spirit of their kickback agreement, thought Bumper. Of course, Bumper could point to nothing in writing.

Nevertheless, the deal was, in exchange for half the kickback, he would get *all* of Tennessee. Herb's attitude was just as depressing. Bumper had been with the company as long as Herb; he was *almost* a Pioneer. Yet here Herb was, WoFing him with some kind of deal with Levy cutting him out of *his* Override! All right, if that's the way they wanted it, he knew what to do. Once you'd had the Iranian Experience – lit cigarettes inserted in your nostrils, swung from the ceiling in a tractor tyre blindfolded, beaten with hoses, beaten on the heels and soles, genitals tied to a door by a string that was plucked like a harp – you knew how to deal with lightweights like Nelson and Herb. He composed a long, detailed letter to the Secretary of the Treasury with copies to the Federal Bureau of Investigation, the Speaker of the House of Representatives and Senator Fulbright and felt perfectly relaxed for the first time in months. His mind was luminously clear. *He* knew how to avenge a wrong.

*

The speedgram reporting Baroque's speech at the Key Associates Conference arrived in the same post as the Special Offer to Pre-Icebreakers – double Volume Credit for 'career-launching' Plans opened within six weeks of the Public Offering. Fitz studied the special offer, wondering if he would be able to squeeze in his first presentation before the deadline, then resumed his study of the WoF Code of Ethics.

'One. I shall at all times place my Client's interest above my own, giving him the financial advice I honestly believe best serves his needs and welfare.

'Two. I shall make certain that my Client fully understands the benefits and terms of his Investment Plan, the special privileges he will acquire as he increases his capital, as well as the acquisition costs involved.

'Three. I shall maintain a high standard of competence in my profession by keeping abreast of changing conditions and legislation that might affect the financial plans of the public.

'Four. I shall cooperate with all WoF Associates in promoting the principles of sound financial planning and improving the quality of service that we provide. . . .'

*

When Alexander the Great entered Orto-spanum (Kabul), the inhabitants poured out of their houses and greeted him with accolades befitting the conqueror of Babylon, Pasargadae and Ecbatana. They removed their turbans, touched their foreheads to the ground, spread rose petals in his path, presented their children to him for his blessing and regaled him with eulogies and baskets of fruit. The Macedonian dismounted and quartered the winter there with all his army and, in a valley nearby, selected for its exceptional beauty, he founded one of the many towns that bore his name, Alexandria-under-the-Caucausus. Zahir-ud-Din Muhammad, son of Omar, descendant of Genghis, surnamed Babur ('the Tiger'), likewise took this sunny Shangri-La in the lee of the snow-crowned Hindu Kush into his exulting heart. Babur was an emperor *and* a poet. 'The goodness of a thousand years would not equal the beauty of Kabul,' he wrote. Belvedere, an English traveller of the twentieth century, met Hunter Sacks.

He had a similar encounter in Lahore. He was strolling along the Mall, past advertisements for Keeting's Powder and Sunlight Soap, the tarmac resounding with the clip-clop of horses' hooves, when a Volkswagen bearing CD plates drove up beside him. 'Hi!' said the driver, a man with mutton-chop whiskers wearing a *dashiki*. It happened outside the barred doors and shuttered windows of Mustafa Khan's general goods store.

'Evening,' replied Belvedere.

'Need a lift?'

'No thanks.'

'I thought you might want a lift.'

'Thanks all the same.'

'Nice evening, eh? It's a little on the warm side, but it's not as bad now as it was. A month ago, can you believe it, it was a *hundred and twenty degrees*.'

'I can believe it,' said Belvedere.

'You sound like you're British. Let me offer you a bite to eat?'

The car stopped, and Belvedere got in.

'My name's Lucivius,' said Lucivius. 'Where you from?'

'London.'

'I was in London once. I stayed in a hotel near a park which wasn't too far from the Thames. You probably know the place?

It cost me only five bucks a night, which included breakfast. How they could afford to do it at that price, I'll never know.'

The subject of Lucivius's London experiences was soon exhausted and led to *the* subject. 'There are quite a lot of Britishers out here, engineers, technicians, teachers and medical people mostly, all earning big salaries without any suitable vehicle for investing their money. The right fellow – a fellow like you, for instance – could make a mint selling them the right vehicle.'

'Just which vehicle is that?'

'The Folkestone Plan.'

'That's funny,' said Belvedere. 'I thought you were talking about cars. I met a girl in London whose vehicle was the Folkestone Plan and a chap in Kabul whose vehicle was the Fiduciary of Fiduciaries. Is your vehicle related to those vehicles?'

'We are a very big company.'

'I'll say! *Ubiquitous*! And, it so happens, you want me to flog this vehicle for you. Is that what you had in mind?'

'Something of the sort.'

Belvedere pushed on after his meal. He reached the border at dusk. There was a light fragrance of flowers breeze-blown from some dark quarter. Passport inspection and forms to complete on the Pakistan side. More forms to complete on the Indian side. No cigarettes, whisky, guns or pets to declare. A policeman gave him a lift to Amritsar. Horns blaring and confusion in the narrow streets around the Golden Temple, a sanctuary set on an island in a therapeutic pond where bearded old men read the *Granth Sahib* incessantly under a silk canopy.

'Guru Ram Das Ji, Fourth Master, excavated *Amrita Saras*, pond of immortality and place *Darbar Sahib*, holy temple, there. Maharaja Ranjit Singh, Lord of Five Rivers, cover dome with purest gold,' a self-appointed guide informed him.

'I think you'll find that it's not really gold,' countered Belvedere.

'Purest gold, sahib!'

A woman in blue satin pantaloons gave him some pellets of coloured sugar.

'Sahib, I am telling you story of how Baba Nanak is telling Hindu peoples bathing and doing *puja* at Benares not to throw water in opposite direction, towards sun. Hindu peoples him want to know why Baba Nanak throw water towards Punjab. Baba Nanak say, "I am watering my field in Punjab." Hindu peoples laugh. "Why you laugh?" say Baba Nanak. "Punjab nearer to Benares than sun worshipped by Hindus."'

Belvedere stayed the night at the *gurdwara*, sharing a dormitory with other sahibs. They all had the Golden Temple in common. They were 'tripping' on Sikhism. Accommodation was free.

He left Amritsar and hitchhiked north, travelling by the winding precipitous road through Banihal, then down into the vale and on by foot into the mountains. The Bakarwals and Gujars in the high pastures were herding their goats and sheep, the water ran in torrents down the mule paths, where bright yellow begonias and orange crown lilies extruded from the dripping foliage. The walk lasted three days. At the end of it was a sacred stone phallus in a cave.

*

Noon in Bombay. The monsoon is one of record intensity, ceaseless, heavy rain, water dripping everywhere, moist, stale cookies with tea.

'They say the first few weeks are the worst,' said Bleitgeist.

'I sware, it jus' dudn't let up.'

'Imagine what it must be like for *them*. Can you imagine it, Bone?'

'I can't imagine it.'

'At least *we* have a roof over our heads and don't have to sleep on the sidewalk.'

'I guess they git used to it.'

Once Bone had formed a clear idea of why he was in India – to help Indians – it might be supposed that it was easier for him to adapt to the very different conditions there. It wasn't easier. India did not perplex as much as repel him. Many small things disgusted him, such as men wearing sarongs instead of trousers and sometimes, even, garlands of flowers around their necks. They even *held hands*. They brushed their teeth with sticks instead of toothbrushes and ate flat, dry-fried brown paddies instead of ordinary bread. Then there was that newspaper report about a politician who 'recycled' his urine to purify his soul.

'Mr Bleitgeist, I don't like anythang about these people.'

'Bone, it's not kindness to people you like that counts. It's kindness to people you don't like.'

'I know. That's whut it says in the Scriptures. But I can't even stand to look at them.'

You don't have to *look* at them. Pretend they're not there. That's the way to get on with them.'

'I guess so.'

'Is it all this emphasis on sanitation that puts you off?'

'You mean the lack of it.'

'Forget it, Bone. Just go about your work. Remember, only two things can happen. The Indian Government will collapse, in which case you will have the satisfaction of knowing that you helped your clients to live abroad, or it will survive, in which case your clients will repatriate their capital, having maximized returns by investing it abroad. "Can you see how this makes more sense than gambling everything on the present Government, Mr Chatterji? You probably have a number of friends who would also like to protect themselves against the danger of a revolution. Would you like me to speak to them? What are their names?"'

*

Belvedere returned to the plains and hitchhiked the muddy roads to the confluence of Holy Jamna and Holy Ganga, staying nights in *dharamsalas*, where the rain tapped incessantly on tin roofs, mushrooms grew out of the rubble walls and lichens coated the wooden bedsteads.

He was accosted by fakirs, astrologers, flesh mortifiers, snake charmers, *yogis* and *saddhus* demonstrating their diverse skills at breathing, stoicism, awkward postures, mastery of serpents and divination. They burned excreta in urns, balanced excreta on their tongues, stuck tridents through their tongues, lay nude on thorns. One demonstrated the science of extruding the large intestine while standing waist-high in water, another the science of coiling the legs while standing on his head, another opened his dhoti to exhibit a penisectomy, black stitches marking his shorn masculinity. 'Manifestation of triumph of *Atman* over sexual desire, sahib.'

'Don't listen to that dirty bugger, sahib. He is not *pukha saddhu*, sahib. I am showing you truth. *Ayie*, sahib.'

'I am Lord Shiva incarnate, sahib. Divine Shiva! God!'

'*Uski bat mat suniye*, sahib. *Wo badmash hai, wo kharab admi hai. Ayie*, sahib, *mere pas ayie.*'

'Divine Shiva, sahib!'

'*Wo jhut bolta hai*, sahib. *Uska bat mat suniye.*'

'I am glory of Maruts. Among Vedas, I am Samaveda. Among senses, I am mind. I am consciousness in living being. Among eleven Rudras, I am Sankara, among eight Versus, I am God of fire. Among generals, I am Skanda. There is no limit to my magnitude.'

'*That bugger is telling you bloody rubbish nonsense, sahib!*'

'Among seats of water I am ocean, among words, Om, among immovables, Himalaya. Among weapons, I am thunderbolt.'

'Fine, but why do you smear yourself with ashes?'

'I am King! When Himalaya was young I already old. Water, air, fire and earth are not older. Only fire within fire can tell you my age, and you cannot speak with fire, because you do not know language of fire. Only stone within stone can tell you my age, and you cannot speak with stone, because you do not know language of stone.'

*

Bleitgeist and Bone dined at a *khannawallah*'s stand in Crawford's Market. Bone was shivering so violently two hours later that Bleitgeist had to cancel a presentation and take him back to their hotel.

'Don't you want me to call a doctor?'

'Unh-unh. I'll be all right. Jus' lemme lie here for awhile. I sware if it don't look like I got a bug.'

Bleitgeist got a thermometer and took his temperature. 'I'd better call a doctor,' he said.

'Don't,' said Bone, not opening his eyes. 'It's jus' some doggone bug.'

'It's probably food poisoning.'

Bleitgeist later persuaded him to drink some tea. 'You need to get your blood-sugar level up,' he said.

'Whut time is it?'

'Ten o'clock.'

'Doggone! I must've been asleep.'

'How do you feel?'

'Cold,' said Bone.

Bleitgeist felt his forehead and took his temperature. 'You must have caught a chill.'

'I wonder how long it takes for one of these Indian bugs to clear you out.' Bone's head throbbed, and he felt like a great weight was pressing on his eyes.

A doctor came next day, looked in his eyes, tapped his chest and listened to his breathing with a stethoscope.

'I don't have much appetite,' admitted Bone. 'All I want to do is sleep.'

'You must be having too many pains in tummy,' the doctor said.

'Maybe so. I guess I jus' slept through them.'

The doctor was one of a list of doctors recommended by the British Deputy High Commission and the American, German, Swedish and Norwegian Consulates. He exuded confidence and professed absolute mastery of Bone's illness. He prescribed suppositories, blue tablets, tea and yoghurt.

He came again next morning and administered an enema. After this visit, there were thunderous noises in Bone's ears, like huge waves breaking against rocks.

The doctor called again and elaborated various theories of Bone's pathology. These included faecally contaminated curry and ingestion of sand. 'Sometimes they are adulterating the sugar, isn't it?' Bone's persistent drowsiness and fever were the classic symptoms of constipation, requiring colonic purification by lubrication and medication, he confidently explained. The tablets were to compensate for destruction of intestinal flora due to change from normal eating habits and climate-induced colonic trauma. 'Sometimes foreigners' pathology is adverse because of amoebic or bacillary dysentery or giardiasis and sometimes owing to constipation,' he said.

When Bone began to talk incomprehensibly ('You gotta watch out for the offside guard 'cause he's liable to pull from the line of scrimmage and lay a cross-block on you. . . .'), Bleitgeist again proposed to take him to the hospital.

'Whut for?' said Bone. 'My laig's okay. It jus' hurts, that's awl. Coach oughta let Les and Blaize play. We need everythang we got in a moment like this. Those ole boys are *rail* tough.'

His delirium continued for two days and nights. Then, suddenly, he seemed normal.

'I thank I'm getting over it, Mr Bleitgeist. I dreamed I was back playing football.'

'You said a lot of things that didn't add up, Bone. You seem perfectly normal now, but last night, frankly, I almost thought you weren't going to make it.'

'I'm sorry to be so much of a drag.'

'You're no drag, kid. I'm just wondering what's best for you, that's all. I still think we'd better transfer you to a hospital.'

'Wail, if you don't really mind I'd sooner stay here. There's no telling whut those Indian hospitals might be like.'

And that afternoon he was back on the gridiron deftly evading pulled guards and annihilating backs behind the line of scrimmage.

*

Benares, and alabaster-white, emaciated cattle dumbly venerated in dung-heaped streets, bloated human and animal carcasses floating in Holy Ganga, the sickly sweet odour of cremation at the burning ghats. Patna, and the sullen, eddying waters of refuse-laden Ganga. Bihar, and teal and egrets breasting the sky, rice paddies and patches of sugarcane and jute.

'He who knows there is no difference between Brahmin endowed with learning, cow, pariah dog or rock endowed with neither sense nor delicate feeling has transcended gross distinction between knowing and not knowing. He has attained wisdom, sahib. He is a yogi – eternal, absolute!'

'Buzz off!'

Successive lifts brought Belvedere to Rauxaul. He spent the night on the platform at the railway station and crossed the border to Birganj the following morning.

*

'People ask why our proprietary funds' management fees are not a fixed percentage of assets under management,' said Sleek.

'Incentive is the reason. If its fee is fixed, Management has no incentive to perform better.'

Noam was not deceived. If the fund gained $100,000,000 in each of the first three quarters and lost $300,000,000 in the fourth quarter, Management paid itself $30,000,000 for its 'Performance' without a corresponding deduction for the fourth-quarter loss. It was not obliged to reimburse the fund's shareholders for losses.

*

Cobalt blue skies portending the end of the rains heralded the Indra Jatra. Observing the clear skies, the Brahmins decreed the moment auspicious, then changed their minds. Devotees thronged the multi-roofed temples of glazed tiles and gilt finials from dawn to midnight petitioning the gods to intercede with Lord Indra, while Tibetan lamas on the surrounding hills chanted *mantras*, banged cymbals, burned votive wicks in bowls of clarified butter and drank buttered, salted tea. Prayer flags fluttered and prayer wheels revolved in the wind before the fierce scrutiny of the Self-Existing One.

The Brahmins thrice made their calculations and decreed the moment auspicious, and thrice changed their minds. Finally, they relented, and Goddess Kumari, a frightened child, was fetched from her palace and borne through the streets on a chariot. She had lived apart and been fed, fanned and adored by her devotees from the moment of manifesting her divinity in her infancy by remaining calm in the presence of men disguised as dragons.

The festival continued for eight days and culminated in an encounter between the Virgin Goddess and Lord Vishnu (the King of Nepal). The excited multitudes drank copiously the grain alcohol flowing from a spout in the mouth of the stone head of the Jan Khana Bhairav. Cows wandered placidly in and out of the temples through studded bronze gates guarded by dragons and goblins.

Belvedere returned to the plains.

*

Hundreds of unemployed or under-employed Indians had responded to Bleitgeist's advertisement in the *Hindustan Times*

('International banking consortium requires executive-calibre leaders to supervise expanding local sales operation. Send full details, including present position and salary to . . .'), and the inaugural Bombay Financial Training Seminar was about to start. Some who responded cited among their qualifications stillborn academic careers ('BA failed'), some stressed genetic credentials ('I am Brahmin of Chittapavan sub-caste married to lady teacher working in Jalgaon District'). Bleitgeist had to sift through all the responses and narrow the list to two dozen or so hopefuls. It was an awkward time for Bone to be on sick leave. Bleitgeist had little time to look after him.

*

The irrigation canals were full now, the rice thick and green in the paddies.

Belvedere crossed the Ganges again at Patna and retraced the Grand Trunk Road west as far as Kanpur, veered southwest as far as Jhansi, then turned east for Chhatarpur and carried on bound for Orissa, before turning southwest, then south for the Carnatic. He saw the pornoglyphs at Khajuraho and Konark ('The main spire, or *shikhara*, is the culmination of a graduating succession of smaller spires representing the philosophical quest for truth which advances by progressively elevated stages of understanding towards the Divine Absolute') and Safar Jang's glass collection at Hyderabad. At Rameswaram, the massive, sombre, arcaded temple on the Palk Strait, pilgrims were pouring vials of Holy Ganga water into holy sea water, baptising each other, dousing one another with absolution and chanting *mantras* to sky and ocean. Monkeys screeched derision at them. Were he to find a philosophy broad enough to command the entire man, he reflected, he would build his own temple for wayfarers here, his Temple of Earthly Contentment, its walls inscribed with all those super-cool moments of the past two months.

And still, there was more to see.

He crossed Adam's Bridge, Rama's route to Ceylon, and travelled through miles of coconut plantations, past happy children presiding over piles of pineapples, and mahouts bathing elephants in rivers. He visited Anuradhapura, Polonnaruwa, Sigiriya and the Temple of Gautama's Tooth at Kandy.

A Burgher put him up at his tea estate near Nuwara Eliya. 'They tried to Sinhalese the telephone service,' he said. 'Look here, I was born in this country and have been here all my life, and, d'you know, I'd be hard pressed to recognize fifty words of Sinhalese. The operators babble away at you, and no one understands them. Now those silly idiots are talking about taking over the tea estates. They haven't the first bloody clue how to run a tea estate. Independence was a formula for disaster.'

He went to Colombo and boarded a ship to Cochin after waiting half a day in a hot shed while customs officers inspected passengers' luggage. 'You were lucky. Embarkation can sometimes take longer than the voyage.'

'What are they looking for?'

'Bribes.'

Another shed and more bumf at Cochin. 'Are you having nothing to declare? No gold, jewellery, cigarettes, alcohol, firearms?'

'Only what I have in my pocket.'

'May I be knowing what is your purpose in India?'

'To learn Telugu.'

He wrote 'Student' in the space after Profession on the entry form and declared that he planned a stay of indeterminate duration.

Part III

Liquidation

10

BAD KARMA

In New York, they were discussing Fenner's dismissal.

'A man who'll cheat at backgammon can't be trusted.'

'*Poy*sonally I never liked the fellow. Still, I can't help feeling sorry for him.'

'Did he resign, or was he shoved?'

'Shoved.'

'Maybe now they'll change the name of the Fenner Biddup Offshore Fund.'

'Gee, Mr Rock, how come Mr Biddup got the sack? Did he steal some money or sumthin'? What's the story? You can tell me. I promise, I won't tell a soul.'

'Just a little family squabble, Ginny. Nothing to get uptight about.'

The rupture followed a sequence of wrong predictions. When the Dow reached 1000, Biddup echoed the chorus of analysts predicting its further advance. The breaking of that psychological barrier heralded an era that continued bullish until the Dow surpassed 1300. Biddup attributed the rise to the promise of increased production implicit in advancing electronic and nuclear technology. Then it dropped to 900. It would rise again, Biddup predicted; 'traditionalists' were engaged in profit-taking. Its drop to 800, although unexpected, was simply an 'overreaction' to the earlier drop, to the 'domino effect'. When it reached 700, Biddup ran out of excuses and joined the traditionalists. It was time to sell.

Baroque, Sleek, Herb, Nelson, Marty, Clovis, Ernest, Jacques, Pierre, Hans, Gerhard, Michele, Vincenzo and Henry were incredulous. 'But you were saying last week that it was time to *buy*.'

'Fenner, it's not the first time it's happened,' said Baroque.

'*Tell* me about it,' said Sleek.

'Gee, Mr Rock, whaddaya think he'll do now he's fired?'

'Get another job, I expect.'

*

The party celebrating the start of the Fall Contest that year was the most resplendent in the history of the Folkestone Plan, but it was not a hundred per cent festive. The sluggish performance of WoF shares depressed the guests' spirits. While the shares had rallied in the past few days, this was due to the company's policy of supporting the price with the proceeds of the underwriting. The general trend was bearish, and already some of the Reps were wondering about the real value of their entitlement under the Stock Option Plan. Opinions varied between irrepressibly optimistic, cautious, cynical and pessimistic.

'The Germans are holding back.'

'The big Swiss banks haven't come in yet.'

'American banks are afraid of the Interest Equalization Tax.'

'The Japanese are selling short.'

'Some of the first investors bought for a quick profit and got out.'

'They'll come back in when they see this year's earnings.'

'Now's the time to invest.'

'Wednesday was the time to invest.'

'I reckon they're a good buy at *any* price.'

'I'm buying all I can lay my hands on.'

'Who's lending you the money?'

'ADB, of course.'

*

'You'll soon see how much of a mug your old man is.'

'Oh Daddy's always getting people's backs up. What's he done now?'

'It's what he *hasn't* done. I advised him to buy, and d'you know what he said?'

'Haven't the faintest.'

'He asked me when the police were going to prosecute Baroque for fraud.'

'Dear me! You two obviously don't get on.'

'When a guy dates your daughter and you don't even bother to offer him a drink, I call it downright unfriendly. He doesn't seem to realize that I make more money than he makes.'

'Don't fret over it, angel. He was *just* as unfriendly to Belvedere.'

*

The sluggish performance of the stock notwithstanding, Sleek was busy flogging used aircraft, geological surveys, oil rigs, pumps, pipes, tanks, NOPIs, even 'dry holes' to the Key Associates – or rather, he was busy defending their acquisitions now that they had to pay for them.

'Herb, you can go on repeating your point until you're blue in the face. You have a tax problem, and the Government allows investment credits on this kind of position.'

'But I don't *need* an aeroplane.'

'You don't need an aeroplane to *fly*. Of course not. You need an aeroplane for an investment tax credit, and you've got one. It's no use crying on *my* shoulder. How was I to know that the bottom would fall out of the market for leasing this kind of machinery?'

'How about you taking over the aeroplane and cancelling my overdraft?'

'Wish I could, Herb, wish I could, but my hands are tied. In your shoes, I'd look for somebody who wants a second-hand plane. Or you could learn to fly. . . .'

'Now look, Sleek, I didn't want these pumps and tanks and stuff in the first place. It was *your* idea.'

'I know you didn't want them, Nelson. You are not in the oil business. But you were facing a very large capital gains tax and an increased tax rate on your other income. This was a way of letting you convert the gain into smaller income increments earned and spread over future years and qualifying for the depletion allowance.'

'Where's the income?'

'That comes from renting the equipment. Okay, so nobody's renting. So don't sweat it. . . .'

'What's a NOPI?'

'I've told you before, Marty."

'Tell me again.'

'Net Operating Profits Interest.'

'That's the promoter's rip-off, right? This guy sets up a drilling fund and keeps a piece of the action for himself. So what do I want with another guy's rip-off?'

'No problem. The interest on the money ADB has lent you to make this investment, together with the cost of prospecting for oil, negotiating the leases, preparing the site for drilling and setting up the rigs qualify as deductible expenses. The cost of the purchase of the equipment qualifies as an investment credit, and any income from oil produced qualifies for a depletion allowance. Then, if you drill a dry hole, it qualifies as a deductible loss. These credits and deductions effectively annihilate your tax liability this year and greatly reduce – if they don't nullify – it in future years.'

'So?'

'So, instead of paying this money to the Government and getting nothing for it, you have bought a piece of the action in six well-drilling ventures. Listen, you schmuck, show some gratitude. We are a *public company*!'

'So what?'

'So, public companies just don't go around lending their directors money to qualify them for tax shelters.'

*

The company's 'offshore' arrangements perplexed not only the flotation's multiple underwriters; they were dimly understood within the company as well. Previously operating under a Panamanian charter, its registered office had been a post office box in Panama City; it was now an address in Toronto. Its largest sponsored fund, Fiduciary of Fiduciaries, was incorporated in Ontario; although its transfer agent and registrar were there, it did no business there. FoF retained a depositary of cash in Switzerland and a custodian of securities in England, while its portfolio manager was WoF Management Company, Ltd, of Nassau. The legal structures of the company's other 'offshore' funds were almost as complex. The Folkestone Plan's Equity

Unit Account was reinsured with WoF Insurance Holdings, SA, of Luxembourg, which invested policy holders' premiums in Fiduciary of Fiduciaries (Sterling) of Nassau. 'These superior technical arrangements are for your clients' benefit,' Reps were told. The main beneficiary, though, was the company, as Sleek explained at a confidential meeting of Key Associates at the Top of the Spirals a fortnight after the Public Offering.

'Immunity from local law. Where we see a situation offering a higher than average return on investment, we are free to act without fear of involving ourselves in complicated, costly legal disputes with regulatory agencies. . . . .

'Managing Fiduciary of Fiduciaries, whose portfolio comprises other mutual funds. is much less expensive than managing conventional funds, enabling us to charge the same for a service costing less to provide, and the proprietary funds in its portfolio also allow us to exact *two* tiers of management fee. The Investment Company Act in the United States and similar legislation elsewhere prohibit this kind of fund. . . .

'You have received Informograms explaining Performance Fees. We don't have to handicap our Reps by expressing our charges in a way that allows unfavourable comparison with our competition. . . .

'Funds that are at least seventy-five per cent owned by shareholders who are non-resident aliens, can retain net income and capital gains, whereas domestic funds are compelled to distribute earnings and gains. We therefore enjoy a price comparison advantage. . . . Retaining earnings and gains also increases assets under management, enhancing management fees. . . .

'Nor are our offshore funds strait-jacketed by laws prohibiting investment companies from borrowing money, buying on margin, selling short, lending fund assets, participating in underwritings and trading in new issues, commodities, real estate and securities of issuers in which their officers or directors have a financial interest. . . .

'Some of you have asked about the classification of WoF Program shares into class A shares and class B shares. Class A shares, which are sold to the public, carry no voting rights, unlike class B shares, which are retained by WoF. We don't anticipate differences arising with our clients, but it is prudent to retain control in case the *perception* of a conflict arises. . . .

'I wonder how many of you know about "give-ups"? Think of them as rebates from brokers. As ADB is the dealer of record for our sponsored funds, we can demand rebates of up to seventy-five per cent of brokers' commissions, depending on the size of the transaction. . . . Of course, we do not abuse our advantageous position by 'churning', trading stock purely to generate commissions. . . .'

Sleek did not allude to that offshore immunity allowing an investment firm to own both an investment bank and a mutual fund. Rumours were rife of Finance Bank and Entrepreneurs Bank flotations induced by bribes and finder's fees and of worthless paper not taken up by the public dumped on the sponsored funds, exciting the anger of those funds' managers. 'Jack put his foot down. He told Sleek that his portfolio was already stuffed with this junk and either to stop interfering in his investment decisions or get another portfolio manager. Sleek apologized. "Forget it and look on tomorrow as another day," he said. Would you believe it, three days later comes this block of Tramways promissory notes! Guess on whose instructions?'

*

Meanwhile, van Zilver directed his efforts at regenerating Asia II. He contacted Lucivius Williams in Lahore and worked with him at polishing his Close. He made a short detour into Afghanistan from Peshawar, found Hunter Sacks at the FAO office and worked with him at polishing his Close. He went to Karachi and demonstrated Closes at a hastily convened Financial Training Seminar, then, venturing into Sind with a briefcase full of referrals from Peace Corps volunteers, missionaries, Red Cross employees and aid workers, tapped, in the imaginative language of the *Bulletin*, the Oasis Market. He made a lightning visit to Kathmandu to tap the Diplomats and UN Markets there, then returned to Karachi to give another Financial Training Seminar. He made a whistle-stop visit to Meshed, then toured southern India, working the great importers, cotton merchants, bankers, discount houses, politicians, even soldiers and policemen. Everywhere that he went, he recruited, trained and sold. If Client needed a mutual fund with Multiple Endowment Protector for his wife and children, he sold him a Folkestone Plan. If Client required Additional Anonymity, he set up an Anonymous Depositors Bank Securities Safekeeping Account for him. If Client voiced a preference for Wider Diversification, he sold him a FoF Dynamic Growth Plan. If Client wanted an investment gratifying national conceit, he sold him Kapitalsfonds, Orbis Fund or Stars and Stripes Fund. If Client sought tax shelters and tax avoidance, he sold him Taxpayers Fund; if Growth Entailing An Element of Risk, Commodities Fund; if Something Specific to Look At, a Redevco apartment in Torremolinos or Honolulu. But the product that he knew and loved above all others, the product that he identified with and invested in himself, was the Fenner Biddup Offshore Fund. FBOF might not do best over the short term, but, over the long term, it was the best.

Occasionally, he encountered a prospect who was familiar with the data compiled by Arthur Wiesenberger & Company. Then he cheerfully cast aside FBOF's performance record and observed that judgements based on past performance alone overlooked the precautions taken by FBOF's management to diversify its portfolio beyond Wall Street.

Of late, he had been encountering prospects who wanted to know why the celebrated Fenner Biddup was no longer associated with FBOF. It was an awkward question, but he rose to the challenge. Fenner Biddup was merely a masthead, he said, a name around which management marshalled their expertise. Orchestrating the minute, delicate music of portfolio management was the work of analysts. The conductor might leave the podium, but the band played on. No one was really intimate with van Zilver, but the few whose acquaintance survived a Call Back sometimes imputed his success to a rich and flexible imagination.

His first encounter with Belvedere was at the General Post Office in Mysore. He had just emerged from the harrowing experience of a Self-Satisfied Industrialist Who Knows I Can Do Better and was in foul temper, violently upbraiding the parcel post clerk for refusing to frank his stamps. Belvedere, in the adjacent queue, was waiting to post a letter to Philippa requesting more money. He sauntered over to van Zilver and said, 'Can't you see that he scarcely understands English?'

'They steal them if you don't get them franked.'

'That may be, but you weren't being very nice to him, were you?'

'Did I raise my voice?'

'Why did you compare him to a chimp? Next time, try using a little courtesy.' Then, turning to the resentful clerk: 'How about overlooking Sahib's bad manners and franking these stamps for him, *tik hai*?'

'I can see that you know how to get things done,' said van Zilver. 'Let me treat you to a cup of coffee.'

Later: 'I take it that you already know something of our company?'

Belvedere alluded to his meetings with Hunter and Lucivius.

'Both decent chaps,' allowed van Zilver. 'Completely hopeless when it comes to presenting the product, though.' Then he made a presentation.

When he finished, Belvedere said, 'I thought you were going to tell me about the Folkestone Plan or Fiduciary of Fiduciaries. However, I can see that Fenner Biddup Offshore Fund is infinitely more formidable.'

'The Fenner Biddup Offshore Fund is the most exciting mutual fund in the world today. . . .'

Belvedere sighed. 'A vehicle.'

'. . . combining maximum diversification with maximum growth potential.'

'Assuming that I were to take you up on your offer, Mr van Zilver, then could I, too, represent the Fenner Biddup Offshore Fund?'

Van Zilver explained the System. 'When your Personal Volume reaches a million dollars, you move onto Branch Schedule. At two million, you rise to Regional and, at three million, to Divisional. Every Financial Counsellor expects eventually to become a General Manager. Each rise in Schedule increases your commission half a per cent and entitles you to buy more shares in WoF under its Stock Option Plan.'

'First you earn these commissions selling the company's Plans. Then you pay them back to the company to buy its stock?'

'Exactly. That's why WoF is *owned and run entirely by the men who created it*. Or at least it was until we went public.'

'Would I be free to hire others to work under me?'

'From day one.'

'What are the advantages there?'

'Overrides. A Manager on Branch Schedule supervising three active Associates on Trainee Schedule can expect to earn as much in Overrides as on his own sales. Put another way, he earns as much from Overrides without doing any work as each of his trainees earns working all the time. Our top Managers earn a million dollars a year in Overrides alone! The other advantage of hiring people to work under you is you get first pick of Referrals. Personally, I generate all of my own business and don't need Referrals, but some Managers keep them for themselves and never make a Cold Call.'

'How are my earnings taxed?'

'They are tax-free.'

'How do you avoid taxes?'

'One way is to pretend that you are fifty different people, each earning twenty thousand dollars, instead of one person earning a million dollars. Another way is to live outside the Territory.'

'And the Company goes along with these schemes?'

'Not only goes along with them; it encourages them.'

'It receives for its stock what the Government loses in taxes?'

'Neat, eh?'

'Who determines the price of shares in the Stock Option Plan?'

'There's a formula. After twenty years with the Company your shares vest. Then you can sell them on the open market.'

'I take it that market price is higher than formula value?'

'Always.'

'Thank you, Mr van Zilver. It's been interesting and instructive. I think I understand everything I need to know. I hope that you won't think that I've wasted your time.'

'When would you like to start?'

'Not soon. But if I should change my mind, where can I contact you?'

'What's to be decided later that can't be decided now?'

'Oh, rather a lot that has nothing to do with financial counselling.'

It was a variant of I'd Like to Think About It that was invincible. Not even Sign or Tear Up could prevail here. Van Zilver helped Belvedere to complete a New Man application form, subscribed his name and gave Belvedere his card. 'Send the form to me, together with a letter referring to our conversation. Then I'll contact *you*.' People at Processing were always intercepting New Man applications and claiming the New Man Bonus. 'Make your own investigation, but remember, no one's really enthusiastic about an idea until he's tried it.'

*

'Now, what's cooking this morning, Ginny?'
'Mr Rubin needs an obituary for 9187.'
'Who's 9187?'
Nelson glanced at the Personnel Record that his far-sighted secretary had brought to him.
'Any idea what he died of?'
'Isn't it on the file?'
'Nothing about it here.'

*

The news of 9187's death covered the entire front page of the *Gibson County Farmers Weekly*. Everyone who read it said it was the most complimentary obituary ever printed about anyone who had ever lived in Gibson County.

Lawrence Saxon Dies in India

Lawrence Saxon, affectionately known to his friends and University of Tennessee football fans everywhere as Bone, of Humboldt, died in his hotel room in Bombay, India on September 3rd after a brief illness.

Until his death, Mr Saxon was employed by World of Finance, the well-known international mutual fund organization. He was a sales representative. The former all-Southeastern Conference linebacker gave up his studies in his final quarter at UT to work in Bombay. He was mainly interested in welfare problems and looked upon his employment with World of Finance as providing him the chance of working among orphans, where he felt he was most needed. He had been in Bombay only a short while before he became ill. He died in his hotel room because he refused until the end to take his illness seriously.

While at UT Mr Saxon majored in Business Administration. He was a member of Sigma Alpha Epsilon fraternity and held the office of Rush Chairman during his junior year. It was his responsibility to organize his fraternity's annual Christmas party for orphans and as an active member of the Wesleyan Club he often volunteered to address boy scouts and other youth groups. He was elected Representative at Large for the University of Tennessee Student Body and in his senior year was tapped for Omega Delta Epsilon, an honorary leadership fraternity.

It is, however, for his performance on the football field that Bone will be best remembered. He was starting linebacker for the Big Orange from his sophomore year, and in his junior year was picked by the Association of Southern Sports Writers as first string All-Southeastern Conference and nominated for All-American. A leg injury put him out of action during his senior year. It was one of the greatest disappointments of Bone's football career that he was unable to play against Texas A & M in the Sugar Bowl.

Mr Saxon was buried in Bombay shortly after his death. The pastor of a local Methodist church, where he was attending services until his illness, conducted the funeral. A memorial service will be held next Tuesday at Bellevue Methodist Church in Humboldt.

Mr Saxon was a bachelor at the time of his death and an only child. He leaves his parents, Mr and Mrs Hays Saxon, and an uncle and aunt, Mr and Mrs Ned Saxon, all of Humboldt.

Most of the letters that Bone's parents received were exuberant tributes to their son. The letter from the company was signed by the President himself. It was the letter of mourning the company used for every WoF bereavement.

Lawrence was one of those to whom the client's interest always came first. His outstanding service to his many clients resulted in one of the finest quality business records of any Associate. His competence, initiative and creative energy were an inspiration to his clients and colleagues alike.

Coach Moose Henning, who loathed sentiment almost as much as he despised curfew-breakers, could not forebear stating that Bone was 'one of the finest defensive players I have ever had the privilege of coaching and one of the nicest fellows I have ever known'. Sarah McCallum's mother wrote, 'I know that you will bear with grace and fortitude this tragic loss. If there is anything I, or any member of my family, can do . . .', while Sarah wrote that 'words alone could never express how I feel'. Bone had always been her 'Number One, and it was so typical of him not to have advertised the fact that he was working with orphans in India'.

*

Belvedere carried on travelling. India paraded its gods: worshipped smoke-blackened idols enshrined in temples and caves, and as snakes, monkeys, elephants and cattle by a multiplicity of confusing names. He brushed his teeth with salt, bathed at public tanks, shaved with discarded razor blades. His food was that of the Indian village: yoghurt, mangoes, rice, chapathis, lentils and milk. The credulous population adored him with the veneration they reserved for itinerant ascetics, bowed their heads and saluted him with pressed palms. They stroked the back of his rucksack for *darshan* and pressed him to attend their marriage celebrations and theatrical performances. 'Come, *sahib*, take rest. Place honour,' they said, offering him a chair or a charpoy, while they squatted on the ground. Then he would sit like a king enthroned under a banyan and accept the homage of musicians thumping tom-toms, rattling timbrels and singing *bhajans* to him in hoarse, ecstatic voices.

'Carnatic is seat of ancient Dravidian civilization, sahib.'

'In Holy Veda, Lord Indra is God of War and Thunder, Bolt of Lightning, Supreme Lord of Devas, sahib.'

'Indra is bolt of lightning who empowers men to put women and dogs to sleep, sahib.'

Belvedere in raptures over nothing at all.

At Melkote, sacred to Vishnu, was the celebrated teaching platform of the venerable Ramanujacharya, 'the incarnation of Adisesha the Primal Snake and constant attendant of Vishnu, whose couch He was when Vishnu reclined and shade when Vishnu stood'.

At Sravana Belgola was the world's tallest monolithic Bahubali, 'the ideal ascetic who stood in meditation till the anthills arose at his feet and plants crept around his limbs'.

At Belur was the Temple of the Beautifully Coiffured One. 'May the god Kesava, whom the Shaivites worship as Shiva, the Vedantins as Brahma, the Buddhists as Buddha, the Naiyayikas as Kartha, the Jains as Arha, the Mimansahas as Karma, ever grant your desires.'

Belvedere wondered if this was not all that mattered, all that there was to make the dumb eloquent and the barren fruitful, these extrinsicalities of the Open Road, these fleeting moments lit with hilarity.

*

Bleitgeist held a sales meeting the evening he received the news of Fenner's dismissal. 'Shake-ups occur in all great sales organizations. Mr Biddup's departure changes nothing,' he said, addressing the nucleus of the Bombay organization, four men representing two opened Plans. The pacemakers were Harbinder Govinda, with volume at $3,000, a Dynamic Growth Plan he had sold to his cousin-brother, and Ram Pal Arjuna, whose father had bought a $1,000 Fully Paid.

'How many presentations have you made this week, Ramchandra?'

'It is very difficult finding prospects, sahib.'

'Are you using the Memory Jogs? Who owns the hotel nearest you? Who owns the *dukan* where you buy your milk and ghee?

'What about you, Mahendra? I suppose there's no point in asking about contacts via your wife. You probably don't let her leave the house.'

'She is illiterate, sahib.'

'I am not talking about *her*, Mahendra. I am referring to her friends. Who sold you the wedding ring? I'm told that weddings are pretty big deals around here. Have you tried selling your jeweller? Who fixes your watch?'

'I will do it, sahib. It is my duty.'

'Gentlemen, it's obvious that you aren't using your Memory Jogs. The company has gone to a great deal of trouble to provide these Memory Jogs. Now let's get cracking. Your earnings will be in direct proportion to the number of presentations you make. Who owns the store where you buy your chappals? Who operates the stand where you buy your newspaper?'

*

That same evening, 7111 reached Bombay. His swing through the Deccan had been so successful that he expected to reach Divisional as soon as Plans in the post opened.

He was confident that 5242 would accept terms. Only if he refused to cooperate would other means be brought to bear. 7111 was not a student of war, ancient or modern. His strategy's resemblance to the Battle of Dien Bien Phu was coincidental. He was merely manoeuvring for *de jure* recognition of what was already his *de facto*.

He took a taxi to Colaba, booked a room at the Salvation Army Hostel, consumed a plate of boiled rice and a bowl of vegetable soup in its dining room, then sat on his bed completing Client Index Cards for the day's take. Outside was all the hubbub and confusion of the Indian metropolis. Here was peace, privacy and a light bulb. The silence was broken by the faint murmur of a missionary couple in the adjacent cubicle saying their goodnight prayers.

*

'I've just heard from ADB, Mr McCool. It seems that another sixty thousand shares were thrown onto the market yesterday afternoon.'

'What's our cash position, Martha?'

'Around the eighteen million mark.'

'Okay, tell them to buy.'

'At yesterday's closing?'

'Affirmative.'

*

'They didn't fire Fenner for poor investment judgement. They fired him for embezzling Clients' money.'

'The schmuck!'

*

Mahe. The splash of sea on sand, the plop of a fallen coconut, rustling palm fronds splayed against a lavender sky and hermit crabs darting sideways along the bright sand. Gin-fogged eyes around a table at the beach bar of the Hotel des Seychelles.

'Sir Vyvyan, I have bad news. The prime minister has invited you to go fishing with him on Thursday.'

'Oh, bother! Wonder what he wants?'

'It's to do with arranging a place at Oxford for his nephew.'

*

A new Territory was a New Promise, a New Opportunity to Bleitgeist. Building his organization, recruiting a New Man here, training a New Man there, was always exciting. Losing Bone, his only effective trainee, however, was a destabilizing development and he had slipped back into exhausting old habits of anxiety and insomnia. A pandemonium of fears assailed him, lying in bed under the *punkah* after his sales meeting with Harbinder, Ram Path, Ramchandra and Mahendra.

Ingrid had instituted divorce proceedings against him for cruelty and desertion. Since when was arguing back cruelty? Didn't he pay the bills on time? And who deserted whom? Would she attach his commissions? Maybe he should ask WoF to pay them to a pseudonym? 'Inter-Office Memorandum to Nelson Rock, Subject: Divorce. What is the company's policy with respect to paying to pseudonyms commissions subject to legal attachment?'

His residual over Tennessee was about to lapse. Aggregate Trainee Volume remained stubbornly stagnant in Asia II. Delhi and Calcutta hadn't sent him a single Plan, despite five days of intensive Orientation. Maybe he ought to make a trip to Kabul? Iran remained shut, and he had heard nothing more from the Top of the Spirals about an Iranian National Fund. Still no response to his demands for Bumper's Activity Reports. How could he evaluate Potential if they didn't send him the Activity

Reports? Was Lucivius Williams a pseudonym or real? He had written to Williams on WoF stationery, introducing himself as the new Area Manager, and back came a curt reply on State Department stationery. 'Thank you for yours of August 10th, which is receiving attention.' Who wanted attention from that quarter? Was Bone's death ominous? Symptomatic of a destructive principle at large? Did his life have no higher purpose than getting rich, than selling bits of paper evidencing title to other bits of paper to obtain more of what he did not really need? Did he still sincerely want to be rich?

He fell asleep.

. . . *Lucivius held his free hand. He was handcuffed to a policeman. 'I believe that he's sorry for what he's done. Aren't you, Bob? Say you're sorry.'*

'I was only doing it to help our balance of payments.'

Lucivius beamed with pride. 'Why this guy's professionally patriotic. He's not in this racket just to make money. Just scratch beneath the surface, and you'll find every American is patriotic.' Then, leaning down, he whispered, 'E pluribus unum.' . . .

About four o'clock, as the sweepers began fanning out over the city with whisk brooms, Bleitgeist turned over onto his other side and, reaching for the sheet, pulled it over his round, bare shoulders.

'There is something else, Lucivius. Can you get Ingrid off my back?'

'She's after your stock, eh? Typical!'

'It's not my stock she's after, and ever since the Public Offering, it's been going down.'

'You have cause to be worried. Tennessee divorce courts are notorious for favouring the wife. Did you desert her because she was fat?'

'Food was the main thing with her. . . .'

A cup rattled in its saucer, and Bleitgeist awoke with a start. It was the servant with his morning tea.

He must pull himself together, he decided. Like Samson in the temple of Dagon, his world was collapsing around him. Now was the time to fight back, not concede defeat. Eschew resentments and, in Bone's heroic phrase, *push on*. The lower the price, the better the buy: wasn't *that* the essence of Vertical

Diversification? It was the same with life. There were Ups, and there were Downs. If he wasn't made of superior qualities, how could he have got where he was? How many WoFers made Divisional Manager? How many owned so much WoF stock?

He bathed, shaved and dressed, then read the *Hindustan Times* on the veranda.

Harbinder Govinda joined him at breakfast. Tom Stamp had such a trainee once. He called him Yul Brynner and used him to prove a ridiculous point at a Managers Conference workshop. Given the right circumstances, Stamp claimed, depilation could exert a positive influence in achieving Situation Control. But there were no two ways about Harbinder's hairlessness: it was an unmitigated disability, its most disconcerting aspect being the absence of eyebrows. '*Boy*! How he's able to get an interview?' Bleitgeist wondered, not for the first time. 'Some people will consent to see anybody.' Breakfast was better spent with his wife even. With Bone gone, though, Harbinder was now his main hope for the Bombay organization. This morning he was his usual plucky self.

'Now he is dead, you must be giving me Referrals you were giving to him.'

'How many times have I told you, Harbinder? Referrals are allocated strictly according to Volume.'

'But since he is not having them, you must be having more, isn't it?'

'I won't help you with Referrals until you reach Basic Schedule. Referrals are too valuable to waste on inexperience. Tell you what I'll do, though. I'll let you have the Maritime Market. I was saving it for Bone, as a present to help his spirits after his fever. But don't let on to the others, will you?'

'It is my duty, sahib!'

'And, for Pete's sake, try and break this habit of addressing white people as sahib. It smacks of servility. Remember, you are a Financial Counsellor.'

'It is habit.'

'Habit or not, it is unprofessional. All right, there's no reason why you shouldn't start at once. Here, let's see your kit.'

Bleitgeist indignantly removed a Redevco *What increased 23.5% in 1968? 'That'*s certainly no use to you! You think these guys want apartments in Spain or Hawaii? They are *seamen*.

They are already paying off one mortgage. They want intangibles, not another mortgage. . . . The main thing is to sell the captain. If he buys, you'll stand a good chance of selling the rest of the ship. I went through an entire super-tanker once just by disclosing that the captain was a Client. Even if he doesn't buy, you can still use his recommendation. "Captain, I can see how your own commitments don't warrant making an investment at this time. However, can you appreciate how fundamentally important it is for your men to understand the value of saving money?"'

*

Noam was breakfasting alone that morning, a mutual fund salesman among missionaries. The price of the lodging at the Red Shield included breakfast. He helped himself to extras of butter and marmalade, wolfed down a bowl of porridge and chased it with inordinate quantities of tea, liberally supplemented with milk and sugar.

Chota hazri for Belvedere that morning was a banana. He had spent the night in a house of the kind that cast such a pall over the last months of Bone's life, an intricate structure of beaten cooking-oil tins, scraps of timber, rags, asbestos and broken panes of glass patched and bound together with mud and string. It had an earthen floor and a palm thatch roof. It was part of a conglomeration next to a municipal dump.

His host, a young man with a pock-marked face and deformed foot, limped back to the road with him, past people relieving themselves. Women with saris raised above their working parts looked up and giggled. Children wearing nothing but G-strings scrambled about scooping up their droppings to use as fuel and mortar. One had to respect the motives of those who tried to alter such things, but their task seemed hopeless, thought Belvedere. India would *never* escape its poverty. If only his club-footed host could pick up a rucksack and walk away from that slum, as he was doing, instead of spending the whole hot day there studying to pass his Cambridge Certificate.

He reached the road and bade him goodbye, then repulsed several taxi drivers soliciting for fares. A Sikh gave him a lift into the city. He had much to see that morning – Colaba Cantonment, the Gateway of India, Crawford Market, Marine Drive, Victoria

Terminus, St Thomas Cathedral; the cranes brightly working in Byculla docks, as in 1928, when a P&O ship brought his parents out with a hearty troop of young planters, boxwallahs, civil servants, soldiers and their wives. He imagined how it was when the last British regiment left in 1947, the precision marching of the troops in khaki, the skirl of the bagpipes, the swinging, white-chevroned beefy arms and roar of a bristle-moustachioed sergeant major, the dramatic last steps at slow march, the crowds silently curious.

A chaos of railway lines, a blare of horns and film music, walls bright with gaudy advertisements, decaying balconies – somewhere in all that bustle, last seen and photographed with the other servants at the farewell garlanding ceremony on the veranda of the house at Poona, flanking his mother and father, were dear, coal-black Ayah with a ring in her nose and lank, dour, infinitely patient Khansaman. Ayah, who chased him around the garden and bathed him in a tin tub, and Khansaman, who dusted his patent leather shoes. Throughout the mixed emotions of the intervening years, he had never wavered in his conviction that they were saints. How sad, rolling back the mists, to think of them now, submerged in that immense floating multitude, ignorant of the proximity of their *chota sahib*.

*

Noam interviewed the Collector.

'Your opposite number in Madras asked me why *everyone* doesn't invest in the Fenner Biddup Offshore Fund. "Frankly, Mr Chaudhary, I had no answer. I don't know *why* everyone isn't invested in it.' He closed the Collector, who gave him a referral to the District Commissioner.

To the DC he said, 'No doubt you are wondering how you will be able to maintain your present standard of living and not become a burden on your sons. I know that a man in your position recognizes that the difference between an *old man* and an *elderly gentleman* is income.'

He closed the DC, who gave him a referral to the Governor.

To the Governor he said, 'Your Excellency, have you given any thought to what happens when your term of office runs out?'

*

Harbinder was less successful than 7111 that morning. First, he had trouble entering the port.

'Hey, *you* there! What are you carrying in that briefcase?'

'Only papers, Sergeant.'

'What kind of papers?'

'Pertaining to business I have in port. It is complex thing. It would not interest you. You would not understand it.'

'Where is your permit?'

'Permit?'

'You must have permit for entering port.'

'I am seeing in your face that you are honest soldier, Sergeant,' said Harbinder, reaching in his pocket for a five-rupee note and giving it to the sentry. 'So why you are causing me needless trouble? Businessmen have no time to arrange permits. They are too busy. You must be knowing, Sergeant.'

By the time he boarded a ship, his shirt was damp, the top unbuttoned, his tie loose and his briefcase heavy. From somewhere quite close came another menacing voice. 'Hey Charley, give Curly some chow before he steals something.'

A middle-aged man with grotesque hairy arms and pink hands, the galley-boy, waddled out onto the deck with a bowl of goulash, presented it to Harbinder and said, 'Don't swallow it all in one gulp.'

'And watch out he don't steal the bowl.'

Harbinder prided himself on having renounced caste taboos, but an appalling thought occurred to him. Was this *beef*?

'You selling sumpthin', buddy?' asked a deckhand in paint-splattered overalls.

'I am Financial Counsellor,' announced Harbinder.

'Yeah, and I'm the King of Guatemala. Wotcha selling, buddy?'

'You must be knowing World of Finance, isn't it?'

The sailor left in disgust.

Harbinder hurried to the taffrail and circumspectly tipped the goulash over the side.

Another prospect appeared. Harbinder proffered a FoF Quarterly Report. 'No need to buy now,' he said. 'Just look. I am Financial Counsellor.'

'Oh no you ain't. You're one of them mutual fund salesmen.'

'You must be knowing Fiduciary of Fiduciaries, sahib. Isn't it?'

'Is that an American fund?'

Hastily opening his briefcase, Harbinder produced a Stars and Stripes Fund Quarterly Report.

'This is American fund,' he said. 'We are representing it.'

The sailor in the paint-splattered overalls reappeared and scowled.

'I am showing your noble colleague Stars and Stripes Fund,' explained Harbinder.

'No kiddin'? And who told you you could come on board? Can't you read? *No Peddlers*.'

'Aw leave him alone, Hank.'

'All I want to know,' said Hank, 'is who let this ugly sonavabitch come on board?'

'How's your fund compare with Allied Investors Fund?'

'Allied Investors Fund?'

'Yeah, that's the fund I got shares in. How's it doing?'

'You gonna stand here and listen to this ugly sonavabitch?'

'Lemme hear what the mother has to say.'

'Fenner Biddup Offshore Fund is better than Allied Investors Fund,' replied Harbinder. 'Of ten leading mutual funds in world in 1968, Fenner Biddup Offshore Fund was top-runner, Fiduciary of Fiduciaries was next to top-runner, Stars and Stripes Fund was standing in fifth place of all leading mutual funds in world, isn't it?'

Hank grabbed Harbinder's briefcase and threw it overboard.

*

'It is very expensive and very difficult market to work. I am feeling it in my heart.'

'Of course you are, Harbinder. I know exactly how you feel. Losing your briefcase like that must hurt.'

'I am thinking Maritime Market is not my cup of tea.'

'Never judge a new market by first impressions,' counselled Bleitgeist. 'Okay, so you had a tough time. Treat it as a learning experience.'

11

SIR VYVYAN TO THE RESCUE

'Ultimately,' stated the *Bulletin*, 'the price of the stock will be decided not by the market's attitude to us today, or even six months from now, but by our expansion over the next decade. That is why the theme chosen for this last year of the decade is Total Financial Service.'

When the price slipped below $14, Baroque proclaimed that the shares were worth at least double that and would probably hit $50; he predicted that WoF was 'destined to become the most important economic force in the world'.

His off-the-record discussions with Sleek, however, were not sanguine. The clouds were gathering: the ignominious expulsions, the long stock market slump, the parasitical Performance Fees, the swindles masquerading as underwritings and property trading, rising costs and the Key Associates' rejection of a Self-Denying Ordinance, the proceeds of the Public Offering squandered on financing tax shelters and supporting WoF's share price, then pledging the shares bought as collateral for Key Associates' loans, Reps' disillusionment when they cashed in their stock options, FBOF's loss of its eponymous founder, shareholders' disillusionment on liquidating their retirement Plans, and the Securities and Exchange Commission now breathing down their necks; bloodhounds were straining their leashes at the floodlit boundaries of the prison, the barometer was falling, the skies darkening.

'Something had better give quick, or I'm going to take the money and run for it. The rest of you guys can look after yourselves. You'd think that, with more than two billion dollars under management, we could at least make a profit.'

'The insurance subsidiary is making a profit.'

'Hell, Sleek, you know that's only because of DGPINS.'

'Sales are thirty per cent up on this time last year.'

'That's *face* Volume. The sales company's bleeding us to death.'

'We're making almost a million a year from the share hocking operation.' Sleek was alluding here to loans of securities to brokers needing them for quick deliveries.

'What's our cash position?'

'Just below fourteen million at nine this morning.'

'Are we still supporting the price?'

'Absolutely.'

'Can't we shift some of the burden?'

'Shift it where?'

'Onto the staff, for example. They responded beautifully to our whisper campaign in August about it being a wonderful investment.'

'A lot of them are deterred by the Interest Equalization Tax.'

'That didn't deter them when Management was hot.' Baroque here was alluding to the flotation of twenty per cent of WoF Management Company. 'Anyway, what's the Interest Equalization Tax got to do with all those Swedish, German and Swiss secretaries? What's been done about them?'

'We sent around an Officegram. Not many of them are exempt. It depends on whether they're technically resident.'

'Can't we call in some of these loans?' Baroque here was alluding to loans to Key Associates. 'What happened to the money *they* got from the underwriting?'

'They used it, plus the money we lent them, to buy more stock. They were furious at having to redeem even ten per cent. Now nobody wants to sell at the current price.'

'Foreclose on the bastards!'

'Not a viable option,' replied Sleek. 'Besides, the indebtedness might come in handy if there's a palace revolt.'

'Has anyone troubled to total up these loans?'

'Yeah, 19.9 million. If we also include loans to people like Sir Harvey, it's 28 million.'

'So, thus far we've spent how much supporting the shares?'

'10.7 million.'

'And the only collateral for these loans is more shares? Like we can't call in the loans for fear of forcing them to sell the stuff, while money received in repayment of the loans has to be ploughed back into the stuff to support its price? *Beau*tiful! We lose no matter what we do, right?'

The Founder had travelled far since PS 112 and recalled that period of his life with the same distaste as Ingrid remembered layering and highlighting. He wasn't about to condemn himself to penury just because someone had goofed and discreetly unloaded a parcel of shares. The price tilted, further eroding the confidence of outside investors, including bankers and stockbrokers privy to the knowledge that the price was now approaching foreclosure ceilings for shares bought on margin.

*

Bleitgeist returned from an excursion into the *mofussil* feeling rather pleased. He had been at an AID site opening up the Hardhats Market, and there were other aluminium-hatted electricians and bricklayers, German as well as American, at other sites scattered around the *mofussil*.

A message on notepaper inscribed *From the desk of Noam van Zilver* was waiting for him at his hotel. Bleitgeist recognized the name, Salesman of the Year in the Year of Growth, awarded the Golden Tie Clasp for Entrepreneurial Excellence in the Year of Professionalism. Bleitgeist rarely made the Bonus List. Van Zilver was always on it. Wasn't he Bumper's trainee? Hadn't he left the Territory? Hadn't he relocated to Africa II? What was he doing in Bombay?

The message proposed a meeting and its tone was friendly, but Bleitgeist was cautious. Could you *ever* trust a Bonus List leader? Probably not, but did he have a choice if the fellow was in his Territory. He pondered the question further and decided that, on balance, the implications were favourable. Most of these Bonus List leaders were migratory types, always relocating, never content to stay put. Perhaps a bout of unpleasantness in Kenya had brought him questing back to Asia II. Well, if he wanted to work in Asia II, a place could be found for him – Andhra Pradesh, for instance.

Bleitgeist unpacked his bag and hung up his blue Madras jacket and green cotton trousers, stacked his pressed shirts in the chest of drawers, undressed, put on slippers and pyjamas, then sat down in the big armchair to savour the last, sweet essences of the past few days. Should he call down to the bar for a *nimbu pani*? He thought not. He sat and reviewed his recent Closes and his battered old heart filled once more with the euphoria of optimism. Then the buzzer sounded.

Who could be calling at this hour? Many years before, when only on Senior Schedule, an enraged client had called on him at such a late hour and accused him of concealing the Front Load. That man wanted to cancel a $30,000 DGPINS. Bleitgeist had already sent his application and cheque to Processing, and a scene followed of such unpleasantness that it had permanently coloured his associations with late callers. He rose, put on a dressing gown and opened the door.

'I've found you at last! I've been looking everywhere for you! I tried your door half a dozen times, at least! But you were always out. I began to wonder if you really existed. Is this a convenient time to call? You look as though you were about to drop off.'

Bleitgeist recognized the style. 'It has been a long day,' he said wearily. 'However, I am always glad to welcome a fellow WoFer. What can I do for you?' he asked after a brisk shaking of hands.

'I could come back tomorrow?'

'I wouldn't consider it. Come in. I mean, you are welcome tomorrow, of course, but you are also welcome tonight. I'm very glad to meet you.'

'And I am glad to meet you, Bob. May I call you Bob?'

The two men sat and stared at each other benignly. With so much in common, so much that was hidden from others, in daily communion with the same great Concepts, it was as though words were superfluous. Each waited for the other to Open.

'Seen any good films lately?' parried Bleitgeist.

'I never have time for the flicks.'

'Me neither. I mean, I never have time for the flicks, either.'

'I saw *The Sound of Music* four or five months ago,' said van Zilver.

'Was it good?'

'It was okay. Depends really on what you're looking for.'

'I heard that it was pretty good.'

'It was better than *Oklahoma*.'

'No kidding!'

Bleitgeist had nothing at hand to offer his adventitious guest and suggested summoning a beer from reception, but van Zilver declined it. 'Never touch the local hooch,' he said.

'I rarely drink myself.'

Bleitgeis offered van Zilver a cigarette. Another gaffe. This fellow, he decided, was the austere type. Not at all like the usual run of WoFers.

Once past these preliminaries, they began talking shop.

'What's your technique with I Don't Believe You?'

Van Zilver repeated what he had said in the Keynote Address at a Regional Managers Conference. 'Closing the credibility gap is often the first step in a presentation, especially with people accustomed to low, fixed-interest returns on capital. I show annual reports, newspaper clippings and our advertisements to prove that we are an established, highly reputable firm.'

'That's exactly what I try to impress on my trainees,' said Bleitgeist. 'How many presentations do you make a day?'

Van Zilver repeated what he had said at a Millionaires Conference. 'My target is a minimum of a dozen client calls a day, including Cold Calls, Call Backs, Referrals and Service Calls. Such a schedule demands advance planning, organization of time and tremendous hard work. It all boils down to the question every WoFer has to ask himself. Am I really serious about wanting to sell more than a million dollars a year?'

'Is a million your target?'

'It's my *minimum* target.'

'What do you sell mostly,' asked Bleitgeist, visibly awed; 'FoF, FBOF, Stars and Stripes Fund, Kapitalsfonds, Orbis Fund, Commodities Fund, Taxpayers Fund or Folkestone Plan?'

Almost all my business is in Fenner Biddup Offshore Fund. But, of course, I tailor the Plan to Client's Need.'

'Of course! What proportion of your business is Fully Paids, and what proportion is contractual?'

'My estimate is roughly one Fully Paid to every five DGPs.'

'You do a lot of insurance business?'

'Not nearly enough.'

'What's your technique with I Can Do Better?'

'The very first person I ever called on thought that, Mr Worth, and not two months later, I'm sorry to say, his creditors forced him into liquidation.'

It was van Zilver's turn now to question Bleitgeist. 'What's the Market like here?' he asked.

Bleitgeist described it in lyrical terms.

'Are you having much success with Parsees?'

'They are a special enclave requiring special handling, a niche market.'

'How are you doing with the Hardhats Market?'

'I have just returned from a pioneering investigation. The untapped potential there is immense.'

'And the other Expatriate Markets?'

'Wide open.'

'Assam?'

'Completely virgin, unpenetrated. I'm told that some of the tea planters up there bank half their pay.'

'Calcutta?'

'I was there in September. It's a real gold mine. Absolutely crawling with European technicians.'

'The Carnatic?'

'Completely untouched and ripe for picking.'

'The Eastern Ghats?'

'Ditto.'

'Rajasthan?'

'Another untapped pot of gold.'

'Orissa?'

'Anyone who can speak German would make a fortune.'

'Tell me something about your Bombay operation. How many men have you here?' asked van Zilver.

'Four.'

'All Indians?'

'I'm afraid so,' admitted Bleitgeist.

'What's their Volume? Two hundred thousand? Three hundred thousand?'

'Nowhere near that, yet.'

'My policy with what I call In-Name-Only Associates, Bob, is termination. They set a bad example for other Reps and create Task Confusion by asserting claims to Markets they aren't exploiting.'

'Yeah, but we're still in the Pioneer Phase, Noam, and these people are tremendously sensitive about job security. They'd bear a grudge against you if you fired them.'

'Any activity in Delhi?'

'I've recruited an Australian there, but he's still a Pre-Icebreaker. His wife's the problem. She's terrified that they won't have enough money to pay their fare back to Australia if he gives up his job to work for us, and, from what I've seen of him, she may have a point. What's your Reluctant Wife Technique?'

'At the very first interview you have to share your enthusiasm for the company. If the husband is sufficiently impressed, he can usually overcome a wife's objections. It's essential to follow up his recruitment with proper training, ideally a Financial Training Seminar concluding in a written examination, and then to start him selling right away. He will begin earning money in a relatively short time. When a wife sees her husband's income grow, she will become his new profession's most ardent supporter. The women behind many of our most successful Counsellors have started out as Reluctant Wives.'

'Look, Noam,' said Bleitgeist, 'are you sure you won't have that beer?'

'Well, perhaps this once,' replied van Zilver in a spirit of compromise.

The beer came, and the two men chatted on about Techniques. Then van Zilver said, 'I'm glad we've had this opportunity to break the ice. Frankly, I was worried that we might clash. Some Managers are completely unreasonable where Territory is concerned.'

'I'm glad, too, Noam. I appreciate your laying your cards on the table. Anybody's open with me, I'm open with him. I take it that you'd like to work in the Territory? Go right ahead. Welcome aboard. I only regret that I can't give you any Referrals. You'll be on your own, but that won't bother a go-getter like yourself, eh?'

'The best test of a real salesman is whether he can generate his own Referrals.'

'Just let me have a list of your sales.'

'I ought to tell you, Bob, I've been working in India for the past month and have recruited and trained men in Chandigarh,

Ludhiana, Patiala, Kanpur, Benares, Patna and Bhagalpur. We have rival organizations.'

'You must be joking! *One man* is in charge in Asia II, and *that's me!*'

'Have you forgotten the commitment that you made when you joined WoF, the Fourth Article of the WoF Code of Ethics? "I pledge myself to cooperate with all WoF Associates in promoting the principles of sound Financial Planning and shall continually strive to improve the quality of the service we provide."'

'The Code of Ethics has never meant a great deal to me. I give it a certain prominence at Orientation and then forget it. In fact, in my long experience with WoF, you're the first person to invoke the Code.'

'Systematic analysis of Total Financial Service in the Territory demonstrates the need for a unified approach to its problems, Bob.'

'I'll admit that you hold some trump cards,' said Bleitgeist. 'However, I'm not sure that we're compatible.'

'Let's discuss the possibilities.'

'What kind of deal have you in mind?'

*

4th day out of Mahe. Wind SSE at 14 knts. A dozen dolphins have been with us this morning. They swim alongside, dive under the bow, then reappear on the other side. Fascinating to watch. . . . Unable to take a sun sighting at noon because the sky was overcast. About 1600, I managed to take a sighting, and it was very disappointing. We have made only 134 miles easting in three days, and normally we should have made that in 24 hours. Our slow progress was due to a heavy head sea and messing about with puffs of wind most of yesterday, tacking and getting nowhere. I suspect that at one time we were even going backwards.

*

There was no letter from Philippa at Poste Restante, but, more disturbing, Belvedere's traveller's cheques were missing. Who took them?

He was also staying at the Red Shield. Could a burglar have slipped through the gap above the partitions between his and the adjacent rooms? Van Zilver occupied one of the rooms, an aged missionary and his wife the other. Belvedere rejected these suspects as implausible.

Had a member of the staff taken them? One of the cleaners perhaps? The hostel was closed to outsiders during the middle of day. Should he inform the manager, a brawny Mancunian whose love for the trombone had lured him into the Salvation Army?

Events clouded his memory. So much had happened in the last fortnight. When had he last seen the cheques? He had exhibited them for the immigration officials at Cochin. Had he returned them to his sleeping bag? When did he last unroll his sleeping bag and put his toes inside? Poona? No, not Poona. Anyhow, a thief couldn't have extracted them from the sleeping bag with him in it. They were in the zipped pouch with his razor and address book. When had he last shaved? Events slowly slotted into chronological sequence. It was at Belgaum that he last unzipped. The cheques must have been there, else he would have noticed. What had happened since Belgaum? There had been many lifts, many encounters, many dark and fleeting opportunities for a thief. But a thief would have nicked the whole pouch.

He mentioned the loss to van Zilver at breakfast. The Dutchman was not sympathetic. 'It's a pity you didn't invest this money in Fenner Biddup Offshore Fund,' he said. 'I shouldn't bother reporting it to the police. Demand a refund from the issuer and open a twenty-five dollars a month FBOF Dynamic Growth Plan. You will never look back. Now, if you will excuse me, I have work to do.' He had finished his second bowl of porridge.

Belvedere had already considered demanding a refund. However, the issuer's nearest office was in Calcutta. Nor had he proof of purchase or the cheques' numbers. 'Must you go at once?' he asked van Zilver.

'I have a busy day ahead, ten Cold Calls and a Call Back.'

'Really,' said Belvedere, giving him a flirtatious wink. 'Are you in such a tearing rush that you can't help a poor laddie down on his luck?'

'Make it brief,' said van Zilver.

'D'you remember that offer you made to me in Mysore? Do I recall correctly that your company pays cash on the nail for Plans sold?'

The two men retired to the hostel's common room, and there, among Third World publicity handouts and pictures of famished and unhappy children, Belvedere completed another New Man application form and signed it.

'Just how much time do you expect to devote to selling mutual funds?' asked van Zilver.

'As much as it takes to get me out of this jam.'

'I recognize that it is unreasonable to expect you to feel keen at this stage, but do not relax until you have mastered the technique.'

'How long will that take?'

'I've known New Men who were proficient in hours and others who have taken up to a week.'

'I might take a week,' admitted Belvedere.

'Have you friends in Bombay? It can be a great help if you know someone.'

He knew only the slum dweller with the deformed foot and the Mancunian trombonist.

'A pity, because we have an excellent technique with friends. You tell me the names of your friends, and I tell you the names of mine. Then we sell to each other's friends. But you'll soon get the knack. Is Belvedere your real name? . . . I was thinking of assuming it when I shed my current pseudonym. Now, please excuse me. I have a small errand. I won't be five minutes.'

Van Zilver left and returned with Belvedere's traveller's cheques.

'The cheek!' exclaimed Belvedere.

'It was obvious that you would not appreciate the seriousness of financial distress until you experienced it.'

'You saw the Need?'

'And acted.'

That morning Belvedere outfitted himself at a tailor's with short trousers, a 'safari' shirt, high ribbed stockings and new Bata shoes; van Zilver also bought him a briefcase. Manager and New Man then made a Cold Call on the Chairman of the Chamber of Commerce, who opened a $36,000 DGPINS and gave them four Referrals.

'See,' said van Zilver, 'it's dead easy. Always remember, he's not doing *you* a favour. You're doing *him* a favour. You can start with the ships in port. It wouldn't do to turn you loose on land before you are fully trained.'

'I know. I'd only spoil the Market.'

*

Belvedere began work next morning and reported to van Zilver that evening, his first Progress Report.

'I ran into stiff opposition at the gate. The guards demanded my permit.'

'How did you get past them?'

'I made a Group Presentation.'

'Did you close them?'

'Not yet. I'm bringing them a Fenner Biddup Offshore Fund prospectus tomorrow. What really impressed them was Vertical Diversification. Then I boarded a Japanese ship. Only the mate spoke English. He agreed with everything I said, bowing every few seconds, like someone at ballet exercises.'

'That's no good. It gives you nothing to grab onto.'

'So I discovered.'

'The next ship was Italian. They were very chummy, invited me to lunch and we drank gallons of *vino bianco*. My presentations were rather droopy in consequence. Italians face an insurmountable problem. Currency control of the lira'

'No problem. I'll show you how it's done.'

'The next ship was French. No joy there either: endemic scepticism. It was almost dark when I left them. Then I found a Greek ship, and things began to heat up. Whoever would have thought old Crabby Cleever's dithyrambs were destined for unit trust presentations?'

'You closed?'

'Three $12,000 DGPINSes. After I closed Platon Papadopoulos, his friends Aristotle Meimorides and Constantine Christianakis had to have Plans, too, couldn't be restrained. Then we drank retsina and danced.'

'There were women on board?'

'No fear. We danced with each other, in the Greek way.'

'Did you get the cheques?'

'Two Bank Instruction Letters. Platon and Constantine have bank accounts in Texas. Aristotle paid in cash. I'm going back tomorrow to sell the Third Engineer, Solon.'

*

8th day out of Mahe. The dense fog that enveloped *Luna* for most of the week has now lifted. Tea at 1600 hrs. Pimms at sundown.

Sir Vyvyan on the poop smoking his pipe, watching the constellations on their voyages and rejoicing in sweet reminiscences of quite trivial triumphs. At 2100 hrs, a navigational reading. 'Easting now 12° a day.' Ovaltine made with powdered milk and late to bed.

The sun rose over a mild sea. Very light winds alternating between calms and light puffs. Breakfast at 0800 hrs. The vault of sky was a mirror of cast metal. Lunch at noon.

*

The professional flatterers at the Top of the Spirals were heaving it to the Top Managers assembled for the Fourteenth Annual Leadership Conference.

Sir Harvey Nobody: 'You succeed because you have a constantly inquiring mind, the gift for innovation, the ingenuity to meet the challenges of today with the solutions of tomorrow. You have shown financial sophistication in the creation of your products, patterned to serve your clients in the international market. You have harnessed the computer to your needs. You have harnessed all that is modern in the twentieth century and invented a great deal of what is applicable to your business. For the Leadership that has brought you to this conference, I salute you, and I want you to know how very proud I am to be part of you.'

Peter Gass: 'Your company has discovered the simplest, most effective way to maintain fund performance – by promoting competition among fund managers. I can assure you that every one of our portfolio managers is keenly aware, not only how our funds are doing, but how they are doing in relation to other funds. That competition is intense, and it's going to get tougher. As the years pass, this competition will continue to improve the calibre of our portfolio managers and keep WoF funds far in the lead.'

Alfonso Ventoso, President of Panama: 'This company's growth is accelerated by Creative Thinking, Hard Work and Leadership, which embodies a drive for success that is part of everyone in this organization. Future growth depends on how much success drive you can impart to everyone you recruit and supervise.'

Herb Beck: 'People have often said to me, "How lucky you were to join WoF in the early days, to get in on the ground floor. That was the time of opportunity." The fact is, the opportunities for growth and advancement in our company are greater today than ever before. We have learned from our experience. We know the way to success and have the tools to achieve it. After all, luck is only a preparation to meet opportunity.'

Sleek McCool: 'Corporations spend a great deal of time and effort creating a public image. Our objective is to let the public know exactly what WoF is, as we know it – the world's largest company in the mutual fund field. A company with more completely trained, better qualified representatives than any similar company in the world. WoF offers the most complete range and best quality of financial planning products. This is a picture of Leadership, Solidity and tremendous Dynamism.'

Nelson pitched in with: 'All of us at WoF are here for just two reasons: to devise the best products that experience, wisdom, ingenuity and imagination can offer your clients; and to give you the best service we can. Everyone works hard to give you the back-up you need to do your job well.'

*

Van Zilver was too busy to attend the Leadership Conference that year. His deal with Bleitgeist recognized the two Managers' shared interest and defined their respective powers. Like Henry of Canossa, Bleitgeist acknowledged the Dutchman as his supervisor but retained the Override on all others working in Asia II, including Belvedere. Van Zilver got GM over Bleitgeist's DM but undertook to recruit and train Reps on Bleitgeist's behalf and to lend him support in disputes with the Top of the Spirals.

Bleitgeist derived great comfort from this arrangement. He relished van Zilver's professionalism and enjoyed the rare experience of working with a colleague he could respect. Van Zilver introduced him to Markets he could not have tapped, to ranking politicians, generals, businessmen, film stars and India's most prominent literary agent, a very with-it maharaja. He imparted an exotic lifestyle to selling that lifted it above the mundane repetition of Model Closes: chauffeured passages through stone gates where uniformed guards rose to full turbaned height and saluted smartly, and palace interiors that were all teak, silver candlesticks and oil paintings. They hit the Diplomats and the UN Markets in Delhi and the Foreign Bankers and Importers and Exporters Markets in Calcutta. Van Zilver generated more business than he could handle himself, and Bleitgeist captured the overspill.

When van Zilver left him at Calcutta to open up East Pakistan, Bleitgeist bade him a joyous Happy Prospecting farewell and returned to Bombay to a report of yet another drop in the price of WoF shares.

*

Noon in Byculla. Flags hanging limp from mastheads and stern jacks, longshoremen asleep under boxcars. Belvedere had been busy all morning making presentations.

'Dear boy, I never expected to see you again – and here, of all places, here you are in Bombay peddling unit trusts.'

The two friends had lots to talk about over asparagus *au beurre*, gulls' eggs, scotch broth and venison St Hubert: Kipling, E. M. Forster and John Masters for starters. Belvedere told Sir Vyvyan about his many wonderful encounters of the past six months, starting with the girl passing out Folkestone Plan literature at Victoria Station.

'Why it must have been my niece, my brother Theo's youngest child, Daphne.'

'She never introduced herself. Funny, I can't remember what she looked like.'

'Not a face to remember. She tried to sell me an insurance policy. Pursued me from port to port, like a U-boat. When I *think* of the *trouble* I've had evading that girl!'

Noting that Sir Vyvyan had a new deckhand, Belvedere asked about Raul.

'There, dear boy, hangs a melancholy tale. Having perpetrated new outrages at every port, the young blackguard crowned his misdeeds by deserting.'

Belvedere inquired cautiously after Sir Vyvyan's writing.

A storm blowing up off the Maldives causing *Luna* to ship water had forced Sir Vyvyan to choose between a crate of Malvern water and his manuscripts. 'It's a *great* weight off my chest,' he admitted. 'Best decision I ever made. Should've chucked the lot years ago.'

They talked gravely and at length about new fiction. Was there really nothing Belvedere could recommend?

No, said Belvedere. Alas, unit trusts absorbed him. He explained the Concept and concluded, 'So, you see, it's possible to combine a high return on capital with the other attributes of a sound investment: security, exemption from tax, freedom from the vexations of administrative correspondence, liquidity, transferability upon death, feasibility in small outlays and, most important of all, Vertical Diversification.'

'I can see that you sincerely believe in your merchandise,' said Sir Vyvyan. 'I wonder, dear boy, if you could spare me one of your prospectuses? Or should I say prospecti?'

Belvedere gave him half a dozen.

'Well, I have to nip off now,' he said after *figues en pernod*. 'Must be getting back to banks and how they make money. See you tomorrow.'

*

The inflation index rose that October, and the Department of Commerce predicted that 'higher prices [were] likely to continue for some time before peaking'. The purchasing power of currency declined correspondingly, and everyone who had ever thought about debased currency knew that the smart way to make money in such moments was to borrow to buy into equities. It was called leveraging. Thus money pouring into the exchanges as a hedge against inflation, much of it from pension and insurance schemes, chased fewer and fewer equities, forcing up share prices until they bore no plausible relationship to earnings.

Anxious to reduce the currency in circulation, while unable to cut its spending, the Government imposed new stringencies on credit, triggering a dip in the market. Then a further rise in interest rates caused another dip. A chorus of distinguished economists paid tribute to the Government for 'responsible management of the economy', but WoF Leadership was furious. A bear market meant poor fund performance, diminished Volume and defections from the Sales Force.

*

Evening in Bombay. Sir Vyvyan on *Luna*'s poop under a mosquito net, naked save for a strip of *chadar* around his waist, mildly intoxicated and re-reading *The Nigger of the Narcissus*. The sky was misty, the air muggy. There was no breeze. Lights from ships moored alongside and floating at anchor, tinsels of silver light on black water. The aroma of lamb roasting in the galley.

Belvedere strode on board, parked his briefcase on the coamings, went below, mixed himself a cocktail, tasted it and approved the ingredients, then joined Sir Vyvyan and waited. He knew that he could rely on the noble knight to reopen the topic.

Presently: 'I have been doing some calculations, dear boy. Looking at your minimum Dynamic Growth Plan for investing $3,000 in monthly instalments of $25, starting with a minimum deposit of $50, I see that your company pays itself $162.50 from the first $325 remitted to it as an Acquisition Charge, and further pays itself $8 as an Administration Fee. Moreover, in "addition to the fees specified", it says in a footnote in small print, WoF *may* charge an "annual service fee of $1.50, either on every Plan or on Plans where the investor falls behind schedule". Does your company, in fact, levy this extra *annual service* fee?'

'I haven't the faintest.'

'In view of the prevailing uncertainty, let us assume that it does. In which case, of the first $1000 paid into the Plan, World of Finance retains a whacking $530 and applies $470 to the purchase of shares in an investment "especially designed to provide sound financial planning for peoples of all nations".'

'The Front Load,' confirmed Belvedere.

'Is *that* what you call it?'

'The acquisition charge diminishes after the first thirteen instalments,' said Belvedere.

'To seven-and-a-half per cent of amount invested. And here we are assuming, are we not, that World of Finance won't increase the service fee. And what happens after these charges? What happens to the customer's money once it's "invested"?'

'Surely, you don't begrudge the experts something for their advice?'

'Tell me frankly, don't you think that three million dollars for allocating money between FoF house accounts is extortionate? . . . Then there are brokers commissions and "incidental expenses". They, too, are defrayed out of the funds' assets.

'But the truly horrifying part of the story is this system of remunerating itself, I quote, "solely on the basis of *true performance*, only out of Fund profits, if any." Let me show you how this works in practice.'

Belvedere began to feel uneasy. He was aware that the front load was heavy, but he had not thought about Performance Fees.

'I don't suppose that you have had the pleasure of meeting Financial Counsellor Grigio?' continued Sir Vyvyan. 'Do you remember that day you called on me before you left Barcelona? You came to see me about looking after your skis for you. We were having lunch and some wretched fellow tried to intrude. Do you remember?'

'Yes, of course. You expelled him.'

'*That* was Financial Counsellor Grigio. He tried to interest me in an investment in Fiduciary of Fiduciaries. He spoke warmly, one might say enthusiastically, of the mineral prospecting rights to millions of acres in the Arctic leased from someone who had leased them from the Canadian Government. He said they contained "the key to the shortfall in our energy supplies". I don't know where he got that from. Something he picked up from your promotional literature I expect. I was sufficiently impressed to consider putting money into this venture. Well,' said Sir Vyvyan indignantly, 'it seems that the whole thing was a kind of trick to create what they call "Performance Fees" to boost their profits. Ten million dollars these scoundrels paid themselves, all on the strength of a sale *between themselves on credit.*

'My bankers looked thoroughly into the whole disgraceful affair. Exact computation is not possible, as detailed accounts have not been published. However, deducing the figures from WoF's annual reports and other data that I am about to show you, FoF's portfolio sustained management fees, brokerage commissions and other expenses amounting to about four per cent of average net assets in 1967 and four and a half per cent in 1968. And that was *before* the venture into "natural resources". The system was so lucrative that it already accounted for more than three-quarters of your company's revenues. Now comes this Nullabor charade. No, dear boy,' concluded Sir Vyvyan triumphantly, 'I am afraid that the evidence rather strongly suggests that you have been *had*. Do they owe you any money in unpaid commissions?'

'About four hundred pounds.'

'Does your contract with them allow you something on account? What can you claim from them *now*?'

Belvedere explained about Advances.

'And can your new boss, this Blight the Spirit chap, advance you this money?'

'He can.'

'Then go get it, dear boy. Go to Mr Blight the Spirit and claim your Advances. Tell him, if necessary, that you are impatient to invest in the Fenner Biddup Offshore Fund or the Fiduciary of Fiduciaries or whatever, but *get the money*! Then report back to me.'

For the first time in his life, Belvedere did as he was told. The operation was almost as prosaic as all others of his WoF experience. Bleitgeist offered no resistance. 'I think it's a fine thing when a New Man still raw and on Trainee Schedule, just after becoming an Icebreaker, shows enough confidence in our Products to want to invest in them himself,' he said. 'It proves to me, as well as to the Company, that he's serious about becoming a Manager himself one day. It shows that he genuinely believes in what he's doing and in the very real advantages of entrusting his money to the safekeeping of people of proven ability to manage it for him. Belvedere, it makes me very, very proud to present you with your very first WoF commissions cheque. My sincere congratulations on your success to date and the best of luck in your future career.'

12

APOCALYPSE

The *Wall Street Monitor* printed the maiden exposé of Operations Thaw and Outback on Thanksgiving morning. Other newspapers followed suit, giving credence to the contention that the financial press always acted in concert. Baroque and Sleek decided to discontinue supporting WoF's shares and the price plunged below margin levels. Banks called in their loans, engendering a stampede of sell orders. WoF's clients, alarmed by the adverse publicity, began redeeming their investments in the sponsored funds. Portfolio managers unloaded unlisted securities and discovered that they were worth a fraction of the values imputed to them; many had to be written off as worthless. The WoF Board of Directors went into session.

The SEC seemed vindicated. What was their function, if not to protect the ordinary man from fraud? Not so, said Baroque. The SEC were 'a lot of mean-spirited men with too little to do'. Preventing WoF's collapse was nothing less than 'preventing the collapse of Capitalism'.

Aggressively untruthful in attack, he was even more so in defence. 'Conspiratorial forces were at work.' 'A consortium of American, Swiss, British, Japanese and German banks was waging a concentrated bear raid with the tacit approval of their governments.' 'Governments had always harboured a hatred of WoF.' 'Speculators were selling the shares short. Buyers should demand the certificates.' 'To suggest that the company was out of money was a pernicious lie. It had enough cash in hand to buy back all the publicly owned stock fourteen times at existing prices' – and long after the Apocalypse was over Key Associates would pretend, as much to themselves as to anyone, that WoF had been the victim of conservative prejudice and senseless errors of judgement, rather than allow that they were accessories to an operation that was comprehensively dishonest.

WoF shares opened at $7 on 7 December, Pearl Harbor Day, and, by close of trading, the dealer at Banque Flonck had marked them down to $6.

Reporters were now barricading the doors outside the Top of the Spirals. While conceding that a plausible case might be made for stiffening controls on company spending, Baroque deplored 'the adverse publicity that has caused so much harm to the small investor'. The press reported that WoF was 'putting its house in order', and the shares rallied a little. On Wednesday, they fell back to Friday's closing at $5 and opened at $4.50 on Thursday.

The WoF Board considered retrenchment measures. As the price of shares was a function of earnings, why not recycle part of the company's equity into debt obligations and distribute earnings over a smaller number of shares? Why not direct the sponsored funds to buy the shares? Why not sell one of the subsidiaries for more than book value and demonstrate thereby that WoF's assets were undervalued? Why not sell the rest of the management subsidiary? As soon as investors realized that WoF had severed its interest in managing the sponsored funds, redemptions would cease and sales resume. 'The basic WoF Concept remains sound,' declared Baroque.

On Friday, 11 December , the shares plunged to a disheartening $4, four-tenths of the offering price. If there was a raid on, it was succeeding. The bold front that WoF had maintained so far now began to crumble under the strain of internal fissures.

'Whatsa happened to alla da money?'

'That's exactly what *I'd* like to know.'

'*Let's have this on the table!*'

Silence and chain smoking in the Leadership Room, while Silas Marner, the new comptroller, read aloud *A Summary of Unauthorized Disbursements*: loans to Key Associates, guaranteeing an ADB loan financing the purchase of another aeroplane for Baroque, loans to trusts and bank accounts to support WoF's share price, a loan to a conglomerate in which

FBOF held a substantial investment and, inexplicably, loans to 'friends of Mr McCool'.

'Look,' said Sleek, 'these guys weren't just friends like other kids on the block. They were business associates. I lent them the money so they could go on doing business with us. That's standard practice, right?'

'How come the rest of us weren't told?'

'Because it wasn't your function to be told. Look, some of these decisions had to be taken at very short notice. Like the shares might take a dive because somebody's tossed a few thousand of them on the market, and the investors might panic and start withdrawing their money from the funds, so you've got a crisis on your hands. So what do you do, call a Board meeting and pass another resolution? C'mon, fellows, be realistic.'

'What I mean is, how does a thing like this happen without *anybody* knowing about it except yourself?'

'That's what I'd like to know, too.'

Was Sleek culpable? If so, was he *solely* culpable? Or was culpability joint? Everyone in the Leadership Room now turned and looked coldly at Baroque.

'What are you looking at me for?' asked Baroque. Having entrusted the financial and legal side of the business to those responsible for the financial and legal side of the business, why, couldn't they see, he was every bit as shocked as they. Had he but known, he would have disallowed these disbursements, but no one had informed him. Sure, he was the guy who was *ultimately* responsible, but no one man could be expected to oversee all the details of a business as complex as World of Finance. His job was to inspire the Reps and close the really big deals. As the company's largest shareholder, he had the most to lose. Obviously, *he* wasn't the schmuck to blame.

The Key Associates were in no mood for excuses. 'You oughta 'ave made it your *business* to find out,' said Sansfoy.

'Last year we made only eighteen million instead of twenty-five million. So, what's happened to the eighteen?'

Sleek explained that a good deal of money had been spent on opening new offices and expanding the underwriting and banking operations.

'We all know about expanding operations.'

'These figures are estimates,' cautioned the comptroller. 'It might not be eighteen. It might be substantially less. We won't know until all the reports are in.'

The crisis brought a deputation from the staff. Mass dismissals were taking place; could the Board confirm that these dismissals were in order? Might some of those fired resume employment once the crisis was over? Was there to be severance pay? These people had families to support.

'A formal announcement will be made soon.'

'Tell them not to worry,' added Baroque consolingly. 'We've got a little technical problem on our hands that we expect to solve soon.'

The dismissals continued unabated.

The company was now losing a million dollars every ninety-six hours, and Reps were decamping to the opposition. In Germany, an RM deserted with his entire team. Publicity was told to get out a *Bulletin* urging the men to discountenance ugly rumours put about by rival financial houses.

A generous loan from the WoF Foundation, a charity Sleek formed for exempting donations from taxation, brought a respite. Flying Key Executives about in the company's planes was abandoned in favour of commercial airlines. The WoF Delicatessen was closed, and imports of kosher salamis for consumption in the staff canteen were stopped; anyone wanting Romanian pastrami on rye would have to walk over to Rabino's. But such economies were nugatory beside Overrides. Everyone accepted that there could be no return to what was now ridiculed as 'infinite pyramiding' – everyone except GMs and DMs, who would tolerate no reduction.

The directors fell to discussing possible rescuers. Outside help might restore confidence. If somebody, *anybody*, could be induced to put up the money ('purely interim financing'), austerity measures would take care of the rest. 'Whatever we do,' said Sleek, 'I am absolutely convinced that we ought to retain control in our own hands.'

Herb moved that, in future, 'the officer or officers concerned put all deals like Operation Thaw and Operation Outback before the full Board *before* proceeding with them'. Meanwhile, the company would counter the adverse publicity by maintaining that 'the essential wisdom of transactions such as our Arctic and Nullabor commitments' would become apparent 'once the auditors' report was in and all the facts known' and that 'plans were already afoot to restore confidence and crush the speculators'.

These were trying times, but not more trying, Baroque reminded them, than the early days of the Company, 'when you didn't know from one minute to the next if you were going to the lock-up, eh Herb?' It was almost the Founder's last statement to the full Board.

Clovis, who had been dispatched to Calhoun, Faloon and Balloon to raise the 'interim financing', now reported on his negotiations. That reputable house was prepared to risk its reputation and buy a controlling interest in the Company for a dollar a share, provided that their offer was accepted at once and Baroque and Sleek resigned their positions on the WoF Board. Clovis had also spoken with Bloom and Basoon, whose offer was similar.

'That's *ridiculous!*' screamed Baroque.

'Don't take it poisonal, man. It's for the Company's image, like. Once things cool down, you'll be reinstated.'

Baroque disagreed. They were trying to get rid of him.

'Speaking for myself,' said Sleek, 'I don't mind resigning. I'm expendable. But no one can step into the Founder's shoes. The Company needs his imagination, his flair, his charisma, his instinct for what is right for the client. Right, fellows? Bringing in outside management is too risky. Do we really want some total stranger poking his nose into our secrets?'

No they did not!

'Sleek's point is, we gotta stick together,' echoed Vincenzo.

*

The adverse publicity continued unabated.

> '*WoF SHARES DOWN AGAIN*' – '*RUMOURS DRIVE WoF SHARES TO NEW LOWS FOR THE YEAR*' – '*WoF SHARE PRICE FALLS 23 PER CENT: SUBSIDIARY ALSO DOWN*' – '*WoF SHARES MARKED DOWN AGAIN: BOARD SEEKS TO HALVE COSTS*' – '*BONN CABINET ASKS WoF FOR*

MORE DETAILS OF ACTIVITIES' – 'WoF SHARES DOWN DESPITE BOARD'S REASSURANCES' – 'SHARES PLUNGE' . . .

The crisis hit Vincenzo the hardest. Baroque was like a father to him, and every morbid headline exacerbated his hurt. Late one night, after a particularly acrimonious Board meeting, he confided his troubles to the Founder. 'Boss, if you don't resign there ain't gonna be no company.'

'Surely *you* don't believe all that stuff they're saying about me, Vick? *You* don't think I'm a crook, do you?'

'No way, boss. But it ain't up to me to decide.'

Baroque's allegation of a concentrated bear raid was true. WoF insiders, Baroque foremost among them, *were* dumping their stock. Similarly, his allegation of malicious rumours. The campaign against WoF proved mortal, because the rumours, albeit malicious, were true. WoF *was* losing business to competitors. Assets under management *were* shrinking. WoF *had* wasted the flotation proceeds supporting the price of the shares. The company's success was predicated on expansion, expanding the Sales Force, expanding Sales Revenues, expanding Management Fees. Everything worked as long as the business was expanding; additional sales defrayed the swelling administration costs. But different ratios ruled in reverse. Administration designed to accommodate a billion dollars in Sales Revenues remained just as costly when Sales Revenues fell by half, and this is exactly what happened. The decelerated pace of cash flow – 15 per cent instead of the 30 per cent increase for the previous year, 4 per cent instead of 42 per cent over the corresponding quarter of the previous year – engendered a 'declining profits picture' coinciding with the moment when analysts everywhere began noticing that WoF portfolio managers were dumping their unregistered securities.

Thus the immediate causes of the company's collapse were technical. Its earnings forecast of thirty million dollars seemed a fair extrapolation from *past* performance, and valuing its stock at 18 times earnings seemed reasonable to the merchant banks that underwrote its paper at ten dollars a share. By late October, though, it was clear to everyone that earnings would be nearer fifteen million dollars than thirty million and substantially less without the Performance Fees from the dubious Arctic and Nullabor transactions.

*

Baroque alone of the twenty-two directors continued to deny the need for a rescuer. 'A staging loan is all that's needed,' he insisted. But neither his nor Sleek's advice was disinterested. That they would have to resign from 'all positions of responsibility in the company' was now *hors de débat*. Their resignations might be useful bargaining chips in negotiations with a rescuer.

Henry Yates made an offer, and the Board invited him to meet them at Mountain Close. Henry arrived the next day, emerging big and beaming from a vast tinted-windows Lincoln Continental saloon. His interest in saving WoF was, broadly, to save himself. Operations Thaw and Outback were his inspiration, and he was the main benefactor. Posterity would debate which was the most to be blamed for WoF's demise, Henry's deals or WoF's squandering the proceeds of the Public Offering, but since the two companies were already linked, there was force in the argument that they should rise or fall together. It was decided to accept Henry's offer.

The press remained sceptical throughout the negotiations.

'*WoF-YATES MERGER AGREED: $40M CREDIT, NEW BOARD* – Allegedly, a consortium of unnamed American financial institutions is backing the deal. Further details are expected this week. . . .'

'*CONFUSION OVER SIGNING OF WoF-YATES DEAL* – A WoF Board member last night disclosed the basis of the deal with the Henry Yates Corporation. "Mr Yates is obliged to introduce partners involving both major American and European institutions," he said. He suggested that Yates would sign the agreement and reveal the names of his supporting institutions today. . . .'

'*YATES IN LONDON TO WIN BANKING SUPPORT FOR WoF DEAL* – The mystery over Henry Yates's American backers and the absence of European support for the proposed deal is clearly a crucial factor in the attempt to restore confidence in WoF. . . .'

'*WoF: BANKERS TRY TO FIND A SOLUTION* – Henry Yates, who spent much of Monday night in meetings with leading merchant bankers who joined in the underwriting of the WoF issue, went to Calhoun, Faloon and Balloon for further meetings on Tuesday and to Bloom and Basoon on Wednesday. Yesterday, he flew to Frankfurt to pacify WoF's German sales force, which has been restive since the Federal government banking commission demanded details of WoF's activities. He told the German salesmen that he had signed the deal with WoF, but that the names of the American banks supporting him could not be released before the Securities and Exchange Commission gave its approval for the deal, and that several leading European organizations were prepared to join him. It is the absence of well-known banking names backing Yates that has delayed the revival of confidence. He then flew to London for further meetings. . . .'

'QUESTIONS STILL TO BE ANSWERED – An official statement concerning Henry Yates's bid to rescue WoF did not reveal the names of the financial institutions that were backing him, as had been promised earlier in the day. . . .'

This farce continued into the New Year. The second week in January, Henry was back in New York.

'YATES LEAVES WoF QUESTIONS UNANSWERED – Mr Yates refused to name any members of the high-powered consortium that he insists he is putting together. In a 50-minute, occasionally rambling address without notes, he stressed that there was "absolutely no doubt" about his company's ability to make up the international group of institutions which will take over the running of the sprawling WoF empire. Everyone concerned is keeping quiet until everything is arranged. . . .'

The SEC denied permission for a merger, and hardly another six months went by before the Henry Yates Corporation was beset with troubles – due, Yates resolutely maintained, to his attempt at rescuing WoF. Others saw his rescue exercise as a 'last mad dash for self-survival'.

Meanwhile, ever more desperate measures were taken to retain the Sales Force. One idea was to divert the salesmen onto selling the real estate subsidiary's products. Thus January's *Bulletin* featured *¿Que es Solymar?*, presenting a 'Costa del Sol Weather Outlook', a 'Gossip Column' showing celebrities 'taking the sunshine in Torremolinos' and a picture of 'a couple from Allentown Pennsylvania relaxing in one of the decorator-furnished suites.

To further promote American tourism to the Costa del Sol,' claimed ¿*Que es Solymar?*, 'the Spanish tourist industry plans to sponsor a 14-day Malaga Week in New York. The Manhattan exposition will feature Spanish handicrafts and art and a full-scale reproduction of a typical Andalusian street and patio.'

*

The letter from Banque Flonck advising Bleitgeist that it had sold his pledged shares to redeem his margin loan reached him on his fortieth birthday. Nine years down the drain, his wife, his house and his shares gone, and he was forty. All his vocational dreams were failures, all his vocational triumphs turned to nightmares. He perceived the past as a long, corrosive postponement, slime floating on a stagnant river, and the future an asylum for the insane, its walls papered with *WoF Monthly Bulletins* and Model Closes. Having counselled others so often about their goals, he was himself bereft of a goal, unemployed, with no one to turn to and nowhere to go. The crack in his bathroom mirror symbolized Bombay, where it was always night. Night in Colaba. Night in Byculla. Night over Malabar Hill where the ravens flew. Night in Breach Candy where the expatriates swam. The thick, humid air hanging still over the inky water of Byculla where the Maritime Market floated, freighted with Plans forever pending; where hirsute, tattooed seamen paced steel corridors and sneered at presentations. Pain was his constant companion, pain in his chest, under his ribs, in his back, as though he had twisted his spine. He broke out in rashes and sores. Unexpected sounds or sudden movements startled him. He drank copiously and resorted to the 'cages', but the expensive imperiousness of the toxin and the crude meretriciousness of girls scarcely larger than dolls deepened his depression.

Then came agonizing reappraisal. Should he attend a religious service? A temple? A synagogue? A mosque? A church? *Which of the two would you prefer to be, Mr Worth? Bust and beaten? Or bust, but not beaten?* . . . Should he surrender to the Eternal Embrace? . . . Should he read the Bible?

The post fetched *Selling through the Apocalypse*, an anthology of reports of salesmen whose tenacity and irrepressible optimism were proof against all adversity. 'I realized that I had to get moving fast and started an intensive campaign of Service Calls. I soon discovered that clients just wanted to be reassured that our internal corporate problems would not affect the value of their investments, and I made it very clear that they had nothing to worry about – no more than the owner of a Ford has to worry about his car's performance if Ford profits decline. I made twenty-nine new sales in February and March, very largely to existing clients. Whatever has happened in the past few months, the many problems of our Company and all the bad publicity, has not changed our business. People must have a safe, convenient place for their money to grow, a hedge against inflation, a means of saving systematically. These are the basic truths of our business and they never change.'

Oh yeah? The mirages of World of Finance no longer deluded him.

'The best way I have found for overcoming *I don't believe you* is to show the prospect old newspapers and clippings from magazines showing past results.'

Do not pile up treasures on earth, where moth and rust can spoil them and thieves can break in and steal, for wherever your treasure is, you may be certain that your heart will be there too.

'I can't afford it.'

Be on your guard against covetousness in any shape or form, for a man's real life in no way depends upon the number of his possessions.

'I can do better.'

On my own? Via acquisitiveness: the Route to False Pride, the Route to Nowhere, the Route to Death?

WoF was false. And he was false. False with his trainees, false with his prospects, false with his clients, false with himself – but the joy of Christian Aspiration and Fellowship was real, so why wait? What was he waiting for? Still, he hesitated. He wanted to think about it.

What would you like to think about, Mr Worth?

Such a range of choices – Quakers, Roman Catholics, Lutherans, Seventh Day Adventists, Jehovas Witnesses, Pentecostalists, Presbyterians, Anglicans, all claiming to be 'casting off fetters mortal to the soul', all borrowing freely from the surrounding paganism, all expounding allegiances to something less than the Inextinguishable Light. The Bible was but one among many scriptures, divine only in that everything was divine. They professed many ways, *not* The Way.

Whether there was life after death, whether the soul floated free or remained attached to some ethereal facsimile of its mortal self, whether the 'essence of conscience' (a grotesque term used by a theosophist at an inter-faith discussion group) was really only 'the net result of all sorts of choices weighed in the divine balance' – all those abstruse questions were for theologians, not for him. There might be many paths to the one True Cross, but the Bible was the highest mediate authority. The ringing certitudes of John's first epistle were clear. *We are writing to you about something which has always existed, yet which we ourselves actually saw and heard, something which we had opportunity to observe closely and even to hold in our hands, and yet, as we know now, was something of the very word of life himself. . . . We saw it, we are eye-witnesses of it.*

John's Gospel was unequivocal.

This is the judgement – that light has entered the world and men have preferred darkness to light because their deeds are evil. Anybody who does wrong hates the light and keeps away from it, for fear his deeds may be exposed. But anybody who is living by the truth will come to the light to make it plain that all he has done has been done through God.

What mattered were the choices that he made *now*. He might or might not reach Paradise, and it might be before or after he died, but deceiving and cheating his fellow man was wrong, as were greed and envy. Fretting over his future depleted the resources that he needed for the present.

The company's collapse thus wrought the best of all possible developments. It freed him from the Stock Option Plan that he might cease *eating the food of the false prophetess* and be no more *afraid of the suffering to come*.

'Lord, I believe,' he prayed. 'Help Thou my unbelief.'

*

Belvedere picked up his rucksack and moved on, only to be engulfed by more staring, rheumy, insatiably curious children, mucus running from their noses. Unremitting, obnoxious interrogation, insulating him from passing motorists.

'Sahib, why not take bus?'

Futile attempts at explanation. 'Please move out of the way, so the traffic can see me.'

A tree laden with roosting vultures. Cattle with hides of sand standing stupefied in meagre shade. Buffaloes wallowing in mud. Sikhs asleep beneath their lorries. Ubiquitous filth.

'May I know your noble name, sir-r-r?'

'Belvedere.'

'How is spelled, sir-r-r?'

'B-E-L-V-E-D-E-R-E.'

'Are you student, sahib?'

Cool at dawn. Wheat fields bounded by canals, mango trees and banyans. Soldiers in their underwear shaving on the bank of a muddy river called out to ask his destination. '*Salam, sahib. Kidar ja rahe hain?*'

'*Angelistan ko.*'

'*Tik, sahib.*'

A long wait outside Quetta. Squandering his remaining rupees on rice and mutton. Old men with beards dyed crimson, women eyeing him through their *burqa* grids. A muezzin's call sputtering and metallic. Night falling over flocks of goats. Cold, crisp air, open sky, nomadic Baluchis camped in black tents. The headlights of a car rounding a bend below, then the ultimate lift with the man bound for Bolton.

'Going flat out, I reckon I average just o'er fifty miles an hour, including stops,' he said. 'Course you've got to arrange your visas aforehand if you want to keep up those speeds. I doan't often stop for 'itchhikers.'

Another dawn broke.

'How long has tha bin away from 'ome, lad?'

'About a year.'

'Is that a fact? And you done it all by 'itchhiking, like?'

'Mmm.'

'Sleep rough, do you lad?'

Bare hills and more bare hills. It occurred to Belvedere that he lacked the fortitude needed for long works of prose, but had all the right fevers for poetry.

*

While Belvedere sped across the wastes of Baluchistan homeward bound, Sir Vyvyan floated alone, saluting the gulls that came to inspect for fish in *Luna*'s wake and sounding his noble ideas to the dolphins. He celebrated each new gigantic sunset and read at night from his favourite author by the light of a whistling paraffin lamp. '*I thought of men who, centuries ago, went that road in ships that sailed no better, to the land of palms, and spices, and yellow sands.*'

In Penang, he visited an old pupil and they played mahjong. The Rector of the University at Singapore invited him to dinner, and they discussed the attrition of talent among the current crop coming up to sit their entrance exams. He swapped gossip with the Deputy High Commissioner, who took him for a tour of the island. The noble knight opined that few of their generation had found what they were seeking. In Surabaja, he sought and identified Schomberg's hotel on one of the tortuous, breathless streets near the harbour. It seemed little altered from the author's description. It had a room with billiard tables which, in the more heroic heat of Axel Heyst's day, would be shrouded in the afternoon, and a gate opening onto a square, now, as then, prettily bordered with oleander.

He sailed on to Bali and the Lesser Sundas and toasted the fishermen returning each evening in their outriggers to plangent wives and made modest purchases of fruit and trinkets from the boat wallahs who came alongside at every roadstead.

A gentle lapping of water against the bulkhead. Moonlight through the porthole. Sir Vyvyan in his bunk still as a corpse, his eyes full of tears. '*A semicircle of beach gleamed faintly, like an illusion. The mysterious East faced men perfumed like a flower, silent like Death, dark like a grave.*' The beneficiary rather than the victim of his heightened longings. Poetry's happy chimera.

*

Selling through the Apocalypse was WoF's last *Bulletin*.

A problem is only as big as you decide to make it. If you spent your time reading newspapers during the past two months, you probably assumed that WoF was finished. If you were busy selling and servicing Clients, however, you probably didn't have too much time to dwell on the problems of WoF. The Associates written up in this issue did as much business in recent months as ever before, which proves that the WoF Concept of offering people professional financial service is as sound as it ever was. Providing, of course, you get out there and offer it.

Harbinder Govinda was surprised and delighted to learn that he was one of those whose Closes were not affected.

I resell the client on the whole concept of long-term investment. Of course, you explained all that when the client opened his Plan. . . . the fact that he should continue his Plan whether the market moves up or down . . . that what the market does this week, or even this year, is of no real importance to him . . . that fluctuations are actually helpful because they help fund managers pick up stock bargains and produce more profits. . . . And through Vertical Diversification these fluctuations enable the client to realize even greater gains. Of course, your client remembers all that. Or does he? Even two months is a long time, and everyone tends to forget. That's why I feel that one of the most important parts of my job is to see my clients as often as I can and give them a fresh supply of confidence.

Harbinder had never seen his name in print before.

*

WoF's losses continued through February, and by March the Top of the Spirals resembled the rump of a fleeing army. Only Liquidations was running at full strength. Each week, another melancholy procession made its way to the Leadership Room to consider another rescue scheme. Sansjoy spoke dryly of the 'tortoise of bankruptcy'.

Cosmopolitan Controls Corporation made tools, dies, rollers and pressers and owned patents for the preparation of low-density gases. Jack Holsome, its chief executive officer and principal shareholder, was the first to offer the kind of financing that pleased everyone. Nor was it considered too serious a mark against him that FBOF's portfolio held a large parcel of Cosmopolitan's debentures. The point was made and accepted that, if Holsome was not what he seemed, the loan that he was proposing was 'one way of getting back part of the investors' money'. An agreement was signed and its terms communicated to shareholders of both the company and the sponsored funds. Holsome was to take no part in the daily running of the saleless organization but, 'as a concession to protect his interest', was to be appointed chairman of a 'Budget Committee' with power of veto over any action of financial import. Although not stipulated in the documentation, it was *understood* that Baroque would be reappointed to the Board and remain in his office with the subdued lighting and speakerphone concealed in the soundproofing, seen as an important symbol of solidarity with the WoF Concept. The directors boasted of their financial adroitness to wives, girlfriends and secretaries once more, and Easter weekend at Mountain Close was almost like old times, minus the pleasures of allocating Territories. For the first time since the onset of the Apocalypse, everyone was friendly and could look back on the past with nostalgia.

'Remember the time Baroque won the Salesman of Free Enterprise Award?'

'And that ridiculous report in *Time*? "From La Paz to Luxembourg, the mutual fund has turned out to be as exportable a US commodity as Coca-Cola or cowboy movies."'

'And how we used to talk about FoF being the ideal investment? Remember those lectures on the Dilemma of the Twenty-five Cents Dollar and the Coming Crisis in College Education?'

'Yeah. "A gift of mutual fund shares is a realistic way of making dreams come true."'

'How *The Times* called it "The phenomenon of phenomena of the investment industry" when Fiduciary of Fiduciaries hit a hundred million?'

'And those marvellous *Bulletin* headlines, "Autumn Leaves Fall, But Fall Sales Rise"? Gee, they were almost like songs from a Dan Dailey, Gene Kelly musical.'

'And how every time somebody got married, or had a baby, or had a hernia operation, it got written up as a major event?'

'When everything that happened in "revolution-torn Saigon" was "Nhu"?'

'Remember Mitzi?'

'Mitzi of the Mail Room? Do I *remember* Mitzi? How could I ever *forget* Mitzi?'

'Remember *The Secrets of Successful Selling*?'

'Sure. It was one of those bonus books back in about 1963.'

'And Gloria Meringue?'

'Code name for Art Schliemann, the first Associate to write three hundred thousand dollars in a single month, who won the Seventh Anniversary Contest and was Salesman of the Year in 1962 and Manager of the Year in 1964. Died of a heart attack on a plane.'

'What about Foster Parent?'

'*Alias* Jeremy Partridge, *alias* Bumper Peabody, Regional, later Divisional, later General Manager Asia II. Present whereabouts unknown.'

It would seem to some that their last holiday together was the best.

Meanwhile, Holsome worked alone, refining and rejoicing in the harmony of his plans. Soon he would pull a lever and a dozen interlocking gears would move. His controlling the Budget Committee amounted to controlling the company, which voted the shares taken up by the Stock Option Plan supporting WoF's share price and shares pledged by Key Associates as collateral for the loans to them to buy more WoF shares. Other shareholders were beholden to him for their jobs.

Why, wondered Holsome, had he not thought of doing business 'offshore' before?

*

A rested and rejuvenated crowd returned to the Top of the Spirals after a noisy end of holiday.

'You know something, Virginia?'

'What, Mr Rock?'

'I have a hunch our new chief's going to pan out better than we all thought.'

'Gosh, Mr Rock, until now you've been saying that you don't trust him.'

'I know, but I've changed my opinion. He's got something up his sleeve. Don't ask me what, because I'm just as much in the dark as you are. Holsome's a pretty private sort of guy.'

'Whatcha think's going to happen?'

'I have a pretty good idea that we won't be selling mutual funds for a while,' said Nelson. 'We'll probably be diversifying into new fields – sales advisory services, public relations, management consultancy. Plenty of people in business want and need our kind of expertise. Of course, we'll have to come to some kind of arrangement with the shareholders, perhaps buy back the flotation on credit and maybe settle a few lawsuits. We'll have to convince those guys down in DC that we intend to play it straight and not horse around with the public's money any more. Everything considered,' said Nelson wistfully, 'I've got a feeling that the worst is over, that we just *may* pull through and that you and your husband and *all* of us are going to get something back after all. Not much, but something.'

'Gosh, Mr Rock, I sure hope so. For *everybody's* sake.'

*

Holsome's loan agreement with WoF increased its debt to him in the event of a breach. The Board's re-electing Baroque as Chairman was such a breach. The vote was inadvertent – and could be nullified, but it allowed Holsome to seize control of WoF's sponsored funds. He threatened foreclosure if Baroque did not divest himself of his WoF stock. Baroque, though, was determined to take back *his* company.

A proxy fight loomed. Intense bargaining ensued.

'How much do you want for your shares?'

'Around fifty cents each. How much do *you* want for yours?'

*

Philippa and Tessa did not repine when Whitehall intervened in the affairs of the Folkestone Plan. They lunched at the Health Juice Bar at Harrods, had their hair styled at Sassoon, bought their boots from Elliott's and telephoned each other incessantly to keep up to the minute on every giggle, as of old.

Ernest and Clovis scattered with their briefcases without even saying goodbye and found employment in Texas selling cemetery plots, funerary markers and monuments. They used for visual aids pictures of stones and plaques engraved with intertwined hands, enscrolled verses from the Bible, ROTC insignia and Rotary Club badges, and their presentations were crude adaptations of the Folkestone Plan Training Manual: 'Mrs Worth, statistics show that, when At-Time Need arises, it is the widow who will have to bear the responsibility for making the arrangements.'

Marty, Herb and Wally were seeking employment. 'Looking back,' said Marty, 'we'd have been better off sticking with Baroque.'

'Hell, *he's* the sonavabitch to blame.'

'Sleek's the sonavabitch to blame.'

Exercising his moral authority, Wally refused to transfer blame: 'We're *all* to blame,' he said. 'We should've got rid of the trash, like I've been saying all along.'

Mafia and Vendetta thought it was outrageous and tragic that the Sales Force, that ubiquitous talent for Total Service they had trained, might generate Overrides for strangers, and formed Soci Finanziari S.r.l. Although the Reps' personnel records were their company's only asset, Mike and Vick were sanguine. They only needed a Product.

Strumpf had accumulated a fortune from his Overrides and invested it in tangibles, notwithstanding his oft-avowed dogma that mutual funds epitomized intelligent estate planning. He owned an alluvium diamond field, the rights to reprocess a gold slag heap, a string of massage parlours, a partnership interest in a cheese store, a riding stable and a ski resort. His responsibilities kept him active, interested in a changing world and immodest.

Handschuh had invested all his savings in WoF and was selling children's encyclopedias.

Sansjoy crowned a singularly dreary life by committing suicide.

Sansfoy was too engrossed with his new duties as FoF's new vice-president to grieve over his oldest friend's death. He greeted the news with equanimity. 'Everybody has a right to choose how and when he dies,' said the ex-Director of Training. He and Sansloy had given Holsome irrevocable proxies to vote their shares in the proxy fight in exchange for jobs. Sansloy was FBOF's new vice-president.

There was work, too, for Nelson and his secretary serving the organization that survived the new chief's 'reforms'. Nelson was in charge of Liquidations.

'What's your opinion today, huh, Mr Rock? D'you think there's any chance of getting our money back?'

'I doubt it, Virginia, I seriously doubt it.'

'How can they let him get away with it, Mr Rock?'

'They can.'

Levy Levin moved to Memphis, took up with Ingrid and started selling municipals.

'Mr O'Brien?'

'That's my name. Don't wear it out. Whatcha you want?'

'This is Levy Levin, First US Corporation. What's the weather like up there? . . . Sunny and dry? *Beau*tiful. Looking at your portfolio, Mr O'Brien, page twenty-two, item eighty. I will buy eighty-four cents on the dollar. Will replace one hundred Scotsboro Alabama IDRs sixes due six one ninety-eight eighty-six cents. That will cost you two thousand dollars plus accrued increase. I'm buying yours at eighty-four, selling you mine at eighty-six.'

'Done.'

'Confirmation will be in the mail.'

'Same page, item eighty-eight. Buy yours at one-C-five replacing with a hundred Albertville Alabama general obligation bonds fours due five one ninety-eight par. Got a free-you-up five thousand dollars.'

'El Paso.'

'Mr O'Brien, let me ask you this. If I can do mine at ninety-nine and three-quarters can we hit it?'

'No interest.'

'Next item. Page fifty, item one-O-one. Buy yours at fifty, sell you fifty Ontario Motor Speedways sixes due one one two thousand at fifty-five. That'll free you up a thousand dollars.'

'Done.'

'Confirmation will be in the mail. I'm doing this just like everything else, okay Mr O'Brien? Everything at the Chemical.'

'Affirmative.'

'Okay, let me check the portfolio to see if you're still clear on these. What about seventy-six?'

'Haven't traded 'em.'

'Okay, can you give me those firm for two hours?'

'You got 'em firm.'

Joe Stamp moved to New Orleans and sold cotton futures.

'Hey Johnny, how's everything?'

'I don't know about everything, man.'

'Okay, how was the ninth race?'

'I dunno about no ninth race.'

'You're okay, Johnny. You're perfect.'

'I brought my kids up. I sacrificed. For twenty-seven years I sacrificed. I never bought myself no new car. I never had nothing but a used car. All these years I got these things hanging over me. Now the kids are educated, and I bought myself a new car.'

'You've sacrificed all these years, Johnny. You're entitled to it. Tell me, whatcha doing with the rest of your savings?'

Having convinced himself, Operations Thaw and Outback notwithstanding, that enlightened self-interest would protect the investors' money, it was not until the disclosures about stuffing the sponsored funds with duds from the sponsored underwritings that the scales fell from van Zilver's eyes. Having liquidated his FBOF shares to buy WoF shares and pledged them to buy more shares, he lost everything. Like Edith Piaf, however, he regretted nothing. He returned to Holland and took up a post teaching economics and business law at Rijksuniversiteit Groningen.

Sleek resumed private practice and steered his new corporate clients clear of offshore funds. 'They're a dead apple,' he advised. A number of variants of the same formula were not 'dead apples', though, and the great legal architect put together package after package, so 'the big tax breaks can be shared by everyone, and not just by the very rich'. He mitigated his losses somewhat by assigning the voting rights in his WoF stock to Holsome.

Holsome, meanwhile, swapped the shares of WoF subsidiaries for minority positions in Bahamian and Antillan companies with notional assets controlled by institutional nominees of 'undisclosed principals'. Herb and Michele instituted legal proceedings to test the validity of the foreclosure clauses of his loan agreement. The court denied their application for a temporary restraining order enjoining 'further alienations pending trial', and after a blizzard of other expensive interlocutory manoeuvres, they withdrew their suit.

Everyone now waited for Baroque. Would he rise from WoF's ashes, expel Holsome and resume command? Alas, whoever looked to him to 'save WoF' learned that he was now a patriarch in myth only. He had mounted a proxy fight with much fanfare, but his terms for proxies, his autograph on a ten-dollar bill for every parcel, were too modest even for desperadoes, most of whom, in any case, had already sold or pledged their shares. The new management then sent Bull and Bear uniformed security men armed with pistols and batons to evict him from his office with the intramural speakerphone. He had always maintained that, if forced to do so, he would sacrifice his entire fortune to protect the small investor. However, when investigative tribunals in Switzerland, Germany and Holland subpoenaed him to answer allegations of fraud, and embittered WoF staff and clients joined as plaintiffs in litigation against him, the company and the sponsored funds, he broadcast one last baseless accusation and retreated to Yucatán in his mortgaged aeroplane. Even the Latvian house cleaners were glad to see the back of him.

After the depressing news of the denial of Mafia's and Beck's application for a temporary restraining order, Marty led a delegation to Baroque. It was just as in former times when the Founder received managers with complaints and petitions. He was at his villa at Isla de las Mujeres. JoAnn, Pam and the other Great Dames were dispersed around a pool drinking Dos Equis and Coca Cola. Everyone was in swimming costume except Marty, who was dressed in a tight suit with uncuffed trousers, a striped blue shirt, a Cardin silk tie adorned with the coat-of-arms of the defunct Folkestone Plan and a gold chain attached to a gold pocket watch. The former Manager of the World was too imbued with the importance of his mission to doff his smart clothes.

The sudden appearance of this rump of the Family minutes after signing the papers disposing of his shares was weird, thought Baroque. What did he want? There was no point in discussing the proxy fight now. It was history. He sighed and, dropping a hand, listlessly caressed the backside of a Great Dame in a sunflower-printed Gucci bikini.

'Marty,' he said, 'have you met Johnny Weisschwarz?'

A bulky, ungainly man asleep under a sombrero, stirred by the sound of his name, rose from a deck chair, proffered a hand and said, 'Have a paw!'

'Put it there!' replied Marty.

'Johnny's writing a book about me,' said Baroque. 'It's going to be titled *My Story*. It's a sort of what you might call ghosted autobiography.'

'You don't say?'

Johnny smiled and sat down.

'How far have you got?' Marty inquired politely. Nothing was to be gained by needlessly giving offence.

'We've just started,' replied Weisschwarz.

'Written many books before, Mr Weisschwarz?'

'Plenty.'

'Johnny's okay,' said Baroque. 'Johnny's published in *Time*, *Fortune*, the *Atlantic Journal*, you name it.'

'Sounds pretty impressive. How long d'you think this book's going to take, Mr Weisschwarz?'

'Dunno,' said Weisschwarz.

This guy, thought Marty, was no worse than the Founder's other parasites.

'It's a big job. It might take weeks, it might take months. Who can tell? Man, at the rate we're going, we might *never* finish.'

'Mr Weisschwarz's very careful what he writes,' explained Baroque.

'You *gotta* be careful,' confirmed Weisschwarz.

Weisschwarz's head sank forward and his paunch spread. Baroque gazed at the blank sky, and the normally vivacious odalisques remained one with the scorched flagstones. Marty tried to decipher the meaning of a Mexican newspaper.

At length Baroque said, 'Why don't we order some frankfurters? Anybody hungry?'

No one stirred.

'Coming right up!' said Baroque excitedly, summoning a servant. One thing he wasn't going to do without in exile was hot dogs. Another of life's indispensable comforts was servants. 'Isn't it strange,' he remarked to his comatose companions, 'how peaceful everything is? Like out there in the water, there are sharks – *real* sharks! Sometimes you can see their fins. And the hills over there are full of *bandits*.'

The hot dogs came, but nobody wanted them. Baroque closed his eyes. His fingers sought and resumed their idle caress. 'Strange, isn't it?' Sounds of slumber rose from the sombrero.

*

On Bone's twenty-third birthday, a crowd gathered in the Humboldt High School auditorium for a memorial service and presentation of the Lawrence Saxon Annual Scholarship. Sponsored by the Humboldt Rotary Club, it was to be awarded to that member of the senior class selected by his teachers and classmates as best exemplifying the qualities of Leadership, Sportsmanship and Good Citizenship. Stands had been erected on the stage, and on them stood a choir of girls in white blouses and black mini-skirts exposing knees and legs of every colour and contour. Miss Clark, the music teacher, led it in singing *Land of Hope and Glory*. '. . . *Mother of the Free, How shall we extol thee, who were born of thee? Wider still, and wider, shall our bonds be set; God, who made thee mighty, make thee mightier yet. . . .*'

A curtain descended, and silence followed, save for the stamp and shuffle of shoes as the choir returned to the seats reserved for them behind Bone's parents, Uncle Ned, Aunt Mag and close family friends. Pinned to Sue Saxon's left shoulder was a large corsage of white orchids, a present from 'The Class of '72'.

When the curtain rose again, the stands had been moved back, tables and chairs had appeared and on them, above the hushed audience, sat a number of dignitaries. The school superintendent officiated. Beside him was the mayor and, flanking them, were Judge Wilkins, Coach Simms, the Baptist pastor, Brother Hollinsworth, the Methodist minister, Mr Russell, the Presbyterian minister, Dr Cook, and the president of Rotary. Only Coach Simms was striking in a blue shirt and checked sports jacket. The others wore grey suits evincing grave dignity.

The superintendent asked the pastor to lead them in prayer.

'Let us bow our heads,' said Brother Hollinsworth mournfully.

Silence in the auditorium, except for the remote hum of the electrical system.

'Our Father, we have gathered together . . .'

The president of Rotary, who was a member of the Saxons' adult Sunday School class, had a worrying business appointment later that morning. He glanced surreptitiously at his watch.

The prayer ended. The pastor alluded to the psalters provided to all and invited everyone to join him in reading the 90th psalm. '. . . *Thou hast set our iniquities before thee, Our secret sins in the light of thy countenance. For all our days are passed away in thy wrath: We spend our years to an end as a sigh. . . . So teach us to number our days, That we get us a heart of wisdom. . . .'* Sue Saxon tried to banish thoughts of her son and concentrate on getting the words right. It would be reported to her later that even Catholics joined in the reading.

The superintendent now called upon Coach Simms for a panegyric. When Coach Simms, after apologizing for ineptitude at public speaking, said, 'One thang about Lawrence that stood out above all his other fine qualities was, he never said "quit".' Ned Saxon sighed and, turning to his brother, observed, 'That's *right*, Hays.' 'Nobody,' continued Coach Simms with a hint of malice towards the half-dozen shaggy-haired, glassy-eyed, shabbily dressed, alien and, in coach's opinion, fatuous louts comprising the school's drug set, '*nobody* had to tell *Bone* whut to do. He had whut I call in-built *dissuplin*.'

The scholarship was awarded to Maurice Seward. General applause broke out when his name was announced. He rose from his seat and mounted the stage, beaming, to receive the cheque and shake the hand of the beaming president of Rotary. Maurice was a tall, whip-thin boy with a broad smile who played right end on the football team, centre on the basketball team and pitcher on the baseball team. He hunted, fished and played the harmonica, but it was his wholesomeness that endeared him most to faculty and parents. He spoke briefly of his gratitude. It seemed to Bone's parents that he spoke directly to them. Sue Saxon had known Maurice all his life. She remembered him as a boy who called at the front door on Halloween stipulating 'Trick or treat!'; who enterprisingly ran a snowball stand during the summer; who once cut her lawn and planted some rose bushes for her for five dollars; who worked behind the counter at Ned's drugstore, and whose picture had appeared in *Farmers Weekly* as a delegate to Boys State some time before Bone's death. 'I jus' want to thank everybody here,' he said. 'Although I don't deserve it, this award means a whole lot to me. And it's not jus' the money, either.'

It wasn't just the money. Hays Saxon, administrator of Bone's estate, had been corresponding with a firm in Canada concerning his son's shares in Fenner Biddup Offshore Fund. Every letter from the firm began, 'Dear Investor', and concluded, 'Trustees in Bankruptcy.' *It wasn't just the money.* If you worked like the dickens all your life to raise your boy, so that you could be proud of him – and you *were* proud of him – then some two-bit mutual fund salesman talked him into going out to India just to earn *overrides* on him, and your boy died, and the paper he was selling turned out to be worthless. . . . There ought to be some kind of law against it, thought Hays Saxon bitterly. But there wasn't.

Maurice returned to his seat to more applause. Dr Cook led everyone in the Lord's Prayer. Judge Wilkins gave the final word and Miss Clark played a vigorous recessional on the piano. Hays and Sue Saxon, who led the exodus, were moved not so much by what had been said as by the presence of so many people so well disposed to Bone. Even a company of Bone's old Boy Scout troop had turned out. All these people who admired their son. It was so nice of them all to come.

Outside the auditorium friends came over to exchange greetings and compliments. Maurice's mother said, 'Sue, I jus' wanna hug-*g-g* you!'

'Esther,' Sue replied, 'you know I'd rather have seen Maurice get this scholarship than anyone else in the world. And Hays thanks so too. We're so *proud* of him.'

'Why you're the sweetest *thang!*'

The Saxons returned to their house. It was full of souvenirs: on the piano, Bone's picture on graduation from high school; in the bookcase, his senior high annual and UT yearbooks; on the coffee table, a paperweight with a carnation centre he had made at church camp. Sue Saxon, who had fought her emotions all morning, now went methodically about her duties. It was time for lunch. She opened the refrigerator, removed her corsage and put it in the hydrator, then retrieved a Tupperware container of vegetable soup from the deep freeze and a box of Olde Tyme cornbread mix from the cabinet. She added an egg to the mix and, filling a muffin tin, placed it in the oven then heated the soup, while Hays watched the twelve o'clock news. When the food was ready, she called him to the table.

'This is mighty good soup,' he said.

'Wail, thank you, Hays. It turned out rather wail. I sent a jar to Mrs Lippitt yesterday. She always liked it, and she doesn't get around too wail. Would you like some more?'

'No thanks. That's plenty for me.'

'There's some cherry pie left. I can heat it for you. And there's some ice-cream.'

'No, that'll wait too.'

Sue Saxon cleared the table and put the dishes in the sink. Her shoulder pained her and she felt suddenly tired. The dishes could wait. She would lie down and turn on her electric heating pad.

*

The Safety Patrol in white caps and white vests were still directing traffic in the adjacent streets and driveways, when the three minute bell rang. Mary Lou, Bobbie Jo, Ann, Margaret, Karen and Linda, the twelfth grade gynaecocracy, were at their lockers getting their textbooks for Algebra, English and Home Economics and discussing the award ceremony in the auditorium that morning. Bone was the school hero when they were in the sixth grade.

'I cri-i-ed,' said Mary Lou.

'I cried,' said Bobbie Jo.

'I cried,' admitted Ann, Margaret, Karen and Linda.

A boy in ROTC uniform overhead them. 'Shoot!' he said. 'That's awl yawl ever do is cry.'

*

Indolence was the mood of the moment with Philippa and Belvedere. They were lying side by side on a blanket, she with a book in her hand, playing Cleverer Than Thou. It was a game that he enjoyed and always won. Victory made him feel tender.

Their circumstances had changed, some would suggest improved. He had renounced skiing, Spanish, hitchhiking and promiscuity to acquire marketable skills and was reading for Part I of the Bar Examination, while she, after much consultation with Tessa and her mother and a little encouragement from Belvedere, had taken a job as a receptionist sitting at a brass-inlaid mahogany Regency desk in a Bond Street art gallery specializing in enigmatic ink and watercolour drawings. Both of them felt like impostors, but accepted grudgingly that this New Plan offered better hopes of success against life's great challenge of defeating boredom than the Old Plan of random experiment.

Belvedere's father stubbornly refused to find solace in his son's decision. They remained as intimately estranged as the legs of an egg beater. For heaven's sake, what was *wrong* with the boy? Why didn't he join the Forces? There were opportunities galore in the Forces for a lad of such marked high spirits. If only Belvedere would heed a sensible suggestion for once, *he'd* know how to fix it.

'"Heard melodies are sweet, but those unheard are sweeter; therefore, ye soft pipes, play on."'

'"Not to the sensual ear,"' continued Belvedere, '"but, more endear'd, pipe to the spirit ditties of no tone." Keats, *Ode to a Grecian Urn*.'

'Darling, you are *so* clever!'

'Test me again.'

Philippa kissed Belvedere on his head, like a mother rewarding her child for allowing her to button his coat. She turned the pages of the book, found another poem and challenged him again. 'Okay, I spy with my little eye something that begins with O. In which poem by which poet does a name beginning with O occur?'

'I hear with my little ear something that begins with . . . *Ozymandias* by Shelley, of course.'

'Explain context.'

'Do you want me to explain the circumstances in which the poem was written or our hero's role in it?'

'Recite!' demanded Philippa.

'"I met a traveller from an antique land who said . . ." Can't remember the rest.'

'You can! You can! Recite!' Philippa insisted.

'Let's see, what *did* he say? Was it: "Two vast and trunkless legs of stone stand in the desert. Near them on the sand half sunk a shatter'd visage lies, whose frown and wrinkled lip and sneer of cold command tell that its sculptor well those passions read which yet survive, stamp'd on these lifeless things, the hand that mock'd them and the heart that fed."'

'*Bang on!* Clever, *clever* Belvedere!'

'"And on the pedestal these words appear . . ."' Belvedere paused, sighed and continued, '"My name is Ozymandias, king of kings: Look on my works, ye mighty and despair! Nothing beside remains: round the decay of that colossal wreck, boundless and bare, the lone and level sands stretch far away."

'It's too sad,' he said. Really too sad. It reminds me poignantly of my own glorious prime.'

'Rotter!'

*

He makes his sun rise upon evil men as well as good, and he sends his rain upon honest and dishonest men alike. . . . The narrow gate and the hard road lead out into life, and only a few are finding it. . . . Happy are the utterly sincere. . . . Remember, there are things men consider perfectly splendid which are detestable in the sight of God. . . . If you only knew, even at this eleventh hour, on what your peace depends – but you cannot see it. . . . The kingdom of heaven is inside you.

'Lord, have mercy on me, have mercy on me, have mercy on me. Lord, have mercy on me, have mercy on me, have mercy on me,' prayed the defunct Manager of Asia II. 'I believe. Lord, help thou my unbelief.'

*

It was all local traffic now, the milkman and the postman going about their deliveries. Whenever Belvedere's thoughts reverted to the Open Road, Philippa became censorious. 'Yes, darling, we *all* know that you've had a *Big* Adventure.' So after a while he stopped mentioning it. Philippa had more pressing matters to discuss.

'The chapel at Fencester was Mummy's idea. Don't you remember? I said we wanted something not so old and turrety. And, besides, in January it will be quite damp. We'd all have goose-pimples. Anyhow, the church at Great Cloyscombe is lovely and the village will like it. Darling, I *do* think you could at *least* go and see it . . . Little Maggie is the difficulty. I thought the bridesmaids could carry pink posies. They're absolutely *Kate Greenaway*. But Maggie's red hair, oh dear! . . . I don't want anyone over eight. They might make me look short. I can't have Caspar. He can't keep still. We'll just have the girls. Mummy wondered whether some of your people, maybe your Hereford aunts, she thought, wouldn't mind staying at the Bull? We're going to be overflowing.'

'Aunt Anita, Aunt Peggy and Aunt Prunella won't mind staying at the Bull.'

'Then that's settled. I'm so cross with Franchini's. They've sewed the pearls onto the collar of my dress, and I specifically said only the skirt. Well, they'll just have to take them off. . . . There's another tray, from the Rumbolds. That's *seven*! It's nice of them, really, but they *could* have looked at the list. . . . You won't forget about the bridesmaids' bracelets, will you, darling? I should try Asprey's. Mummy was saying that she thought lobster and chicken vol-au-vents, as well as smoked salmon and turkey. What do you think? That shouldn't be a problem. Searcy's are fairly reliable. I want the cake to have at least four tiers, as I intend to have *at least* three children! And, by the way, you were *beastly* to the Wilkinsons on Sunday evening. I simply dread to think how you'll behave when you're forty. You'll be just like your flashy-teethed Mr van Zilver,' an extraordinary creature Belvedere had picked up on the road who reminded Philippa of Ernest and Clovis. 'And *who* are the Blenkinsops, Mr and Mrs and Miss Pamela? They're no one *we* know.'

'They're some of mine.'

'Well, they're *coming*! . . . Darling, I do think you could have been nicer to the Wilkinsons, as they'd never met you before. He can be very useful to you once you are in chambers and have finished your book. He's *very* important.'

Belvedere had renamed *Our Times*, *The Gospel of Our Times*, then renamed it again, *Of Writers and Vagabonds*. Finishing it was proving painfully truculent with all the diversions going on around him. He promised himself that, as soon as this wedding lark was over, he would resume work on it in earnest.

TOPICAL POSTSCRIPT

I began writing *Client Service* in the late 1970s. Events intervened, and I resumed work on it in 2010.

Meanwhile, three strangely apposite developments occurred. First, stock markets plunged as a result chiefly of leveraging, subprime mortgage lending and the commissions-and-bonuses-for-sales-driven trades in derivatives. Then, an Andover classmate, Yale roommate and close friend reported that he had invested his cash reserves with Bernard Madoff and seen them disappear. 'Madoff made off with my money,' he said.

The stock markets crash and Madoff's Ponzi scheme have been widely reported and are well understood. I will dwell a moment on the other development: the Australian Government's decision, acting in tandem with the Australian Stock Exchange (ASX), to allow Australian companies to enrich their resident shareholders at the expense of their non-resident shareholders. All the company need do is (1) 'conduct' an 'accelerated non-renounceable' offer to its resident shareholders of rights to buy further shares at a price below the market price; (2) 'decide that it is unreasonable' to offer non-resident shareholders these rights, owing to 'the number of [such] holders; the number and value of shares that otherwise would have been offered [to them]; the cost of complying with the laws and legal requirements of the place where [such shareholders live]'; and (3) 'send details of the offer' to them with the advice that 'it will not be extending the offer to them'.[1] It is entirely up to the company to decide whether the inclusion of non-resident shareholders is 'unreasonable'; nor is there any provision in the

---

[1] Corporations Act 2001 §9A and ASX Listing Rule 7.71.

statute or the Listing Rules for reviewing this decision. Australian companies that have made rights offers excluding non-resident shareholders under these provisions include Wesfarmers, One Steel, Blue Scope Steel, CSR, Suncorp-Medway, Mirvac Group, Goodman Group, Incitec Pivot and GPT Group.

Thus, Wesfarmers announced an offer on 22 January 2009 entitling 'eligible' shareholders to buy three shares at A$13.50 a share for every seven shares held. Their shares were then trading at A$15.98 a share and, four months later, on 28 May 2009, traded at A$20.96. One Steel announced an offer on 16 April 2009 entitling 'eligible' shareholders to buy two shares at A$1.80 a share for every five shares held. Its shares were then trading at A$2.34 a share and six weeks later at A$2.64. Blue Scope Steel announced an offer on 5 May 2009 entitling 'eligible' shareholders to buy one 'new share' at A$1.55 for every share held. Its shares were then trading at A$2.06 and three weeks later at A$2.32.

The chief beneficiaries of such discrimination, of course, are the major Australian shareholders. According to Wesfarmers's FY 2008 annual report, the four largest shareholders on its Board held between them 2,500,038 shares, which entitled them under the 22 January rights offer to buy 1,071,445 shares for A$14,406,458. Four months later, they were worth A$22,451,199, a gain of A$7,390,741, and are now worth A$31,200,478, a gain of A$16,794,020.[2] We do not know how much of the gain derives from the dilution in the value of 'ineligible' shares. The company has ignored my request for the percentage of its equity that non-residents hold, nor is there any means of forcing it to provide this information, other than by filing suit against it. Ineligible shareholders must accept on faith that the company's decision to exclude them from the rights offer was 'reasonable'. All of which is curiously evocative of Investors Overseas Services.

Client Service is drawn from my brief employment in the mid-1960s as an IOS 'Associate' or 'Financial Counsellor'. I invested my winnings in the company's paper when it went public in

---

[2] At A$29.30 per share, the price at close of trading on 27 February 2012.

1969 and watched them evaporate when it collapsed during the spring and summer of 1970.

IOS 'Key Associates' who remained on friendly terms with its founder, Bernie Cornfeld, compared its collapse to an elephant drowning in an inch of water. Never mind the lavish spending that depleted the company's reserves, or the ensuing panic that led them to vote Cornfeld out of office and deliver IOS into the hands of Robert Vesco, a veteran confidence trickster. Their explanation was characteristically inspired: the press 'exaggerated' the cash crisis, because it was 'blatantly anti-Semitic'.

Most people who are familiar with IOS's sales materials, its monthly *Bulletins* and its sponsored funds' prospectuses and who have read the interim exposés, including almost all of the company's former salesmen and clerical staff, now believe that its collapse was inevitable, the consequence of dishonest dealing so pervasive that, by the spring of 1970, nothing could have saved it from extinction, and that the Board's choice of 'rescuer' *had* to be someone such as Vesco, who had a like interest in keeping his affairs private. The important thing to remember about IOS, it seems to me, is not its collapse, but that it succeeded so long and that *none* of the men responsible for defrauding the public of hundreds of millions of dollars has been convicted of securities frauds.[3]

The notion that IOS was Bernie Cornfeld's personal creation is hagiographic fantasy. Nor was he a natural leader with a magical touch, another popular fiction. No one who knew him before he left New York for Paris in the autumn of 1955, I suspect, could have foreseen that he would become the 'King of Europe's cash' (*Newsweek*), commanding an army of salesmen subservient to a financial Napoleon. He had no craftsman's gift for altering the shape of base materials. He was merely the company's first tout, in that he, rather than Gladis Solomon, first suggested that they motor down to Fontainebleau and test the Air Force Base Market. IOS owed its early success to circumstances, not to Bernie's 'genius'. The 1950s and early 1960s in Europe was an era when investing in the

---

[3] Six years after IOS's collapse, Cornfeld was convicted of using 'blue boxes' to cheat the Pacific Telephone Company 'on long distance calls from his luxurious 40-room Beverly Hills mansion', an offence unrelated to IOS. *San Francisco Chronicle*, 14 June 1978, p. 57.

American economy was beguiling and the open-ended investment trust (mutual fund or unit trust) was in its untested infancy there. It was also an era when a lot of Americans were eager for any employment enabling them to live in Europe. Allen Cantor, IOS's sales manager, first encountered it in Paris as a rare book dealer, Victor Herbert as a buyer for a rare music and musical manuscripts dealer, Ben Heirs as an officer in the United States Air Force, Lester Hayes as a ballroom dance instructor, George Landau on vacation. The inspiration that journalists imputed to Cornfeld was for them the stimulus of earning staying-on money.

This is not to deny the creative imagination of Area Managers such as John Jessen, George Tregea, Werner Kunkler and Alain Berrier; salesmen such as Victor Herbert, Philip Bell, Lou Ellenport and Adel Gennaoui; and public relations impresarios such as Wilson Watkins Wyatt, James Roosevelt, Erich Mende and Eric Wyndham White. Most notable of all was the company's Mephistophelean lawyer, Harvard Law School-trained Ed Cowett, who in the competition for according blame for the 'Apocalypse' became its chief villain, but without whose talents IOS could never have developed from a minor sales organization representing the Dreyfus Fund into a complex of more than fifty companies with a cash flow of nearly a billion dollars, which on some days accounted for four per cent of the trades on the New York Stock Exchange.

The structure of IOS's Fund of Funds (FoF) perhaps best exemplifies Cowett's skills at eluding Government surveillance, financial regulation and taxes. Incorporated in Ontario (although its shares were not sold in Canada), it purchased securities registered in the United States for its investment portfolio, lodged the certificates in the Netherlands (later England) and directed all cash transactions through Switzerland. IOS clients bought non-voting 'preference' shares, held 'in trust' for them by a Panamanian entity known as the IOS Investment Program, while voting commons vested in IOS 'Key Executives'. Another Panamanian (later Canadian) entity managed FoF's portfolio. A Luxembourg entity handled life cover for clients subscribing monthly instalment share-buying schemes, while a Bahamas entity served as share registrar. IOS was registered in Panama (later Ontario).

Such offshore arrangements, claimed IOS, enabled 'the smallest investor, anywhere in the world, to profit from all the professional expertise that two billion dollars can buy'.[4] However, as partly reflected in *Client Service*, they also allowed IOS and certain IOS insiders to:

- lend to themselves money deposited with IOS banks to invest in tax shelters and buy IOS shares;
- guarantee a loan of $4.9 million to Cornfeld to buy an aeroplane;
- mislead IOS clients about the performance of the company's sponsored funds and what IOS was charging them for brokerage, expenses and as management and 'performance' fees;
- channel into IOS-sponsored funds and IOS-owned banks hundreds of millions of dollars of 'flight capital' from undeveloped countries;
- falsely present FoF as offering two tiers of investment management expertise;
- invest FoF money in real property and lettered stock (unlisted securities), bought on margin and sold short for FoF, notwithstanding restrictions against such trading in FoF's prospectus;
- unload at inflated prices securities held by themselves and their cronies onto IOS-sponsored funds;
- exploit their insider knowledge to buy FoF shares in advance of profits announcements;
- dump commercial paper underwritten by IOS's merchant banks on the company's sponsored funds;[5]
- direct to IOS, rather than to its sponsored funds, give-ups (rebated brokerage commissions) and fees paid by brokerage houses for loans of securities to cover short sales;
- use sponsored funds' money to defray legal expenses incurred in the company's litigation with the Securities and Exchange Commission;

[4] Charles Raw, Bruce Page and Godfrey Hodgson (1971) *Do you sincerely want to be rich? Bernard Cornfeld and IOS: an International Swindle* (London: Andre Deutsch), p. 119.

[5] IOS-sponsored funds absorbed about a third of the combined value of the bond issues underwritten by IOS banks (ibid., p. 319), to be written off, along with the lettered stock dumped on the funds.

- misrepresent to merchant banks underwriting the flotation of IOS shares the sales subsidiary's prospective profits and the performance of IOS's largest sponsored fund, the International Investment Trust;
- spend $13.2 million of the $52 million raised by the flotation supporting the price of the shares, $8.3 million providing a market for shares redeemed by IOS's employees under the company's Stock Option Plan and $3.5 million supporting the shares of IOS's sales subsidiary after advising the underwriters that IOS planned to use the proceeds of the flotation to expand its business;
- lend $15.2 million of the flotation proceeds to themselves to finance their tax-avoidance schemes and $5.3 million to John King, his companies and business associates.

Perhaps the most audacious of the company's swindles was a venture with King Resources Corporation in the Canadian Arctic. Both companies were engaged in creating captive markets for their services, and their common client here was the Natural Resources Fund, a 'proprietary fund' sub-account of the Fund of Funds's portfolio. King Resources sold it 'exploratory properties', while IOS paid itself a 'performance fee' assessed as a percentage of notional gains. Seemingly complex, the particulars of this scam were really quite simple. First, King Resources acquired from the Canadian Government *free* permits to prospect for minerals in the frozen islands and seas stretching north from latitude 74° N, where any activity was all but inscrutable. The permits lapsed if a specified amount was not spent on exploration. The Natural Resources Fund then bought half of the permit acreage for $11 million – acquiring thereby an obligation to spend another $10 million on exploration and still more if King Resources defaulted on its obligations. In the unlikely event that oil was extracted (existing drilling technology precluded production on roughly four-fifths of the acreage), the Natural Resources Fund was to keep half of the profits, less a 12½ per cent override reserved to King Resources. King Resources next arranged a sale of seven per cent of the Natural Resources Fund's acreage for a consideration amounting to fifteen times the *average* per acre cost to it.

Nor was this a sale between third parties negotiating at arm's length. The purchasers were two business affiliates of King Resources, a syndicate in which John King himself was a member. Only 8½ per cent of the purchase price, moreover, was paid in cash. The balance, including a pledge to relieve King Resources of some of its exploration undertakings, was secured by a 'purchase-money mortgage', King Resources retaining the permits as security for the purchase price. Nevertheless, based on this transaction, IOS 'conservatively' revalued the 93% of the mineral prospecting rights acreage retained by the Natural Resources Fund and paid itself $9.7 million for procuring a gain of $156 million to its Fund of Funds's portfolio. Operations Thaw and Outback in *Client Service* are modelled on these transactions.

There are other similarities. WoF's Fiduciary of Fiduciaries (FoF) corresponds to IOS's Fund of Funds (FoF): both invested in other mutual funds, including in-house 'proprietary funds' rather than equities, and rewarded management with 'performance fees' rather than a percentage of assets under management. Natural Resources Fund, a proprietary fund in the Fund of Funds's portfolio investing in real estate ventures, corresponds to the Natural Resources Fund in the Fiduciary of Fiduciaries's portfolio. The model for WoF's Folkestone Plan was IOS's Dover Plan. WoF's two investment banks, Finance Bank and Entrepreneurs Bank, parallel IOS's Investors Overseas Bank and Investors Bank, whose 'main function seemed to be to pick discounts, underwriting fees and commissions off securities on their way into the [sponsored] funds' . . . portfolios'.[6] Anonymous Depositors Bank corresponds to IOS's Overseas Development Bank, which managed 'special collections' to enable IOS clients to evade exchange controls. Presentations, call backs, informograms, speedgrams, monthly *Bulletins*, Big Game Contest, University of Modern Money Contest, Professional in Action Contest, WoF Olympiad Contest, Citation for Entrepreneurial Excellence, Salesman of the Month features, New Man Bonus, pyramidal selling structures, Million Dollar gold watch, Stock Option Plan, Financial Training Seminar, Advanced Training Seminar, Money

---

[6] Ibid., p. 288.

Makers Lounge, Model Close, Three Types of Objections and How to Overcome Them, putting your prospect in a Yes-Frame-of-Mind, successful supervisory experience (SSE), Trainee Schedule, Basic Schedule, Senior Schedule, Branch Schedule, Regional Manager, Divisional Manager, General Manager, Area Manager, the Year of Growth, the Year of Professionalism, the Year of Total Planning, Automatic Withdrawal Plan, Financial Worksheet, Coinage of the World calendars, Activity Reports, Easy Money Referrals, Continuings and many other details were lifted *verbatim* from IOS.[7] Even the book's title draws on the *IOS Bulletin*'s designation of IOS's last functioning year as 'the Year of Total Financial Service' and, like IOS, refers to the company's collapse as the Apocalypse. IOS's last *Bulletin* was titled 'Selling through the "Apocalypse"'.[8]

---

[7] IOS called its Dynamic Growth Plan a Capital Accumulation Program and its DGPins a CAPINS.

[8] October 1970. It comprised a prologue, testimonials from twelve salesmen, volume list and an epilogue. Panagiodis Tsobanidis, working in Germany, stated: 'Like every other associate in the Company I have met sales resistance because of adverse publicity. My strategy was to explain the true facts, interpret them, and move directly into the products I am offering. . . . My presentation is extremely simple: a sheet of paper, a pen, an annual report and a hundred mark bill are all I use. The paper is to jot down figures and diagrams, the annual report for statistics, and the hundred mark bill to explain the problem of inflation. I point to the figure 100 on the bill and ask the Client what it means to him: "Does it mean a hundred loaves of bread? Or enough gasoline to travel a thousand kilometers in your car? No, it is just an abstract number . . . The real value keeps going down and down. Only through a sound investment can you protect yourself against this loss."' K.W. Cheung, working in Hong Kong, stated: 'Whatever has happened in the past few months, the many problems of our company and all the bad publicity has not changed our business. People must have a safe, convenient place for their money to grow. . . People needed our products before the crisis; in today's market, they need them more than ever.' According to the volume list presented in the same *Bulletin*, the cash sales of neither of these associates reached $10,000 during the preceding month.

Inertia was the prevailing mood in the lower ranks of the Sales Force, most of whom were content to subsist on as few presentations as possible. For weeks on end, the blare from head office at Geneva was scarcely audible. Then a local supervisor, stung by a dismal Activity Report, would chivvy us into calling on prospects, who were often names chosen randomly from telephone directories. If you sold in countries such as Spain, Morocco, Afghanistan, Pakistan and India in the mid-1960s, you understood that Cornfeld's and Wyatt's rhetoric about 'people's capitalism' meant that anyone rich enough to afford a telephone could buy a mutual fund. We inhabited a dream compounded of youth, freedom and a naive conviction about the social value of what little work we did. Most people are perfectly serious about paying off mortgages, educating their children and providing for retirement. What better way of accomplishing these laudable goals than a Capital Accumulation Program with Insurance (CAPINS), where Dollar Cost Averaging (Vertical Diversification) guarantees a profit whether the market rises or falls and affords their families financial security whether the clients live or die? To bring home the point, we used as a visual aid a grid listing various kinds of investments (savings accounts, gold, commodities, bonds, equities, real estate, business ventures, mutual funds) in a vertical column and the advantages appurtenant to such investments (small capital outlay, low risk, high return, anonymity, tax avoidance, liquidity) in a horizontal column. Correlating the data in the two columns demonstrated that only IOS-sponsored mutual funds featured all of the listed advantages.[9]

Nor were we blind to the skills employed in the funds' design. I remember a presentation to a New York corporate lawyer. Although he did not buy a programme, the Fund of Funds's technical excellence fascinated him. His firm had tried to form

---

[9] I learned after IOS collapsed that this technique bears affinity to 'the Winston Churchill Close'. A prospect agonizing over whether to buy is advised that Churchill resolved such decisions by drawing a line and listing all the pluses on one side and all the minuses on the other. The technique is known in America as the Benjamin Franklin Close. Raw *et al.*, pp. 217–18.

such a mutual fund but ultimately abandoned the project as impossible.

My brother introduced me to IOS in April 1964. He rose eventually to become a vice-president of the company, but in the spring of 1964 he was living at Cap d'Antibes supervising a modest operation encompassing himself and two part-time salesmen, one of them a portrait painter, working the Maritime Market in France, Spain and Italy. The US Navy's Sixth Fleet had sailed from Naples bound for Cannes. My training lasted about twenty minutes. I read the prospectus of the Dreyfus Fund, which IOS sold to American military personnel, and asked my brother some questions. He showed me how to complete the application forms, then gave me a printed model presentation reputed to be 'Bernie's Own'. It began, 'Mr Prospect, if I had seen you ten years ago and you had given me a check for $10,000 payable to the Bank of New York, and now I gave you a check for $20,000, would you be happy? [Wait for answer.] You'd be even happier if I gave you back $50,000, wouldn't you?' This was my introduction to putting the prospect in a Yes-Frame-of-Mind. IOS salesmen devised their own presentations from this premise.

My brother drove the painter, the other part-timer and me to Cannes, where 'the Market', US Navy ships' crews, was disembarking from lighters. Every sailor was a prospect – unwittingly, for none can have formed any intention of planning his financial future during shore leave. Our task was to intercept them between dock and local amusement spots and sell them a $25-a-month programme. Glancing at the painter from time to time to ascertain if he was having any success, I experimented with various opening gambits, including Bernie's Own, and eventually settled on 'Are you over 21?', implying that maturity qualified my prospect for the prestigious privilege of participating in a mutual fund. I also fashioned the How Do Banks Make Money presentation that Bleitgeist uses with Mr Hill and wrote about $150,000 of business with the unthreatening assurance, 'You don't have to send in your cheque if you change your mind.' Only one of the forty-odd sailors who signed applications that I filled out for them remitted money into the account, and even he discontinued payments. Nevertheless, that did it. The next

IOS Bulletin included my name among the Icebreakers, and Cornfeld sent me a letter enclosing a certificate emblazoned with the company's red seal welcoming me to IOS and praising me for the wisdom of choosing it as a career.

IOS was small in those days, with two to three hundred active salesmen. The salesman was responsible for his expenses and could work almost anywhere he chose. Geneva abounded in salesmen who had just returned for six months of amusement in Europe after a fortnight's labour in Elizabethville or Caracas. As local managers received Overrides on our work, their supervision consisted of enticing us to their territories, greeting us on arrival and discouraging us from ever leaving. We obtained authorization from Geneva, reported to the area office (it might be Amsterdam for Elizabethville) and set off with stocks of the current sales literature and application forms. In the course of perhaps twelve months of activity during four years as an IOS salesman, I sold programmes in France, Spain, Morocco, Italy, Romania, Bulgaria, Cyprus, Iraq, Saudi Arabia, Iran, Afghanistan, India and Nepal.

My first destination was Geneva to attend a Financial Training Seminar, five days of promotional antics devoid of technical instruction. Nine of the ten three-hour sessions were devoted to rehearsing stratagems for overcoming Objections and the remaining time to the commissions that we could expect to earn.

My arrival in Geneva coincided with a party at a house formerly belonging to the Colgate family, where I met Cornfeld and suggested that the party was to celebrate the accession of 'Icebreaker Tucker' to the IOS Sales Force. This so exhilarated him that he summoned several of his cronies to share the joke, and, next day at Headquarters, called me over to share the joke with Ed Cowett. It is a job to say whether such behaviour derived from genial impulses or a dearth of humour, or instanced the blatant flattery that characterized Geneva's dealings with its salesmen. I met Cornfeld half a dozen times after that. He was always polite, without the alarms associated with his reputation, and he twice paid for my lunch, but I never received the impression of being in the presence of a genius.

Bill Bunting, who was touring Europe after retiring from the Canadian Air Force, had given me a lift to Geneva and decided to accompany me to the Financial Training Seminar. After the concluding session on prospective earnings, we departed for Spain together. He thereby became my 'trainee', although I was only on Trainee Schedule with four days of professional experience. We fulfilled a rendezvous with Thor Thorsson, another alumnus, and the organization quickly grew to five men. Our territory was the port of Barcelona. Each morning, we set forth from humble pensions in the odoriferous streets flanking the Ramblas, boarded ships tied up alongside and made presentations to their crews in Italian, Greek, Swedish, Danish, Norwegian, French, German and English, the working vocabulary of these exchanges being 'bank', 'money', 'little', 'much', 'you', 'knowledge' and 'how much'. We relied heavily on visual aids of the kind depicted in *Client Service*.

Evenings we dined together at a cheap restaurant frequented by Larry Humphries, a tall Canadian who was in Barcelona to learn Spanish and the art of the Spanish guitar. Like Belvedere, he supported himself by teaching English at a local language school. It was Larry who taught me the drill: 'I put the pencil on the table.' 'I poot thee peenzil on thee *tay*bool. . . .' For about three weeks, he heard with dismay how much we were earning selling mutual funds – $600 on Monday, $800 on Tuesday. Although, his material ambitions were modest, venality gained upon him until the day when he was outfitted with a briefcase and escorted to the bottom of a gangway. Following an unprecedented number of saleless presentations ('I just don't see how anyone in a completely strange port is likely to buy an investment costing thousands of dollars from a complete stranger'), I decided, as his 'manager', to impress on him the reality of a Close, and we made a round of the ships together. 'Try to disabuse yourself of *theoretical* objections to the technique,' I told him. 'If it works, it works. Right, Larry?'

Our first prospect that morning was the master of an American freighter. ('Always call on the skipper first. If you sell him, you can use the sale to sell the rest of the ship.') He received us cordially and asked who we were.

'If you could bear with us for just *one* minute, Captain, our purpose will become absolutely clear,' I replied.

His mood darkened. 'You didn't answer my question. Who are you?'

'We're financial counsellors. Tell me this, Captain. Do banks make money?'

It was IOS technique to prompt prospective clients who did not reply to questions. I prompted him. 'Of course they do, Captain. My question was so simple that you misunderstood it. You were probably wondering *how* banks make money.'

He picked up a telephone and shouted into it, 'Who let these salesmen on board? *Fire that guard!*'

By the time I made my first Close that afternoon, Larry was no longer counselling. We had been expelled from one ship, denied access to two others, made a presentation to a stoker who was naked and called at the cabin of a tattooed deckhand with eyes red and furious from drink who grabbed Larry by the collar, thrust him against the bulkhead and said, 'The life of Riley, of whom I think highly!'

We had been in Barcelona about four months when arrived one Emile Giubelli of Milano, Montreal and Mexico City. IOS was to distinguish him from other rising types in the company by accusing him of stealing over $100,000 of clients' money, and a Spanish judge would convict him of 'a monetary offence, committed and repeated, of a complicated nature', by which time his entire organization had fled the country, Giubelli heading the exodus. Signora Giubelli stayed behind to greet the Guardia Civil. However, his sponsors in Geneva in 1964 were more powerful than my brother's.

After introducing himself, he told us of the many advantages that would accrue to the territory reconstituted under his supervision, one of which was the ease of converting pesetas into dollars: just give him the money and he would spirit it across the border. We discussed this between ourselves and decided that Giubelli was bad news. Thor and I applied to Geneva for reassignment, and our little organization disintegrated. My brother, bereft of six-ninths of his organization, left soon afterwards for Canada, precluding an Override dispute.

Thor's and my next assignment was Dhahran. We bought a Volkswagen and drove out with two girls in tow, our trainees. We sold funds at various embassies en route and in Cyprus, provoking a bitter dispute between the General Managers for Italy, Greece, Turkey and the Middle East. (GMs seemed to spend most of their time quarrelling over Overrides.) We drove on through Lebanon, Syria, Jordan and Iraq to Kuwait and there turned south, paying the head-tax imposed on non-Muslims entering the land of the Prophet's birth.

We arrived at the Saudi border simultaneously with the Kuwaiti emir's brother leading a cortège of Cadillacs and open-backed lorries full of pilgrims. For the next hundred miles or so, the road was a maze of tracks on sand. Shortly before sundown, some people at the crest of a dune hailed us. Ibn Jiluwi, the governor of the Hasa, an unshaven man with one jellied eye, reputedly illiterate, had come out into the desert with his entourage to greet his cousin. I ascended the dune and said, 'All my life, *sharifna*, I have *longed* to meet a desert prince.' '*Merhaba!*' he reciprocated with great dignity, and the conversation continued in this way. The Kuwaitis arrived. The two cousins went forward, embraced, then returned to their followers to lead them in the *salat al-maghrib* (sunset prayers). The bodyguards removed the curved daggers on their hips and cartridge belts across their chests and laid their hand-hewn rifles on the sand. After praying, the bodyguards retrieved their weapons, then Ibn Jiluwi and his entourage got into Cadillacs and sped to his palace in Dammam.

One of his counsellors instructed us to wait for him outside the palace gates. He then led us to another walled compound and through a huge garden full of palm trees, roses and marigolds irrigated with imported water to an almost empty room the size of an Oxford college refectory. Its vast floor was covered with a hand-woven carpet, and an enormous Saudi flag encrusted with precious stones covered one of the walls. When a slave fetched a jar of Planter's peanut butter, tins of Hawaiian pineapple juice and Scottish salmon for us, we protested that such luxury was beyond our means. This was his guest house, not a hotel, our host replied. His name, Darwish Darwish, meant 'Peasant Peasant', but he was a very rich man, and we were to be his guests for as long as we were in Saudi Arabia.

Alas, we were not there long. We were writing about $30,000 a day, all fully paids, 'tapping the Aramco Market', when a telegram arrived from the Area Manager: '*Leave Saudi Arabia immediately!*' followed by a more cautiously worded message from Geneva. A rival salesman coveting the Aramco Market had whispered into the Area Manager's ear that the girls' presence endangered the rest of the Saudi operation, and, as our visas were dependent on his Saudi sponsors, we had to comply.

The return journey dispelled any resentment we might have felt. Back to Jordan between the brown rivers and across the plain of polished boulders; by boat from Beirut to Alexandria; the Red Sea, Luxor, Karnak and back to Alexandria via the Nile; rows of white crosses at El Alamein; Greek, Roman and Phoenician ruins at Cirenaica, Leptis Magna and Carthage – we made a leisurely tour of half of the ancient world and, on reaching Geneva, Cornfeld apologized to us for a 'misunderstanding', reimbursed our travel expenses and awarded me India and Nepal. Thor returned to Sweden, which was 'opening up' at that time. 'To keep Thor from his motherland would be like denying Poseidon the sea,' remarked the IOSer who arranged the assignment.[10]

I spent some time in a Capuchin monastery at Bracciano near Rome writing and studying Italian, a typical IOS intermezzo, then departed for my last territory with one of our trainees, to whom I was briefly engaged. We drove through the Ukraine, Georgia and Armenia to Erevan, consigned our car to a chauffeur and proceeded by train. There were black screens over the windows, but they did not conceal the Russian soldiers clad in great coats and armed with automatic rifles posted at 50-yard intervals along the track, which ran along the border first with Turkey, then with Iran. Other soldiers met us at Djulfa and handed us over to Iranian soldiers at the middle of the inevitably named Friendship Bridge spanning the Araxes.

Reunited with our car, we drove on to Teheran and met our new Area Manager, whose office door proclaimed: 'Guide of Foreign Investors Company, Limited'. A teacher by profession, he told us that IOS to him was a means of saving enough money to open his own school – a man of hidden dimensions, we thought. He suggested that we try working Meshed, which was on our route, extolling it in IOS-speak as a 'market of unlimited potential, completely untapped'. We did as he suggested, with some success, but received no confirms. This jovial idealist stole the programmes.

---

[10] Thad Lovett.

After the volume of two of my trainees in India reached $150,000, I needed one more successful supervisory experience to reach Branch Schedule, that magical moment when an IOSer's achievement was recognized by the gift of a Patek Philippe gold wrist-watch engraved with the IOS logo and leave to participate in its Stock Option Plan. Having played the donkey pursuing the carrot long enough, however, I did not wait for the remaining SSE and, instead, followed one of my SSEs, who returned to Tennessee to go to medical school.

'Let me tell you how I see your five stars of leadership,' roared Mr Wilson Watkins Wyatt, ex-Lieutenant Governor of Kentucky, addressing an assembly of salesmen in 1966, the IOS Year of Leadership. 'First and foremost, I see quality, and this means character, integrity, dignity, judgement, professional skill. Quality has been and will continue to be the very keystone of IOS. Second, I see the scope and the great range of your leadership. In IOS you make no little plans.'

'People who do the impossible are the people who write the history of the world,' proclaimed Allen Cantor, head of'sales at IOS. Were they too late for stock options, he asked us tauntingly? Had all the growth already occurred? By 1975, he opined, the Sales Force would comprise 75,000 associates.

'I feel safe in predicting that, by 1974, we will be the world's biggest insurance complex,' added Richard Hammerman, the company's insurance maestro.

'The job that each of you has accomplished so far,' trumpeted Cornfeld in 1969, 'is nothing short of spectacular. More than a hundred members of the firm became millionaires at the time of the Public Offering.' Not because they were 'concerned with the process of becoming a millionaire for its own sake', he explained, but because they were 'primarily concerned with doing an important job well'.

The main reason for going public, asserted Ed Cowett, was 'to demonstrate the true value of IOS stock to the thousands of associates who have acquired shares under the Stock Option Plan.'

The hallucinated salesmen invested their winnings to buy the company's paper, some even mortgaging their homes as collateral for loans to buy more paper, and, after the Apocalypse, found themselves with obligations they could never redeem, no longer in their prime and without attractive credentials for future employment. At least one was murdered by his clients. Nor were the Key Executives entirely spared, although most of them remained wealthy men. Cornfeld's wealth shrank to a modest 15–25 million dollars, and he still owned the aeroplane bought on credit guaranteed by an IOS bank and 'fitted out to rival Hugh Hefner's all-black Big Bunny'.[11] A press release from the prison where he underwent a brief 'rehabilitation' for defrauding the telephone company described him as 'a financier'.[12]

A few months after the Apocalypse, a group of ex-IOSers were at a house party near Paris, when the question arose: what was Bernie doing? One of the party was in a benevolent mood about his former employer, although he had good reason to feel otherwise, as the only thing left to him from nine years in IOS employment was his gold watch, worn now as a kind of artefact.[13] He got up from his chair and, to everyone's immense enjoyment, performed a little dance while singing, 'tea for two and two for tea, and you for me and me for you'. He explained that he was resorting to a Zen technique of pantomiming foolishness to overcome rage. 'Bernie's just doing a little tap dance,' he said.

A similar antic for me was writing *Client Service*. I hope the divergences between my World of Finance and its prototype will convince the reader of the fictional character of the book. None of my characters are representations of IOSers I knew and, in the main, liked. Baroque, emphatically, is not Bernie, who died in London on 27 February 1995, broke, sustained in his final hours by the charity of his remaining friends. Sleek McCool is not Ed Cowett, who is also dead,[14] nor is Marty Rubin Allen Cantor.

During my moment as a Financial Counsellor, I was privy to none of the decisions made at the higher levels of IOS management, nor was my brother. The facts most confidently presented in my novel pertain to the craft of selling mutual funds. I was not an executive. I was a salesman.

---

[11] Raw *et al.*, p. 457.
[12] *San Francisco Chronicle*, op.cit.
[13] Bob Patterson.
[14] Cowett died in April 1974, age 44.